OF FIRE AND LIONS

Center Point
Large Print

Books are produced in the United States using U.S.-based materials

Books are printed using a revolutionary new process called THINKtech™ that lowers energy usage by 70% and increases overall quality

Books are durable and flexible because of Smyth-sewing

Paper is sourced using environmentally responsible foresting methods and the paper is acid-free

Also by Mesu Andrews and available from Center Point Large Print:

Isaiah's Daughter

This Large Print Book carries the Seal of Approval of N.A.V.H.

OF FIRE AND LIONS

A NOVEL OF PROPHETS & KINGS

MESU ANDREWS

CENTER POINT LARGE PRINT
THORNDIKE, MAINE

This Center Point Large Print edition
is published in the year 2019 by arrangement with
WaterBrook, an imprint of Random House, a division of
Penguin Random House LLC, New York.

Copyright © 2019 by Mesu Andrews.

Scripture quotations and paraphrases are taken from the
Holy Bible, New International Version®, NIV®. Copyright
© 1973, 1978, 1984, 2011 by Biblica Inc.® Used by
permission. All rights reserved worldwide.

This book is a work of historical fiction based
closely on real people and real events. Details that
cannot be historically verified are purely products
of the author's imagination.

The text of this Large Print edition is unabridged.
In other aspects, this book may vary
from the original edition.
Printed in the United States of America
on permanent paper.
Set in 16-point Times New Roman type.

ISBN: 978-1-64358-155-2

Library of Congress Cataloging-in-Publication Data

Library of Congress Cataloging in Publication
Control Number: 2019002807

To our twins, Rory and Asher.
You were a gift to our family
during the writing of this book.

CHARACTER LIST

Abednego (see also Azariah) Twin of Meshach (Mishael); one of three brothers, Daniel's friends, taken from Jerusalem in first exile to Babylon

Abigail Hebrew handmaid taken from Jerusalem in first exile to Babylon; Daniel's maid

Allamu Belili's son with Gadi

Amyitis Nebuchadnezzar's wife; queen of Babylon; daughter of King Astyages, king of the Medes

Arioch Commander of the king's guard; King Nebuchadnezzar's personal bodyguard

Ashpenaz Chief eunuch; overseer of palace

Azariah (see also Abednego) Abednego's Hebrew name

Belili Gadi's wife; Daniel's wife

King Belshazzar Last king of Babylon; grandson of Nebuchadnezzar

Belteshazzar (see also Daniel) Daniel's Babylonian name

King Cyrus King of Persia; nephew of Amyitis, Nebuchadnezzar's wife; grandson of Astyages, king of the Medes

Daniel (see also Belteshazzar) Hebrew boy taken from Jerusalem in first exile to Babylon; becomes governor of the Chaldeans (chief wise man) during King Nebuchadnezzar's reign

King Darius (see also General Gubaru) A Mede; sentences Daniel to lions' pit

Gadi Belili's first husband; chief magus; Allamu's father

General Gubaru (see also King Darius) A Mede; leads army that conquers Babylon in one night

Gula Chambermaid for twins Meshach and Abednego

Hananiah (see also Shadrach) Shadrach's Hebrew name

King Jehoiachin King of Judah; taken into captivity in Babylon during second exile; son of King Jehoiakim

King Jehoiakim King of Judah 608–598 BC; king during the first exile

Kezia Eldest daughter of Daniel and Belili; Sheshbazzar's wife

Laqip Chief astrologer

Mert Shadrach's Egyptian chambermaid; becomes Daniel's family servant

Meshach (see also Mishael) Twin of Abednego (Azariah); one of three brothers, Daniel's friends, taken from Jerusalem in first exile to Babylon

Mishael (see also Meshach) Meshach's Hebrew name

Nabonidus King Nebuchadnezzar's son-in-law; king of Babylon 556–553 BC and then co-reigns (from undisclosed location) with his son, King Belshazzar, until Medes invade in 539 BC

King Nabopolassar Nebuchadnezzar's father; died 605 BC

King Nebuchadnezzar King of Babylon 605–562 BC (approximately)

Orchamus One of the three overseers in King Darius's kingdom; responsible for satraps in Phoenicia

Princess Rubati Classmate of Daniel

Shadrach Eldest of the three Hebrew brothers, Daniel's friends, taken from Jerusalem in first exile to Babylon

Sheshbazzar Kezia's husband; Daniel's son-in-law; chief scribe at the Esagila, temple of Marduk

Zakiti Baker's daughter

King Zedekiah Last king of Judah before Babylon destroyed it; taken captive during the third exile; Daniel's uncle

Zerubbabel General Gubaru/King Darius's personal bodyguard; grandson of King Jehoiachin (Daniel's cousin)

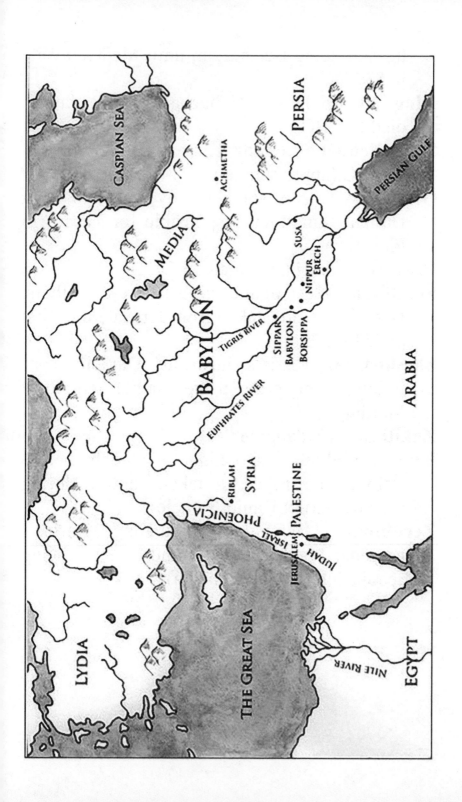

PART 1

Then Isaiah said to Hezekiah, "Hear the word of the LORD: The time will surely come when everything in your palace, and all that your predecessors have stored up until this day, will be carried off to Babylon. Nothing will be left, says the LORD. And some of your descendants, your own flesh and blood who will be born to you, will be taken away, and they will become eunuchs in the palace of the king of Babylon."

—2 Kings 20:16–18

1

King Belshazzar gave a great banquet for a thousand of his nobles. . . . He gave orders to bring in the gold and silver goblets that Nebuchadnezzar . . . had taken from the temple in Jerusalem, so that the king and his nobles, his wives and his concubines might drink from them. . . . As they drank the wine, . . . the fingers of a human hand appeared and wrote on the plaster of the wall.

—DANIEL 5:1–2, 4–5

Babylon
October 539 BC

I'd never seen a sesame seed grow until I came to Babylon almost seventy years ago. At harvest time my husband, Daniel, looks to the tiny seed as cause for great celebration. How inconsequential is a miniscule seed? How incomprehensible its yield? How unbearable the process of growth? A seed is buried. It dies. Then sprouts. And grows. It blossoms. Dries and dies again to be plucked up and used for the purpose of its planting. My husband's purpose in celebration was to mark the passing of years toward prophecy's fulfillment—

now just futile poetry. But it caused me to remember things I'd rather forget.

It was a day I dreaded all year long.

I picked up my polished-bronze mirror and tucked a stray tendril of gray curls beneath my new linen head scarf, noting in the reflection his fidgeting behind me. He always had trouble tying a jeweled belt, but his fingers seemed more trembly this morning. Was he nervous too?

I set aside my mirror and crossed the bedchamber, nudging his hands aside. "Let me do it." Though both his hands and mine were spotted with age and lined with bulging blue veins, at least mine were still nimble.

He cradled my head and placed a kiss on my forehead. "Thank you, love. What would I do without you?"

I finished the knot and gazed into his rheumy eyes, as smitten as I'd been sixty-six years ago. "Let's hope you never find out." I laced my arm through his. "Let's go downstairs. The children are waiting."

He opened our chamber door, and lively family sounds floated up from the courtyard below. We descended the stairs slowly since Daniel's feet pained him. Waiting in our lush green courtyard were three generations of our descendants seated around four long rectangular tables. Four daughters with their husbands. Twenty-one grandchildren. And thirty-two greats.

Two conscientious grandsons met their *saba* Daniel at the bottom of the steps, one supporting each elbow. I was left to follow—alone. The snubbing had begun.

"I'm fine," he protested. "Tend to your *savta*."

"But *Ima* said your feet have been paining you, Saba." Our oldest daughter's firstborn offered an obligatory nod at me. "*Shalom*, Savta."

I returned the nod with a half smile but remained silent, refusing to mock the peace such a greeting offered. One glance at our oldest daughter, Kezia, assured me there would be no shalom today. She stole sullen glimpses at me while standing beside her husband, Sheshbazzar, the prince of Judah's exiles in Babylon. Our other three daughters stood arm in arm with their husbands, eyes trained on the *abba* they all adored.

"Abba and Ima!" Sheshbazzar, whom we lovingly called Shesh, shouted over the dull roar of chattering children and our fountain's happy splashing. "Take your place at the head of the table." He'd already arranged two brightly colored cushions at the end nearest the stairs and rushed over to support Daniel's arm while he lowered himself. I mouthed a silent thank-you and sat quietly beside my husband.

Shesh took his place at Daniel's right. Kezia sat beside her husband with several of her children and grandchildren filling spaces at the large table around us. She avoided my gaze.

15

"You look lovely today, Kezia." I spoke across Daniel. "Is that a new robe, dear?"

Her eyes sparked. "Are you implying I spend too much money at the market, Ima?"

"No, dear. I . . ." Nothing I said to Kezia would be safe. "You are beautiful, Daughter. That's all."

Her cheeks pinked, and she looked quickly away, beginning a conversation with one of her daughters about the toddler on her lap. A great-grandson I'd met only a few times. Kezia's eyes crinkled with a smile that lit her features. She was a good ima, at her best when her children surrounded her. Had she learned anything from me—before her hatred sprouted and grew?

The servants began a triumphant march with pitchers of juice and wine and platters laden with various meats, fruits, and vegetables. This was a day our dear Egyptian servant, Mert, anticipated all year long, a day when her best recipes from both Babylon and Jerusalem found their way to our table.

My husband hoisted his silver chalice in the air, repeating his annual vow. "If I forget you, Jerusalem, may my right hand forget its skill. May my tongue cling to the roof of my mouth if I do not consider Jerusalem my highest joy." Adults lifted goblets of wine and children their cups of juice. Our children had seen Jerusalem only in their minds through the stories Daniel told of his childhood in the palace. The rugged

16

beauty of Zion. The grandeur of Yahweh's Temple. With our first sip came the rattle of the courtyard gate, and I caught the glint of morning sun off a soldier's shield. Ten of King Belshazzar's guards charged into our celebration.

One, wearing a captain's gold breastplate, marched straight toward my husband. "King Belshazzar commands the presence of Daniel, exile of Judah, chief of King Nebuchadnezzar's counselors."

"I am Daniel." He stood, and the captain gripped his arm and fairly dragged him toward the gate.

"Wait!" I lunged for my husband, but the other soldiers blocked my way.

My Daniel looked over his shoulder, offering a weak smile. "I'll be back, love. Save some roast lamb for me."

Panic clawed at my throat while ten strong soldiers led away the beating of my heart. I turned to the fruit of my womb, who moments ago had shunned me. Now everyone stared at me, pleading silently for direction. Angst filled my belly. Who needed food when my Daniel had been taken to the banquet of a madman? "I'm going upstairs to pray. No one eats a bite until Daniel returns."

The captain's fingers bit into Daniel's arm, pulling him into the narrow street. Daniel tried to hurry his pace, but his feet were too

17

tender. Perhaps conversation would slow the man down. "I haven't visited the palace since Nebuchadnezzar released me from service twenty-four years ago. Did King Belshazzar mention his reason for summoning me?"

The only sound came from rippling water in the canal alongside the street. Silence was typical of a loyal eunuch. The captain's wide gold collar proclaimed his vow to serve the king unto death and the king's reciprocal commitment to lifelong provision.

Daniel stumbled, landing hard on his right foot. He braced his hands against his knees, wincing in pain.

"Are you well?" The captain's concern was rather surprising.

"Yes, thank you. Could we slow our pace a bit?" Before the eunuch could answer, his stomach growled, and Daniel chuckled. "You and your men should have joined us for this morning's meal. Mert is a fine cook."

The captain's features remained grim. "The king needs you now, Lord Daniel. Please." He extended his hand in the direction of the palace, and Daniel felt the prickly flesh of urgency.

Continuing in silence, they left the walled city of Babylon's wealth and nobility and ascended the marble stairs to the Processional Way. While crossing the wide avenue splitting Babylon's municipality, they passed the three-storied Ishtar

Gate, the military complex, and finally entered palace grounds through its southern gate.

The pounding of drums and trill of a flute floated on a chill autumn breeze, and a sudden presence pressed Daniel to his knees. With both hands over his ears, he blocked out distraction and held in the silent whisper:

"*MENE, MENE, TEKEL, PARSIN.*

"*Mene*: I have numbered the days of Belshazzar's reign and brought it to an end.

"*Tekel*: He has been weighed on My scales and found wanting.

"*Parsin*: I have divided his kingdom and given it to the Medes and Persians."

"My lord!" A huge hand lifted Daniel to his feet. "My lord, are you well?"

Shadows cleared from the prophet's eyes, and he gazed into ten pale faces. "Yes, yes. Thank you. We must hurry to the king."

The captain placed a giant arm around Daniel's waist and fairly carried him toward the grand stairway. "I've heard you are a seer. Did you have a vision, my lord?"

Daniel sensed something genuine in this man but knew a eunuch's loyalty was first and always to his king. "If you have any family in Babylon, Captain, they should leave the city tonight."

His brows shot up, but a slight nod communicated understanding. Any Babylonian with a measure of sense knew King Cyrus of Persia had built an army that would someday overtake Babylon—the empire King Belshazzar had weakened by overspending, poor council choices, and constant revelry during the past fourteen years.

The captain hoisted Daniel up the grand stairway and into the main entrance. They hurried through what had once been pristine hallways, now covered in dust and frayed tapestries. Music grew louder as they neared the throne hall but with no accompanying sounds of laughter or merriment.

"I thought the king was hosting a banquet," Daniel said.

"He was." Was it fear or loyalty that kept him from saying more? Guards at the throne room opened the double doors, revealing the colossal space filled with tables, terrified noblemen, and musicians whose timid notes tested the eerie silence.

A man wearing a gold crown rushed toward Daniel. He'd seen the young king only once, on the day of his coronation, when Belshazzar entered Babylon in a chariot on the Processional Way. He was much shorter up close and much older tonight.

"Are you Daniel, one of the exiles my grandfather brought from Judah?"

Daniel barely had time for a nod before the king aimed a shaking finger at a side wall. "The inscription. See it? None of my wise men could interpret it."

Daniel followed his gesture and stared at the exact words from his vision blazing with an unnatural fire on the plastered wall. "I've heard the spirit of the gods lives in you," the king said, his panic-stricken features but a handbreadth away. "Interpret the message, and I swear by my father's life I'll dress you in purple, place a gold chain around your neck, and make you the third highest ruler in our kingdom."

Sickened by the king's stale sweat and fetid breath, Daniel was grateful he hadn't eaten. How many promises had this regent broken? Many believed Belshazzar had killed his father to take Babylon's throne. Shrugging off Belshazzar's hands, Daniel stepped back and bowed with forced habit.

"You may keep your gifts and reward someone else. The Most High God gives glory and splendor to whomever He pleases—as He did to your forefather King Nebuchadnezzar. But when the king became proud, he was stripped of his glory, driven away from people, and given the mind of an animal. He lived with wild donkeys and ate grass like the ox until he acknowledged that the Most High God is sovereign over all kingdoms on earth and sets over them anyone He wishes. But you, Belshazzar, though you knew all this, have not humbled yourself."

Shocked whispers rolled like a tide over the noblemen in the hall, confirming that King Nebuchadnezzar's transformation had not been widely known. Daniel scanned the crowd, noticing for the first time the glint of gold set before each guest.

Righteous indignation loosed his tongue again. "You set yourself against the Lord of heaven by allowing your nobles, wives, and concubines to drink wine from the goblets taken from Yahweh's Temple. You have not honored the God who holds your life in His hands, so His hand wrote your doom on the wall."

Daniel pointed to the blazing words and read aloud:

"MENE, MENE, TEKEL, PARSIN. The Lord has numbered the days of your reign and brought it to an end. You have been weighed on scales and found wanting. Your kingdom is divided and given to the Medes and Persians."

He bowed once more and turned to go.

"Wait!" Belshazzar grabbed his arm and then lowered himself to one knee, inclining his head. "Please. I believe everything you've said, but please have mercy." He stood and lifted his voice to the gathering. "Daniel will wear a purple robe from my chamber, and only my commands and those of my father carry more authority than Daniel's in the whole empire."

Belshazzar removed the gold chain from his

neck and lifted it over Daniel's head, letting the chiseled granite seal rest on the prophet's chest. Lingering near, he spoke in a voice meant for only the prophet. "You're now a son of Babylon. Surely your god won't destroy an empire governed by one of his own."

Daniel answered in an equally quiet voice. "My God will destroy many empires to bless His own."

King Belshazzar recoiled, stiffened, and studied him. "You will remain at my side until I'm convinced you haven't somehow conspired against me."

"As you wish." Daniel followed him to the elevated table, eating food prepared by palace cooks instead of the meal made by Mert's loving hands.

Yahweh, protect my family when You bring Cyrus into Babylon.

2

One courier follows another
and messenger follows messenger
to announce to the king of Babylon
that his entire city is captured.
—JEREMIAH 51:31

When I fled to my bedchamber after Daniel
was taken, my daughters glared at me, and their
husbands—temple scribes, all of them—gathered
in a corner, whispering. What were they plotting?
Could scribes rescue my Daniel? Their whispers
did nothing but add to the tension.

I fell onto the couch beside our bed and buried
my face against the armrest. *Yahweh, protect
my Daniel. Only You know why he's been taken.*

My chamber door opened without a knock, and
Mert entered with a tray of samplings from the
delicacies she'd prepared. I was furious. "I told
them we weren't eating until—"

"You're being ridiculous." She plopped the
tray on the couch between us. "The babies were
fussy, and the adults were about to revolt. Master
Daniel wouldn't want us to waste all this food,
and you'll feel better after you eat."

In stubborn silence, I stared into her wintry-
gray eyes. Why was she always right? "Sit down

24

and help me eat it, then." I scooted over to make room for the woman who was servant, comforter, counselor, and friend. "My children hate me."

She spread a generous portion of goat cheese on a piece of bread and handed it to me. "They can't hate someone they don't know."

"They can't know someone who abandoned them." I threw the bread onto the tray and inhaled sharply, driving away unwelcome emotions. I'd cried enough for ten lifetimes.

Mert picked up my bread and took a bite. "You didn't abandon them. Explain what happened. They're adults now. They'll understand."

I shook my head, still not trusting my voice, and prepared another piece of bread with goat cheese. After a few bites, I was ready to proffer another plan. "I'll go down after they've eaten and try to salvage the day. Perhaps Daniel will return soon and provide the balm for any additional wounds I've caused."

Mert reached for my free hand and squeezed it. "Perhaps when others are stingy with forgiveness, you should direct them to your god. Master Daniel comforts them by praying with them."

Surprised and a bit convicted by my friend's suggestion, I set aside my bread. "I've tried, Mert. Anytime I've suggested prayer or asking for Yahweh's help or wisdom in a matter, my children have made it clear—they see nothing in me to warrant that kind of trust." The gaping

25

hole inside nearly swallowed me. I bowed my head and cradled Mert's hand in mine. "I fear their scars are too deep."

"Nonsense." She drew her hand away and presented my bread to me. "Your girls have their own little circle to depend on, so they've held their grudge tightly. But one day, Belili"—she winked—"one day, they'll all come around. You wait and see."

Her optimism, though likely misplaced, brightened the mood, and we chatted of lighter things while finishing our meal. She took the dirty dishes downstairs, leaving me alone to return to prayer. *Yahweh, I know You've forgiven me, but how could others—when I can't forgive myself?*

My silent plea revealed a hidden truth I hadn't even acknowledged in conscious thought. Could I ever forgive myself for the mistakes I'd made as an ima? Unsettled, but feeling the draw of obligation, I straightened my robe and returned to the courtyard to play hostess to a house full of family who loved each other and barely tolerated me.

I spent the day with the youngest in my clan, babies and toddlers who cooed and laughed on my lap, as yet untainted by family stigmas. By nightfall, fussy little ones filled all our villa's beds, and the adults gathered in huddles to share horrible possibilities of my Daniel's fate.

I wandered through our courtyard alone. The splashing fountain calmed me, and the cricket song assured me that Yahweh cared for even the most insignificant in His creation. I sat on the bench in the garden between our courtyard and street, counting the winking stars.

"Are you all right, Ima?" Son-in-law Shesh stood in a shaft of moonlight beside me.

"Not really, but I'm trying to remember that Daniel's absence doesn't mean he has come to harm. He would stay at the palace for weeks if a king asked it of him."

Shesh shifted awkwardly from one foot to the other and waited as if he had more to say, so I patted the bench. "Join me, if you like."

We sat in companionable silence for a while. I closed my eyes, inhaling Babylon's night air and thanking Yahweh for our oldest daughter's husband. Shesh was a leader of men with a heart of compassion. He'd been kinder to us than seven sons and was generous to show Daniel deference in our old age, though he and Kezia were now master and mistress of our shared villa. He adored Kezia, had been a loving abba, and was now a doting saba of their nine grandchildren. Every Jew in Babylon respected him, and as chief scribe of the Esagila—Marduk's temple—he'd cultivated a healthy connection with Babylon's religious community as well.

"Sheshbazzar!" Kezia's voice grated like a cat's claws on tile. "Why didn't you tell me you were waiting with Ima?"

27

"Come, my love." Shesh offered his hand, calling her to join us.

I scooted to the bench's edge, and she squeezed between us, bringing a wave of tension with her. "We should send one of the servants to the palace. Check on Abba. See if he's all right."

Shesh pulled her close. "If your abba hasn't returned by morning, I'll call Israel's elders together and send a delegation to inquire of the king."

I patted her knee and joined my support. "Sending a single servant would be dangerous, but a delegation of Jews who hold powerful positions in the city won't be ignored. Shesh is very wise."

The moonlight showed Kezia's lips pursed into a thin white line, but she held her tongue. An improvement over her early days as wife of Judah's prince. I locked my lips as well, proof that Yahweh had done a work in us both.

Sudden splashing in the canal across the street stole my attention, and before I could voice concern, soldiers emerged. Dressed in foreign armor. Swords drawn.

Kezia screamed, and I jumped to my feet. Shesh clamped his hand over her mouth, while other shrieks echoed down the street. Then wailing.

"Get inside!" My strangled whisper mingled with the invaders' shouts, and my feet halted on the tiles. "They're Medes."

Startled that I still understood the language after all these years, I silently interpreted an officer's instructions. "Kill those who resist. Displace the others and send them across the river to find housing."

I hurried to catch up with Shesh and grabbed his arm as we reached the courtyard gate. "Listen to me. We must leave willingly when they come. They'll send us to the unwalled part of the city across the river."

He looked at me as if I'd grown horns. "You understand their language?"

My children and adult grandchildren gathered around us inside the courtyard. "What language?" one of the grandchildren asked. "How does Savta know—"

"You!" Four Medes rushed toward us. "All of you! Out!"

Without thinking, I bowed deeply and answered in Median, "We will obey, Master. May we retrieve the others from our household?" All four soldiers stopped in their tracks, exchanging odd glances. I bowed again before they had time to think. "I was a friend of Queen Amyitis, the great Median princess. She taught me to speak."

Seeming satisfied, the leader nodded to the darkened villa behind us. "Get the others and get out."

I turned and faced my terrified family. "The soldiers are Medes. They'll be too busy killing to attack women right away—"

"What? Ima, no!" Kezia's shriek spread hysteria to the other women.

Shesh drew her to his chest, silencing her, and turned to me. "Have they joined Cyrus's army?"

"He didn't say, but Daniel has feared Belshazzar's careless reign would draw Cyrus's army like a wolf to an unshepherded flock."

The ashen faces of my own flock screamed silent terror in Daniel's absence. He was the rock on which we stood. *Yahweh, please. Give me Your wisdom.* While waiting for divine help, I stalled with what I knew for certain. "Whether the Medes acted independently or under Cyrus's command, we must get everyone—family and servants—to a safe place. Fleeing across the river won't be safe for my daughters or the children."

My girls whimpered, drawing their children closer. Shesh's brows dipped in consternation. "What do we do?"

I saw Mert standing at the back of the gathering and felt the gentle wind of wisdom blow across my spirit. "Mert, gather the servants while the family collects our little ones. Shesh, go to the Esagila and speak with the high priest. Surely he'll allow you, as chief scribe, to shelter your family there until the invasion is over."

One of the other sons-in-law asked, "Won't the Medes attack the temples?"

"They will raid other temples, but not the Esagila. Because of the Medes' respect for Nebuchadnezzar, they fear his patron god, Marduk, so the Esagila remains sacred." I shoved Shesh. "Go, Son. We'll meet you there."

My decisiveness stiffened resolve and propelled parents to collect their dear ones. Within moments, we ventured out the side door into the dark, chaotic streets. It had been years since my old legs moved so quickly and even longer since I'd seen this kind of carnage. Swords clanged. Women screamed. Children cried over their parents' corpses. The canal ran red with noble blood, those who had been passed over or who snubbed their invitation to the king's banquet. The Medes would have almost certainly attacked the palace by now, but I refused to let myself believe my Daniel lost.

Invading armies showed no mercy to conquered kings and their nobles. Daniel had been led into Belshazzar's presence this morning in nobleman's clothes. But this couldn't be the end Yahweh intended for my husband's faithfulness. *Yahweh, show him Your mercy. Deliver my Daniel by Your power as You delivered our friends from the furnace years ago.*

Kezia cupped my elbow, nearly dragging me through the street. "Ima, hurry. I'm worried about Shesh. You should never have sent him alone." I bit my tongue, feeling the weight of twenty millstones around my neck. If anything happened to our dear Shesh, Kezia would never forgive me—nor would I forgive myself. It would be a relief when I could return the weight of family patriarch to my husband.

31

We passed through darkened side streets, staying off the Processional Way, until we were directly opposite the temple complex. Hurrying up the stairs, across the wide avenue, and down the stairs on the other side, my cherished brood slipped past the towering ziggurat in darkness, its heavenward height blocking the moonlight, helping us to reach the sprawling Esagila in safety.

Shesh was already there, speaking with Marduk's chief priest in hushed tones, while the rest of us waited with other anxious families in the main hallway. Without permission, my eyes wandered to the yawning chamber at my right and found the glistening gold statue of Marduk mocking me. I hadn't stepped inside this temple since my first days in Babylon.

"Ima, come." Shesh tugged at my arm. "We have permission to hide in one of the treasury rooms where I work."

"A treasury room?" My heart jumped into my throat. "No. I can't."

Shesh's brows drew together. Kezia rushed past him and grabbed my hand. "Ima, we must go before they offer the room to someone else."

"No!" I pulled away, blinking back tears.

Soft hands cradled my shoulders from behind. "The mistress and I will follow everyone else." Mert's voice was like honey on a wound. "We won't get lost, Master Shesh. I promise."

"All right," he said, holding my gaze. "Abba Daniel will look for us here first, Ima." Righteous, pious, tenderhearted Shesh. I lowered my head, suddenly siezed by the fear and shame that paralyzed me as a child in this dark place. Mert stepped in front of me, looking fiercely into my eyes. "You are the wife of the nobleman Belteshazzar, who was chief of Nebuchadnezzar's wise men and governor of the Chaldeans. The priests here have no power over you." She looped her arm around mine and instructed the servants to follow our family. Shesh's position as chief scribe had secured shelter for our seventy-plus-member household, but I felt anything but safe in the southeast treasury, where my skin crawled with memories. I held my breath while passing every priest's and priestess's chamber and almost fainted as we approached the room that stored some of my deepest pain. Thankfully, Shesh opened a door two chambers before we reached it.

My family's gasps ushered Mert and me into a world so different from the chaos and blood we'd left in Babylon's streets. Gold, silver, gemstones, purple robes, exquisite furs, gilded armor, and large chunks of precious metals lay in piles around the large room.

"Some of these chunks look familiar," I said to no one in particular. While others oohed and aahed, I found Shesh and pointed to an ornately carved bronze piece. "Is that what I think it is?"

"It's one of the bronze capitals from the two pillars of Jerusalem's Temple. See the pomegranates in rows around it?"

I nodded, heart pounding as I pointed out other treasures. "That's a golden lampstand, and over there is the golden altar."

Shesh turned to face me. "How do you know what the lampstand and altar looked like?"

Excitement had overtaken my senses. I'd been careless with my words. Though my son-in-law had been born in Babylon, he'd been faithfully taught the Law and Torah and understood the Temple restrictions. A jumble of emotions tied my tongue. Fear of past secrets warred with the joy of seeing Yahweh's sacred items again.

Kezia heard our exchange and drew close, brows lifted. I refused to offer more grain for her gossiping hens at the market. "Are all the treasures from Jerusalem housed in this single room?" A slight shift of subject might work. "Surely this isn't everything Nebuchadnezzar brought from the palace, the Temple, and all the wealthy landowners in Judah."

Shesh grinned, acknowledging my redirection. "No, of course not. Though it was logged before my time, the records show King Nebuchadnezzar divided most of Jerusalem's treasure between all the temples in Babylon. Some of it was also given to his father-in-law, King Astyages of the Medes, to aid in military campaigns. King

Belshazzar, however, has squandered most of the other temple treasuries with his banquets and revelry. He'd left the Esagila's valuables largely undisturbed until two days ago, when he requisitioned all gold and silver goblets from Solomon's Temple to serve wine at his banquet."

Fear vied with shock, and my mind began to spin. "No wonder Yahweh brought judgment on Babylon tonight."

Shesh's eyes grew wary, glancing from me to the Temple items. "You think Yahweh sent the Medes to attack Babylon because Belshazzar used the sacred goblets?" He folded his arms across his chest and gave me a forbearing smile. "If Yahweh was so quick to protect His holy items tonight, why didn't He strike down the Babylonians when they destroyed His Temple?" His expression said he thought he'd confounded me.

Kezia, too, waited for my answer. Fully aware that whatever I said could lead to more questions, I walked away to inspect the piles of treasure. Some mounds rose higher than two men. Some had been sorted according to composition—gold, silver, or bronze. Another pile held only more manageable chopped pieces of what had once been larger objects.

Shesh and Kezia followed close on my heels. My son-in-law took a piece of hand-sized gold from the pile and placed it in my hands. Its

35

weight nearly toppled me. Appreciation shone in his eyes. "We don't often realize how heavy the golden Temple items would have been. Imagine the Ark of the Covenant, for instance."

I swallowed the instant lump in my throat. "Yes, imagine."

He took the gold from my hands, giving me a sidelong glance. "It's been recorded that much of Jerusalem's wealth—including the Temple items—was cut into pieces this size." He held it before me. "Which makes it impossible to identify the original items."

Renewed panic gripped me. First my Daniel had been taken and now Yahweh's Ark? "Yahweh's presence cannot be cut into pieces, Shesh. He would not allow it." But even as I said it, I felt the hypocrisy of my words. Hadn't He allowed His Temple to be burned? And His cherished people to be scattered and made a mockery among nations? "There must be a way to trace the journey of the Ark from its capture in Jerusalem to wherever it sits today."

The son of my heart gazed into the windows of my soul. "We can only trace the Ark if those who have seen it tell their stories."

He knew. Somehow he knew I'd seen the Ark. Mert's hand slipped into mine. "Tell him."

"Tell us what?" Kezia's tone was clipped, her eyes flitting from Mert to me.

Sadly, I could more easily confide in my

son-in-law than my gossiping daughter. But she feared family shame more than tonight's invaders. Perhaps Kezia's life as daughter of King Nebuchadnezzar's chief wise man and wife of Lord Sheshbazzar, with the pomp and privilege those roles ensured, was more important than her standing among her gossiping friends.

Reaching out to cup her cheek, I couldn't even imagine my eldest spending a night cold or hungry, homeless or enslaved. She could have withstood only a portion of the memories flooding my mind. "When *Crown Prince* Nebuchadnezzar invaded Jerusalem to steal the young nobility, I saw the Ark in the Temple. In his following two attacks—eight years later and eleven years after that—the priests included in both of those exiles spoke of their continuing sacrifices and annual Day of Atonement celebrations. How could they without His presence above the Ark?"

Turning to Shesh, I placed my hand on the piece of gold in his hand and held his gaze. "I've imagined all these years that Yahweh's presence still rested on that Ark tucked away somewhere in a king's treasury. I can't bear to think it may have been chopped into . . ." I squeezed my eyes closed, and Daniel's sweet face came to mind. I couldn't forfeit my husband and Yahweh's presence in the same night. I lifted my chin. "Please, Shesh. Will you try to discover in which of the exiles the Ark was captured and where it might be?"

3

In the third year of the reign of Jehoiakim king of Judah, Nebuchadnezzar king of Babylon came to Jerusalem and besieged it. And the Lord delivered Jehoiakim king of Judah into his hand.

—DANIEL 1:1–2

Jerusalem
August 605 BC

The morning was already steamy, the sun barely peeking through the tattered curtains in our single-windowed servants' chamber.

Ima jostled me awake. "Hurry, my little joy. We must clean the king's private chamber before he returns."

I was on my feet before fully awake, knowing I couldn't delay. King Jehoiakim prowled his wives' chambers through the night and often returned to his private chamber shortly after dawn.

Ima slipped my sleeveless woolen robe over my tunic, and I tied a rope around my waist for a belt. She called out as we hurried without a lamp toward the door. "I freshened the linens last night so we need only replace the water in his washbasin, empty his waste pot, and tidy the room. You can fluff the pillows on his couch and sweep the floor."

"Yes, Ima." I followed her through the darkened hallways as I'd done every day of my life. At least every day I could remember. I tried to count the number of steps between our small chamber and the king's but always lost count. King Solomon's palace was enormous, but at three hundred years old and neglected by our king, Judah's royal residence was rather run down.

We arrived at the king's private chamber. Ima and I set to work feverishly. I pounded the couch pillows hard, remembering the one time King Jehoiakim returned while we worked. Abba had been with us, and the king had burst through the heavy cedar doors, startled at our presence. Then, donning the look of a predator, he advanced toward my ima with a smile that seemed more mean than happy.

My abba stepped in front of her. From my place beside the washbasin, I saw only the king's back and watched Abba fall to the floor, his blood soaking the tapestry. One of the king's guards took me outside the chamber, but I could hear Ima crying inside. We hadn't spoken Abba's name since—or the king's.

Trying to erase the memory, I reached for the hyssop broom and swept the floor as if an army chased me.

"Finished yet?"

"Yes, Ima." I scuffed the pile of dust under the bed. I could return this afternoon to finish while the king was at court.

As Ima reached for a tray of half-eaten food, I felt the floor vibrate under my feet. "Ima, what's happening?" Before I crossed the room to her open arms, the vibration grew to a rumble. A silver goblet on the tray skittered sideways on the slanted table.

She reached for my hand and led me onto the king's balcony that overlooked the Kidron Valley. Below us, speeding toward Jerusalem's Horse Gate, was an army so vast it looked like ink spilling onto a page.

"You must hide!" She shoved me back inside the chambers, but she returned to the balcony, watching the activity below.

"Ima, come on! We must hide!"

She rushed inside, her eyes wild. Looking back at the balcony and then at the chamber door, she seemed confused. Undecided. "He let them in. Why would he open the gates for them?"

"Who let who in, Ima?"

She shook my shoulders. "King Jehoiakim! He opened the gate to let in the Babylonians." She pulled me into a fierce embrace, praying her panic through hysterical sobs. "Yahweh, You must save my child. You must. Show me where to hide her. She's all I have. Please." She laid her cheek atop my head, whispering words I couldn't hear, while I clung to her middle.

"The Temple!" she said suddenly, slipping my hands from her waist to hold them in hers and then looking into my eyes. "Abigail, the Babylonians surely won't harm the priests." She ran with me toward the door. "Go to Yahweh's Temple. The priests will save a child." Before I realized her intention, she pushed me into the hallway, slammed the door, and locked it. "They would care little about a woman, but they'll have mercy on a child."

"No, Ima!" I kicked and pounded the door. "Ima, come with me!"

"Go, my precious girl. Go now before the Babylonians enter the palace. I love you. Go!"

Chaos surrounded me. Palace guards, servants, women, and children screamed in terror through the hallway. Having no choice but to obey her, I gave the door a final kick and ran toward the servants' wing. I kept my my head covering low, eyes averted, and hugged the wall. Sounds of invasion rose as I neared the servants' entrance. Men shouting in Hebrew were joined by myriad foreign tongues I'd never heard and didn't understand. Swords clanged and death cries echoed in my ears as I emerged from the palace onto the street leading to Yahweh's Temple.

Panic threatened to swallow me, hysteria beginning a low moan and weakening my knees.

Run to the Temple. Run to the Temple. I ordered my feet to move and focused on the Guard's Gate, which connected the palace grounds to the Temple courts. *The priests will save a child.*

I ran through the upper city's market, while soldiers fought, merchants fled, and women huddled with their children in dark corners. The Temple's gate was unguarded, so I rushed into the Great Court and found both priests and Levites busy at the far reaches of the large building, filling wagons with gold and silver from storerooms. The Temple guards were gone, probably fighting in the streets with Judah's army.

But who was guarding Yahweh?

Looking right and left to be sure I wasn't seen, I skittered across the outer court and up the stairs toward the Bronze Altar, where the high priest made sacrifices. I hid between the twelve bronze bulls that held the Bronze Sea on their backs. I'd seen these sacred items when Ima took me to daily sacrifices, but we watched from balconies and porticos. It all seemed more *real* now as I scraped the blood from the altar with my fingernail. I stood at the doorway to the Temple, studying the colossal bronze pillars—named Jakin and Boaz—and wondered for the thousandth time what lay beyond. Did Yahweh truly dwell on top of a gold box in the Most Holy Place?

Panicked voices drew my attention, and Temple guards flooded the courts, followed by foreign soldiers, swords clashing. Angry priests left the storerooms and their wagons, trying to escape the advancing violence. Fear sped my heart and choked my breathing.

I glanced at the pillars and the forbidden door between them. *Yahweh, if I must die today, I'd rather die by Your hand than by the sword of an enemy soldier.* With a little more faith than courage, I bolted across the upper court to the doors meant only for priests.

To my shock and great relief, the handle opened easily. I slipped into a silent world of glittering golden lamplight. Tipping my head back, I examined floor to ceiling glory. I ran to one golden lampstand, my fingers tracing the etchings of pomegranates, lilies, and almond blossoms. Then to the table, where gold bowls, dishes, censers, and wick trimmers were carefully placed and two stacks of sacred bread—each pile of six warm loaves—filled the room with a fresh-baked aroma. I snatched a loaf to quiet my rumbling tummy as the noise outside grew louder. If I was to die, I wouldn't die hungry. The sounds of fighting grew nearer, driving me closer to the One whose holiness would likely thrill me—to death.

I hesitated outside the Holy of Holies, separated only by a floor-to-ceiling curtain with cherubim woven in golden thread, and called out in a strained whisper, "Yahweh, if You're in there, please have mercy on me. I'm simply obeying my ima." As if I were swallowing a spoonful of fish oil, I broke through the curtain and ran inside. Eyes closed, I waited for the death blow.

Nothing. No rumble of thunder or fire from the sky.

I opened my eyes, repositioned the large flat loaf of bread under my arm, and scanned the wide room. Two gargantuan golden cherubim extended their wings over the famed golden box that ima called the Ark of the Covenant. She said Yahweh dwelled atop it, but I saw no cloud or fire of our invisible God—which I supposed made sense. He was invisible. I walked under the cherubim's wings and around the gold box, studying the greatest treasure of my ancestors. Dare I touch it?

I broke off a piece of bread and placed it on top of the Ark. Maybe Yahweh would appear if I gave Him small bites.

"No! You must not enter—" A priest's Hebrew warning was cut short by an enemy's blow as sounds of war erupted on the other side of the curtain.

I crouched low behind the Ark, but there was nowhere else to hide. *Yahweh, if You're here, save me!*

More pleading priests. More mocking replies.

I covered my ears and stared at the gold box. Waiting. Praying. I squeezed my eyes shut, imagining the God of my forefathers sweeping away the enemy as He'd done to the Egyptians when they chased the Israelites into the Red Sea. But the screaming continued. There would be no divine rescue today. No righteous anger when soldiers entered Yahweh's Temple. Why?

An iron grip cinched my waist. "Noooo!" I kicked and flailed at the monstrous brown arm that held me against a broad chest.

A huge hand clamped over my mouth and nose, making breathing impossible. "You can fight me now and die or serve the chosen royal princes of Judah under Babylon's protection." My captor spoke in broken Hebrew, but I understood.

Spots formed in my vision. Desperate for air, I searched the top of the golden Ark again. *Please, Yahweh. Show me Your presence.*

In little more than a blink, I saw a glimmer, a shimmering of air above the Ark, and then it was gone. *You are real!* My arms and legs relaxed, and the giant's hand fell away.

I gasped sweet breath. "What protection can Babylon offer?"

Strong arms whirled me to face a grinning giant. His black hair was close cropped, and I tried not to stare at his thin-plucked eyebrows and beardless chin. "You think you're in a position to negotiate, little wildcat? You're not. Babylon offers protection from Judah's primi-tive culture and the constant threat of invasion." The dimple in his chin made him seem almost human. "I am Ashpenaz, Prince Nebuchadnezzar's chief eunuch. I serve him with unswerving devotion in exchange for Babylon's protection. You see? We are not so different."

"I must find Ima and tell her I'm leaving so she won't worry."

All traces of humanity fled as he leaned to within a handbreadth of my face. "You have no ima. You have no abba. You have only Babylon, and no one will ever worry over you again." He straightened his fine linen robe and took two quick glances at the sacred bread I'd dropped. "That's a strange looking loaf of bread. You can take it with you if you like."

I noticed the piece I'd laid on top of the Ark was gone. "Did you eat the piece I placed on the Ark?"

His eyes narrowed. "I would never steal an offering to any god."

I bent to retrieve the bread from in front of the Ark and gasped. It was whole—as if I'd never offered a bite to Yahweh.

Ashpenaz shoved me toward the curtain, and I cradled the loaf as if it were as sacred as the Ark itself. Yahweh was *real!* He hadn't saved Jerusalem from the Babylonians, but He'd shown Himself to me.

4

The LORD sent Babylonian, Aramean, Moabite and Ammonite raiders against him to destroy Judah, in accordance with the word of the LORD proclaimed by his servants the prophets.

—2 KINGS 24:2

Ashpenaz delivered me to a soldier on the other side of the Temple's dividing curtain, and I cast a betrayed glance at the chief eunuch. He was far from kind, but he'd promised to protect me. The eunuch ordered three other soldiers to accompany us, while my new captor, a skinny and surly teenager, cut my rope belt and tied my wrists with it. Legs shaking, I followed Babylon's chief eunuch out of the Temple, with the other four soldiers surrounding me. Was a nine-year-old girl so dangerous that she required five grown men to escort her?

The moment I stepped into the Temple courts, I realized Ashpenaz had kept his promise and recruited the other men for *my* protection. Yanking the rope around my wrists, he pulled me closer. "Don't lag behind. The Arameans, Moabites, and Ammonites are hired armies and here only to fill their pockets. They'll see your slave value as worth a fight."

The hired soldiers' savagery was beyond imagining; they killed who they wished and stole what they wanted. Curved swords drawn, my saviors led me through the chaos of foreign tongues and grisly celebration. The smell of blood and waste caught in my throat, and I braced my hands on my knees, retching in the street.

Ashpenaz paused our escape, towering over me. "It was *your* king who opened the city gates, Wildcat. He offered up his guards in exchange for his own life." He lifted a thin-plucked brow. "Survival is a strong instinct. You'll need it."

We resumed our hurried pace past a Judean soldier whose lifeless eyes stared up at me, testifying to his misplaced loyalty, reminding me to award my trust wisely. Over my shoulder, I glimpsed Yahweh's Temple.

Do You see all this death from atop Your golden box?

"Eyes forward." One of the soldiers shoved me through the Horse Gate. Would I ever return to Jerusalem again? Could I worship Yahweh in a foreign land? Would I ever again hear King David's psalms?

The prophet Jeremiah had predicted doom for Judah's sins for as long as I could remember.

Captivity. Exile to foreign lands. But there were just as many prophets—more, really—who said Yahweh would never destroy us.

I turned once more to look at my city, but one of the black-eyed monsters poked the blunt end of his spear into my back. I cried out and then gritted my teeth. Was this what Ima meant when she said Judah was Yahweh's chosen people? Chosen to be captives? What good was it to be chosen if armies could destroy your home, your family, your life?

"Where are you taking me, Lord Ashpenaz?"

No answer. I chanced a look at the four soldiers. Each one marched without expression, eyes forward, jaws clenched. I dared not ask again.

We walked through the Kidron Valley and crested the hill east of the city, pausing while Ashpenaz pointed at a large encampment three hills away. "That will be your home until we depart for Babylon. It's a difficult trek, but we'll make it before dusk." His hard expression brooked no argument.

I lowered my head. "Yes, my lord."

The eunuch released his grip on the rope around my wrists as we descended the first hill, and I was grateful for the small mercy. The sun beat down, and hunger gnawed at my stomach. I caressed the loaf of bread, wondering if I dared eat it or if it had become sacred since Yahweh mended it. By afternoon, I was too hungry to care and nibbled at the loaf. Without yeast, it was firmer than Ima's brown bread, but it had a hint of sweetness I'd never tasted before. I received every bite as a gift from Yahweh.

The soldiers shared their water, and the eunuch led us with a resolve that left me breathless. When we finally reached the encampment, dusty, tired, and starving, the guard on duty bowed to Ashpenaz as if he were Babylon's king. The words he spoke were foreign, but they were offered with the deference of a servant to his master.

Ashpenaz acknowledged him with a nod and shoved me forward, answering in broken Hebrew. "This girl will serve the royal boys we take to Babylon. You will show the same care to her you've been ordered to give the boys. If she ends our journey with a single mark, you die."

The guard bowed and answered in the language I didn't understand. Ashpenaz strode away with the four soldiers, and I was left in the care of the stranger, who nudged me in the back with his spear, jabbering his foreign words and pointing toward a cook fire.

As we neared, I saw three women crouched low at the fire. Though their backs were toward me, their dingy-brown woolen robes were a familiar Judean weave. The sight pierced me afresh with grief. None of them were my ima. Would I ever see her again?

My captor shoved me, and I stumbled on a rock, falling hard against one of the women. She grabbed her side, and I began an apology, but the words caught in my throat at the sight of her. Glancing quickly at all three, I saw their bruised and swollen faces and was glad Ima wasn't among them. Each wore a bronze ankle shackle with a heavy chain as long as my arm that linked her to the next. One kneaded bread. Another prepared mounds of fresh fruits and vegetables, likely harvested from Judah's rich lands. The third woman turned a deer on the spit over the fire.

The bread woman spoke, her hands in constant rhythm, kneading the dough. "You'd better stop ogling us and get to work, or they'll do the same to you." Her voice broke, but she cleared her throat and continued. "You're young, but these animals don't care. You're too beautiful to leave alone."

"Stop it. Can't you see she's frightened enough?" The woman I'd fallen into scowled and patted the dirt beside her. "Come. Tell us your name, little one. We'll plot how to poison their food." A wicked grin lifted the corners of her lips, but she winced and touched a freshly open cut before reaching for another cucumber.

I liked her immediately and sat down by her. "My name is Abigail." Glancing left and right, I conspired with a whisper, "Can we really poison them?" Embittered silence replaced fleeting grins, but I'd earned their trust by my willingness to hate.

I snuck dates and cheese and offered them bites from my sacred loaf while we worked. I was sure Yahweh wouldn't mind.

The camp swelled with returning soldiers and their captives as the sun sank into the western hills. We worked long into the night, chopping vegetables, shelling pistachios, and baking bread. The Babylonians didn't care that our Sabbath had begun.

When I ate the last bite of sacred bread, I closed my eyes, laid my head on a rock, and thought of Ima. Was she safe inside our chamber? I couldn't bear to consider anything else. Then I remembered the Ark, the broken piece of bread, and the loaf that fed me and the beaten women.

Thank You, Yahweh. If You never show me Your presence again, at least I know You're real. The thought made me smile, and I don't remember falling asleep.

5

Then the king ordered Ashpenaz, chief of his court officials, to bring into the king's service some of the Israelites from the royal family and the nobility—young men without any physical defect, handsome, showing aptitude for every kind of learning . . . to serve in the king's palace. He was to teach them the language and literature of the Babylonians.

—DANIEL 1:3–4

"Wildcat." Someone kicked my side. "Wildcat!"

I jumped to my feet and looked up at the giant, Ashpenaz. Memories of yesterday's horrors rushed back like a flooding wadi in a desert rain, and I swallowed back instant tears. Breathless, speechless, I could do nothing but stare into his sharp black eyes.

"Follow me." He turned quickly and strode away. Had his smug expression softened, or had my yearning for kindness tricked me?

I followed him past gawking soldiers and weary women. I kept my eyes averted and walked a pace behind my protector. Weaving through an inner circle of blazing-white tents, I tried not to stare at the finery. Tapestries lined the dusty ground. Two Babylonian soldiers guarded the occupants of each dwelling, and a golden image of a strange-looking creature stood outside every tent.

"What's that?" I pointed at the dragon-snake-lion-eagle statue at the tent before us.

The chief eunuch eyed me as if I were a mosquito. "*That* is Sirrush." He bowed to the image as he spoke. "The earthly representation of our god Marduk." He clapped twice, and four Hebrew boys immediately emerged from the tent, eyes wide and fearful. Two boys appeared to have reached manhood. The younger two were about my age, faces mirroring each other identically but height and hair color quite different.

Ashpenaz stepped aside to introduce them. "You will tend to the needs of these four princes. They must arrive in Babylon with no scratches or bruises, or you will die. They must be well fed, or you will die. Give them whatever they want, or—"

"Or I will die?"

Ashpenaz raised his hand to strike me but halted when I flinched. "Interrupt me again, and you will die."

I bowed, my heart pounding, and he walked away. *"Give them whatever they want . . ."*

"You're very brave." The oldest-looking boy stepped toward me.

Another boy raised his eyebrows. "Very brave or very stupid."

The first boy elbowed him and then nodded respectfully. "I'm Daniel, and my rude friend is Hananiah. What's your name?"

"I'm Abigail, my lord." I bowed, noticing the younger two boys nudging Hananiah.

"These are my twin brothers," Hananiah said, pointing to the obvious resemblance, "and we will all be careful not to scratch ourselves or get bruised." There was a gleam of mischief in his eyes that unsettled me.

Daniel looked past me, and I turned to see what was so interesting. But he appeared to simply be observing the camp. "How old are you, Abigail?" he asked, still calculating our surroundings.

I hesitated. What if he thought I was too young and rejected me? Perhaps avoiding an answer was safer. "How old are you?"

His attention snapped back to me, a grin curving his lips. He stepped closer and lowered his voice. "Old enough to find a way to escape."

Fear tightened like a rope around my neck. "They'll kill us all if you attempt to escape. You're in the very center of their camp, surrounded by trained soldiers."

Daniel exchanged a glance with Hananiah and

then studied me. His thoughts shone through his eyes, windows to his mind. I could see him sorting through possibilities, and I knew when he'd reached a conclusion. With a sigh, he said, "Hananiah, it's too risky with Mishael and Azariah—and now Abigail's life is at risk too. If we fail . . ."

Hananiah kneaded the back of his neck. "I know you're right, but we can't leave Jerusalem." He looked up, tears in his eyes. "It will be forever, Daniel. If we can't find a way to escape, we'll never see Jerusalem again."

Daniel grabbed his friend's robe. "Not forever. Jeremiah said a remnant would return from captivity in seventy years. We could come back, Hananiah." He looked at the twins. "You believe, don't you? We could come back."

"Seventy years?" My interruption startled them. "A king or prince may live seventy years, but you're captives now. Servants and slaves don't reach that age." My candor washed the color from the twins' faces.

"Slaves?" A frightened squeak came from the one with golden curls. "I don't want to be a slave."

"We aren't slaves, Mishael." Hananiah shot a dark look my way.

"Of course we're slaves," I said, wondering at his intelligence. "Haven't you heard them calling us captives?"

Hananiah, leaving me seared from his burning glare, turned to brace his brother's shoulders. "Yes, we're *captives,* but they're choosing the best princes and nobility of Judah to join young nobility from other nations to attend school in Babylon. The best minds from every culture in the empire are being invited to the capital, where we'll study for three years and then be assigned roles in government." He shrugged and aimed a defeated look at Daniel. "I suppose if we stayed in Jerusalem, we'd learn less, live in fear of invasion, and be assigned roles in Jehoiakim's court."

"Yes, a *puppet* government," Daniel said, "that obeys the same king we're following to Babylon. We'd be more captive here than in Babylon."

Regretting my harsh words to these would-be officials, I bowed before the four princes. "Forgive me, my lords. Perhaps royal families live longer." I didn't believe it, but maybe the simple apology would save me from a beating when Ashpenaz returned.

Daniel lifted me to my feet and stared at me with a grief so raw, it startled me. "My abba was killed in battle four years ago. My ima was killed yesterday while I watched. Royal families die too, Abigail."

"I didn't mean . . . I only meant . . ." Mouth dry as a desert, I couldn't escape his gaze. Pain washed with compassion met me. *Please,*

Yahweh, God on top of the Ark, let all our suffering be over.

My ima's sad face appeared before me. She told me suffering lasted a lifetime. "I don't mean to be harsh, but it's better to be honest with Mishael than let his hopes be dashed by bronze shackles."

"Do you see shackles?" Hananiah held out his wrists, shaking them in frustration.

I remembered Ashpenaz's instructions not to scratch or bruise them. Of course they wouldn't be shackled. So how had the eunuch escorted them to camp without a fight? And how would they be forced to walk to Babylon?

"What gifts did Ashpenaz promise if you went to Babylon without a struggle?" It was more accusation than question.

The boys averted their eyes, and I felt all the more justified in my mounting disdain. They were no different than Judah's king. Selfish, greedy, and arrogant.

Daniel, their self-appointed spokesman, finally lifted his eyes. "Nebuchadnezzar ordered every member of the king's court and their families to report to the throne room, including the king's relatives and council members. He chose young men who he determined to be 'without physical defect, handsome, showing aptitude for learning, and quick to understand' to answer questions. When we answered correctly, members of Judah's royal court lived. If we answered incorrectly, someone from our family died."

I felt my face drain of color, realizing I'd misjudged their suffering. "How many questions did you answer correctly?"

"All of them," Daniel said. "But they weren't as fortunate." He pointed at other Judean boys, emerging from their tents after the first night of captivity. "Some of our friends saw their entire families killed."

I had no more words. I could only stare at the empty-eyed boys huddled together near their tent flaps.

Azariah, the smallest twin, stepped forward with boyish determination. "If we could escape and return to the palace, we could search out Jerusalem's secret tunnels. I know they're real. We could access them and travel almost to Jericho with our families." His eyes sparkled with adventure, and I marveled that a boy so close to my age could be so naive. Had he heard nothing Daniel and Hananiah said?

When I turned to see Daniel's response, he was studying me again. This time, his eyes were shuttered, and I couldn't quite decipher his thoughts. Before I could ask, he met Azariah's enthusiasm with a wan smile. "I fear the tunnels are only a boyish dream, my friend. We must live in Babylon so our families won't die in Jerusalem. Nebuchadnezzar made it clear. We submit to his *invitation, or those we love die.*"

He turned to me, challenge in his eyes. "You see, Abigail, our bronze shackles are self-imposed. By choosing integrity and honor, we will follow the Babylonians into captivity and trust Yahweh to bring us back to Jerusalem at the end of Jeremiah's prophesied seventy years."

Hananiah growled his frustration at the cloudless sky. "Daniel, what are the chances we'll live to be eighty-two years old? And of Mishael and Azariah living to eighty? If we choose to save our families by going to Babylon, we need to go and not look back."

"Oh no, my friend." Daniel extended his hand. "The royal court ignored Jeremiah's warnings, but we won't ignore his promise. Yahweh said a remnant of captives would return to Jerusalem in seventy years. Why couldn't we be with them?" He offered his hand, and it lingered in the air, like a bleating lamb waiting to shed its blood for a covenant.

Hananiah's fingers twitched, his eyes searching Daniel's so long I thought I might grip his wrist if Hananiah didn't hurry. Finally, he grabbed Daniel's wrist, and they locked grips, sealing their vow. Hananiah drew in his brothers with his free hand. "We trust Yahweh can bring us all back in seventy years." Mishael and Azariah each placed a single hand atop the older boys' grip, eyes wide with adventure.

Their camaraderie shifted something deep inside me. Less than a day after my world had been shattered, I found myself hoping against all hope that these boys could do as they'd promised. Perhaps the God who had restored the sacred bread could keep these boys whole until the remnant returned.

"Abigail, come!" Daniel reached for me, grasping my hand and placing it atop theirs. "You will return with us."

His wide smile humbled me. My throat tightened. Perhaps I could serve in one of their households when we arrived in Babylon. Maybe someone under these masters could live to return in seventy years. The tiny seed of hope dared to sprout, despite my grief and fear for the future.

Shame for my previous assumptions drove me to my knees, and I let my dusty brown hair form a curtain to hide my tears. "Forgive me, my lords, for speaking to you with anything but the utmost respect. I will serve you faithfully my whole life."

An uncomfortable silence replaced the jubilant moment, and one of the younger boys whispered, "Why is she crying?"

Feeling foolish, I swiped at my eyes and turned my back, wishing I could disappear into the sea of white tents.

I felt a presence draw near and was certain

it was Daniel, but curiosity forced me to peer behind me. "Go. Please. I'll find water for your morning—"

"I'm glad you're coming, but you don't need to fear us." His voice was kind, massaging my battered heart.

I sniffed back more emotion while stiffening my spine. "Thank you."

"Will you look at me?"

Squeezing my eyes shut, I wiped the last drop of moisture away and turned to face my four masters. Daniel offered his hand. "What we've endured here strips away any pretense. Ashpenaz has assigned you to serve us, but you'll also be our friend. Friends help friends."

I stared at his hand as if it were a viper. He was young, but he was a man. If I gave him my hand, would he take all of me? I looked up, searching his face for trickery or deceit but found only clarity in those warm brown eyes. Nothing hidden, nothing held back.

Placing my hand in his, I felt his warmth seep into my fingers, my palm. All the way up my arm. I closed my eyes, letting the safety of his presence wrap me.

Since I'd shared the last of my loaf of bread with the women, perhaps serving these descendants of David could keep me on the path of Yahweh's blessing when we left Jerusalem.

6

Some of the Israelites from the royal family . . . were to be trained for three years, and after that they were to enter the king's service.

—DANIEL 1:3, 5

We lingered in the captive camp, waiting for the mercenary armies to sate their thirst for violence and fill their pockets with gold. I tended to my princes' laundry, their hair, their nails, all the while searching every captive woman's face for Ima's features.

She wasn't here.

After my chores were finished, the princes included me in mindless games to pass the time. Still I searched for her.

"Who are you looking for?" Daniel asked on our fifth day in camp, a stone poised in his hand. The other three princes waited eagerly to hear my answer.

"My ima." I looked down at three smooth stones in my hands and tossed one into a basket twenty paces away.

A Babylonian messenger on horseback rode past us, kicking up rocks and dust. I choked and waved away the cloud. We paused our game as his horse skidded to a halt outside Prince Nebuchadnezzar's white tent. The rider leapt off the horse and ran inside. A wrenching roar followed that sent a shivering dread through my bones.

Within moments, Crown Prince Nebuchadnezzar emerged with Ashpenaz and another man wearing the wide gold collar of a eunuch who looked even fiercer than the one I knew. The warrior eunuch demanded Nebuchadnezzar's horse be brought immediately, and Ashpenaz marched resolutely toward the guardian of the princes' camp.

Daniel exchanged a conspiratorial glance with Hananiah, and they wandered closer to a fig tree and hid underneath to eavesdrop. I followed my prince, taking our game basket so we could pretend to be picking figs. We arrived just as Ashpenaz explained the messenger's news.

"King Nabopolassar is dead. Our crown prince is now King Nebuchadnezzar, but he must ride for Babylon immediately to ensure a smooth ascension to the throne." The guard slammed his fist over his heart. Ashpenaz nodded his approval. "Arioch and I will accompany our new king with a thousand soldiers and return to Babylon in haste. King Nebuchadnezzar trusts you, Nebuzaradan, to lead the Judean seedlings home *unblemished* within forty days—or we'll send out troops to find you. Is this understood?"

"Why am I not among the thousand returning to Babylon with Nebuchadnezzar?" Though Daniel and I saw only his back, anger singed the man's tone.

"He trusts you—and only you—to deliver the best of Judah's young minds with caution and care. Our new king will build an empire, Nebuzaradan, not simply destroy nations." Ashpenaz hurried away, and Nebuzaradan whirled to find us picking ripe figs behind him. "What did you hear?"

I fell to my knees immediately, but Daniel faced his fury. "Please accept our humble concern at the death of King Nabopolassar, my lord. We'll collect our simple belongings and be ready to march at your command." He reached for my arm, pulling me to my feet as we scurried away from the silent commander.

My four princes were the first in a line of captives that stretched farther than I could see. I counted our traveling days with small pebbles placed in a basket as we traversed mountains and valleys, rocks and plains, deserts and rivers. Our feet bore the burden. The servants bartered goose fat like gold, and I was grateful my princes had secreted small palace valuables in their pockets for trade. Three sets of earrings, five rings, and three bracelets saved my life and theirs with the goose fat they purchased.

Each night I mixed a small ceramic pot of goose fat with the olive oil we'd brought from Jerusalem and then massaged it into their feet to stave off blisters. Each morning I smeared more of the mixture on their lips to prepare for our day's march in the unrelenting sun. I wrapped their heads with light-colored cloth, moistening the turbans with water to keep them cool. All this and more I did to save our lives, yes, but also because I wished for them to become my friends. The only family I now had.

The realization that we were nearing Babylon came when I first glimpsed the sparkling waters of the Euphrates.

"Look, Hananiah!" Azariah hopped up and down like a desert hare. "Will they let us bathe in it?"

Hananiah exchanged a wary look with Daniel. The two older boys then turned to me for an answer. I shrugged. How should I know?

Azariah, the smallest but boldest twin, looked at me with wide, expectant eyes. I didn't want to disappoint him, but the thought terrified me. I'd kept my princes healthy and unmarked for the whole journey. What if they cut their feet? Were caught in the river's current?

Thankfully, the decision was made for me. Our military escort was in too great a hurry to loll in the river. Instead, they loaded us twelve at a time into *quffas*, circular woven-reed vessels, flat bottomed and coated with pitch, the side walls bowing outward. The river was full of them, crossing over the mighty Euphrates with their human cargo and the livestock that had been driven with us for food. As those of us who crossed were driven south, Daniel spoke quietly behind his hand. "It would be easier to line up the quffas and walk across them to the other side of the river."

I covered my mouth to hide a grin. The tedious process of crossing the Euphrates had exasperated our captors. One soldier had already been killed for whipping a young prince. What an odd people, the Babylonians, to kill one of their own to protect a prisoner. A child, no less.

For the next three days on our final approach to Babylon, my friends and I noticed everything about the country that would become our home for the next seventy years. Everywhere we looked, something new winked back, and my princes' curiosity demanded answers. Hananiah, who was curious enough to ask a rock questions, approached a soldier whose missing front teeth made pronouncing the *s* sound rather comical. The poor soldier had no peace as Hananiah asked about everything from plowing and planting to the barrel-shaped reed houses lining the river-banks.

Nearing the end of the third day, I'd used up nearly all the olive oil I brought from Jerusalem.

"I've seen no olive trees, my lord. How can you live without oil?"

The soldier glared at me and turned his attention to Hananiah. "In Babylon we grow sesame seeds and use their oil. You'll find it equally useful." His tone said he was finished with our questions.

Farther south, the waters split into tributaries, and we followed the eastern branch, marching into drier, dusty terrain. On the final morning of travel, I counted forty pebbles in my basket and sighed with relief, thankful Ashpenaz wouldn't be sending troops to find us. I woke before dawn and mixed goose fat with the last of the olive oil. Before mixing, I rubbed a drop from our last vial between my fingers and inhaled the pungent aroma of home. Goodbye, Judah. I emptied the rest into the pot of goose fat and squished the mixture between my fingers, memorizing the sensation and wondering if sesame oil would feel different.

Too soon, the captive train was moving again, equal measures of hope and dread pulling our nerves taut in the stillness. Every day we had marched farther from the life we knew and closer to a life we must build. Today we would discover if it was better or worse.

By midday, the vague outline of a walled city appeared on the horizon, looming ahead like a vision in the heat waves. Exhaustion battled with apprehension, the eerie silence lingering over the captives in our caravan. Even my curious young princes remained speechless as the vision became reality.

The dirt roads on which we had traveled became packed and smooth. Farmland was marked in squares by perfectly dug canals that both nourished the soil and protected the crops from animals. City walls stood higher than the cedar trees we passed on our journey. Once inside the first wall, we saw more crops surrounded by canals. Barley, no doubt. Only a few houses dotted the sprawling fields before we reached a second, even higher wall that protected what I supposed was the city of Babylon itself. Soaring above everything else was a giant mountain of bricks, its peak rising to the heavens, higher than any structure I'd imagined men could make.

Daniel slipped his hand into mine, and only then did I realize I was trembling. "It's the Tower of Babel," he said. "There was talk King Nabopolassar had been rebuilding it. We'll see if Nebuchadnezzar continues—or if Yahweh stops him as He stopped the nations so long ago."

I couldn't speak. Could barely breathe. The ingenuity of our captors was breathtaking.

The soldiers on horseback led the captives onto a bricked road. Inside the first wall of the city, we approached what appeared to be a huge tunnel. Above it stretched a platform for guards, running the whole width of the tunnel, which was broader than a house. The city's second wall extended from both sides of the tunnel, and I wondered if the wall was that thick all the way around the city.

As we marched closer to the tunnel, a trumpet sounded from one of the mammoth parapets above us, the sound sending a shiver that worked down my spine. The clopping of hooves echoed off the walls, drowning out the pounding of my heart. I saw, deep inside the tunnel, gargantuan cedar-paneled double doors—each door the height of fifteen stacked camels. Every step took us closer and closer until finally we were swallowed into the belly of Babylon. The cedar doors swung open, each door hung with seven iron hinges, each hinge the size of a grown man.

The horsemen emerged into the light. I released my breath and slowed my steps, wishing I could postpone the first glimpse of the world that would swallow my past.

Daniel squeezed my hand, infusing me with his courage. "I'm sure what waits for us inside Babylon can't compare to what we've endured outside it."

I offered a half-hearted smile, reminding myself he had been raised a prince. When he was taken prisoner, it was to enter a three-year education and then a government position.

But what lay ahead for me?

7

Then they said, "Come, let us build ourselves a city, with a tower that reaches to the heavens, so that we may make a name for ourselves."

—GENESIS 11:4

Inside the sanctuary of Babylon, hundreds of Babylonians poured from their homes to line both sides of the wide city street, shouting and jeering with upraised fists. Having learned bits of the Akkadian language in the forty-plus days of our captivity, I understood the denigration aimed at us and feared for those of us who weren't royalty.

For the hundredth time, I wondered about the three women I'd met my first day in camp. I hadn't seen them since being assigned to care for my boys. Had they survived the journey? Would they rather die than live as I'd seen them?

Resolving to ignore the angry citizens, I looked beyond them to the city I would call home. It was like stepping from earth to the moon. Everything glowed with subtle glory, yet a film of dust dulled its brilliance. Construction and progress infiltrated every detail of the city around us. Workers hauled wheeled carts full of bricks everywhere I looked, and I thought of

71

Ima's stories of Egypt and the brickmakers under Pharaoh's torturous rule. Who made all these bricks that were placed in the streets below this wide, elevated avenue on which we marched?

Lovely villas lined the streets below us, where new canals were being dug to parallel nearly every one. Walls and buildings, all made of bricks, received a facade of tile in vibrant colors. Outside two-storied homes, at various levels of terraced gardens, men shoveled dirt from large wagons, creating a paradise for each family with plants I not only couldn't name but also had never seen.

A sudden bump into Hananiah's back told me fascination had overtaken my senses. The procession halted in a columned outer courtyard of what must be the palace. The engraved marble columns bore images of unimaginable creatures—half man, half beast.

Hananiah looked back at me while I continued gawking. "It's a good thing Daniel has you to protect him." He winked at his friend, motioning to our joined hands, and I ducked my head, pulling away from Daniel's grasp.

"Immigrants of Jerusalem!" The familiar voice with its broken Hebrew saved me from further humiliation. Ashpenaz, Nebuchadnezzar's chief eunuch, stood atop the tall, wide staircase, commanding the attention of both captive and captor. In addition to his wide gold neckband, he now wore a purple sash over his left shoulder, cinched at his narrow waist with a lion-headed broach. "Your journey is over," he said, "and your true service to the empire now begins."

He nodded to the men on horseback, who had led us from Jerusalem with such care and respect. They dismounted, shouting orders and moving quickly into the crowd of captives, swords drawn. A wicked gleam appeared in the lisping soldier's eyes. Daniel stepped in front of me, but the soldier shoved him aside. "You, girl. You're going out the south gate." He gripped my arm as if it were a twig he would break without remorse.

"Abigail!" Daniel reached for me, but a line of soldiers separated all the maids from their princes and ushered Judah's young royalty up the palace stairs. I saw Daniel searching the crowded courtyard with the same panic I felt. Our eyes met for only a moment before the lisping soldier shoved me through a wooden gate and the sting of a whip kissed my back.

I'd reached the end of my protective custody.

A contingent of soldiers drove the worthless captives through the streets amid a hateful throng. I don't remember the route. I know only the pelting of rotten fruit, the humiliation of spittle in my hair, and the blinding sun that assaulted us on our way to the quay. My body ached—but not like my heart. Would I ever see my princes again? Would they remember me?

"Wait here for your assignments." We captives formed a line on the street along a canal. The smell of rotting fish convulsed my empty stomach, but I swallowed again and again, refusing to show my weakness. At the front of the line a short, plump eunuch wrote on a wax tablet and seemed to be assigning the captives destinations and placing them in quffas. I recognized none of the soldiers surrounding me and had only nightmarish inklings of what might be required of a nine-year-old slave girl.

The fat eunuch wore a purple sash like Ashpenaz. Could I somehow gain his favor? When the woman in front of me was placed in a quffa, I fell at the man's feet, my hands outstretched. "If it pleases my lord, I would serve wholeheartedly under your protection."

I heard nothing except his labored breathing and counted seven breaths before the handle of his whip slipped under my chin. Prodding me to stand, he removed the whip's handle and inspected me with his small black eyes. "You will serve wholeheartedly or you will die, pretty one."

Every instinct screamed to pull my sleeveless robe tighter around my neck, but I stood without flinching. The fat eunuch smiled, reminding me of a jackal I saw in the desert on our journey. "You will serve well at the Esagila, the temple of Marduk. For now, you can empty the priests' waste pots and scrub their floors. When you get a little older, you're pretty enough to become a priestess."

I dared not appear pleased, though emptying waste pots sounded better than other assignments I'd heard given out. The older girl ahead of me would gut and section animals in a butcher's shop. The three women before her were sent to the limestone quarries in the Zagros Mountains.

"Thank you, my lord," I said in halting Aramaic. "I am in your debt."

He leaned close and lifted his brows as he spoke. "Indeed. And I'll collect that debt from your earnings as a priestess." His breath smelled of garlic and rancid fish.

He pushed me toward another guard who seemed happy to escape the quay. Tall and slender, my new guardian was younger than other soldiers I'd seen and not quite as fierce. His hand was gentle on my arm as he led me back toward the wide bricked street that seemed to split the city in two.

"This is called the Processional Way," he volunteered. "The king, visiting dignitaries, or captives enter the city on this street." I only nodded, hoping my silence would win his favor. But as we neared what Daniel had called the Tower of Babel, I couldn't hold back. "What is that?" I pointed at the seven-level structure that nearly touched the clouds.

75

"That is the Etemenanki. I've heard your people call it the Tower of Babel, and your myths say a god confused the world's languages when our ancestors built it." He looked down at me with a condescending smirk. "Have you heard such nonsense?"

"It isn't nonsense." My response clouded his good humor, so I quickly added, "I mean, we believe the story is true, my lord, as surely as you believe the myths about your gods." I smiled as I said it, hoping he would attribute my forthrightness to childishness.

He grinned, steering me around a corner and through another guarded gate. Mouth gaping, I halted at the sight of another impressive structure. It wasn't covered in gold like our Temple in Jerusalem, but it was at least three times the size. "What is this one?"

He nudged me forward. "This is where you'll serve, little one." The sadness in his voice confused me. It was like a paradise. Date palms abounded in the courtyards, and the beautiful gardens with their shaded benches created peaceful and inviting settings. Bald, clean-shaven men tended bronze braziers that emitted the smoky sweet aroma of incense. I paused when my escort approached the sprawling stone building, but he nudged me forward—and no one stopped us.

"Won't we be struck dead?" I asked, taking

mincing steps as we drew closer to the double doors.

"Of course not." My guardian flung open a door and hailed a tall young priest, who looked as if a strong wind might knock him over. "I have here a serving maid for the Esagila."

The young priest gazed down a long, slender nose. "Do you worship Marduk, girl?"

I glanced first at my captor and then back at the priest, thinking it best to simply shake my head no.

"Our supplicants enter the temple and immediately proceed to the altar, where they receive a gift from Marduk before offering their petition." The priest moved into the dimly lit chamber to our right, where a looming gold dragon-like statue stood over chanting priests.

My captor whispered as we followed. "This priest is devout and will treat you kindly, but others won't. Learn who you can trust, girl, or you won't live long." He shoved me at the tall priest and interrupted the man's instruction. "I need no lessons on Marduk." He was gone before either the priest or I could protest.

I stood in the shadow of the gold idol, choking on the cloying odor of foreign incense, and noted a gold table beside the altar. On it sat a single platter stacked high with pieces of broken bread. *Broken bread, not whole loaves as in Yahweh's Temple.*

"What's that?" I asked the priest.

"The pieces are Marduk's gift to the supplicants. You're old enough to bake. Perhaps the high priest will assign you the job."

I wanted to ask why Marduk didn't bake his own bread but was sure it would earn me a beating. Returning my attention to the pieces of broken bread, my dread turned to despair. Yahweh would never find me here. Could Yahweh find me anywhere in Babylon?

8

Fear of man will prove to be a snare,
but whoever trusts in the LORD is
    kept safe.

                    —PROVERBS 29:25

It had been a week, and the kind soldier hadn't returned. I was silly to hope. His advice, however, had become my best friend. The first priest I met delivered me to the chief priest, who was as corrupt as a festering sore. He ordered me to clean until I became of age and then turned me over to the chief priestess, who assigned my daily duties.

This morning after sacrifices ended, I was given a new job in the worship chamber—cleaning the blood from Marduk's image and disposing of animal entrails after a divining session. The sound of sandals scuffing on tiles whirled me around, a wet cloth my only defense.

The chief priest's chambermaid met my fear with a smirk. "Take that attitude to my master, and you'll be flogged before you speak. He commands your presence immediately."

She turned to go, and I followed, leaving my dirty cloth and murky water at the altar. Winding through hallways and darkened corridors, she led me into the bowels of Babylon's wealthiest temple. We passed busy scribes and arguing priests, primping priestesses and happy noblemen. Finally, we turned down a window-less hallway with a single doorway at the end. My breath quickened, and I felt as if I could reach out and touch the walls on both sides.

"Please, tell him you couldn't find me."

I turned to run, but she captured my arm. A single torch on the wall gleamed in her eyes, making her appear unreal. "Too late." She lifted her hand and knocked.

The door opened before a second quick strike, and the high priest pulled me inside, ignoring his maid. "Here's the little beauty I've been telling you about, Lord Laqip. She'll be ripe for initiation by the Akitu festival in the spring. What better way to celebrate Nebuchadnezzar's coronation and Marduk's ascension to supreme god over all the earth?"

The priest held my back against him, one arm across my chest and the other locked under my chin, forcing me to face the nobleman.

"Why would I pay for a child who has no idea how to please me?"

"Because with her initiation you'll name her. Define her nature and character for the duration of her earthly life." The priest pressed his hand tighter against my throat. "Just as the gods bestowed fifty names on Marduk when he conquered Tiamat, so you become like the gods when you name this little goddess—for a mere fifty talents of silver."

"Fifty talents? You're mad!" The nobleman started toward the door.

The high priest turned me to face him, hissing a threat. "If he leaves, you'll beg on Babylon's streets by sunset." He shoved me toward the angry nobleman.

"Please!" I whimpered, stumbling over my feet and clutching at the nobleman's robe to keep from falling.

He shrugged off my hand and looked down at me as if I were a crawling insect.

At least he stayed to listen. I straightened my dingy robe and met his gaze. I couldn't beg on Babylon's streets. Slavery to one man was better than torture by an angry mob. I had six months to escape the Esagila before the Akitu festival.

"I may not know what pleases you, my lord, but I'm no child, and I'm worth every shekel of fifty talents."

Lord Laqip arched a manicured brow and again let his eyes roam my form. This time I put my hands on my hips, lifted my chin, and stared back. Surprise lit his expression. Then something more frightening than desire.

Tenderly cradling my cheeks, he drew to within a handbreadth. "I'll call you Belili, like the consort of the shepherd god, Tammuz. All

of Babylon will know you as *my* little lamb."
My skin crawled at the look in his eyes, but I
stared back without flinching.

He released me and reached for the pouch at
his waist. I bowed my head, trying to control
my shaking. The priest shoved me toward the
door. "Leave us, girl."

I stumbled in my hurry to the door, opened
it, and ran out of the chamber—only moments
older but vastly wiser.

9

Among those who were chosen were some from Judah: Daniel, Hananiah, Mishael and Azariah. The chief official gave them new names: to Daniel, the name Belteshazzar; to Hananiah, Shadrach; to Mishael, Meshach; and to Azariah, Abednego.

—DANIEL 1:6–7

For six months I'd kept to myself, emptying waste pots, dusting idols, clearing ashes from altars, and dumping more animal entrails than I ever imagined a single city could produce. Every day I prayed to whatever god would listen that I might stay a child forever, but my body changed without permission, and I'd thought of no way to escape the Esagila.

Spring came and with it barley sowing and the feast of Akitu. Nebuchadnezzar returned to Babylon, having conquered the Hatti nation, and prepared for his official coronation as King of the Earth. On the fourth day of Nisannu, the high priest opened the Akitu ceremonies by presenting King Nebuchadnezzar with the divine scepter and sending him to Borsippa, a half day's sail downriver, to spend the night in the temple of Nabu.

Waiting for the summons of Lord Laqip, I curled into a ball on my sleeping mat in the chamber I shared with five other chambermaids, shaking and nauseous. The maids told the temple's chief steward I was too ill to eat, and since so few would visit our temple today, he excused me from my duties.

The summons from Lord Laqip didn't come.

The next day, King Nebuchadnezzar was scheduled to return and make an appearance at the Esagila. We maids cleaned every room, every nook and cranny. Though dread of my initiation still loomed, busyness dulled my anxiety and carried me through another day without a summons from the lord who had purchased my name.

So it continued each day of the festival, and over the course of the week, my dread slowly lessened. Perhaps Laqip had a change of heart— though I questioned if a man like him even possessed the vital organ. More likely, he had a wife who'd discovered his wandering and threatened him with the loss of something more precious. I spent the last day of the festival considering all the wonderful ways Laqip's wife might torture him if she discovered his temple antics.

Just after midday, the temple steward called

me aside. "The southeast treasury is a mess, and the high priest is furious. I told you this morning to clean up the room on the far end of the hallway. What have you been doing all day?"

I fell to my knees, arms extended overhead. "Forgive me, master. I'll clean it right away." Was he losing his mind? He hadn't told me to clean it this morning, but I didn't dare argue. I feared another beating.

"Go! Now!"

I fled his presence, rushing first to get my cleaning supplies and then through hallways that skirted the temple proper. Finally, I reached the treasury wing. Priests were replacing goblets and dishes in small closets after their use in the festival. I tried each of the treasury room doors lining both sides of the hall, but they were locked. How was I supposed to clean when the priest neglected to unlock them? Only one door stood ajar at the end of the hall, a dim light shining from within.

I pushed open the door and stepped cautiously over the threshold, finding a single lamp sputtering on a table in the far corner. Strange. I took two more steps inside, enthralled with the glittering gold and silver stacked in piles from floor to ceiling. What faraway kingdoms had these beautiful treasures come from?

"There's my little lamb." A deep voice.

I whirled and dropped my cleaning basket.

Lord Laqip stood behind the door—and closed it. Panic rose, but if I cried out, who would save me? The blood pounding in my ears answered. No one. No one. No one.

Terror knocked me to my knees. "Forgive me, lord. I was sent here to clean the treasury." Quick breaths fought back tears, and I hoped feigned innocence would purchase time to devise an escape.

"You are the treasure, little Belili." I sensed his approach and wanted to flee when dirty bare feet rested by my fingertips. He reached down to help me stand, but I let my body go limp, refusing to be lifted. I couldn't run, but I wouldn't make it easy.

"Ah, a stubborn one." He gripped my arms, digging his fingers into my flesh, and lifted me off the floor, pulling my face to within a handbreadth of his.

I closed my eyes. He could not make me look at him.

The sound he made was like a growl—and then came the blow. The pain in my cheek brought an explosion of light. I fell, knocking my head on the floor. Instantly, Laqip's heavy bulk smothered me. I wriggled beneath him, trying to breathe, to scream, to escape. I realized in that moment, no matter how invincible a woman's resolve, a man's sheer strength can break it.

"The high priest said I could find Lord Laqip and his new initiate choosing jewelry from the treasury." A male voice from the hallway sent the nobleman rolling to his feet, smoothing his oiled hair and beard.

I crawled to a corner and curled into a ball, pressing my throbbing cheek against the cool tiles. I heard the door squeak on its hinges, then footsteps.

"Lord Laqip, greetings from the palace and your new king." The voice was familiar, floating on the edges of my consciousness. "I'm taking the girl to her new master."

I kept my face hidden, wishing I could disappear among the treasures.

"But I paid fifty talents for her!" the nobleman shouted. "She's mine. I named her Belili."

"It is a fine name." I knew that man's voice. Ashpenaz. "I'll be sure to inform her new master."

A grip like iron siezed my arm. I cried out and was released. Falling to the floor, I heard scuffling and grunts. I covered my head and tried to block out Laqip's shouts and protests.

Then there was silence. Blessed silence.

A hand touched my shoulder gently, and I screamed again, my eyes squeezed shut. "Don't touch me! Stay away!" Shaking, I scooted away blindly until the treasure blocked my retreat, unable to bear a man's touch.

"Shhh, Wildcat. Laqip is gone." I opened my eyes and saw the eunuch. "I'm taking you home."

"Home?" My naïveté had nearly destroyed me. Now suspicion whirred at the awful things a eunuch might do to a ten-year-old girl. "Why would you want me?"

"I don't want you," he said with a lopsided grin. "But your friends—Belteshazzar, Shadrach, Meshach, and Abednego—sent me to find you."

He was trying to trick me. I gathered my torn robe and pressed myself against the treasure at my back. "I have no friends, and I've never heard of those men."

10

The king assigned them a daily amount of food and wine from the king's table. . . . But Daniel resolved not to defile himself with the royal food and wine, and he asked the chief official for permission not to defile himself this way.

—DANIEL 1:5, 8

Ashpenaz led me through the dimly lit halls of the Esagila. "Belteshazzar, Shadrach, Meshach, and Abednego are the Babylonian names of the princes you served on the journey from Jerusalem." He slowed only long enough to give me a disparaging glance. "They still call you *friend*."

I ducked my head, walking quickly past every priest and priestess, afraid any one of them might snatch me from my dream. When we stepped into the outer courtyard, I closed my eyes and lifted my face to the Babylonian sun, feeling its warmth replace the chill that penetrated my bones. Daniel sent Ashpenaz to find me. Shadrach and the twins hadn't forgotten me. The sounds of children playing and the smell of spring blossoms ushered me back into the land of the living.

A hand on my back shot terror through me, and I shrieked, drawing unwanted attention. The eunuch glowered at me. "You are in need of a new robe, little Belili."

"Don't call me that," I shot back, sounding like a petulant child.

"You will walk two steps behind me and address me as 'my lord' or 'Lord Ashpenaz,' and I will call you anything I wish, Wildcat."

He started down a bricked path toward the river rather than the Processional Way, and I hurried to match his long strides. The sun, shining directly overhead, had already turned the brick-lined street into a griddle, burning my bare feet. An elegant quffa, lined in purple silk, awaited us at the quay, and I groaned my relief when I stepped into cool water in the bottom of the vessel. Ashpenaz lifted a single thin-plucked brow, and I detected a softening in those hard lines around his mouth. He crossed his arms over his muscled chest, and we sailed the short distance to the palace without speaking.

The royal quay wasn't nearly as crowded as the dock where I'd been given my assignment six months earlier. No haggling traders or deck slaves to avoid, only finely dressed palace servants, busy with daily tasks. No one even glanced at the king's chief official leading a young girl toward the palace. This time, I walked toward the three-story mud-brick building knowing who awaited me. I wanted to run and see my four boys.

Instead of taking me through the public southern gate, where I was separated from my friends last autumn, the eunuch led me to a long staircase that took us below ground level. He opened a secluded door surrounded on all sides by ivy. Warning bells rang in my mind, and my newly honed suspicions rose.

Ashpenaz had said he was taking me to my friends' home. Why had he taken me to the palace? "Where exactly do the boys live?"

No answer. He continued walking down a long hallway as servants shuffled here and there through doorways lining both sides. We had apparently entered the servants' quarters of Babylon's palace.

"Are my princes here? What will I do for them? Cook? Clean?"

Again, no answer. Ashpenaz turned a corner, where a single door waited. He opened the door and entered, but I stopped three paces from the threshold. Eunuch or not, I was determined never to be alone with a man again.

Before I could declare my decision, he emerged with a folded garment of finer linen than anything I'd ever owned. "Here." He shoved it at me. "This should fit." And then he began another journey to who knew where.

Through two hallways and the kitchen, up

a winding staircase, and down another hall, we somehow eventually emerged in the same courtyard in which we captives had originally been deposited on our arrival in Babylon. We descended the majestic staircase, and I hopped from brick to brick, avoiding the scorching-hot glazed tiles that were being installed.

"Your feet will grow accustomed to the heat, Wildcat." Ashpenaz chuckled, a strange sound. "Maids don't wear sandals."

We exited the palace courtyard's east entrance, crossed the Processional Way, and walked on a lovely street where two-story villas sat in neat rows. A small canal—more like a stream— followed the bricked street, each home looking much the same with a fenced garden separating it from the street.

"Do the boys live in one of these?"

Finally, Ashpenaz stopped, ramming his fists at his sides. "You must stop calling them boys. They are to be members of the king's Chaldeans, Belili, and you must show them the respect of their office."

The weight of his words settled over me. He was right. Who was I to imagine that princes of Judah would deign to call me *friend?* They would become officials in Babylon, and I was nothing. Less than nothing. Laqip taught me that. I bowed to King Nebuchadnezzar's chief eunuch, perhaps realizing for the first time how gracious he'd been to me. "Forgive me, Lord Ashpenaz. They deserve not only my deepest respect but also my lifelong service—as do you, my lord."

"Get up, girl. Humility doesn't suit you." He stormed past me through an intricately designed iron gate and entered a well-manicured garden. I followed closely, but Ashpenaz stopped me, pressing his finger to his lips and then pointing at a man clipping dead branches from one of the bushes. He spoke in hushed tones. "You must realize the great honor you've been given to serve Belteshazzar. He will be a great man one day. Already he uses his influence for the benefit of others. He's rescued several Judeans from fates as dire as yours." Ashpenaz nodded at the gardener. "That man was sent to the temples as you were but for . . . well, let's just say he will never again lie with a woman."

My cheeks warmed, and I ducked my head—but felt silly. I'd lived for the past six months in a temple of eunuchs, and the man standing with me had undergone the same humiliation. Why was I suddenly embarrassed to hear the reality of Babylon's royal life? Confused, I crinkled my brow at Ashpenaz. "Why do you feel sorry for the gardener when you share his fate?"

His magnanimous demeanor clouded to disdain. "I am a eunuch by choice. For honor. My manhood wasn't taken by force."

A sudden horror gripped me. "Daniel? The others? Have they been made . . ."

Ashpenaz looked down the slant of his long nose. "Belteshazzar and your other three friends have not yet been given the opportunity to come under the king's protection as eunuchs. They must complete their three years of study and face King Nebuchadnezzar's personal testing before they're approved for a life at court. Only then can they choose between a family or a life of royal honor."

Royal honor? I didn't want to offend him again, but I certainly didn't understand the pride shining from his eyes.

My thoughts must have betrayed me. Ashpenaz straightened his spine and gritted his teeth. "Are you still so ignorant of what's truly important in this life, Wildcat?" Without warning, he shouted at the gardener. "Come and meet the new chambermaid."

I wanted to dig a hole and hide in it. "Please don't talk about—"

The gardener arrived and gripped Ashpenaz's wrist, nodding his head in a respectful but familiar bow. "Peace and health to you, my friend," he said as if the two men had known each other for years. His wide gold neckband gleamed in the sun, and his face still bore a faintly uneven tan where his Hebrew beard once grew.

"Peace and health to you," Ashpenaz answered. "I was telling Belili why a Hebrew might choose to become a eunuch."

Without hesitation, the man began his explanation. "When the king chooses to honor a boy or man with the opportunity, it is a privilege. If that man or boy accepts the honor, he then dedicates his life to the king alone, shunning family, friends, and societal norms. In return, a eunuch comes under the king's sovereign protection and provision for the rest of his days. He is favored, blessed, and regarded by his lord forever." The man looked to Ashpenaz and back to me. "Do you question my decision?"

"No! No." I looked away, hoping to hide a disapproval I couldn't dislodge from my chest. The gardener couldn't have been more than twenty years old. How could he choose to throw away his whole life in exchange for a foreign king's promises?

Ashpenaz placed a fist over his heart, and the man returned to his work.

"Thank you for your explanation," I called after him. Ashpenaz's kindness toward him warmed my heart and bolstered my hope. "You're a good man too, Lord Ashpenaz."

Something unreadable passed over his face, and he nudged me toward the villa. "It's too bad you can't choose to become a eunuch."

I followed Ashpenaz into the villa, pondering

his cryptic words. This man was both bread and gall, life and venom. "Why would I choose to be a eunuch when I have you and Daniel to protect me?"

He halted at the courtyard gate, pinching the bridge of his nose, as dramatic as a priestess. "I am not your protector, little Belili. And Dan—uh, Belteshazzar—will soon be one of the king's Chaldeans who even I will call 'lord.' " He shook his head. "You Hebrews are a troublesome lot."

I reached up and cautiously tugged at his arm, effectively ending his tantrum. "Tell me what trouble you've had with the four princes. Perhaps I can speak with them about it."

He seemed almost startled by my concern. "Thank you, Belili, but Belteshazzar has already taken care of the matter. Upon arriving, he and the other three refused the special diet ordered by the king, though it included the finest cuts of beef and lamb and wine from the altars of the Esagila."

I silently cheered my boys' devotion but tried to hide it. "What did you do?"

"I thought to force the meat down their throats, but your Belteshazzar has the tact and wisdom of the gods. He proposed a test, asking me to give them only vegetables and water for ten days."

Grinning, I waited to hear the outcome.

"And by the gods, they were healthier looking than the other royal students after only ten days." His laughter sounded as I imagined a playful lion's roar would.

This compassionate yet powerful man was winning my respect if not my trust. "Will I prepare and serve these vegetables then?"

"No, little Belili." His eyes wandered to his sandals. "All meals are prepared in and delivered directly from the palace kitchen."

Puzzled, I laid my hand on the gate, ready to enter the villa. "What will I do then? Clean?"

Ashpenaz stepped around me and led me inside. "Yes, clean and tend to Master Belteshazzar. Let's get you settled."

Tend to Master Belteshazzar? What did that mean? I clutched the folded robe in my arms and walked through the arched entry of the two-story home. Immediately inside the doorway was a private well. Its beautiful stonework stood waist high, and a bucket hung on a rope wound around a crossbar that was suspended between two beams. Beyond the well was an expansive open-air courtyard, shaded only by long slanted beams stretching across the roof. The slanted wood allowed light and yet provided slivers of shade to protect both people and plants from the punishing rays of Babylon's sun. Gathering areas with bright-colored cushions and lush green plants filled the lovely space.

At the other end of the courtyard sat a cooking area, cold and unused. Beyond the courtyard, on the ground level, archways led to darkened hallways with rooms and closed doors that captured my curiosity.

"Belili, you really shouldn't gape," Ashpenaz said, nudging me forward. "A bug could fly in at any moment." I closed my mouth, preferring his sarcasm to disapproval. "The masters' bedchambers are upstairs," he said, beginning our journey up a staircase. Matching stairs bordered the other side of the courtyard. The second-story balcony formed a horseshoe, accessing an entire floor of closed doors.

"Are all the upstairs rooms sleeping chambers?" I asked when he stopped at the last door.

"Yes, and all are occupied by Judean nobility who arrived with your princes. Belteshazzar, Shadrach, Meshach, and Abednego are the occupants in these three chambers." He pointed to the last three doors.

He opened the last door without knocking, and I peeked inside. A raised bed frame with a straw-stuffed mattress sat against one wall, and a reed mat was placed against the opposite. A hammered-bronze washbasin perched on a three-legged stool between them. I saw two large baskets in the corner, and three pegs held robes—two of white linen and one of brown wool.

"You will serve as Belteshazzar's chambermaid."

I chuckled to myself, looking again at the mattress and reed mat, wondering which of the boys got the soft mattress and which slept on the reed mat on hard tiles. Perhaps Daniel and Hananiah took turns. They were nobility, after all, and had been more polite than other boys I'd known.

"Does Hananiah have a chambermaid?" I asked.

Ashpenaz stepped into the hallway. "Of course. In the room next door."

The door was ajar, and two large dark eyes peeked out. When I approached, the door slammed shut. "What . . . ?" I turned my question on the eunuch. "Why can't I go in?"

Ashpenaz grimaced. "That's not your chamber. You serve Belteshazzar."

"Not my cham—?" Before I could say more, the eunuch pointed to the third room.

"Not that it's any of your concern," he said, "but I did keep Meshach and Abednego together in the room closest to their brother." He opened the door and I peered inside. Two straw-stuffed mattresses and one reed mat.

The realization came with sickening clarity. Daniel and Hananiah wouldn't share the first chamber. They wouldn't take turns on the soft mattress. "Tell me where I am to sleep, Lord Ashpenaz?" For some reason, I needed to hear him say the words.

"By the hair on Marduk's toes, Wildcat, I showed you Daniel's cham—"

His suspended rant told me he'd only now comprehended my stupidity. Would I always be so gullible? I couldn't raise my head and reveal the emotions clawing at my heart. Any sign of compassion from Ashpenaz, and I would dissolve into self-pity. Had I been saved from one Babylonian lord to be forced into the bed of a friend? Was Daniel requesting the same service the Babylonian nobleman tried to steal?

"Little Belili, look at me." Ashpenaz's voice was gentle. He didn't touch or command me.

With a defeated sigh, I swiped at tears and obeyed.

The eyes that met mine were as black as obsidian but as good as rich soil after a soaking rain. "Belteshazzar is a wise young man. You are now his maid, his possession. He may do with you as he pleases—"

I covered a gasp and turned away.

"Look at me, Belili. You must look at me."

Yahweh, give me strength. Did the God of my ima still hear me? I could see only the mounds of bread in Marduk's temple, broken pieces like my life in Babylon. But I inhaled a sustaining breath and met the gaze of the man who held my future. "Yes, my lord."

He nodded with approval. "Though Belteshazzar may do with you as he pleases, I have seen him act with unwavering integrity. I believe he will treat you with respect."

Obedience was my only option. Perhaps Daniel would be a kinder master than Laqip. Perhaps. I bowed and remained in the submissive pose. "Thank you, Lord Ashpenaz, for rescuing me. I am forever in your debt. Now if you'll excuse me, I must prepare the chamber for my master's return."

I hurried past the eunuch into Daniel's room and closed the door. Pressing my back against it, I held my breath and listened until his heavy footfalls receded on the tiled balcony and down the stairs. Fear twisted at the center of my chest and kept wringing my insides until my body lay in a heap on the floor. Writhing changed to quiet weeping for the life of a girl once named Abigail.

Dragging myself to the bed, I climbed onto the raised mattress and buried my face in Daniel's feather-stuffed pillow to muffle my screams. Later, throat raw and body too weak to keep pounding the mattress, I rolled on my back and stared at the ceiling, weeping until exhaustion carried me into darkness.

11

Pharaoh said to Joseph, "I had a dream, and no one can interpret it. But I have heard it said of you that when you hear a dream you can interpret it."

"I cannot do it," Joseph replied to Pharaoh, "but God will give Pharaoh the answer he desires."

—GENESIS 41:15–16

I woke in a strange room, and terror stole my breath. A moment later, memories of the day's attack at the Esagila rushed back like a river released from a dam. Ashpenaz had arrived in time to save my honor. To bring me here, to Daniel's room—where I would lose it. My throat burned with the irony of it. Did Yahweh see me? Did He even exist? Or had the stories been pretty little bedtime stories Ima told me when I was young to soothe my nighttime fears?

Ima. Would she have sent me away if she'd known I would go to a land where Yahweh was silent?

Daniel's room glowed in the haze of dusk. He would surely be back soon. The thought both pleased and terrified me. Would he still be my kind and inquisitive friend? The gentle protector

I'd come to know on our long journey? My heart ached at the alternative.

I scooted off the bed and set the washbasin on the floor. I moved the three-legged table to the single window and stood on it to glimpse the setting sun. The city below was still buzzing with Akitu revelers. A few market booths near the palace had begun folding their canopies, sunset marking the end of Babylon's greatest annual feast and the second worst day of my life.

Cleanup had already begun along the Processional Way. Servants and slaves of all sizes, shapes, and colors worked under the watchful eyes of Babylonian masters with whips in hand. Were some of those who marched from Judah in the sorry lot below? Probably.

My stomach grumbled, reminding me I hadn't eaten since the night before. Daniel's evening meal hadn't yet arrived from the palace— nor mine. Ashpenaz hadn't mentioned my provisions, and I didn't dare venture from the chamber with drunken Akitu revelers still in the streets.

I climbed off the table, determined to forage for a morsel of bread or dried grain. One large basket in the corner held the contents I expected: extra linens and winter tunics. But the second was filled with scrolls, loosely tied with leather strings. Though I couldn't read, I'd always been fascinated by the scrolls I'd seen in King Jehoiakim's chamber. As if handling a thin-shelled egg, I carefully lifted one scroll from the basket and pinched the string between two fingers. Gently tugging, I—

"Abigail!"

"Ah!" I dropped the scroll and fell to my knees, hands stretched overhead in the familiar pose. "Forgive me! I can't even read. I'll never do it again. I promise." Heart pounding, breath ragged, I covered my head when he neared, bracing for whatever blow might come.

A moment's hesitation, and then his hand caressed my hair. "It's just a scroll, Abigail."

No, Yahweh. Please, no. I hadn't known until I saw him which would be harder to bear, his violence or his violation. His anger I could forgive. "Please, Daniel. Don't—"

Thundering footsteps stole my attention, invading the room, and then a shrill voice. "Abigail, you're back!" Two bodies piled on top of my penitent pose and then rolled off, wrestling each other to their feet.

I stood too, straightening my hair and tunic, but kept my head bowed to avoid Daniel's gaze. He stood behind me, and I faced the twins.

"You've changed, Abigail." Azariah grabbed my hand. "You're really pretty." Mishael elbowed his ribs about the time Hananiah arrived at the doorway. A dark-skinned girl, not much older than me, stood beside the oldest of the brothers, her gray eyes inquisitive but cautious.

Still not ready to face Daniel, I asked Azariah, "How do you like your classes?"

"We get to look at sheep guts and use fancy gadgets to look at the stars."

"I'm better at star gazing." Mishael, the quiet one, puffed out his chest. "But Dan—I mean, Belteshazzar—is better than anyone at dreams."

"Dreams?" I asked Hananiah instead of Daniel. "What does he mean, 'better at dreams'?"

The oldest brother shot a grin at his friend. "It seems Belteshazzar inherited our ancestor Joseph's gift. Remember the ancient stories of Jacob's son Joseph, who interpreted Pharaoh's dreams? Belteshazzar spends a few moments in prayer each day and then explains to diviners and magicians the dreams they bring to class."

I turned on the only one I had yet to face and felt a strange sense of betrayal. "You're practicing sorcery?"

Daniel winced as if I'd slapped him but stood silent, staring at me with those penetrating eyes completely unshuttered. I'd wounded him deeply.

The twins scurried toward the door, and their maid followed.

Hananiah shooed the twins out the door, but I reached for them like a soldier for his shield. "Please, don't go."

The oldest stopped at the doorway. "It's as if

105

you don't remember us at all, Abigail. How could you think Daniel would practice sorcery?" And then he was gone.

Fear sent my knees to the floor and my face to the tiles. "Forgive me, Lord Belteshazzar. Please, *please* don't send me back to the Esagila." My throat tightened, cutting short my pleas, but I would do anything—yes, anything—to stay here. Body trembling, I hardened my heart for what must come next.

I heard the disturbance of Daniel's straw mattress. He was waiting for me to join him. I sat back on my knees and, without looking up, wiped my face on my sleeve.

I'd taken only two steps before Daniel stopped me. "Go sit on your mat, Abigail. You are never to sit with me on my mattress. This is my space, and the reed mat is yours." I glanced up then, testing what I'd heard. His handsome face was weary and sad. "Whatever you learned in the Esagila, you will unlearn in my care. You will unlearn fear. You will unlearn distrust. And you will unlearn oppression."

My feet felt rooted to the floor. Was he tricking me? I looked at the reed mat and then at his basket full of scrolls. I backed away a safe distance before asking. "While I'm unlearning, will you teach me?"

He rewarded me with a grin, looking like the boy I'd met six months ago. "Of course, but let's start tomorrow. Tonight, we'll eat our meal, speak of Jerusalem, and remember Yahweh's faithfulness."

Still suspicious, I kept my distance as he crossed the room to untie the leather string on the scroll I'd been holding. I lit a lamp, and he began reading, interrupted only by a knock on the door from a palace servant who carried a tray with two bowls of stew on it. One for the royal student Belteshazzar. One for his new maid, Belili.

12

[Ashpenaz] was to teach them the language and literature of the Babylonians.

—DANIEL 1:4

Six Months Later

Babylon's coolest months were warmer than Jerusalem's winter, and my small world of friendships was warmer still. Hananiah's dark-skinned Egyptian maid, Mert, became a quick friend and valuable teacher. The twins shared Gula, a maid who was more aloof, but her quiet, gentle nature seemed to instill a sense of peace over them.

Each of the noble youths in the eastern chambers was slowly assigned a maid as well. All the princes ate evening meals together in the gargantuan courtyard of our main level, while we maids sat at a respectable distance and enjoyed their stories about the day's learning.

My four princes and we three maids enjoyed an almost immediate bond; however, during my first week of service, Ashpenaz surprised us with a morning visit and caught us breaking our fast together in Daniel's room. Furious with our familiarity, he forced the boys to watch as we maids were beaten and told we must always use their Babylonian names. Our masters cried harder than we did, and we've called them Belteshazzar, Shadrach, Meshach, and Abednego since.

"What are you thinking about?" Mert nudged my arm as we bent over our laundry stones. Gula looked up too, pausing her scrubbing.

I took a moment to appreciate these girls who had been so kind. "I was thinking how fortunate I am to have friends like you."

"Then I've hidden my true self well." Mert cupped her hand into the canal and splashed me.

I splashed back, and even Gula joined the fun before we returned to our chore. Rinsing the imported Egyptian natron from Daniel's white linen robe, I rolled the fine fabric and set it aside to wring out later. My small pile of laundry nearly gone, I reached for the last item—Daniel's woolen cloak—and made sure the girls weren't watching. I pressed it against my face, drinking in the aroma of frankincense mingled with his musky scent, and let it massage my heart. The image of his smile danced in my mind, and I submerged the robe in the canal's cool waters.

A moment of regret tainted my joy. Barely a year ago, I'd lived in Jerusalem's palace with Ima. I'd come to accept that I would never see her again, but knowing that others lived out the nightmare I'd escaped in the Esagila was a reality

I could hardly bear. What right did I have to be so happy?

"Belili?" Mert's hand rested on my arm. "Are you well?"

I nodded, lifting Daniel's dripping robe to the rock and sprinkling it with natron before scrubbing away the beloved scent—and my sadness. Our masters were training to be leaders in Babylon. Perhaps they could help the Judeans who were being mistreated as I had been. And though I missed Ima, she would be happy for me. The freedom I had in Daniel's service and the education he gave me was far beyond what I would have gained in Jerusalem. But more than that . . . he was wonderful. When I slept, I dreamed of him. While he attended his classes on palace grounds, he consumed my thoughts. And when we were together, my heart was so full, I felt as if it might burst.

After our evening meals, when Belteshazzar and I were alone, we studied his scrolls by the light of a lamp, and I called him Daniel. In those moments, I gave him my heart on the wings of first love, unmarred by the cruelties of our world. In his small chamber, in a villa so far from the city of our birth, I fell in love with my best friend. He taught me the world from his scrolls and said I was every bit as bright as the Babylonian princess Rubati, who sat beside him in class.

Rubati. The girl was the sum of everything evil in my world. Though I didn't know her, I hated her. Though I'd never met her, she was my fiercest enemy. She spent her day, every day, with my Daniel, learning the language and literature of Babylon. He gave me only scraps of his knowledge after our evening meal, while she feasted at a banquet I would never attend.

Mert finished rolling Shadrach's last robe, and we helped Gula finish double the laundry for the twins. My frustrations were well spent as my friends and I twisted out every drop of water from the sopping-wet clothes. Robes hung to dry, I said goodbye to my friends for the afternoon, suddenly in no mood for chatter. The thought of a Babylonian princess fawning over my Daniel stuck like pine sap in my mind.

By the time he entered our chamber at dusk, I'd grown especially cross. He didn't even notice. "We studied the Babylonian story of creation today. Would you like to hear it?"

I set aside the scroll I'd been reading, thinking this my opportunity to prove myself Rubati's equal. "Yes, of course. I'd like to discuss it with you."

"The Enuma Elis begins very much like our creation story and actually predates Moses's written records. The Babylonians agree that the earth was formless and void, a dark and watery chaos. Their supreme god, Marduk, created light the first day, then the heavens, and then set the cosmos in place. Finally, Marduk created man to tend all he'd made." Daniel stopped, lifting both brows. "What do you think of their story?"

Indignant, I shot to my feet. "It was Yahweh, not Marduk. They're trying to make you love everything Babylonian and throw away everything Hebrew." Did he know I spoke of more than just Yahweh?

Daniel stood, pressing a single finger against my lips. "I know that is their intention, but I will always serve Yahweh and love all things Hebrew."

I smelled the ink on his hands and the cloves on his breath. The sensation of his finger on my lips warmed me, and his eyes lingered too long on mine.

He removed his hand and stepped away quickly. "Let's talk about how our creation story differs from theirs." He crossed the room to the basket, searching for a scroll. "Their story begins with a battle between their many gods for supremacy. Yahweh doesn't need to battle since He's the only true God." He found a scroll, brought it to our small table, and unrolled it. Searching out the story and then following with his ink-stained finger, he showed me the progression of the Babylonian creation. "Here, Marduk creates the sky by splitting open the goddess Tiamat and then creates man by draining the blood from the god Kingu."

"Ick! Why so much blood?"

"There's shedding of blood in all religious rites, but at least our God requires it of animals, not humans, and only for our eternal good. It's Yahweh's goodness that sets Him apart from other gods."

I hadn't considered Yahweh's nature as a difference, only His laws, the procedures of our worship. I was suddenly struck by the memory of Jerusalem's Temple and the Ark inside it. "Wasn't the Temple created so Yahweh could dwell on earth again, like He once did in the Garden of Eden?"

Daniel looked at me as if I were a king's crown. At moments like this, I didn't feel like his maid. I wondered if I should tell him that I'd seen the cherubim and the Ark. That Yahweh took my broken piece of bread and made the loaf whole again.

"I explained the story of Eden to the council of Chaldeans today." His eyes sparked with excitement, so I decided not to interrupt. "At first, my instructor patronized me and my archaic Hebrew legends. So I asked how he would reconcile my Hebrew 'legends' with our shared Chaldean ancestry."

"Shared Chaldean ancestry? You were born in Jerusalem like me."

"Yes, but Father Abraham came from the city of Ur, in the land of the Chaldeans. He was a great prince who would have been taught the same story of Marduk's creation epic that my instructors were teaching me today. But when Yahweh led Father Abraham to Canaan, the Lord revealed Himself there as the one true God. Abraham and his descendants have been commissioned to serve and carry His blessing to all nations." Daniel grew pensive, his eyes searching mine as if looking for answers inside me.

Unnerved, I crossed my arms. "What? What are you thinking?"

"What if part of Yahweh's covenant with Abraham—to bless all nations through him—involves our exile to Babylon?" Before I could answer, he rushed on, excitement building. "What if choosing to educate the princes of Judah and place us in government positions throughout the empire is to fulfill Yahweh's ultimate purpose of spreading the truth of the one true God?"

"But you said Yahweh was good. The things we saw in Jerusalem weren't good, Daniel. What happened to me at the Esagila . . ." My throat constricted, and I turned away. If everything that had happened to me was God's will, what kind of God had my ima served?

Daniel reached for my hand, pulling me around to face him. "People make choices to sin and disobey Yahweh every day. Like a good Abba,

He must follow through on His promised discipline and tolerate the consequences of a sin-sick world. Perhaps a good God can take something as terrible as our exile and make it beautiful."

The thought salved my wound, though I wasn't completely convinced. I could at least face him again. "How did your council of Chaldeans react to the argument?"

The satisfied grin on his handsome face told me more than words. "We spent the rest of the day going through Babylonian legends, while I explained how each related to Yahweh's revelation of Himself to Abraham."

"Brilliant!" I applauded.

His smile suddenly stricken, he reached for my hands to still them. "No, Abigail. No. It wasn't me. Only Yahweh could argue so shrewdly and grant me favor among the council. They actually requested more stories about our God tomorrow."

Without another word, he rerolled the scroll and placed it in the basket, seeming weighted by our conversation. I sat in quiet wonder at how real Yahweh was to him. "How can the God of the Hebrews speak to you in Babylon when the Ark still resides in Jerusalem's Temple?"

He offered me a devastating smile. "How do you know the army didn't bring the Ark to Babylon?"

I swallowed hard, feeling my palms grow

sweaty. Would he think me brave or a blasphemer? "Ashpenaz found me hiding in the Holy of Holies. My ima told me to hide with the priests, and when I saw the army attack them in the Temple courts, I decided to die by Yahweh's hand in His holy place instead of by an enemy's sword." I shrugged. "I even tore off a piece of sacred bread to offer Him. Yahweh made it whole again."

He gaped at me, wide eyed and slack jawed, for more than five heartbeats.

"Well? Say something."

"Shadrach!" He hurried to the door, shouting, "Meshach, Abednego! Get in here!" I feared he was angry, but he returned laughing and lifted me into his arms and twirled me in circles. "You must tell us everything! The Holy of Holies. The miracle of the bread. You must tell us all of it."

He set my feet on the floor but my head still spun. Was it his nearness or the doubts that still nibbled at my heart? "Daniel, I'm not sure about the bread. Perhaps I only thought I tore off a piece."

The princes arrived with their maids, and Hananiah was first to speak. "Abigail, you look flushed."

Daniel brushed my cheek and then took my hand, leading me to our cushions beside the small table. "Come. All of you. Abigail has much to teach us about Yahweh's Temple in Jerusalem."

13

In the second year of his reign, Nebuchadnezzar had dreams; his mind was troubled and he could not sleep.

—DANIEL 2:1

The morning was cold and damp. Mert and I were among the maids hanging our masters' linens on hemp ropes tied between two poles in the court-yard, while Gula prepared a midday snack for us of bread and date paste. We each wore one of the boy's extra woolen robes under our own for warmth, hiding their generosity lest Ashpenaz inspect the villa unannounced. I heard the garden gate rattle open but didn't look up, expecting the Hebrew gardener I'd met my first day at the villa. Instead, I heard the panicked voices of our masters.

"How could you promise to interpret his dream?" Shadrach's voice held a disturbing tremor I hadn't heard before.

Hurrying through the rows of billowing sheets and tunics, I watched all four young men march upstairs toward their chambers.

Daniel shouted over his shoulder at the three who followed, "What should I have done? Let them kill us?" Our masters didn't notice the line of maids peeking from behind the hanging sheets. The other boys trickled in, sullen and silent, and climbed the opposite staircase without a glance into the courtyard, where we watched with growing concern.

Mert shoved me forward. "Go talk to Belteshazzar. I've never seen Shadrach so upset." She felt about her master as I did for Daniel but would never admit it.

"Enough!" Daniel shouted, drawing our attention again. He stood outside Shadrach's chamber, where the twins were huddled behind their brother. "You know I can only interpret a dream when Yahweh gives me its meaning. Stop badgering your weak friend on earth and start pleading with our powerful God in heaven." He turned on his heel, entered his chamber, and slammed the door. Shadrach spoke something quietly to the twins, and all three disappeared into the oldest brother's chamber.

I emerged from my hiding place, startled by Daniel's uncharacteristic rudeness. The other maids looked to me, but I was at a loss.

"Go!" Mert nudged me again. "He'll tell you."

I wasn't sure she was right, but her confidence emboldened me. With similar encouragement from the other maids, I padded upstairs to Daniel's chamber and tapped lightly on the cedar door. No answer. I knocked harder and heard a muffled, "Come."

When I entered, no lamp was lit, but enough sunlight shone through the window to see my master's red-rimmed eyes. He knelt in the middle of the chamber. Looking up, he wiped his nose on his sleeve. "What is it?"

His coolness wounded me. I bowed. "I'm here to help, but first you must tell me how." I dared not look up in the silence.

"Come in then, and close the door."

With a measure of relief, I entered and knelt opposite him, hands in my lap, eyes averted.

"King Nebuchadnezzar experienced some sort of nightmare last night. He summoned the council of Chaldeans—every magician, enchanter, sorcerer, and astrologer in his kingdom—and asked them to tell what he had dreamed."

I lifted my gaze. "You mean to interpret the dream?"

"No. To tell what he dreamed."

"Can they do that?"

Daniel shook his head. "When the council tried to explain that no one could do such a thing, the king said they were merely stalling for time and ordered the execution of *all* wise men in the kingdom—including the students of the Chaldeans."

"No!" I covered a gasp.

"We are safe."

Confusion. Fear. Hope. I couldn't make sense of his report. "Did the king change his mind?"

"The council sent Arioch, commander of the

king's guard, to our class. He planned to begin executions with the most easily expendable. I recognized him from Jerusalem and approached him, asking what brought him to our classroom." Daniel offered his first slight grin. "I think he was intrigued by a fourteen-year-old boy foolish enough to talk to the executioner. He actually listened to me."

Captured by his story, my heart was beginning to brighten. "What did you say?"

"I told him Yahweh could tell me King Nebuchadnezzar's dream and interpret it, but I needed until tomorrow morning to pray and hear from Him."

Momentary relief was swallowed up in anxiety. "So, Yahweh has done this before—I mean, told you the dream before interpreting it?"

He reached for my hands and held my gaze. "No, but I'd never heard of Yahweh mending a loaf of bread in the Holy of Holies until we were faced with exile."

I yanked my hands away and bolted to my feet. "He did that in Jerusalem. In His Temple. How could you even imagine that Yahweh will hear and answer a prayer in this pagan city?"

Annoyingly calm, he offered his hand, bidding me return to my place opposite him.

"No! You must tell Arioch you need more time. You must find another way." His hand waited in stubborn tenderness. I knew he wouldn't answer until I resumed my place, so I refused his hand but knelt. "Well? Will you rescind your promise?"

"Yahweh created the heavens and the earth, He divided the waters of the Red Sea, and He summoned a fish to swallow Jonah. I think He can reveal a king's nightmare to those who trust Him in Babylon."

"We think so too." Shadrach stood in the doorway, his brothers huddled around him. "I've sent Mert and Gula to cancel our evening meal so we can fast and pray."

A slow, wide smile bloomed on Daniel's face. "The God of heaven will reveal this mystery, and the whole empire will hear of it." The three princes closed the door behind them and joined Daniel and me on the reed mat, ready for an all-night vigil if necessary.

"Thank you, my friends," Daniel said, looking around our circle.

"May we join too?" Mert asked, standing at the doorway with Gula.

Daniel exchanged a glance with Shadrach, who scooted over to make room for the newcomers between himself and Meshach. Daniel welcomed them with a nod and offered a word of instruction. "Focus your prayers on what you know of Yahweh. Praise Him and consider how it might bring Him glory to reveal this mystery to King Nebuchadnezzar." Without another word, he bowed his head and left us to find Yahweh in prayers of our own.

On the floor of that small villa, seven children cried out to a Hebrew God whose presence rested on a golden box far away in Jerusalem, asking that He reveal the dream of a king who had killed their families.

And He did.

The moon was well past its zenith when Daniel fell on his side, eyes fixed on a distant nothing. His pallor faded to the color of fresh cream, almost translucent in the lamplight. He pawed the air, grasping for something we could not see. Fearful he'd fallen ill, I retrieved the washbasin and thought to cool his face with the cloth.

Shadrach hovered over him like a mother hen. "Don't touch him. I think Yahweh is speaking."

"Well, Yahweh won't mind if I hold him." I sounded more certain than I felt, but surely if He didn't strike me dead in His Temple, He'd let me comfort my friend.

The others moved away, but I cradled Daniel's head in my lap. His breathing grew erratic. Huffing, then panting, and then nearly stopped. I shook his shoulders to wake him but to no avail. Terrified, I began rocking and singing a psalm of David my ima had taught me. The others joined me, eyes closed, lost in the soothing words and rhythmic tune.

Daniel stirred, and I looked down to see a sweet smile curve his lips, though his eyes remained closed. His breathing calmed. We continued singing. He lingered between two worlds, and I wondered if he would be changed when he came back to us. Dawn peeked through the single slender window, and my Daniel yawned—a yawn as if he'd enjoyed a peaceful night's rest. He blinked a few times, looking left and right, and he bolted upright. Red splotches appeared on his neck, as though he was embarrassed about lying in my lap. I wanted to hug him and ask a million questions, but Shadrach was quicker at both.

"Are you all right?" the older boy asked, pounding Daniel's back in a ferocious hug.

"I saw myself in a sheep pen; the shepherd's song kept the wolves away all night." Daniel nudged Shadrach away and looked at all of us. "Yahweh showed me Nebuchadnezzar's dream. Not just the interpretation—He showed me the dream! I must find Arioch!" He rushed out the door, his voice echoing in the cavernous courtyard. "Praise be to Yahweh, my God and my Deliverer! He showed me the king's dream!"

"We're saved," Shadrach whispered and then looked at the rest of us in wonder. "Has any Chaldean *ever* revealed the dream *and* its interpretation?"

"Yahweh has done it!" The twins jumped up and hugged their big brother.

Mert looked longingly at her master, and I pulled her into my arms, wishing she were Daniel. "You see, my friend. Nothing is impossible with

Yahweh," I whispered. "Perhaps someday, we'll hug the ones we love." It was the first time I'd revealed my knowledge of her secret.

She pulled away, startled and about to protest, when Shadrach announced, "Hurry! We must make sure we're dressed and in class when Belteshazzar shares Yahweh's revelation with the king."

As it turned out, our masters had plenty of time to prepare. When Daniel told Arioch he was ready to present the dream and its interpretation, Ashpenaz sent him back to the villa to prepare for his first official audience.

We laid out our masters' tunics and robes, then waited on the balcony while they dressed. "You can come in," my master called from within our chamber. I opened the door, catching my breath at first glance. Shoulders back, chin high, and dressed in his finest linen robe, Daniel wore a wool cloak to protect against winter's chill and a confident air to deliver Yahweh's message.

"You are beautiful." The words escaped on a breath without my permission. Feeling heat rise to my cheeks, I covered them with both hands. "I mean . . . What I meant to say was . . . Aren't you afraid?"

With a devastating grin, he drew me with his gaze. "Yahweh is faithful. I have nothing to fear."

"But aren't you nervous about meeting the king?" I wanted to straighten his beaded collar but didn't trust my shaking hands. Perhaps I was nervous enough for us both. Why was he looking at me that way?

Those dark brown eyes held mischief, yes, but something more. As if he held a secret that begged to be told. I had the strangest feeling he wanted to kiss me—or was it my own desire I felt? Eleven now, I was old enough to be betrothed had we still lived in Jerusalem. Had he ever considered such a thing? Or was he practical enough to know that in Jerusalem, our circumstances would never have allowed it?

"I am a little nervous, yes," he said, finally. "It's hard to remember that King Nebuchadnezzar is only six years older than Hananiah and me. Our teachers say his youth is what makes him so fickle."

Fickle? Shadrach said he'd threatened to cut his wise men into pieces and demolish their houses if they couldn't reveal the dream. "I think he's more dangerous than—"

"Good morning, Arioch." Fear shadowed Daniel's glance over my shoulder. "My maid speaks of the king's prowess in battle and how dangerous he is."

I stood like a stone, my heart in my throat. The king's bodyguard had slipped up behind me as silent as the wind. No wonder he was the king's chosen protector.

"Your maid would do well to keep her opinions to herself." Arioch's voice was the middle tone of a eunuch. I turned to face his abdomen and let my eyes drift up to see the giant glaring down at me. He smiled, which looked more like a snarl, and sent me to my knees.

"Forgive me, Lord Arioch. As you care for your king's safety and would give your life in his stead, so I am fiercely devoted to my master, Lord Belteshazzar. I meant no disrespect to our lord, King Nebuchadnezzar."

Before my next breath, two meaty hands grasped my throat and lifted me off the floor, pulling me close to his face. "You think you are as loyal to this child as I am to my king?"

"To my death," I choked out, no hesitation.

Our eyes battled while the pressure in my head mounted. His snort preceded my release, and he laughed as I crumpled to the floor, rubbing my neck. "She would have made a fine eunuch," he said to Daniel. "The king is waiting."

Daniel followed Arioch from our chamber without a backward glance.

The other princes left for their classes soon after, and the morning crept by. The other maids and I completed our tasks with bittersweet anticipation. I'd returned to our chamber to read a scroll, but I couldn't concentrate on anything but Daniel. Yes, Yahweh had been faithful. He'd displayed His presence in Babylon, and we'd witnessed a powerful answer to our prayers. But would Daniel's revelation of the dream and its interpretation sufficiently impress Babylon's king?

Yahweh, forgive my fear and doubt. You've shown Your great power, but can I really trust You? The words had barely crossed my mind when I heard footfalls on the bricked walkway outside the villa. Sandals hurrying across the courtyard tiles. Now up the stairs. I huddled in the corner of our chamber, terrified that Arioch had come to kill Daniel's impudent maid. Had King Nebuchadnezzar rejected Daniel's revelation? *After all our prayers, Yahweh, have You removed Your protection?* I squeezed my eyes shut and covered my head, making myself as small as possible.

"Abigail?"

I looked up to find my friend standing in the doorway. At least, the face was Daniel's, but the clothes and sandals were those of a nobleman. I left my hiding place in the corner. "What happened?"

He looked into the hall before closing the door behind him. Still, he kept his voice low. "See these clothes? Fickle. Yesterday I was to be executed. Today, the king dresses me as a noble and says I rule the whole province of Babylon."

I thought surely he was teasing, but his eyes held a glint of fear, and he began to pace.

"Daniel, how can you rule Babylon when you haven't yet finished your training?"

He took two giant steps back to where I stood, stopping barely a handbreadth from me. "Nebuchadnezzar honored me, Abigail. *Me.* Even though I told him repeatedly only Yahweh could reveal *and* interpret his dream. I tried to reflect all the praise to Yahweh, but he wouldn't listen. When I began describing the statue revealed in the king's dream, everyone in the throne room acted as if I were a god. It was terrifying!"

Curiosity distracted me from my friend's distress. I wanted to know what the dream was, but the fear in his eyes sobered me. "Daniel, you were faithful to point others to the true God, but you can't make them believe. Perhaps revealing the dream and interpreting its meaning is the first step, but it may be a long process."

He stared at me for a long moment and then brushed my cheek. "Thank you."

My cheek burned like fire where he touched it. Heart pounding, I needed a distraction. "What was the dream?"

"It was about a strange statue. It had a head of gold, chest and arms of silver, belly and thighs of bronze, legs of iron, and feet partly of iron and baked clay. Suddenly, from out of nowhere, a rock was cut out—but not by human hands—and it struck the statue on its feet of iron and clay, smashing them, and then a great wind blew them away," he said, his arms flailing. "And the rock that struck the statue became a huge mountain that filled the whole earth."

He shrugged and waited, as if I was supposed to comment, but I was dumbfounded. He'd seen all that while we prayed for him? "And Yahweh revealed its meaning as well?"

"Yes, Yahweh was showing King Nebuchadnezzar the future world empires. Each piece of the statue represented a new conqueror. The gold head is Babylon; the silver, bronze, and iron portions are three more kingdoms that will someday rule the earth. The feet of iron and baked clay is a divided kingdom that will be crushed by a divinely created Deliverer who will rule forever."

I stood in awe of this boy, who had become a man before my eyes. Belteshazzar, Yahweh's revealer of dreams. I lifted the pendant around his neck. Gold mixed with silver and copper, a stunning masculine piece. "And the king rewarded you—as he should."

"No, Abigail!" He slipped off the heavy necklace and tossed it on his mattress as if it were a dirty rag. "I deserve none of it. I thought you, of all people, would understand that. Only Yahweh could have done this great thing. After I gave Yahweh's revelation and interpretation of the dream, the king paused for an excruciating moment, and I wondered if he would order my execution after all. Then he descended the dais and fell prostrate in front of me."

Daniel's face filled with wonder. "Finally, Nebuchadnezzar, King of the Earth, acknowledged Yahweh before his whole court as God of gods, Lord of kings, and a Revealer of mysteries. And then he ruined it by making me ruler of the whole province of Babylon."

I instinctively laughed but covered the outburst when Daniel looked hurt.

"You must celebrate, Daniel. The king of Babylon praised our God and made you ruler. Why are you so upset? It seems like a—" But his arched brow and solemn features silenced me.

"When I complete my last year of training and pass his personal examination," Daniel explained, "I'll become chief of his wise men, governor of Chaldeans."

The gravity of it finally landed in my gut. I stepped back, felt dread rising, and bowed to hide it. "Congratulations. Yahweh be praised." Nausea gripped me, and my arms instinctively wrapped my waist. The governor of Chaldeans would need a household of servants and have no use for me.

"Abigail."

"I need to do laundry." It was a lie.

"Abigail." He seemed hesitant, almost fearful to speak. "Abigail, you've been very dear to me."

Was he dismissing me?

He swallowed, and I heard the crackle of a dry mouth. "At the end of my training, you will be of an age to marry. Would you consider being . . . I mean, since you don't have an abba in Babylon to arrange our betrothal . . ."

I stepped back, covering my mouth and shaking my head at the impossibility of this moment. Had the obsession of my heart asked me to marry him? Daniel looked as if I'd slapped him. "I understand. We need never discuss it aga—"

I realized I'd been shaking my head and nearly leapt into his arms. "No! I mean, yes! Yes!" I willed my feet to stay rooted, though I desperately wanted to kiss him. "Yes, Daniel ben Johanan, I will marry you."

"Lord Belteshazzar." Ashpenaz filled the doorway, disapproval darkening his brow. "Lord Laqip has invited you to join him, his wife, and his daughter, Princess Rubati, for the evening meal." Ashpenaz watched me, knowing what his revelation had done. The two names I hated most dug into my chest like dull blades.

Tears scalded my throat, but I swallowed them back and confirmed the awful truth. "Lord Laqip, the nobleman who . . . at the Esagila . . . he's Rubati's abba?"

Confusion veiled Daniel's face, glancing first at Ashpenaz and then at me. I'd never told him what happened in Marduk's temple. But he was a wise man, now chief among them. "I'm sure this is a misunderstanding," he said. "Rubati lauds her father's good deeds among the poor. He's a decorated soldier." Daniel reached for my hand, but I recoiled. "Abigail, whatever happened to you at the Esagila, Rubati's father couldn't have been the man responsible." He turned to Ashpenaz again as if pleading.

131

"Belili doesn't know anything about Marduk, his rituals, or the noblemen who worship him, Lord Belteshazzar. Marduk's followers don't use his temple like a brothel as do the Medes in their worship of Mithra. Lord Laqip is a respected member of the council, the king's chief astrologer, and he would never attack a young girl." He pinned me with a stare. "Belili appears a bit weary. She can accompany me to the palace tonight for her meal while you join Lord Laqip and his family." He offered his hand to me, a polite but commanding invitation.

I bowed my head, mind whirring. What fate awaited me at the palace?

Daniel stepped between us. "Belili will remain in my chamber this evening."

Ashpenaz was twice our age and stood two heads taller, but he would obey the new governor of Chaldea. "As you wish, Lord Belteshazzar, but might I have a word with your maid sinceshe is under my care—a palace servant dispatched to a student of the Chaldeans?"

Tension grew in the silence, my fate growing darker with each moment Daniel delayed. "You may speak with her, Ashpenaz."

I followed the chief eunuch into the hallway, and he closed the door behind us. Ashpenaz hooked his large finger under my chin, and I looked up into surprisingly caring eyes. "I cannot protect you, little Belili, if you stay in Daniel's chamber tonight."

14

Then the king placed Daniel in a high position and lavished many gifts on him. He made him ruler over the entire province of Babylon and placed him in charge of all its wise men. Moreover, at Daniel's request the king appointed Shadrach, Meshach and Abednego administrators over the province of Babylon, while Daniel himself remained at the royal court.

—DANIEL 2:48–49

I set about cleaning our chamber after watching my Daniel walk away as a nobleman, two steps in front of Ashpenaz instead of two steps behind. The revelation of his love and intent to marry me gave me wings, yet tonight he would dine with a Babylonian princess and the man who had tried to steal my soul. Did Babylonian women eat at the same table with their men? Surely if her father allowed her to attend classes with boys, she would dine with them. And why had Laqip invited Daniel tonight?

As if my own insecurities weren't enough, I remembered Ashpenaz's final warning. "Keep watch at the door, little Belili, for any stranger lurking in your hallway." He seemed utterly sincere, but why would I be in danger? Who in Babylon cared enough to harm a Hebrew chambermaid?

When I asked, Ashpenaz refused to answer, claiming loyalty to other eunuchs superseded fondness for me. With a heavy sigh, I returned to straightening the mess Daniel had left. Dirty tunic on the floor. Ivory comb on the bed. Pots and jar lids strewn across the shelf where his lotions and perfumes were kept. I smiled. He required more maintenance than some of the priestesses I'd known.

Dusk had fallen like a curtain over our latticed window, so I lit three lamps to finish my cleaning. My heart skipped at the sound of heavy footsteps on our side of the villa stairs. I hurried to open our door a crack and peeked through. A stranger, dressed as a royal messenger, approached. Quietly closing the door, I wished for the first time it had a lock. I pressed my back against it and closed my eyes, praying that Ashpenaz was only trying to frighten me.

I heard a knock, but not at our chamber. Refusing to be tricked, I suppressed the urge to fling open my door. I heard voices. Male voices. Then footsteps receding. Now I flung open the door and found Shadrach reading a small scrap of parchment.

"Who was that, and what did he want?" I

sounded far more demanding than intended and then realized my friend was dressed in robes similar to Daniel's. "Are you a lord now too?"

Shadrach raised his brows, the look of a true nobleman. "Which question would you like me to answer first, Lady Belili?" A grin punctuated his gentle reprimand.

Since he was holding an actual message in his hand, I was no longer concerned about the messenger. "Did King Nebuchadnezzar make you a nobleman like Daniel?"

The twins heard my voice and joined Shadrach, dressed in similar fine robes, gold necklaces, and jeweled belts. "Look, Abigail!" Meshach's usual bashfulness was forgotten amid his splendor. "Daniel is friends with the king now, so he asked if we could be administrators." He looked up at Shadrach. "What does an administrator do anyway?"

I wondered the same thing. The oldest brother heaved a sigh. "An administrator is like an abba who cares for a whole family of people. When we finish our training, we'll remain in the nation of Babylon, but we'll each be assigned a city of our own to care for." His forced joy failed. Had he forgotten his brothers, like him, were Judah's brightest boys?

Abednego blinked rapidly, sniffing back emotion. "Will we get to visit each other?"

"Of course." Shadrach held up the newly

received message. "Tonight, we'll attend a special dinner, where we'll make important friends and create more reasons to return to Babylon and visit each other."

"A dinner?" I interrupted.

Shadrach handed the invitation to me. "One of our instructors invited us to a celebration for his daughter. Rubati's father has chosen a husband for her and is making the betrothal announcement tonight."

I covered a gasp, gaining the attention of all three. "Betrothal?" The word slipped out as my throat tightened. "Daniel left for Lord Laqip's villa earlier this evening."

Abednego missed the connection. "Good! Daniel will hear the news too."

But Shadrach rushed his brothers into Meshach's room. "Gula, prepare the boys quickly."

Gula cast a sympathetic glance in my direction before following the boys inside and closing the door.

Mert stood behind Shadrach, her eyes downcast. Her future had been shaken by today's events too. Would Shadrach take her with him when he was reassigned to another province? Or would they separate at the end of the boys' training?

"Daniel loves you, Abigail." Shadrach's affirmation surprised me.

"He told you?"

"He's not afraid or ashamed to declare it. If he can refuse the betrothal, he will. My brothers and I will lend whatever support we can tonight at dinner. Try not to worry." He offered a less-than-inspiring smile and disappeared with Mert into his chamber, leaving me standing alone in the hall.

My sorrow instantly turned to anger. If he can refuse the betrothal? Daniel was a nobleman now, ruler of Babylon. Not just a Hebrew boy in training. Of course he could refuse the betrothal. He would rule the wise men soon—including Rubati's father.

Fuming, I stomped back to Daniel's chamber and slammed the door, ignoring the sounds of the boys' hurried departure. Mert tapped on my door. I sat on the bed, arms folded, pouting and silent.

The door opened slowly, and my friend's lovely dark face peeked around it. I dared not speak, lest I completely lose control of my emotions. Mert slipped through the door and joined me on the bed. "I wish Shadrach loved me as Daniel loves you." She reached for my hand and stared at some nondescript spot on the wall. "When Shadrach came back to our chamber wearing the linen robe and jewels, he spoke of joining the royal house of eunuchs to secure the king's protection for himself and the twins."

137

"Mert, no!" I pulled her around to face me. "It's an abomination for a Hebrew man to do such a thing."

Her eyes glistened. "Which is worse? Becoming a eunuch or loving an Egyptian chambermaid?"

I stumbled over the question, seeing my friend with new eyes. Of course, I had known she was Egyptian when she shared her story on the day we met, but now I saw her as a woman. "It is worst of all," I answered, "to love and never share it."

Beautiful and exotic, Mert's stunning gray eyes, short-cropped hair, and lithe form made her alluring in a way I could only imagine. But to my knowledge, Shadrach had treated her with only respect and dignity—showing not a shred of emotion. Neither had he taught her to read or write. Mert spent her evenings seated outside his chamber, carding and spinning wool, while Shadrach quizzed his brothers on their studies.

"Have you ever hinted at your feelings for him?"

She rolled her eyes. "Of course not!"

"Why not be the first to risk your heart if the alternative is to be separated forever?"

Another knock on the door saved Mert from answering my question, and Gula peeked in. "May I join you?"

"Of course." Mert waved her over to join us on the bed and then glared at me with a silent warning. I understood and would keep her secret safe.

Chattering like sparrows, we talked until our stomachs protested. "Has the palace kitchen canceled all our meals since our masters are dining elsewhere?"

"I'll go find out." Mert scooted off the bed, but Gula halted her.

"No, let me." She was off the bed and at the door before Mert could argue. "I know the cook. Maybe I can get some leftovers from the king's table." She rushed out the door and slammed it behind her.

Mert scrunched her face. "Why wouldn't a friend of the palace cook serve a tidy princess? Why clean up after messy Hebrew twins?"

I shrugged, thinking of a hundred easier jobs Gula could get with a friend in the palace, but I was far more interested in our conversation about Mert's heart. "Why wouldn't a smart Hebrew prince marry his lovely Egyptian maid?"

My question was equally absurd, and we must have realized the gap in my reasoning at the same time. We both spiraled into full-bellied laughter. I'd never seen my friend so hysterical. In that moment we became two silly girls without a care in the world. When our joy wound down like a spool of thread, we wiped away tears in a pleasant silence.

Suddenly, Mert pressed a finger to my lips and

hers in warning. I hadn't heard anything, but she slid off the bed without making a sound. Her bare feet massaged the floor, and she pressed her ear against the door.

Still, I heard nothing. "It's probably one of the other maids. They're starving too."

"Shhh!" Mert waved away my noise. Listening again. She rushed back to me and hauled me off the bed like a sack of grain and shoved me to the floor. "A maid doesn't wear sandals. Get under the bed and stay quiet." She pulled a dagger from a leather sheath strapped to her thigh, and I realized Mert was not a simple chambermaid.

I sat beside the bed, shocked and confused at my friend's sudden skill. "Where did you get—"

"Shut up and get under the bed. Now!" She shoved my shoulders to the floor, pushed me beneath the raised mattress, and moved like a desert cat toward the door. Finally, I heard the faint scrape of a sandal approaching. I almost shouted at her to come away. All four of our boys wore sandals now. What if she sliced their throats by mistake?

My enigmatic friend grabbed a towel, covered the dagger, and waited.

A heavy knock sounded. "I have a message for the handmaid Belili, from her master, Lord Belteshazzar."

Hidden by overhanging covers, I watched as she opened the door and a strange guard appeared.

He spoke too quietly for me to hear, towering over Mert, and then tried to step past her. The moments that followed were a blur of confusion and horror. I knew it had been Mert's quickness that surprised him because when the guard fell beside the bed, I saw life drain from his shocked face.

"Belili, hurry!" Mert whispered sharply. "There could be others on their way." She struggled to scoot the heavy guard aside so I could squeeze around him from beneath the bed.

I tried to avoid the pooling blood, but some of it stained the front of my robe as I crawled around him. Trying to wipe it away, I began to cry and tremble, my hands now coated with blood. Standing beside the man's body, I couldn't move. Couldn't look away from his wide eyes and gaping mouth, frozen in death with the same surprise I'd seen in his last moments. "Look what you did, Mert! Look . . ."

She rushed to the doorway and glanced up and down the hallway. "Hurry!"

I trembled violently, black spots threatened my vision, and I retched on the floor. Mert grabbed my arms and shook me, her gray eyes glistening. "We don't have time to be frightened or think about what happened—not if we want to live." She swiped fiercely at a traitorous tear, then dragged me into the hall.

I followed her down the stairs, and then we

hesitated before exiting the iron gate. She looked both directions down the darkened street and walked at the pace of a chariot race, whispering more to herself than to me, "Gula must have sent the assassin when she went to the palace for our meal. I knew there was something suspicious about her."

The notion jolted me. "Why would Gula want to kill me?"

Mert pushed me into a dark alley. "It wasn't Gula. She worked for someone very powerful."

Stunned, I was certain Mert had lost her mind. "No one cares about a simple Hebrew maid."

"Are you really so blind, Belili? Daniel has never hidden his feelings for you, and King Nebuchadnezzar wouldn't want his chief wise man to marry his maid."

I felt another gorge rise in my throat but swallowed it down, forcing myself to think instead of react. "Ashpenaz warned I'd be attacked tonight. He knew."

Mert's hands went to her hips. "And you're just mentioning this now?"

Why hadn't I believed him? I'd placed Mert and myself in danger with my stupidity. "I'm sorry, Mert. I couldn't imagine why anyone would try to harm me."

Moonlight reflected the sadness in her eyes. "Belili, King Nebuchadnezzar will ensure his governor of Chaldeans marries a woman who represents the elegance and culture of Babylon's finest society. Ordering your death was like swatting a fly."

Her worldy wisdom shocked me. "How do you know this?"

"My mother was beautiful—like you. She was a fly in the court of King Nebuchadnezzar's father." She lifted the bloody dagger. "I've carried her dagger ever since he decided she was a pest to be destroyed. When I took it from her lifeless body, I vowed to kill or be killed before I became a fly to any king or nobleman."

"Oh, Mert, I'm sorry." I squeezed her hand, terror seeping into me. "What should we do now? If the threat came from the king, who can help us?"

"What about Ashpenaz?" Mert asked. "If he warned you about the attack, perhaps he would be willing to help."

We found Ashpenaz sitting on a cushion in his chamber, bent over a wax tablet with a stylus. "Since you're still alive, come in and close the door." He did not turn to greet us. "Do you believe me now, little Belili?"

My cheeks warmed. "Yes, Lord Ashpenaz. I'm sorry. I . . . Mert protected me, and . . ." Emotion strangled me. I dared not cry and let him think I'd come for sympathy. "We seek your wisdom . . . and protection."

"Ha!" He turned slowly, a sneer on his face, but

143

jumped to his feet at the sight of my bloody robe. "Are you injured, Belili?" He inspected my arms, turning me side to side like a fussy mother hen.

"I'm all right. Mert protected me."

"Of course she protected you." He heaved a sigh, seeming satisfied I was unharmed. "She wields her mother's dagger as if it's a spoon in her gruel. I placed her with the four most talented Hebrew boys, certain they'd need her protection from jealous classmates or bigoted councilmen." His eyes lingered on me, his features softening. "I never imagined the trouble would fall on you, Wildcat." He cleared his throat, leaving the room in stillness.

What a puzzle he was, this roaring lion with a heart of gold. I reached for Mert's hand and knew we would be all right. Ashpenaz would protect us. He would find a way.

Even as the thought crossed my mind, he spoke, all tenderness gone. "You must leave Babylon tonight, Belili. I will send you with two eunuchs—men I trust—who will deliver you to a safe destination that even I won't know."

Mert's hand tightened around mine. "Surely Mert could come with me. She's—"

"No." He looked at Mert. "Go. Now."

She bowed and left without a word. No argument. No pleading. No goodbye.

I was alone again. "How long before I can return to Babylon?"

Ashpenaz clenched his teeth and then turned his back on me. He reached for a piece of parchment and began writing what I assumed were orders for my escort. "You will never return to Babylon."

At Lord Laqip's villa a servant escorted Daniel into the library, where scrolls filled three walls of floor-to-ceiling shelves and astrological diagrams covered every visible surface of a large wooden table. Daniel had nearly memorized one of the maps by the time a servant arrived, carrying a tray of delicacies and two goblets of wine. Laqip followed her with a six-month betrothal contract for Daniel to sign. "I see no reason to delay when my daughter is in love," he said, scooting the food and wine aside to offer Daniel quill and ink.

Stunned to silence, Daniel was forming his tactful refusal when a second servant ushered in his friends, Shadrach, Meshach, and Abednego. It took only a moment before he realized Laqip had invited them to celebrate a betrothal to which Daniel had not yet agreed.

"Excuse me, Lord Laqip," Daniel said. "I'm deeply honored you would consider me worthy to join your family, and I am very fond of Rubati; however, I cannot marry your daughter." He bowed in the awkward silence and rose to find the man's smile unaffected.

"It's been an eventful day, Belteshazzar, and I shouldn't have broached the subject this evening. Let's enjoy our meal together, and we'll talk of the future later." He rolled up the betrothal contract, placing it back in its leather binder, and tucked it away on a shelf. "Come. Let's eat." He motioned toward the courtyard.

"No, Lord Laqip." Daniel wouldn't be cajoled. "Now or later, my answer will be the same. I love another, and it would be unfair to Rubati to marry her. I'm sorry." Offering a perfunctory bow, he spun on his heel and fled the villa.

Letting the cool evening air fill his lungs and clear his head, he took long, quick strides, hoping to return to his room in time to eat the evening meal with Abigail. Perhaps now that he was governor of the Chaldeans, he could eat every meal with her. Once they were betrothed, however, she'd need to sleep in another chamber until they married.

The thought brought a smile, and his shoulders relaxed. His strides slowed, and he breathed deeply of the Babylonian life Yahweh had given him. Abigail would be his wife when his training concluded in less than twelve months, and he would be assigned a villa on palace grounds—perhaps one as splendid as Laqip's. Abigail would become the mistress of her own household. She would miss Mert, of course, and he would miss his three best friends. But he would assign them as governors over nearby provinces, and as governor of the Chaldeans, he would also have authority to place other Judean friends in key positions throughout Babylon. His sacrifices had been worth it. Leaving Jerusalem. Relinquishing worship in Yahweh's Temple for seventy years. Never seeing his family again. *Thank You, Yahweh, for blessing our lives here.*

As he approached their villa, he noticed his window was dark. *Odd.* He walked through the garden and entered the courtyard, where his other Judean friends were just sitting down to their evening meal. Their maids served bowls of stew with bread and cheese, but Mert, Gula, and Abigail weren't among them.

Daniel waved off invitations to join the meal, a sense of dread beginning to stir as he jogged up the stairs. Shadrach and the twins were still at Laqip's, but he knocked on both doors to rouse one of their maids. No answer. He moved to his door, which was slightly ajar, the interior dark. He hesitated at the threshold. Perhaps Abigail was ill and the other two girls had gone for help. Heart beating faster, he pushed the door open, letting his eyes adjust to the dim light of the moon through the single window.

"Abigail?" No answer. Feeling his way along the wall at his left, he came to the shelf where she kept the lamp and flint stones. Striking the stones together, he lit the wick and lifted the clay lamp to disperse the light. Their small table was knocked over, their cushions askew. When he stepped toward the bed, he noticed something spilled on the floor. Something . . . red. "Nooo!" Terror drove him to his knees, hovering over the smeared pool of blood. He lowered trembling fingers but couldn't touch it. Was it Abigail's or someone else's?

"Belteshazzar, what—" Friends from downstairs huddled at the door.

Gasps and whispers grated at raw nerves. "Get Ashpenaz!" He fell against the bed, staring at proof of something despicable. Then searched the faces of those at the door. "Have you seen Abigail or Mert or Gula? Did you hear anything?"

"Tonight's meal was late," one of them said. "We thought it was some sort of punishment or test. When I sent my maid to ask you or Shadrach about it, she said this side of the villa was empty."

Daniel's mind whirred with frightening possibilities. If someone purposely delayed tonight's meal to keep the young nobles in their rooms, the attack was coordinated by someone at the palace—or someone with power over the palace.

"Take your meals and eat them in your rooms tonight." Daniel stood, careful to avoid the blood. "No matter what you hear, don't come out of your chambers. If anyone asks you later, tell them you saw nothing tonight." The frightened eyes of his friends mirrored Daniel's mounting suspicions. "Go!"

Students and maids hurried down the stairs, gathered their food, and disappeared into their chambers, the last door closing only moments before Ashpenaz rushed into the villa with a contingent of palace guards. "Have you been harmed, Lord Belteshazzar?"

"No, I left Laqip's home early and returned to this." He pointed at the pool of blood, and the eunuch squinted—as if it were difficult to see a stain the size of a goat. In that moment, Daniel knew the chief eunuch was involved, and if Daniel had been equal in size and stature, he would have killed him. "Send your men outside, Ashpenaz. We will speak in private."

His thin brows arched, and he nodded permission to his men. They retreated to the balcony, closing the door behind them.

Daniel flew at him furiously, fists aimed for the eunuch's face, but the bigger man effortlessly deflected every blow. Growling, kicking, crying, hitting, Daniel exhausted himself in futile rage. His body spent, he sagged against the wall and slid to the floor, covering his face and sobbing like a maiden. "Did you kill her?"

"She's not dead."

Like a clanging cymbal, the three words brought his head up. "What? Where is she?"

He held Daniel's gaze. "I do not know, my lord,

where she was taken." Carefully chosen words. Ashpenaz was telling the truth.

"Whose blood is this?"

"No one of import, my lord."

Daniel stared into the cold eyes of truth and felt the utter helplessness of captivity. He would never know what happened in his chamber tonight. Releasing a frustrated groan, he curled into a ball and turned away from his tormentor. "Leave me, Ashpenaz."

"I'm sorry, my lord, but King Nebuchadnezzar has summoned you."

He closed his eyes and fought back tears. He was too old to cry and wise enough to know that tonight was the king's doing. Rubati's betrothal. Abigail's disappearance. How could a king who had praised Daniel—and his God—this morning carry out such a despicable plan tonight?

Because this is life at court. He remembered the days before the exile, when his ima had warned him of the games kings played with people's lives. The only difference between Babylon's courts and Judah's was Daniel's new position. He would soon carry the authority to save Judean lives throughout the empire—and he would use that power to find Abigail and help other Judeans who suffered injustice.

He scrubbed his face and offered a quick prayer to the God who reigned over all the earth. Then stood to meet his captor. "I'm ready to face the king."

PART 2

I, Nebuchadnezzar, was at home in my palace, contented and prosperous. I had a dream that made me afraid. As I was lying in bed, the images and visions that passed through my mind terrified me.

—DANIEL 4:4–5

15

That very night Belshazzar, king of the Babylonians, was slain.

—DANIEL 5:30

Babylon
October 539 BC

I woke in the windowless treasury chamber and felt as if my family had waited here for days. Mert snored like a dragon beside me. We rested well on the soft cloaks Shesh had thoughtfully gathered from family to keep our old bones from aching on the hard marble floors. Could any son-in-law be kinder?

The door squeaked, and my lazy lids flew open. Shesh rushed to meet a bald-headed priest who carried a basket mounding with round loaves of bread. I strained to hear their whispered conversation but heard nothing. The priest smiled kindly before leaving—with perhaps a hint of sadness or disappointment—and placed the full basket of bread in Shesh's arms.

I waved to my son-in-law, demanding his attention. He glanced over to where Kezia was still sleeping and soundlessly hurried my way. "Good morning, Ima. Did you sleep well?"

How could I sleep well in the Esagila? "Of course not, but thank you for the cloaks. What did the priest say?"

"The fighting has ceased in the streets."

"And the palace?"

"No word."

I felt the news drop like a boulder in my stomach.

"The priests were up all night, baking for the refugees in the temple." Shesh reached for a loaf of bread, tore it, and gave me half. "We must leave by midday. Do you know of anyone who could house all of us?"

"We can't leave," I said. "Daniel won't know where to look for us when he's released from the palace."

"Ima . . ." Shesh tilted his head, his eyes communicating his doubts.

I looked away, scanning my displaced family. The babies and toddlers were waking, cuddling with sleepy parents. My children and grandchildren lay in each other's arms, whispering and afraid. We couldn't stay here forever. Even if Daniel was released, we'd need new homes since the invaders confiscated our villas. The answer to our dilemma was clear, but stuck like a fishbone caught sideways in my throat. How could I tell Shesh our secret— the secret that had stolen my children's love and respect from me so many years ago?

Yahweh, what should I do?

Mert sat up, yawned. Shesh tore another loaf and offered half to her. "Tell him, or I will."

"I was going to tell him." *You old goat.*

"Then tell him."

"I will."

"Go ahead."

"Daniel owns an estate in Borsippa." I blurted out the secret I'd kept for over thirty years.

I saw relief in Shesh's raised brows instead of the anger I feared. "That's wonderful, Ima. If we leave soon, we can be in Borsippa before dark." He started to leave us, but hesitated. "Perhaps someday you'll tell me why you and Abba kept the estate a secret from us."

I brushed his bearded cheek. "When Daniel returns from the palace to find our villas occupied by Medes, Borsippa will be the first place he looks. Perhaps Daniel can explain then."

His eyes misted, and he held my hand against his cheek. "May Yahweh guide him to us." He stood and clapped his hands, gaining the family's attention. "Ima and Mert will deliver bread to each family. Please take only a half loaf per adult and only as much as your children will eat. We leave for an estate in Borsippa as soon as possible. When you're ready, line up at the door. We'll gather as many waterskins as possible from the priests on our way out."

Mert carried the basket, and I began offering

bread and a blessing to each of my family members, drinking in the intimacy such urgency creates. I'd nearly finished rationing the provisions when I heard a beautiful sound.

"Abba!" one of our daughters exclaimed.

"Saba has returned!" The little ones ran as a mob, nearly knocking Daniel over, and the adults clapped and shouted.

"Daniel!" I said with a delighted cry. Almost immediately, I stumbled back into Mert at the sight of a man wearing the robe of the Mede's chief magus. "Gadi?" The name escaped on a whisper, heard only by my friend.

"It has to be Allamu," Mert whispered to me in reply. "Not Gadi."

The man's eyes locked on mine. He took three steps toward me, and I matched them. Ten paces separated us now, but a greater chasm was riven years ago.

He raised one brow with a mocking grin. "Hello, Mother."

The pain on Belili's expression tore at Daniel's heart. He'd never imagined Allamu would announce his kinship so bluntly to their unsuspecting family.

"Allamu, please step into the hall where we can speak privately," Daniel said, but Belili's son stepped farther into the room.

Approaching Shesh, Allamu extended his hand.

156

"You must be my sister Kezia's husband. Daniel told me you're an elder of the Jews. General Gubaru will be anxious to speak with you and the other elders of standing."

Shesh glanced at Daniel before gripping his hand. "I would be honored to meet your general. May I ask your position among the Medes?"

Allamu clucked his tongue. "Forgive me, Lord Sheshbazzar." After an exaggerated bow, he raised his arms and spoke to the whole family. "I am Allamu, chief magus and General Gubaru's personal seer. Babylon now belongs to an empire ruled by Cyrus the Great."

Daniel, seeing his wife's cheeks pale, moved across the room to support her. He kissed her temple and whispered, "When the soldiers invaded the banquet, Allamu recognized me and advised the general to let me live. They slaughtered everyone else in the throne room. Afterward he demanded to see his mother. I'm sorry it came out this way, my love. I'm so sorry."

She leaned into him, eyes closed, voice a hushed groan. "I'm so thankful you're alive."

Allamu's shout invaded the tender moment. "Zerubbabel!" A short but stout Hebrew emerged from the hallway. Allamu patted his muscular shoulder. "Zerubbabel is the grandson of a Judean king but is somewhat less devout in his beliefs than I remember Daniel being." He chuckled, but the guard looked as if he wanted to crawl back to the hall.

"Zerubbabel now serves as General Gubaru's personal guard and escorted us here because he expected danger in the streets." He flashed a smug grin. "I suspect I may face more peril from this family than the people of Babylon."

"Allamu," Daniel said, hoping to interrupt his inane chatter, "simply tell your ima about our homes."

The man covered the distance between them in two long strides and looked down with a cold stare. "She's my *mother,* not my *ima.* I'm a Mede, not a Hebrew."

"You have as much Hebrew blood as Median in your veins," his mother said.

"He has the manners of a Mede." Mert huffed and crossed her arms.

Allamu's features darkened as he spun toward the voice. "Who . . ." He studied her for only a moment. "Mert!" He smothered her in a hug.

"This is absurd!" Kezia pinned her ima with an accusing glare, and even Shesh's gaze held uncharacteristic suspicion.

Daniel pulled his wife closer. "Please, everyone. Listen. We'll explain everything in time, but right now we're all feeling shocked. Allamu has arranged for us to keep our villas." A relieved buzz fluttered through the gathering.

Daniel noted Allamu's reunion with Mert

had ended and nodded at Allamu, hoping his stepson would divulge the rest of the news. But Allamu pursed his lips, shifting the task to Daniel.

With a resigned sigh, he spoke the words that would change their lives. "General Gubaru has again deemed me Lord Belteshazzar and appointed me to serve on his high council."

"No, Dan—" His wife tried to interrupt, but he raised his hand to silence her and continued. "I am to serve him for the rest of my days."

Belili stepped away from him, wrapping her arms around her middle. He couldn't comfort her now.

"All the king's officials are required to live on palace grounds. Other than that, the living arrangements in the family villas will remain unchanged."

"Why must you live on palace grounds?" Kezia lifted her chin. "Does this general think himself our new king?"

"They have strapped on your yoke. Does it matter who drives the plow?" Allamu's glint of satisfaction muzzled Kezia.

Daniel tried to assuage the panic that began to spread. "All the king's officials will live on palace grounds to be able to answer his summons immediately, day or night. I couldn't do that if I lived on this side of the Processional Way. Our family villas remain personal property belonging to us. We must be grateful for the gift." He met the gaze of each of his children and added, "Belili and I will move to a villa of my choosing today."

His wife's head snapped up with a look of betrayal that pierced him. Her eyes searched his for answers he didn't have. Finally, she lifted her chin and turned to Allamu. "What kind of general would allow his adviser to choose the villa? A wise leader would ask the adviser's *wife* to make that choice."

Her son's stony expression cracked with a faint smile. "Follow me then, Mother, and we'll find a palace villa that suits you."

Daniel and his wife left the chamber, a thousand unanswered questions trailing behind them.

16

King Nebuchadnezzar made an image
of gold, sixty cubits high and six cubits
wide, and set it up on the plain of Dura in
the province of Babylon.

—DANIEL 3:1

Achmetha, the land of Medes
Spring 598 BC

Every priest and priestess of Mithra's temple
dashed about in preparation for the evening's
initiations. The annual event was celebrated
throughout Media, but in Achmetha—the nation's
capital—the underground temple thrummed with
activity for a week before and after.

I rounded a corner carrying two pitchers of
wine and bounced off the high priest's belly,
staining both our white gowns with the sweet
nectar.

"Forgive me, Highness." I bowed awkwardly,
still balancing the heavy pitchers.

He took one from my hands and began walking
beside me. "Are we on our way to the initiates'
chamber, Belili?"

"Yes, thank you for helping. I thought I could
manage two pitchers, but clearly I was mistaken."

"You were doing fine until you bumped into a white bull coming around the corner." His eyes sparkled with friendly mischief, referring to himself as the poor animal we'd sacrifice tonight for the festival.

My thoughts dashed over the order of ceremony, the litany of recitations I'd memorized, the sacred bowls, towels . . .

"Madam High Priestess!" The high priest stepped in front of me, sloshing the wine again.

Had he spoken to me more than once? "Yes? I'm sorry. My mind—"

His smile turned leering. "It's normal to be a bit nervous before performing your first ceremony as high priestess, Belili, but you'll do well." He drew his finger along my jawline, and I leaned into his repulsive gesture, feigning enjoyment. "You've soared past every expectation."

"It is my honor and oath to serve with the strength returned to me by the great and mighty Mithra." The practiced words slid from my tongue like well-oiled wheels.

Not that Mithra had saved me. No god had. Nor any man. When Ashpenaz's eunuchs abandoned me on the streets of Achmetha, I realized the folly of faith—in anyone or anything. Trust led to betrayals, and betrayals crushed hope. By the time an old woman found me huddled in a trench with other waste, I was starving and had been beaten nearly to death. Even if I'd known she was Mithra's temple midwife, I was too weak to reject her ministrations. Too desperate to refuse the warm broth she ladled into my mouth. How could I know—Abigail, a naive Hebrew girl—that this woman's kindness would indenture me to a life of servitude to Mithra?

The day I was declared healthy, she offered me two choices to pay for her services: the slave market or priestess training. After six weeks as a low-level priestess, I knew I could survive temple service only as high priestess—a woman treated with the respect due Mithra himself.

"Here we are." The high priest allowed me to enter the expansive initiates' chamber before him. Like bees in a hive, priests, priestesses, and slaves busied themselves at seven stations, where would-be initiates would prove their devotion before the feast began.

My slave, Laleh, ran to meet us. "Both highnesses! Your robes!"

The high priest shoved his pitcher into her arms. "You worry about the chief priestess's robe. She must look perfect for tonight's festival." He lifted my hand to his lips. "I have no doubt you'll outshine any other highness before you." I suppressed my shiver till he released my hand and left, having become an expert at delayed revulsion.

"I didn't mean to make him angry." Laleh's lip quavered.

"He's not angry. He's the high priest. He always speaks like that." *To slaves.* It was how he'd treated me five years ago.

I walked past her to assess the progress made on the seven stations around the outer perimeter of the room, each designated by an image etched into a marble column. With the progression of images—raven, bridegroom, soldier, lion, moon, torch, and red cape—a priest or priestess rose in status and commitment to Mithra, the god of oaths. The rite at each station was sealed by an oath of silence, all seven oaths known only to the high priest and priestess. Any oath taken tonight was lifelong and punishable by death if broken.

"Let's begin with the lowest station." I advanced to the column of the raven, dictating instructions on necessary preparations while Laleh made notes with her stylus on the wax tablet. Educated Persian slaves were valuable and Laleh doubly so, for she was also beautiful.

Moving to the second station, I made my way to the altar and picked up one of the clay lamps, symbolic of the sacred bridegroom's oath. "I see only ten lamps. Where are the rest?"

The girl's eyes widened. "I thought you said you only needed ten."

"What if all twenty qualify?" I raised my hand to brush her cheek, but she flinched as if I might strike her. My heart constricted, but I couldn't let her see it in my expression. "I don't hit slaves for honest mistakes. Only willful rebellion will get you a beating, and one of my guards would do it so you'll never disobey again."

The fear in her eyes bludgeoned me, and I turned away quickly. I would never order any slave beaten, but I'd done worse things. And much worse had been done to me. Laleh's beauty would undoubtedly force her into priestess training. I'd clawed my way through all seven rites of Mithra in only five years. Now, as high priestess, I lived in nearly as much comfort as our Median queen. Splendid food. A spacious chamber. And a warm bed—only occasionally trespassed by the wealthiest men of Achmetha, come to offer their "oaths" to Mithra. How long would it be until Laleh, or another girl even more beautiful, displaced me?

What happened to Mithra's discarded high priestesses? I could never return to Yahweh. Apparently, He didn't dwell among the Medes. I'd cried out to Him every time a man abused me in the streets of Achmetha, every time I grew faint with hunger. I thought surely the God who had revealed Himself in the Holy of Holies and protected me from death in Jerusalem would show Babylon's new chief of wise men where to find me.

Perhaps Yahweh had never meant to protect me. What if He saved my life only because He was protecting the four princes? Fear, abuse, and starvation had created shrewd Belili and put trusting Abigail to death forever.

"Highness? You look pale." Laleh's luminous eyes blinked her concern. "May I pour you a cup of wine?"

"Yes. I need a little something to help me through this inspection." I reached into my pocket for a little goose fat to smooth my unruly curls beneath Mithra's tiara. Spouting like a fountain from behind the tiara, my riotous curls cascaded down my open-backed gown.

Warm fingers slid under my curls, and I whirled, ready to lift my knee into the tender parts of any man who touched me without paying for an oath. "How dare—" I froze, then quickly bowed before the chief magus, a frequent worshipper and King Astyages's dearest friend. I amended my words and tone. "How are you today, Lord Gadi?"

"I'm sorry, Belili." He cleared his throat. "I shouldn't have disturbed you on such a busy day."

I looked up and saw him retreating. "Wait, please!" If I offended the chief magus, it would be I who endured a beating. I caught up and fell to my knees before him, kissing the large gold ring on his hand. "Forgive me, Lord Gadi. I wasn't expecting you in the initiates' chamber. I'm always happy to see you." It was true. Of all my worshippers, Gadi was one I might have even called a friend if we'd met outside these walls.

He lifted me by the hand and then met my gaze. Something troubling swam in the eyes I knew so well. "What is it, my lord? Are you ill?"

"I'll know after I hear your answer." He hesitated, so unlike the decisive chief of Media's wise men. "I've already asked the chief priest, and we've settled on a price. Now the only question is your willingness, Belili."

Settled on a price? My willingness? Prickly flesh lifted the small hairs on my arms. I'd performed all the priestess's prescribed oath ceremonies. What more could he—

"Marry me, Belili."

"Marry you?" I waited for him to chuckle and even glanced behind him, checking for a nobleman who had likely dared him to play a trick.

He released my hand, real hurt blazing in his eyes. "Are you looking for someone to come to your rescue? I can see you have no intention of—"

"No, I thought someone . . . I mean . . . Why would you wish to marry *me?*" The whole chamber fell silent, and I realized we'd become entertainment. "Please, can we go into the hallway to talk?"

He accompanied me, placing his hand at the small of my back. It felt possessive but secure. I liked it. The hall was busy too, but at least people were bustling past rather than standing to listen.

I lifted my eyes to appraise this familiar stranger. In his early thirties, he wasn't unpleasant to look at. His hands had always been gentle and kind. How could I express my fear and distrust to the man Gadi? Not the chief magus or friend of the king. "Don't you want to marry a Median maiden who's never known another man?"

He grinned, and at first I thought he would mock me. "You're seventeen, vibrant, and clever." With a feather-light touch, he traced a line from my earlobe down my throat and paused at the hollow of my neck, where he placed a kiss that sent my heart racing. I inhaled a ragged breath, daring to feel a moment's pleasure. He brushed my lips with a teasing kiss. "I want you, Belili. Tonight. After the sacrifice of the white bull. Come to me at the pinnacle of your service to Mithra, you, the most beautiful high priestess in Achmetha's records, and wed the chief magus."

His words shattered any delusions of his affection for me. This marriage, like everything else in my life, would be about my survival.

"I've heard King Astyages has asked you to represent the Medes when King Nebuchadnezzar unveils a giant statue on the Dura Plain."

Surprise lit his features, then a wry smile. "You want to see Babylon."

"More than anything."

He slid his arm around my waist and pulled me against him. "After we're married."

I pulled his head down and kissed him thoroughly, then pulled away, leaving him breathless. "I'll marry you when we get to Babylon."

Eyes narrowed, he placed both hands on the wall near my head, trapping me with a steady gaze. He knew I was gambling. When would a high priestess get a better offer? "We leave for Babylon tomorrow."

"I'll be ready." I slid out to my right and tossed a smile over my shoulder. Let Gadi think it was for him. He didn't need to know I was imagining Ashpenaz bowing to me.

Daniel was too nervous to sit still. He marched out of his bedchamber onto the second-story balcony and leaned over the railing to see farther up the mighty Euphrates. "They should be here by now. Surely they'd come straight to our villa, wouldn't they?" He let out a huff and returned to his chamber.

Zakiti remained quiet, a wry grin on her lips, while she finished embroidering his new belt for today's dedication ceremony.

He paced another lap around her couch. "Aren't you going to say something?"

His wife laid aside her embroidery and rose with the grace of a willow tree. "What do you wish me to say, my love? Shadrach, Meshach, and Abednego will move heaven and earth to find you if they're in this city. But look at all the people." She pointed to the river, clogged as it was with rafts and quffas of every size. "If your friends didn't plan for the crowds, they'll likely miss the big event."

He pressed both hands against the rail, releasing his frustration in a long, slow sigh. "Sometimes Babylon's chief wise man needs to hear the obvious from his wise wife."

Zakiti snuggled into the bend of his arm, and he pulled her into a long-overdue embrace. He'd been working too much—again. For the past five years, Nebuchadnezzar had demanded every one of his council members' full attention to design and build the monstrous statue in the Dura Plain.

Nebuchadnezzar's obsession began on the night Abigail disappeared. Daniel had been summoned and reluctantly stood before the king, who had both betrayed and blessed him. Nebuchadnezzar vowed, "I'll build the statue in my dream and dedicate it to your god." Leaving his throne, he descended the dais and met Daniel face to face. "How old are you, Belteshazzar?"

"Fifteen." Teeth clenched, Daniel still burned with rage.

"I had a wife and son by the time I was fifteen. Now I'm twenty-one and rule the world. Do you believe your god is more powerful than me?"

"Yes," Daniel said without hesitation. "Yahweh can do anything."

"Can he find you a Babylonian wife, or will he make you a eunuch in my service? These are your god's choices, Belteshazzar. He should make the decision before you're sixteen." Nebuchadnezzar lifted a single brow. "Or I'll make the choice for him."

Daniel tightened his arms around his wife. She was indeed a gift from Yahweh, introduced to him a year before that fateful night, a day when he'd accompanied Abigail to buy bread in the city market. Zakiti's father was the best baker in Babylon. A shrewd haggler too. His daughter, even then, sat quietly with her embroidery, her pleasantness balancing his hard bargaining. Zakiti had visited Abigail occasionally at their villa after that, striking up friendships with all the maids.

When Daniel named his choice of bride, King Nebuchadnezzar grudgingly agreed, since Zakiti wasn't a nobleman's daughter. He arranged their betrothal and even paid the baker an enormous bride price. The wedding had been simple, as had been their lives. Daniel worked. Zakiti maintained their home. She was caring, quiet, kind, and . . . childless. *Yahweh, make my wife's womb fruitful.*

Daniel tried to remember when he'd fallen in love with her. At least he thought it was love. His chest didn't constrict with that passionate yearning he once felt for Abigail, but perhaps those feelings came only in youth.

"Lord Belteshazzar, the lords Shadrach, Meshach, and Abednego have arrived and await your greeting in—"

"Yes! Finally!" Daniel grabbed Zakiti's hand and fairly dragged her down the stairs. "I thought you three might miss the ceremony. What took you so—" The wide gold collars on their necks stole Daniel's breath. When had they become eunuchs? Why?

Shadrach scuffed his sandal on the tiles, refusing to meet his gaze. "We weren't sure . . . well . . . that you'd want to see us."

Daniel glanced around his courtyard at the six eunuchs assigned by the king as his personal guards. He couldn't speak freely in front of them. "Zakiti, would you bring some wine and cheese up to our bedchamber so my friends can enjoy some refreshment while I review last-minute administrative details about their cities before the dedication?"

"Administrative details . . ." Confused, she started to argue, but realization dawned. "Oh, yes. Of course. I'll bring a tray up in a few moments."

"Come, gentlemen." Daniel led the men dressed in red administrator's robes to his chamber and closed the door behind them. Without a moment for pleasantries, he pulled them all into a fierce embrace. "How could you think I wouldn't want to see you?" They huddled together, letting the balm of friendship heal the uncertainties of four long years apart.

Meshach, the quiet twin, broke the huddle first. "You should have no regrets about your decision to marry Zakiti. She's lovely and seems to have maintained her kind spirit—even after marriage."

The awkward approval opened the door for Daniel's question. "Thank you, Meshach. I have no regrets. What about you three? How did you decide . . ." Struggling to find a way to phrase it, he kept it vague. "About your future?"

Shadrach glanced at his brothers, who coaxed him to speak for them—as he always had. "It was actually quite simple. When you assigned our cities, we were alone for the first time in our lives. Nebuchadnezzar proved his negotiating skills when within a month, each of us received a message from the king giving us the choice of marrying a Babylonian maiden or taking the vow as his loyal eunuch."

Abednego, the feisty one, broke the tension. "None of us found a girl like Zakiti, so we opted for the brotherhood."

The brothers laughed and Daniel joined them, but Meshach sobered quickly. "Each of us came to the same conclusion independently. To marry a Babylonian in a strange city meant we'd become even more captive. Slaves to a wife's needs, her family's demands, and eventually our children's legacy. To choose the ultimate form of Babylonian brotherhood felt simpler, since we knew how to be brothers. We serve Yahweh first, then the king and each other."

For the first time, Daniel saw the brotherhood of eunuchs as more than disfigurement, but what about Yahweh's law? Again, he searched for words that wouldn't offend. "Have you considered the law of Moses? The command that says, 'Do not cut your bodies.'"

Meshach nodded with a mischievous grin. "Recite the whole verse, Daniel."

Daniel's memory was sparked by the use of his Hebrew name, and he recited it easily. "Do not cut your bodies for the dead or put tattoo marks on yourselves. I am the LORD." His heart lightened immediately. "The cutting is in the context of grieving!"

Shadrach nodded. "Yahweh also forbids priests to cut themselves, but we're of Judah's descendants and could never be priests. Each of us heard Yahweh's wisdom on the matter and wrote the exact same points in a message to the other two, receiving the messages on the day we took the eunuch's vow."

Gooseflesh rose on Daniel's arms. "Though we cannot worship our God in Jerusalem, He has come to Babylon with us, my friends. In little proofs like this, I feel His presence." The three exchanged approving glances, and Daniel felt as if they were young princes again in the captive camp. He placed his hand in the middle of their circle, and the others piled their hands on top as they'd done seven years ago.

Only Abigail's was missing. A stab of loss closed Daniel's throat.

"Have you looked for her?" Shadrach's voice, barely a whisper.

Daniel shook his head. "I gave her into Yahweh's hands. He will protect her." It was the only thing he could do. The alternative was insanity. What mortal could oppose the King of the Earth?

Shadrach placed his other hand atop the pile. "Yahweh is faithful, friends, and He has placed us in key positions at strategic locations. Daniel teaching the king's advisers in Babylon. My brothers and I secretaries to governors in Sippar, Erech, and Nippur."

Daniel's heart soared. "Our scattering is our strength, brothers. Those who trained with us also serve throughout the empire. They'll teach their children and their children's children about Yahweh's laws and His ways. We'll grow stronger in faith, in number, and in loyalty to each other while we await our deliverance."

"And we'll return with the remnant in only sixty-three years," Meshach added, surprising them all with his humor.

"Indeed, my friend." Daniel's smile felt traitorous. How could they celebrate without Abigail? Where was she? Where would she be in sixty-three years?

17

[King Nebuchadnezzar] summoned the satraps, prefects, governors, advisers, treasurers, judges, magistrates and all the other provincial officials to come to the dedication of the image he had set up. . . . Shadrach, Meshach and Abednego replied to him, ". . . If we are thrown into the blazing furnace, the God we serve is able to deliver us from it."

—DANIEL 3:2, 16–17

Gadi ransomed me from my underground tomb of secret rites and life-threatening oaths and bore me on eagle's wings into a world I'd never known. Cold, clear water gushed from rocky crevices as the snows thawed in the Zagros Mountains. Wildflowers bloomed on soil-crusted plateaus. New life chirped, mooed, and baaed around us on our journey to Babylon. Beside our evening campfires, Gadi wrapped me in blankets and taught me to recognize the constellations of the Dog, the Hunter, and the Twins. He lauded my cleverness and filled my mind with knowledge of plants, animals, herbs, cloth, dyes, governments, languages, and geography. His intellect astounded me, and I planned to capture his affections as I'd done with dozens before him.

But on the first night of our journey, when the moon rose high and camp sounds stilled, he delivered me to the threshold of my private white tent and pecked a chaste kiss on my cheek. "Are you suddenly so concerned about my virtue?" I said it with a teasing pout, certain he'd swagger into my tent with little coaxing.

Instead, he held my face gently between his hands. "While you were a priestess, your body was a representation of Mithra to me—and to others—but when you come to our wedding bed, you will be as a maiden to me." He kissed the tip of my nose, as if all his other kisses had never happened.

The next morning—and each morning after—twenty servants met our every need before we spoke, and 150 guards ensured our safety. We journeyed over mountains, through a desert, and over plains, the experience far different than my torturous journey with Ashpenaz's eunuchs years before.

Ashpenaz. The closer my camel lumbered to Babylon, the more I wished to avoid the dedication ceremony altogether. Why had I wished to humble Nebuchadnezzar's chief eunuch? And why had I imagined it was even possible? I should be utterly content as Lord Gadi's wife in Achmetha. But like a moth to a flame, I continued, swaying in the plush sedan on the back of the slowest Bactrian camel on earth, imagining what I would say when I came face to face with . . . Daniel. Not Ashpenaz, but Daniel.

I hated Ashpenaz. But I was terrified of seeing Daniel. Would his discerning eyes see more than I wanted to reveal?

Had the boy I loved become King Nebuchadnezzar's governor of Chaldeans—a role equal to Gadi's position in Achmetha? Or had Babylon's king reneged on his promise and betrayed my dearest friend? *Friend.* It seemed a rather empty word for all we'd shared.

After our fifteen-day journey, I noticed a glimmering reflection on the horizon before we crested the hills of Babylon. We plodded forward, and the mammoth statue seemed to grow taller as our beasts climbed higher on the hills. The landscape southeast of Babylon was scarred by the hideous image, nearly as high as the temple's ziggurat but ridiculously narrow. Its golden top had a slight protrusion with several indentations. Was it supposed to be a head?

"What is it?" I asked my nobleman but kept my voice low. He shot a warning glare my direction. Even he knew better than to question mighty King Nebuchadnezzar.

Gadi swatted his camel's rump, sending its hooves into flight. I urged my lazy beast into an urgent trot toward the massive crowd on the Dura Plain. Bowl-shaped hills bordered the northern edge of the flat green expanse, where the enormous statue stood guard over earth, men, and sky. At the pinnacle of the hill and directly beneath the gold monstrosity, King Nebuchadnezzar and a woman I supposed to be his queen rested nobly on their thrones, presiding over the largest crowd I'd ever seen.

Gadi had weaved his camel expertly through the crowd and halted at the northernmost point of the plain. He gestured wildly for me to hurry. My camel was skittish though, hesitant to advance through the cheering crowd and drunken revelry.

"Come, my dear!" Gadi pointed at two large platforms flanking the king's dais, formed by graduated terraces in the hillside, where men and women in various foreign costumes and regal dress sat in places of honor.

When my camel finally ambled up to meet him, a Babylonian eunuch grabbed its harness. "What are you doing?" Panic nearly launched me from my sedan.

"He's leading us to the nobility terraces beside the royal dais." Gadi tossed a scroll, imprinted with King Nebuchadnezzar's seal, into my sedan.

I opened it, read it, and felt like a nine-year-old girl again, waiting for Babylonian guards to expose my true identity.

My bridegroom chattered like a hoopoe, changing from the distinguished chief magus to an excited little boy. "I had no idea King Nebuchadnezzar would honor King Astyages by placing us on the nobility terraces. We'll stand by kings, Belili. Kings and their queens."

"Yes, what an honor." With a trembling hand, I secured my red veil across my face. The matching red head covering and robe—the color of Mithra's high priesthood—were a gift from my bridegroom proclaiming the status of his prize to any who had experienced the underground world of Mithra's worship. I paraded through the crowd like a dazzling red banner, but at least I was covered—all but my eyes—in the land of my enemies.

Two brick furnaces bordered the nobility terraces, built into the downward slopes at the far edges of the hills. Perhaps they were the excuse I needed. "Gadi, I'm frightened of the furnaces." My pitiful lie interrupted his elation. "Why are there flames in them? Does the king need to fire bricks while nobility stand no more than two hundred paces—"

Our guiding eunuch interrupted, shouting over his shoulder. "King Nebuchadnezzar has thrown two food vendors into the furnaces this morning."

"But why?" I sputtered, horror gorging at the back of my throat.

"They charged too much, and the king believes in setting an example." The eunuch spoke as if he'd informed us of the weather.

I turned to Gadi, hoping to see the same revulsion I felt, but his attention was fixed on the steady stream of ox-drawn carts carrying wood up the hills. The insanity of Babylon became clear, like water filtered through a tightly woven cloth. The carts delivered fuel to stoke ever-burning furnaces to make more bricks to build ever-taller towers so Nebuchadnezzar could grow an ever-larger empire to, presumably, increase his ever-cruel executions. I turned my head and spit on the land of my first exile, wishing I'd never come.

Familiar grousing stole my attention, and I caught my first glimpse of Ashpenaz at the front edge of the king's dais. Gesturing wildly toward us, he shouted at our guiding eunuch, "Off! Get those two off the camels! They're too close to the king."

Well, his passion for his king certainly hadn't waned.

Gadi tapped his camel's front shoulder and called to me, "We'll walk from here." He winked, a little mischief twinkling from his eyes. "That eunuch needs a lesson in manners."

If you only knew. I, too, tapped my camel and accepted Gadi's hand as I stepped onto Babylon's soil for the first time in over five years.

Only twenty camel lengths separated the viewing terraces from the king's dais; a wide staircase rose between them on both sides. I reached up to hold my veil securely fastened before taking my first step. I had no desire to reveal my identity until the moment I chose. Arioch, the king's bodyguard, stood at the king's right. And at the king's left . . .

Daniel.

My breath caught.

Gadi gripped me as if I were a shield, looking down. "Did you see a snake?" He hated snakes.

Floundering for an explanation, my attempted deception was pathetic. "No, I just remembered the high priest warned me of King Nebuchadnezzar's disdain of Mithra. It's caused difficulty in his marriage, so we dare not reveal that I'm a high priestess."

Gadi pulled me close. To any other, it would have appeared a touching embrace, but his whisper was a threat. "How could you keep this from me until now? What if Nebuchadnezzar recognizes the red robes of our high priestess?" He cast me away and climbed the stairs alone. I followed, refastening my veil.

Why did it matter if Daniel knew I was Mithra's high priestess? My indifference lasted only until the memory of his brown eyes pierced my heart. Until the warmth of his tenderness and protection flooded my chest. Of course it mattered. The thought of his shock and sadness that I'd turned away from Yahweh after my experience in the Temple and witnessing his first vision . . . my stomach filled with knots. I couldn't face him.

Gadi halted at the foot of the king's dais, and I stood beside him, head bowed. Hopefully, the king and queen would interpret my act as honor, not rudeness.

"Lord Gadi, it's good to see you again." King Nebuchadnezzar's welcome was both warm and familiar. Many in the crowd quieted, perhaps hoping the ceremonies were beginning. "I see you've brought a lovely companion."

"More than a companion, King Nebuchadnezzar. I plan to marry the most beautiful woman in Achmetha." He reached for my hand. "In fact, she has agreed to marry me this evening after the dedication."

"We are most honored." The queen's voice. "I know your family is gone, Gadi, but is your wife alone as well?"

"We have each other, Queen Amyitis, and are eager to celebrate our union in your lovely city."

"You must let us provide a wedding banquet for you after the ceremony. We'll invite all the nobility."

"You are too generous, Queen Amyitis." Gadi bowed deeply and I matched his deference. "I am honored to bring you greetings from your father. Achmetha anxiously awaits your annual summer visit, my lady."

"You'll have your own wife now. Stop trying to take mine away," Nebuchadnezzar teased. An uneasy silence filled me with foreboding. "Gadi, you say your bride is beautiful, but I have yet to see her face. Surely she doesn't dress in red and then pretend to be bashful." The king laughed, and the crowds on the platforms beside us joined him. My cheeks burned at the mocking. The hills around us echoed our voices so everyone could hear the slightest sound.

Gadi answered above the noise. "It was I who chose her wedding dress, King Nebuchadnezzar, because I want the world to notice my Belili."

Without warning, he tugged my veil away, and I looked at the king who had so handily disposed of an eleven-year-old girl deemed unworthy to be Belteshazzar's wife. The name Belili meant nothing to him, nor would the name Abigail, so he and his queen smiled their approval at Gadi's betrothed. Gathering my courage, I turned to Daniel and saw his face pale with recognition. His forehead etched with the deep lines of judgment I feared as he appraised my robe, ruby necklace, and dangling earrings. Whatever was left of Abigail hid behind Belili.

I returned my attention to the king, stiffening my resolve and hardening my heart. "In answer to your question, King Nebuchadnezzar . . ." I swept my hand in an exaggerated bow. "I am not bashful."

The king laughed aloud, and the queen sprang from her throne, applauding my boldness and speaking to those gathered on the plain below.

"Meet a true daughter of the Medes! Belili, bride of Gadi."

The crowd applauded, and my bridegroom lifted our hands like victors. "You are remarkable, my dear," he said to me quietly. "Utterly remarkable."

A eunuch approached us, indicating where Gadi and I should stand on the terraces. We took our places among other men of high rank, some with their wives—or other companions. Once settled, I scanned the nobles on the platform opposite us, mostly representatives from other nations. No one I knew. What had happened to Shadrach, Meshach, and Abednego? What about the other Judean youths who lived in our villa? My eyes flitted to the royal dais again, careful to avoid Daniel. I found Ashpenaz staring at me, his lips quirked in an appreciative grin— and then he bowed. I inclined my head as a noblewoman would, but the victory felt hollow.

Without permission, my attention wandered to Daniel, who stared at me, his features dark and brooding. When he turned his head away, it felt like a blade to my heart, regret seeping out like blood. So many *if onlys* separated us. The queen's promised wedding banquet came to mind, and I almost groaned aloud. Daniel would no doubt be invited.

Trumpets sounded, and the king's guard lined the edge of his dais, partly obscuring my view of the thrones—and Daniel. Hadn't Ashpenaz and his eunuchs always come between us? *The eunuchs!* Every man serving in Nebuchadnezzar's court was either married or a eunuch. But Daniel didn't wear a eunuch's collar. I worked to keep my expression placid, refusing to show the emotions roiling inside. He'd probably forgotten me within days of my kidnapping. Lord Laqip probably convinced him to marry Rubati, and they now had a villa full of little Laqips. The thought sickened me.

"I am feeling unwell," I whispered to my nobleman. "I can't manage a large wedding banquet after such a long journey."

He gathered me under his arm. "You're nervous, my dove. It's to be expected. But the queen adores you." Nodding toward the dais, he shushed me.

The king's herald cleared his throat. All grew still. His words carried across the bowl-shaped setting like the voice of God. "Nations and peoples of every language, by the decree of the great and mighty King Nebuchadnezzar, when you hear the sound of horn, flute, zither, lyre, harp, pipe, and all kinds of music, you will fall down and worship the image before you. Whoever does not fall down and worship will immediately be thrown into a blazing furnace." Stepping back, he allowed the royal guard to close ranks, forming an impenetrable shield across the front edge of King Nebuchadnezzar's elevated dais.

Sparks flew heavenward from the crackling flames in the furnace. I shivered despite the heat and began to search the crowded plain. Were Shadrach, Meshach, and Abednego among the thousands of satraps, prefects, governors, advisers, treasurers, judges, magistrates, and other provincial officials gathered there? Surely my Hebrew friends would bow. It was only a giant lump of metal. It meant nothing. Would Daniel kneel to an image of gold? Daniel would never, but would Belteshazzar? Had he become Babylonian—submitting to all that required—as I'd become a Mede?

When music rent the air, I glanced at the dais to see the man at the king's left. Please, Daniel, bow!

I heard my sleeve rip before my knees landed smartly on the limestone platform. A grip of iron had pulled me down. "Has your head covering made you deaf, Belili? Now, worship!" Gadi released my arm, but the sting of his rebuke remained. Hands raised to the image, my bridegroom spoke adorations to the image as if it could hear him.

As for me, I lifted my head slightly to peer over the crowd, thinking how ridiculous everyone looked. I'd given up on Yahweh long ago, sure He'd given up on me. But while others complimented and cajoled, begged and bargained with a mammoth piece of metal, I remembered the day I'd hidden beside the Ark in Jerusalem's Temple and I vowed to never worship a god who was too weak to save the men who created it. Long ago, I'd seen Yahweh protect my four boys when Nebuchadnezzar's dream threatened their lives. Perhaps He would still answer if I prayed for them and not for myself.

Yahweh, I'm too stained to expect an answer, but please protect my friends in this dangerous land.

Amid the inane mumbling around me, the loudest voice was the one that rumbled in my chest. Was Daniel kneeling? Gadi pulled me to my knees before I'd glimpsed the king's platform. Why did it matter to me? Daniel was Nebuchadnezzar's governor of Chaldeans. Probably married. But I had to know.

Turning my head slightly, I still could not see him, and my heart skipped. Had Yahweh given Daniel power and position, removing him from the need to choose? The idea that Yahweh might save him felt completely true and settled in my deepest parts.

But why would Yahweh save Daniel from such a decision and not me? I found the answer in the droning worship of those who joined me on our knees. I'd never been worthy of Yahweh's blessing. I'd been useful for a time and cast away when no longer needed. I slipped my hand into Gadi's and felt his fingers tighten around mine.

At the herald's command, musicians throughout the plain began to blow, bang, and strum, creating such a cacophony that Daniel wished he could cover his ears. He refused to kneel, but dare he not? Nebuchadnezzar motioned for both he and Arioch to bend near but kept his gaze fixed on the plain. "You two will remain standing. Alert the guards to anyone who refuses to bow to my image."

With Daniel's relief for himself came a sinking dread for Abigail. Would she stand or kneel? Standing meant she would die in a furnace. Kneeling proved she'd died in Achmetha. Reluctantly, Daniel let his eyes wander to his right, the third terrace down . . .

Her vibrant red robe was easy to spot. Its matching head covering brushed the ground, while the bride-to-be knelt beside her groom. Why was he surprised at her kneeling? The Median woman Belili was nothing like the Abigail he knew. Brash and calculating, Belili had learned to manipulate royalty during her six years away. She'd drawn in Babylon's king and queen like a spider to her web.

Yahweh, what could have changed her so profoundly? Grief and guilt pounded in his chest. *"Friends help friends,"* he'd promised, but he'd been helpless the night she needed him most. At times like these, the bitter taste of exile tainted even the sweetest memories and stirred his hate for the king he'd vowed to serve.

"My king, look there." Arioch pointed to a disturbance on the plain.

Daniel shaded his eyes against the sun and saw a group of black-robed astrologers shoving three red-robed administrators. Steadying himself against the throne, Daniel felt as if the earth trembled beneath him. Shadrach, Meshach, and Abednego marched with heads held high through a crowd of curious worshippers. The music dwindled to dissonant tones, and people stood as Daniel's friends walked by.

"Burn them!" one man jeered, and like water through a hole in a dam, others on the plain erupted in vehement prodding for the violent deaths of three men unknown to the masses.

The eunuchs lining the dais drew their weapons against their brothers who had broken a vow of loyalty to the king. Daniel sucked in a breath as his friends approached the dais. Would the king's guard kill them before they reached the throne? Of course not. That, too, would be a betrayal. They would allow the more brutal death in a furnace. The eunuchs split their line, allowing the offenders and their escort to pass through. Closing ranks and turning their backs to the crowd, they provided a private audience for judgment on the elevated dais.

The astrologers shoved Shadrach, Meshach, and Abednego to their knees before the throne. One of the black-robed men bowed to the king before he spoke, his lips pinched in disdain. "May the king live forever! When the music sounded, these exiles from Judah, who neither worship our gods nor pay any heed to your commands, refused to bow down and worship the image of gold you have set up." His voice echoed off the hill, bouncing back over the plain below. More jeers and heckling stoked the king's rage. "Is it true, Shadrach, Meshach, and Abednego, that you do not serve my gods or worship the image of gold I have set up?"

They lifted their heads, looking only at the king. "It is true, my king" came Shadrach's humble voice.

"You made a vow. Your loyalty for my protection. Yet on the day I ask you to publicly show loyalty, Shadrach, Meshach, and Abednego, you refuse to bow down or worship my image?" The king's voice rose on the last word, sounding incredulous.

In the ensuing silence, Daniel silently cheered his friends' courage. But could he have made the same choice? When the music began, he'd hesitated. Even now, when they needed help from the chief wise man in Babylon, true wisdom eluded him.

Still, none of them glanced in his direction.

All three eunuchs focused only on their king. "Because of your vow," Nebuchadnezzar said, voice trembling with rage, "I offer one more chance. One. The next time you hear the instruments, you will fall down and worship. If you do not, you'll be thrown immediately into a blazing furnace. Then what god will be able to rescue you from my hand?"

Shadrach spoke, remaining calm and respectful. "My king, we do not need to defend ourselves before you in this matter. If we are thrown into the blazing furnace, the God we serve is able to deliver us from it, and He will deliver us from Your Majesty's hand."

"But even if Yahweh chooses not to deliver us," Abednego added, "we want you to know, Your Majesty, that we will not serve your gods or worship the image of gold you have set before us."

The collective gasp sounded like a wind sweeping the plain. Shock threatened to send Daniel to his knees. Nebuchadnezzar's fury shook him back to awareness. "Stoke the furnaces seven times hotter!"

"But, my king," Daniel pleaded. "The fires will consum—"

"Bind them!" he shouted. "And throw them into the fire immediately!"

Daniel's friends finally lifted their eyes to meet his gaze as their brother eunuchs wrenched their arms behind them and tied leather straps around their wrists. Three princes of Judah, trained as Chaldeans of Babylon, to be burned in a brick kiln at the whims of a maniacal king.

"Get them out of my sight!" King Nebuchadnezzar screeched. His queen laid a gentle hand on his arm and nodded toward the furnace. Absolute power need only whisper to show its strength.

Yahweh, let the increased heat be a mercy to my friends. Take them quickly, Lord. Walk with them into paradise.

The king watched as the procession of eunuchs neared the furnace at the far end of the hill's slope. Slaves stoked the flames with small chunks of wood to quickly raise the temperature. Daniel could feel the increase in heat where he stood more than half a city block away. In that moment, he wished he'd been forced to choose and could die with his friends rather than serve the evil king.

"Throw them in!" someone shouted from the plain, and Daniel's attention snapped toward the furnace.

Flames rose as tall as an oak tree from a huge hole on top of the furnace. The royal guards paused ten camel lengths away, glancing back at the king for direction. Even standing on the dais, Daniel's cheeks were flushed from the intense heat. How could the guards carry out this execution?

King Nebuchadnezzar waved his arm toward the furnace and bellowed, "Throw them in! Burn them!"

"Yahweh, please stop this," Daniel whispered as the first set of eunuchs, obedient without flinching, led Shadrach toward the flames.

The guards lifted their hands over their faces in an attempt to shield themselves from the heat. But Shadrach, hands tied behind him, walked undaunted and without slowing. Barely two paces from the furnace, the guards' clothes and hair burst into flames. In final screaming obedience, both guards shoved their prisoner into the fiery abyss.

"The other two," the king demanded, having backed up several steps. "Now!"

True to their vows of loyalty, the second and third sets of eunuchs led Daniel's friends to the furnace entry. They, too, gave their lives for their king while shoving the twin brothers into the flames as the smoke carried the stench over the plain.

Unable to bear the swirl of stink, sorrow, and horror, Daniel ran to the back of the dais and retched on the hillside. He braced his hands against his knees, waiting for the agonizing screams to die with his friends. How could he continue to serve as governor of Chaldeans? What could he teach young minds under his instruction about an empire led by such a perverse king? *Yahweh, how could You . . .*

"My king! My king! Come quickly!" Panicked voices from the plain below drew King Nebuchadnezzar to the front edge of his dais. Daniel cared nothing about the newest crisis in this vile kingdom. He wiped his mouth and beard and stood with a weary sigh.

"Lord Belteshazzar! Come immediately!" Nebuchadnezzar shouted. He jumped from the dais and ran down the steps toward the furnace where it opened to the plain. Daniel and Arioch followed, only a few steps behind. Daniel strained to see why a crowd gathered at the ground-level arched opening of the furnace, but too many people blocked his view.

Descending the steps, he passed Belili and Lord Gadi. The chief magus cried out, "By all the gods, it can't be!" Others shouted similar astonishment, but Daniel still couldn't get a good look at what they'd seen.

Royal eunuchs gathered around the king, who stood twenty camel lengths away from the furnace's ground-level opening. Arioch grabbed Daniel's right sleeve and dragged him toward the king.

Daniel felt a sudden tug on his left sleeve and looked behind him. Gadi clutched the blue cloth of his robe, countenance bright with a mischievous grin. "I want to see this miracle up close!"

Had the whole world gone mad? Daniel would

have ordered his arrest had Belili not peered over his shoulder, eyes swollen, face wet with tears.

"Get her away from here, Gadi!" Daniel's heart shattered that the girl he once loved had witnessed the atrocity of these deaths and another of his failures to protect his friends.

Gadi scoffed. "Seeing the wonder will erase her tears, Lord Belteshazzar."

Completely bewildered, Daniel shielded his face from the heat and stumbled to the king's side. "Lord Belteshazzar, look in that furnace and tell me what you see."

Daniel would rather have run into the flames than see the remains of his friends' bodies, but, coward that he was, he lifted his eyes and saw.

"Four." He could barely comprehend it. "Four men." He gasped for breath. "Yahweh, God of heaven, I see four men in the flames. Walking around. As though unharmed."

Arioch stood behind them and whispered, "Oohh." A sound Daniel had never heard from Nebuchadnezzar's hardened bodyguard.

Lord Gadi stood at Daniel's left and placed Belili between them, her head bowed. Daniel felt her trembling against him and could barely resist taking her hand. Gadi placed his hand in front of her face to shield her eyes from the heat. "Lift your head, Belili, and see a true miracle." She shook her head, failing to stifle a sob.

"You should listen to your bridegroom," Daniel

said gently. "It isn't often one experiences Yahweh's presence." She shot a pained glance at him full of emotion. Betrayal? Accusation? He didn't know what to say. "Look, Mistress Belili. They're alive."

Her shock was easily recognizable—and the joy that spread across her face once she looked. "There are four men in the furnace!"

King Nebuchadnezzar grabbed Daniel's arm and took a step toward the furnace, repeating Belili's words. "There are four men in that furnace."

Sparks flew heavenward through the hole above, and Arioch pulled them back. "They are safe, my king. You are not."

Nebuchadnezzar, eyes wide, turned to Daniel. "One of them looks like a son of the gods!" He shoved Arioch's hand away, almost giddy.

Wonder spread like a wave, men and women pointing. Some nudged their way closer to see the sight they could hardly believe. There, in the red-yellow-orange of the blazing flames, were four men. One stood, arms raised, His white robe a protective covering over Daniel's beloved friends, who knelt in worship to the only One who could save them. The only God deserving praise.

Amid the clamor, King Nebuchadnezzar shouted into the furnace, "Shadrach, Meshach, and Abednego, servants of the Most High God, come out! Come here!" His voice invaded the holy moment like cymbals in the dead of night.

The fourth Man in the furnace walked deeper into the flames and disappeared, uninvited by Babylon's king to enter his council. But the three brothers looked up as if waking from a dream. Still deep inside the furnace, their faces perfectly at peace, each one rose from his knees and stepped from the flames onto the sunbaked soil of the Dura Plain. Unhurried, they walked across the twenty paces that separated them from the gathered crowd and bowed humbly to their king.

A great clamor of celebration greeted them, and the king shouted over the melee, "Praise be to your God, Shadrach, Meshach, and Abednego, who sent his angel to rescue you this day!"

All the observers around Daniel echoed, "Praise be to the God of Shadrach, Meshach, and Abednego! Praise be to the God of Shadrach, Meshach, and Abednego!"

Daniel couldn't take his eyes off his friends. No wounds marred their bodies; no hair was singed. Not even the smell of smoke clung to their robes. Daniel shook his head in utter delight. *Yahweh, You have proven Your power to Babylon and its king!*

The king raised his hands to silence the crowd and addressed the three eunuchs. "You were willing to defy my command and give up your lives rather than serve or worship any god but your own. Your loyalty is well placed." He lifted his voice to address the crowd. "I hereby decree that the people of any nation or language who say anything against the God of Shadrach, Meshach, and Abednego be cut into pieces and their houses be turned into piles of rubble, for no other god can save in this way."

Daniel suppressed a groan. Why must he ruin Yahweh's praise with the threat of brutality? The king pulled the three into a tight circle, speaking in quiet tones meant only for the brothers.

Gadi nudged Daniel's arm, offering his hand in friendship. "We'll see you at our wedding feast tonight, I hope." Belili ducked her head, and Daniel was caught speechless. Gadi seemed oblivious, bubbling with enough enthusiasm to carry the conversation. "I hope to meet your wife, Lord Belteshazzar. You are married, aren't you?"

Belili's head shot up, waiting for Daniel's response. "I, uh . . . yes, of course. Tonight, then."

"We have much to prepare before the banquet." Gadi bowed, his countenance bright. "My Belili will be the most beautiful bride you've ever seen."

Daniel bowed, keeping his head lowered. "Of that I have no doubt."

18

Then the king promoted Shadrach, Meshach and Abednego in the province of Babylon.

—DANIEL 3:30

Daniel walked on clouds from the Dura Plain to Babylon after his friends' dramatic salvation. He and Arioch took their customary positions at the left and right of the king's palanquin as they marched on the Processional Way. Nebuchadnezzar honored Shadrach, Meshach, and Abednego by placing them directly behind him.

The crowd cheered the great miracle they'd witnessed, repeating, "Praise be to the God of Shadrach, Meshach, and Abednego! Praise be to the God of Shadrach, Meshach, and Abednego!" When the processional arrived inside the palace courtyard, King Nebuchadnezzar and Queen Amyitis exited their palanquins and walked hand in hand up the grand stairway. Daniel followed them to the top of the stairs and waited for his friends, feeling a growing angst to begin preparations for tonight's feast. A stab of sorrow robbed his joy over God's miracle salvation. How, and when, would he tell his three friends about Abigail—rather, Belili?

The brothers climbed the grand staircase to join him, their faces beginning to show the weariness of both the trauma and victory they'd borne today as the center of attention. Daniel opened his arms like a welcoming ima, anxious to embrace the men who had been in the physical presence of the Lord.

"You must tell me everything!" he said as all four fell into a circle of embrace. "I want every detail but *after* tonight's wedding banquet."

They moaned wearily. "What *wedding* banquet?" Shadrach asked, at least mildly conversant. "We were told the king plans to introduce us at a banquet and announce our promotions to the nobles." He wiped sweat from his face. "All we want to do is sleep."

Daniel tried not to sound demanding. "I'm sure Zakiti will have your bedchambers ready for you to rest before the banquet."

"No need," Shadrach continued for his brothers. "The king has reserved chambers in the palace for us to be fitted with our new governor's robes."

Abednego finally spoke up. "What wedding banquet is so important that we must attend?"

"You're considered nobility since the king promoted you to governors of your cities." Again Daniel felt like a scolding ima. "You're required to attend every royal function while in Babylon."

Abednego straightened his spine, and hard lines formed between his brows. "You didn't answer my question. Why must we attend *this* wedding?"

Daniel looked around to be sure he wasn't overheard but still avoided the news he dreaded sharing. "Because after today's great deliverance, you're Yahweh's mouthpiece to Babylon."

"Answer the question." Abednego's eyes sparked. "Whose wedding is it?"

Suddenly, Daniel's mouth felt full of sand. "It's Abigail's wedding." Their faces looked the way his insides felt. "She's marrying Gadi, the Medes' chief magus."

Shadrach was first to recover. "How did she get to Media? And how does she know the chief magus?"

Daniel shook his head, having wondered about God's sovereign hand all afternoon. "She goes by the name Belili, and by all appearances she's become a noblewoman in Achmetha. Make sure you address her accordingly."

"Did Zakiti see her?" Meshach's question knocked the wind from Daniel's chest.

"I'm going home now to find out. Why don't you three come with me to greet Zakiti before preparing for the banquet?"

"No thank you." Abednego's eyebrows shot up. "Eunuchs don't have to witness fights with wives over past betrothals."

"Go then." Daniel nodded them toward the entrance with more happiness than he felt.

The short walk to his villa felt even shorter this afternoon. He'd been too distracted to notice where his wife stood in the crowd at the dedication. Had she seen Abigail? She would surely recognize her since they'd become friends while Daniel and the other princes trained and Abigail bought bread from her abba.

Too soon, he stood at his courtyard gate, wiping sweaty palms on his best robe. He was being ridiculous. Nebuchadnezzar's chief wise man needn't slink into his villa. Shoulders back, he strode through the gate and into the courtyard, where servants scurried past him and up the stairs bearing his wife's finest robe and the box of gemstone necklaces. Zakiti obviously knew about the banquet. He climbed the steps slowly to their bedchamber, thinking through what he'd told his wife before they married—she knew of Abigail's disappearance, the bloodstain in his chamber, and Ashpenaz's involvement, and she knew that Abigail was taken to an unknown destination.

Abigail had been in Achmetha all this time. How had she risen to the status and privilege of betrothal to the chief magus? And why were her eyes filled with anger?

Daniel paused outside his bedroom door, listening to his wife's familiar humming. He'd been honest with Zakiti from the beginning, telling her Abigail still held his heart. He'd even told her he couldn't marry her if she continued to worship Marduk. It only made sense. If he refused food sacrificed to idols, how could he join himself in marriage to a woman who worshipped those idols? Zakiti married him anyway. Not because she trusted Yahweh or believed Daniel's heart would be hers but because he'd promised to always be honest with her.

Abigail was his first love, and Belili was beautiful, but Zakiti was his wife, his life, his world. He pushed open the door to assure her of it.

I waited in the palace guest chamber Queen Amyitis assigned me. She'd forbidden Gadi to let his bride spend her wedding night in a tent, and I was delighted. Standing alone on the balcony of the second-floor chamber, I perused the city I'd first seen as a captive almost eight years ago. I remembered standing in the palace courtyard below, terrified when I was taken from my four young princes. Memories assailed me, as did unanswered questions. Why had Shadrach, Meshach, and Abednego chosen to become eunuchs? Who was Daniel's wife? Did they have children? Where was Mert?

I settled the uncertainties into a small chamber of my heart and closed the door, whispering only one question on the night breeze. "Am I marrying the right man?"

I heard the quiet swish of footsteps slip into my chamber and whirled on the intruder, wishing I still carried my dagger. Queen Amyitis observed my defensive stance with a smirk. "No one born to nobility has those reflexes. You've had to fight your way into Gadi's heart."

I inclined my head, offering neither assent nor dissent to her observation. She seemed intuitive. Why risk a lie? "Is my bridegroom ready to receive me?"

"I daresay he's been ready all day." She winked. I liked this queen. Older than Nebuchadnezzar, she wore her nobility naturally but discarded it for moments like these, when a woman needed a real friend.

"What advice would a queen give to a new bride?"

She held my gaze before answering, letting me know her words carried meaning. "Serve him. Love him. Teach him to treasure you, and he'll be happy you did." Without waiting for a response, she looped her arm through mine. "Come. I have a feeling we're going to become good friends."

The queen led me to my bridegroom's chamber, where he waited in a stunning gold-trimmed robe with five of his chosen friends, one of whom was the king of Babylon. Since we had no family to pronounce a blessing, and the contract with its dowry had been exchanged in Achmetha's temple, only the consummation was necessary before the banquet began downstairs. I stared into the face of Nebuchadnezzar and suddenly felt nine years old again. I was in the elegant chamber of Judah's dangerous king. Where my abba was killed for defending Ima. Where my ima locked me out, hoping I'd be safe at the Temple. Safe? My whole life seemed a jumbled heap of pottery shards, jagged and dangerous, and one little slip could cut me to pieces.

Suddenly unable to breathe, I stepped back, intending to make my escape. Amyitis's arm locked around mine. "Steady, girl. It will be over before you know it."

The moment struck me as absurd. The queen of Babylon reassuring a high priestess about consummating her wedding night? A nervous giggle escaped, and Amyitis joined me. The men thought we were ridiculous but offered bawdy congratulations to my bridegroom. He stepped to my side, placing a possessive arm around my waist, while four of his friends filed out of the chamber.

The king and queen lingered in the doorway. "Be kind to her," Nebuchadnezzar said. "If Amyitis loves her, she's a treasure worth keeping." They closed the door, and I lowered my head to hide a grin, lingering in the irony.

"Are you all right, my dove?" Gadi gently lifted my chin.

I saw the face of a friend, whom I hoped someday I could come to love. "I am well, Gadi, because I am yours."

He loved me with tender passion—as a bride should be loved—keeping our banqueting friends celebrating long into the night before we joined them. When we entered the throne hall, the herald met us at the door and led us to the dais, where two dining tables were arranged. The king and queen reclined beside one table, leaving two open places, presumably for Gadi and me. At the second table reclined the other three guests of honor: Shadrach, Meshach, and Abednego. Daniel lounged beside them with a woman who looked rather familiar. But she was not Rubati, to my great relief.

"Nobles and noblewomen of Babylon," the herald began, "it is my privilege to be the first to present the highly revered chief magus of our queen's beloved homeland, Lord Gadi, and his new bride, Lady Belili. Let the newlywed banquet officially begin!" Warm laughter and applause welcomed us to Babylonian society, and the herald directed us to the royal table.

As I settled onto a cushion beside the queen, arranging my crimson robe around me, I looked up and found Daniel waiting. His arm rested comfortably around the waist of a woman I now recognized. "Lord Gadi, Lady Belili, I was unable to introduce my wife, Zakiti, this afternoon, so please allow me to do so now."

"A pleasure to meet you both." She bowed cordially, and Daniel's pointed gaze told me he'd cautioned her to use discretion. Zakiti immediately turned to the queen. "The banquet is, as always, beyond measure." She lifted Amyitis's hand to her forehead in fealty, a melody of elegance.

Gadi stood to greet Daniel and began discussing something about a joint project for their schools of wisdom, and I tried not to stare at the baker's daughter. I listened politely to her conversation with the queen and marveled at her refinement.

She turned to me. "How did you meet the chief magus, Lady Belili?"

The simple question drew both Daniel's and Gadi's attention. My husband placed his hand on mine. "We met in the market," he said. "I saw this lovely woman buying a red scarf, my favorite color."

"In the market?" Daniel nodded. "That's where Zakiti and I met as well." Everyone chuckled politely, only three of us fully grasping the awkwardness of the moment.

Feeling safely sheltered in our secret, wicked curiosity got the better of me. "How long have you and Lord Belteshazzar been married, Zakiti?"

The smile left her eyes, turning into a mask of decorum. "We married shortly after another girl betrayed him. I believe he's much better off with me, don't you?" Pink cheeks and misty eyes told me the confrontation required all her courage, and I hated myself for baiting her. Even her attempt at malice was tainted by decency.

"Yes, Zakiti. Lord Belteshazzar is much better off with you."

Daniel nodded coolly, and they returned to their table.

Gadi informed the king of his and Daniel's plans to integrate the wisdom teachings of both nations into their respective curriculums, and I let myself drown in my new world.

After a week of feasting, Gadi and I returned to Achmetha as husband and wife. I left Babylon with two precious gifts. One would arrive nine months later—a son named Allamu. The other would visit me in Achmetha each summer, Queen Amyitis, the dearest friend of my life.

19

The king of Babylon killed the sons of Zedekiah before his eyes; he also killed all the officials of Judah. Then he put out Zedekiah's eyes, bound him with bronze shackles and took him to Babylon, where he put him in prison till the day of his death.

—JEREMIAH 52:10–11

Babylon
October 586 BC

The trumpets blared, and Daniel stood in his customary position at the top of the grand stairway of Babylon's palace, waiting once again to feign congratulations for another of King Nebuchadnezzar's conquests. This time the victory for Babylon's king meant devastation for Daniel's homeland. Jerusalem and Yahweh's Temple had been burned, razed to the ground, and now lay in total ruin. When Nebuchadnezzar climbed the stairs to lift victorious hands to the crowd, could Daniel suppress the anger and hatred that had been building for nearly twenty years and bow to the gloating king?

The roar of celebration moved like a wave of

the sea as the king paraded toward the palace on the Processional Way. With every conquest, large or small, Nebuchadnezzar led his captives in a train with the wealth of their conquered kingdom trailing behind them on camels and ox-drawn carts. As a twelve-year-old boy, Daniel hadn't realized that he'd been part of Nebuchadnezzar's first train, but since then he'd witnessed every one. Nearly every autumn, the king added captives and treasure-laden carts to his burgeoning empire. And waiting at the palace entrance on every occasion were his royal counselors, Daniel included, to heap praise and glory on the best military mind in history.

The inner city gates opened slowly, and Daniel's stomach clenched, remembering the sound of their creaking iron hinges when he entered Babylon in the first of Judah's three exiles. Eleven years ago, Nebuchadnezzar brought ten thousand more Judean captives to Babylon—the finest soldiers, artisans, and scholars, as well as the rebellious King Jehoiachin, his officials, his wives, and even his ima. Daniel had begged for the royal lives to be spared. Nebuchadnezzar agreed but placed them in the palace prison, where they remained to this day.

Gasps and cheers erupted from the crowd of noblemen gathered in the courtyard when the first splash of sunlight reflected off gold and silver.

Daniel swallowed what felt like a boulder rising in his throat as the king's royal guard escorted a line of treasure carts mounded with gold, silver, and bronze. A surge of anger pressed Daniel's teeth together while he squinted against the sun's glare, trying to recognize the treasure from his days in Jerusalem. Were they palace furnishings? The pieces were too small to be sacred items from the Temple.

As the carts paraded past the grand staircase, Daniel's breath caught. Small pieces of bronze—engraved with pomegranates—filled one of the carts. They were undeniably pieces of what had been the stately pillars outside Yahweh's Temple. Another cart held equally small chunks engraved with gourds unique to the sacred Bronze Sea. Other pieces were gold and engraved with almond flowers, buds, and blossoms.

Fury coursed through his veins. How could this king that Daniel had coddled, calmed, and cajoled have chopped into pieces the sanctuary of Yahweh's presence on earth? Daniel had bowed to him, appeased him, even aided him in furthering his empire whenever Nebuchadnezzar returned to Babylon between military campaigns. Thankfully, the king was a warrior and builder, so he was gone often and for extended periods, allowing Daniel time for his true passion—coordinating records of their Jewish nation in exile.

Shortly after the miracle of the fiery furnace, while Nebuchadnezzar was favorably disposed to the Hebrew God, Daniel suggested an empire-wide census to discover where Yahweh worshippers dwelt. If a remnant of God's people were to fulfill Jeremiah's prophecy at the end of seventy years of captivity, they must know how far their people had been flung. The king had given his permission, hoping to curry the favor of Daniel's powerful God, and placed Shadrach, Meshach, and Abednego in charge of the project. Had Nebuchadnezzar forgotten it was the same God who dwelt in the Temple he'd just destroyed?

Why won't You release me, Yahweh? Daniel had prayed for Yahweh's permission to escape Babylon and its insanity. But where would he go? And would Zakiti come with him, leaving all that was familiar to her, to follow Daniel and the God she'd only recently begun to trust?

The cheering surged, drawing Daniel back to the moment. King Nebuchadnezzar, the victorious conqueror, entered the courtyard riding his sleek black stallion and pulling a prisoner bound with bronze chains. A long captive train followed behind them to the jeers and taunts of the gathered noblemen. The king's personal captive was barely recognizable, his face swollen and bruised, body caked with dirt and blood. But sweat gathered on Daniel's brow despite the morning breeze as recognition dawned. Bearing the broad square shoulders of King Josiah's descendants, Nebuchadnezzar's prize was King Zedekiah—Daniel's uncle.

Today, Nebuchadnezzar fulfilled centuries-old prophecies that Daniel had studied when he was six years old—that the temple would be destroyed. Daniel could never have imagined he would stand at the right hand of the king who would fulfill them—and be forced to honor his conquest.

Ashpenaz barked orders at the cart drivers, checking a scroll the king had sent in advance with orders to count and catalog their contents. Some of the loot went to the palace storehouses and other carts were directed to various temple treasuries. Most were sent directly to the Esagila—the temple of Marduk, Nebuchadnezzar's patron deity.

The king reined his stallion to a stop at the foot of the grand stairway and dismounted. He charged up the steps two at a time, leaving his prisoner facedown in the street, too near death to cause trouble.

Nebuchadnezzar stopped toe to toe with Daniel and whispered through clenched teeth, "Will I be punished or rewarded for destroying Jerusalem? You didn't reply to my messages."

Daniel met the wild-eyed stare of the King of the Earth. "Our Chaldeans read the stars. We charted your travel. We sanctioned your battles.

We even advised the king on which women to bring into his harem." Daniel stepped forward and moved the king back. "But I cannot—I will not—relay a message Yahweh doesn't give." Daniel swallowed hard, refusing to look away. "You are the chastening stick in Yahweh's hand, but even sticks are thrown into a fire and burned."

The king's eyes narrowed. "After all I've done for you, Belteshazzar, you wish me harm?"

Nebuchadnezzar had massacred Daniel's family, burned Jerusalem, and destroyed Yahweh's Temple. Without a Temple, why would a remnant return? How could they worship? Daniel looked at Zedekiah and felt as if the promise he'd made with Hananiah, Mishael, and Azariah had been gouged out like his uncle's eyes.

Did he want Nebuchadnezzar to be destroyed? Yes. But what then? Judah no longer existed. Was there another Babylonian whose rule would be kinder? Nebuchadnezzar was cruel and arrogant but also occasionally generous and open to wise counsel.

Daniel swallowed his rage and turned to face the king. "I wish you no harm, King Nebuchadnezzar. In fact, I pray for your peace."

His expression turned to stone. "You might as well pray for my death, Lord Belteshazzar. A king who yearns for peace will lose his kingdom faster than a maiden her virtue on a ship full of sailors."

This revelation—the fear behind his madness—was staggering. "It saddens me to think peace is such a tyrant for you. I hope someday you and Queen Amyitis can enjoy your eight children and their children after them."

The personal comment seemed to disarm him, and Daniel hoped the small crack in his heart would widen to allow compassion for the captives. He pointed at the line of weak and sickly prisoners. "Many appear to be feverish and with open sores. Perhaps we could treat them before dispersing them throughout the empire."

Nebuchadnezzar waved a dismissive hand. "They're all sickly. More died inside Jerusalem than by our swords after the walls fell. We've no need to use up Babylon's medical supplies when most will die before reaching their assigned provinces."

"What about King Zedekiah?" Daniel pointed at his uncle. "Will we at least provide treatment for the royal family?" *The rest of my family?* Daniel wanted to shout.

Nebuchadnezzar glared at Daniel with the coldness of a warrior. "I killed most of those who lived in the palace but took Zedekiah's sons to our camp at Riblah, where I had them killed slowly in front of him. Then I took out his eyes so the last thing he saw was his sons' torture." He held Daniel's gaze, challenging him to react, to show any sign of disloyalty.

20

In the first year of Darius son of Xerxes (a Mede by descent), who was made ruler over the Babylonian kingdom, . . . I, Daniel, understood from the Scriptures, according to the word of the LORD given to Jeremiah the prophet, that the desolation of Jerusalem would last seventy years. So I turned to the Lord God and pleaded with him in prayer and petition, in fasting, and in sackcloth and ashes.

—DANIEL 9:1–3

October 539 BC

After choosing our villa on palace grounds, Daniel and I were exhausted, but my husband insisted Allamu return to our family villa in the walled noblemen's city to help us decide what we should transfer to our new home. *As if I don't know what I'll need in my new villa.* It was a ploy to spend more time with my son. I knew it and so did Allamu.

My son stood atop the Processional Way and watched Daniel lean on my arm, struggling to climb the steps. He watched. He didn't help.

I ground out a vow. "If he doesn't help you down the steps on the other side, I'll find a switch and beat him with it."

"That should make him feel welcome for his first visit to the family's villa." His mischievous grin ruined my sour mood, and I had to kiss his cheek. How had he put up with me all these years?

We crossed the Way, and Allamu offered his arm to my husband for the climb down. I followed them, two steps behind. We'd lived in our neighborhood since returning from Borsippa nearly twenty-five years ago. The thought of moving back to the palace complex with all the tensions of life at court sent a chill down my spine, but this General Gubaru had given Daniel no choice.

As we walked through our familiar streets, unfamiliar Medes now acted as overseers of Babylonian troops who removed corpses, scrubbed away blood, and tried to restore some level of normalcy. I recognized some servants who worked in the gardens, but which of Babylon's nobility would remain in their homes? Many of the men had been murdered at Belshazzar's banquet, leaving wives and children unguarded. Were the survivors sent to the unwalled city, or had they become servants when their villa was confiscated by a new Median owner? Would they be slaves sold at market? Or had unwitting widows become unwilling brides on the night of their husbands' deaths? *Oh Yahweh, have mercy on them.*

Heart breaking for our friends, I asked Allamu, "Who decides which noblemen get to keep their homes?"

He stopped and glared at me. "Who decides? The Medes, Mother. Because we have the biggest swords." He gave a condescending snort and started walking again. "Can't you simply be grateful your *real* children kept their homes?"

Slapped by his bitterness, I swallowed my own pain and spoke gently to a son too angry to see me. "I'm deeply grateful that all *five* of my children have homes and thankful for whatever part you played in securing them."

"Hmm." He resumed his trek, following Daniel's direction to our family villa twenty paces ahead.

Our garden had been partially harvested by hungry soldiers, our terraces destroyed, and the courtyard disheveled. All in all, we suffered little. Shesh was in the courtyard, organizing the servants into cleanup teams, while Kezia and Mert worked diligently at the cook fire.

Shesh was first to spot us. He raised his hand. "Welcome, Lord Allamu. Thank you for escorting Abba and Ima home."

"This is no longer their home," he said and then turned to Daniel. "Twenty men will arrive this evening to transfer whatever personal items you've packed." He offered a curt nod and turned to leave.

Daniel caught his arm. "Surely you can take a few moments to come upstairs and help your mother and me know what we should take to the new villa." Silence passed between them, and Daniel released his arm. "Please, Allamu. A few moments of your time."

He glanced at me, then extended his hand. "Lead the way, Lord Belteshazzar."

I followed the two men again, this time up the stairs into the chamber where my secret memories were hidden in plain sight. Familiar objects—a small pitcher and clay lamp—that had deeper meaning only to me. And Allamu. Why hadn't I thrown them away or at least hidden them? Because I'd grieved for my son every day for over forty-five years, and I never imagined he'd return. Would he expose the only secret I'd kept from Daniel just to spite me?

My husband pushed open our bedchamber door, and Allamu entered as if he owned its contents. He began inspecting Daniel's robes, offering comment on which were appropriate for Median court and which were *too Babylonian*. He then moved to our large baskets of linens. "You'll need none of this," he said, waving his hand over them distastefully. "The palace provides the finest Egyptian linens for all the noblemen's homes."

Next he approached the large wooden trunk at the foot of our bed and opened its intricately carved lid. How would he react to its irreplaceable treasures? Our daughters' first sandals. Copies of their wedding contracts. Our grandchildren's handprints in baked clay. He stepped back and lowered the lid quickly as if a cobra might strike him. "I suppose you'll want all this." I saw the pain on his face, and my chest constricted. He sniffed and moved on.

"Do you have a family, Allamu?" I asked, showing considerable restraint. I really wanted to ask, *Do I have a daughter-in-law or more grandchildren?*

"No." Without further comment, he continued the inspection, opening a basket beside Daniel's couch, where he kept two ancient scrolls.

"Those were written by the prophet Jeremiah," Daniel offered. "It's only a small portion of his writings, but Shesh came across them when King Belshazzar requested the goblets from Yahweh's Temple for last night's banquet. These scrolls were found with items taken from Zedekiah's palace." He picked up one from the basket and unrolled it. "You see? Hebrew is read from right to left."

"I'm not interested in reading Hebrew, Lord Belteshazzar."

Allamu hurried to escape, walking straight toward my dressing table. My heart rate set my feet into motion. "I'll decide for myself which personal items to take, Allamu. You can help Daniel."

But I was too late to block his path. He picked up the pitcher and lamp, one in each hand, and turned to me with a dangerous gleam in his eyes. "Why aren't these hidden away in your treasure trunk, Mother?"

I glanced at my husband, who was absorbed in Jeremiah's scroll, and lowered my voice. "Please, Allamu." Shaking my head, I tried to communicate my plea for discretion without speaking.

His eyes widened with delight, and he drew close, stepping between me and Daniel. "He still doesn't know you were high priestess?"

"Shhh. No one but Mert knows." I looked over his shoulder. "Daniel, my love, I'm going downstairs with Allamu to find more baskets to pack our smaller items. He'd like a chance to see Mert again."

"Of course, of course." My husband, engrossed with Jeremiah's text, waved us out of the chamber without looking up, and I tried to conjure words that would convince my son to keep my secret.

Daniel heard Belili say something before she and Allamu left, but his heart and mind were consumed by the words on Jeremiah's scroll. He'd randomly pulled one from the stack and opened to these words: " 'But when the seventy years are fulfilled, I will punish the king of Babylon and his nation, the land of the Babylonians, for their guilt,' declares the LORD."

Had the Medes' invasion been Yahweh's punishment on Babylon for their barbaric and inhumane attacks on Jerusalem? Daniel tried to swallow, but his mouth was as dry as the waste-land Judah had become. In the early years after Judah's destruction, traveling merchants regularly mocked the once-great land of legendary King Solomon. Daniel had burned with indignation, but as the insults continued, he'd become calloused to their comments against the Jews, the term used now for Judean exiles in the empire.

But he'd also become numb to the passion he once felt to return to his homeland, believing that without a Temple in which Yahweh dwelt, there was no need to return. Had he been wrong? Was Yahweh now coaxing him back to the vow he made with his friends as a youth? A fist tightened in his gut, and he was forced to admit that if Yahweh actually fulfilled His portion of the vow, it would be difficult to leave the life he'd built here with his family.

Three more years. It was but a breath away.

A wave of grief drove Daniel to his knees. Oh, how he missed his friends. He pressed the heel of his hand against his forehead, wishing he could change the past.

After Nebuchadnezzar's death, his heir had released the Judean prisoners from the second exile, and King Jehoiachin found special favor. In fact, hundreds of Jews were raised to positions of authority, including Shadrach, Meshach, and Abednego, who returned to Babylon to serve as Jehoiachin's advisers. But danger and intrigue at the Babylonian court rose to boiling, and Daniel resigned his position as governor of the Chaldeans. He begged his three friends to step down as well. They refused, and a week later, the heir's uncle staged a coup, seizing the throne and killing Nebuchadnezzar's heir, Jehoiachin, and many high-ranking Judeans. Shadrach, Meshach, and Abednego were among them. The loss hit Daniel like a mighty storm.

Jews scattered throughout the empire to escape the insanity of an imploding royal family. Those living in the cities where Daniel's three friends had governed continued sending meticulous census records to his villa, detailing as many of the twelve tribes and their families as they could discover.

On his knees, Daniel dropped Jeremiah's scroll as he lifted his hands and face toward heaven. "Should I have pronounced judgment on King Nabonidus's cruelty, Lord?" Nebuchadnezzar's son-in-law had ascended Babylon's throne through a river of blood, and his son, Belshazzar, had become co-regent in the same manner. Yahweh felt so distant during those years, but in the first and third years of Belshazzar's reign, the Most High had spoken to Daniel through visions. "Should I have declared the messages to King Belshazzar, Yahweh? Should I declare them to the Medes and Persians?"

Silence answered, and Daniel relived the staggering exhaustion he'd suffered after the vision came in Belshazzar's third year. He hadn't understood the interpretation by the heavenly being named Gabriel, so he'd kept silent, returning quietly to teaching a few students assigned by the king.

Weeping now, Daniel stretched out on his belly and reached his hands over his head. *Was I faithful to You, Yahweh? Have I done all You required of me? Have we, Your people, kept You at the forefront of our minds and hearts while in this foreign land?*

In an overwhelming brokenness of spirit, Daniel cried out to the God of his childhood. The God who had heard his vow in that captive camp in Jerusalem and who knew the deepest longings of his heart: *Lord, the great and awesome God, who keeps His covenant of love with those who love Him and keep His commandments, we have sinned and done wrong. We have been wicked and have rebelled;*

we have turned away from Your commands and laws. We have not listened to Your servants the prophets, who spoke in Your name to our kings, our princes, and our ancestors, and to all the people of the land . . .

He had no idea how long he lay there, weeping, calling out, and repenting for himself, his ancestors, and his descendants, when suddenly Gabriel—the man he'd seen in his last vision—appeared before his eyes, saying, *"Daniel, as soon as you began to pray, I was dispatched, and I've come to give you wisdom and insight because you are highly esteemed."*

Daniel tried to lift his head but the glory of the messenger's presence was too great. He could do nothing but listen.

"Seventy 'sevens' are decreed for your people and your holy city to finish transgression, to put an end to sin, to atone for wickedness, to bring in everlasting righteousness, to seal up vision and prophecy, and to anoint the Most Holy Place."

Mind reeling, Daniel tried to make sense of it. Was he talking about the length of their exile? *Seventy sevens?* Were *sevens* to be considered weeks—seven days? Couldn't be. Seventy weeks would have lasted barely over a year. He must have meant seventy *years*—confirming Jeremiah's earlier prophecy. *Anoint the Most Holy Place?* Was he talking about a new

Temple? Before Daniel could even get excited about the prospect, Gabriel's words rumbled in his chest once more.

"From the time the word goes out to restore and rebuild Jerusalem until the Anointed One, the ruler, comes, there will be seven 'sevens,' and sixty-two 'sevens.' It will be rebuilt with streets and a trench, but in times of trouble. After the sixty-two 'sevens,' the Anointed One will be put to death and will have nothing. The people of the ruler who will come will destroy the city and the sanctuary. The end will come like a flood."

The messenger poured out more words of war, another covenant, more destruction, and another end to offering and sacrifice in a temple that would be rebuilt. But an abomination would defile it before the final wrath would end it all. Daniel covered his head, mind spinning with such deep and weighty matters.

By the time he lifted his head, having formed questions about the Anointed One, the sevens, and the identity of the ruler who would destroy a restored temple, Gabriel had vanished. The room was silent. And Jeremiah's scroll lay open beside him. Daniel was sitting on the floor. Perspiring. Confused. Exhausted.

But his faith had grown a hundredfold.

Two things he knew with a certainty that could move a mountain: The Jews' seventy years in exile was quickly coming to an end, and the returning remnant would rebuild Yahweh's Temple.

Remembering what Gabriel said about the power of prayer—*"As soon as you began to pray, I was dispatched"*—Daniel dropped his face into his hands. He inhaled a fortifying breath and exhaled the power to move the hand of God.

Yahweh, direct my steps. Give me Your words. And grant me courage to do what I've believed impossible since the destruction of Your Temple.

21

This is what the LORD, the God of Israel, says: I am about to turn against you the weapons of war that are in your hands, which you are using to fight the king of Babylon and the Babylonians who are outside [Jerusalem's] wall besieging you. . . . I will strike down those who live in this city—both man and beast—and they will die of a terrible plague.

—JEREMIAH 21:4, 6

Babylon
October 586 BC

The long, lonely days of Nebuchadnezzar's war travels sent Queen Amyitis to her homeland each summer, where she could escape Babylon's heat and enjoy Achmetha's mountain air. She stayed at her father's palace, of course, but she spent so much time at our villa that Allamu called her "Auntie," and we became like sisters. Gadi welcomed our endearing friendship, eager to strengthen his relationship with our king and hear her latest gossip from Babylon's court.

When King Nebuchadnezzar's travels neared their end each autumn, Allamu and I would occasionally return with Amyitis to Babylon. The fall breezes hadn't yet begun when a Babylonian messenger arrived at our villa, bringing news of her husband's early arrival and his request for her presence. I'd never seen her so excited, nor had she ever been so persistent about Allamu and me returning to Babylon with her. "You simply must come to discover what great conquest Neb has made."

We'd known Jerusalem had been under siege for over a year, so I made every excuse for why I could not accompany her. However, Allamu was relentless, begging to see what Auntie promised would be her husband's best captive train yet.

So there we stood, Amyitis, Allamu, and I, on a third-floor balcony of Babylon's towering palace, the queen pointing out her husband's valor and eleven-year-old Allamu joining her accolades. I focused on something else in the pathetic Judeans parading before us. Open sores riddled the captives' bodies, along with blackened lumps and bruises. I'd lived with the Medes' chief magus, expert in magic and medicine, long enough to recognize the black mark of an angry god.

Three days later, two eunuchs in the palace reported similar symptoms. They died a few days after, and dozens more fell ill. Nebuchadnezzar barricaded himself in his private chambers, sending Ashpenaz to plead with his magicians, enchanters, sorcerers, and astrologers to find a cure. When many of the wise men also fell ill, rumors spread faster than the plague. Among them rose a general fear that Belteshazzar, chief of the Chaldeans, had cast a spell of vengeance on the city responsible for his people's destruction.

"Lord Belteshazzar can't be trusted." Amyitis rocked back and forth, rhythmically spinning her wool. "I told Nebuchadnezzar he should cut him into pieces and feed him to the dogs."

I remained passive on the stool beside my loom, hiding the screaming fear inside. "A woman's intuition is not to be ignored, of course, but do you have anything on which to base your suspicions?"

She set aside her spindle. "Belili! He's Judean. And he has repeatedly wielded the power of his god."

"Has he ever wielded that power to harm the king or this kingdom?" I noted the rising suspicion on her features and wished I could take back the words.

"Why are you defending him? Don't tell me he's charmed you." She stood and crossed the room in a few long strides, towering over me. "I think he looks rather silly with that light-brown hair oiled and curled like a Babylonian. It's obvious he's not one of us."

"Need I remind you that you aren't Babylonian either?"

She glared at me, trying to remain cross, but a grin broke her sullen features. "I suppose he isn't so hard to look at."

"I'd say he's rather handsome." Why did my heart still flutter when I thought of him?

She resumed her seat and took up her spindle again. "The only handsome man I trust is Neb."

In all my visits to Babylon, I'd been careful to avoid both Daniel and Neb—as she called him. Both reminded me of a life I longed to forget. I worked hard at loving Gadi. He'd treated me like precious pottery during the months I carried our son, but when Allamu was born, my husband refused to let me nurse him. He insisted my body should return to the way it had been as quickly as possible. I lost two babies within the next three years, and though I'd conceived Allamu easily, I worried the herbal packs I'd used as a priestess to block conception somehow damaged me internally. Gadi suggested we sleep in separate chambers until I'd fully recovered. That had been seven years ago. Now he visited the temple to sate his desires.

"Belili!" Amyitis's strained voice wrenched me from my thoughts. Allamu stood in the doorway. Face crimson. Covered in sores.

I leapt to my feet, toppling over my stool, and covered the distance in two strides. "Is your throat sore?" I tried to lift his arm. "Do you have lumps under your arms or in your groin?"

He shoved me away weakly. "Mother, I'm eleven. I'm not a child."

"You're my child!" I grabbed his elbow to lead him to our chamber, but he cried out in pain. I scooted up the sleeve of his robe and found more sores and a large lump under his arm.

Amyitis stood frozen in the doorway, her eyes flooding. "He's going to be fine. Take him to your chamber. I'll send the king's physician."

I could only nod, my throat too tight to speak. Why had I brought him to Babylon? I hadn't wanted to come, but I'd bowed to Amyitis's pleading, and Gadi hadn't dared deny the queen. I thought a long journey with Allamu would strengthen our bond and perhaps loosen the stranglehold Gadi kept around his heart. I led my man-child to our chamber, heat emanating through his Egyptian linen robe. He was warmer than if I'd wrapped him in three woolen blankets, his cheeks redder than Judah's finest wine.

"I want Father." His eyes rolled back, and he fell against me.

I heard footsteps behind us as we entered our chamber. Marching footsteps. I turned to see a contingent of guards, the royal physician leading them. They stopped ten paces from us. "Queen Amyitis sends her regrets. King Nebuchadnezzar has commanded all those showing symptoms of the gods' judgment to evacuate the palace complex immediately."

I took a step across the threshold into our chamber. "We'll stay inside our room. It's on the opposite side of the palace from the king's—"

"I'm sorry, Mistress Belili, but the king made it quite clear. No one is allowed to stay on palace grounds if they show a single symptom of the plague, and, um . . . your son . . ."

"My son is sick! You can't possibly expect a sick child to—"

"Not I, Mistress Belili. The king." The physician stepped aside and swept his hand into the hallway as if I'd forgotten where to exit. The guards placed their hands on their swords. What was I? An assassin with a hidden dagger?

Mind reeling, I tried to think of any other shelter, but who would take in a plague-ridden boy? Amyitis, my dearest friend, was abandoning me, allowing her brute of a husband to displace my son when he was weak and dying. A fiery ball of fury rose in the pit of my belly. "At least let me gather our belongings."

"Of course."

The men stood there and watched me while I lowered my son onto a couch, stuffed our personal items into a shoulder bag, and considered the God I no longer knew. The God who could accept a bite of bread and still restore the loaf to wholeness. The God who stood inside a furnace and kept three men from burning. *That* God could heal my son's burning plague.

But that God would never hear my prayers. Not anymore. Not after what I'd done. To eat. To live. To survive. But if *Daniel* asked, Yahweh would surely answer. Daniel was worthy. He was good.

Resolve filled me. I must find my old friend.

"Father? Father, I'm thirsty." My son reached into the air, delirious with fever.

Marching over to the physician, I spit in his face and then offered him a linen cloth. "Only a peasant would leave a man in his humiliation, but a noblewoman offers escape." I glared at each of the guards. "Which of you will escape the disgrace of leaving a nobleman's wife and son homeless? Who will carry my son to Lord Belteshazzar's villa for me? I would hate to see all of you fall under his displeasure."

Less than a heartbeat passed before one of the eunuchs stepped forward. "I will carry your son to Lord Belteshazzar's villa, Mistress." He lowered his voice, leaning close as the other guards melted away. "Lord Belteshazzar's wife fell ill a few days ago. Are you certain he'll receive you?"

White-hot terror shot through me. How could his wife be sick when Yahweh always blessed Daniel? "Lord Belteshazzar and I are old friends. We'll help each other care for those we love." He accepted my word without hesitation, lifting my baby's limp frame into his arms.

Allamu touched the man's face, calming some. "Father, you're here."

"Go. Hurry!" I prodded the eunuch through the palace halls and out the south gate. I followed him through narrow streets lined with villas, still on palace grounds but outside the king's family residences.

Please, Yahweh! You must hear Daniel's prayers. You must.

We turned right on the first street and followed it to the end, arriving at the largest villa situated directly on the canal. I lifted the heavy iron ring on the courtyard gate and let it fall. Again and again until finally a servant girl opened the gate only a crack. "I'm sorry. My master isn't receiving guests."

She started to close the gate, but I lodged my sandal against it. "Your master must see me."

I pushed past her, and the eunuch followed through the weaving path of the expansive courtyard as I shouted, "Daniel! Daniel, it's Belili. I need you."

The girl chased me. "Please, Mistress. You must leave. My master cannot be disturbed." Ignoring her, we veered left and found an empty dining hall with a stairway leading to a balcony. "No, stop!" She blocked my path to the stairway. "My mistress is dying."

I stared at the girl, and up the long stairway, and then back at my son. I was sorry about Daniel's wife, but only Yahweh could heal Allamu—and only Daniel could reach the God of my childhood.

I shoved the girl aside and hurried up the stairs, shouting, "Daniel? Daniel, it's Belili. I'm sorry to bother you, but my son is—"

A chamber door opened as I hurried down the hall, and Daniel appeared. Startled at first, he looked at me as if dreaming. I walked over and stood before him, silent. Would he command me out of his home?

His face twisted in grief, and he fell into my arms. Broken. Sobbing. "She's gone, Abigail. My Zakiti is gone." His weight nearly pressed me to the floor, so I guided him to a nearby stone bench. Still he held me, his shoulders heaving.

I looked beyond him and saw the girl showing the eunuch into a neighboring chamber. Had Allamu heard Daniel use my Hebrew name? My son was delirious. Surely he didn't hear. Wouldn't notice. The eunuch kicked the door closed behind him, and I knew my son could rest while I sat with my friend. I cried with him, remembering the breadmaker's daughter who had been my friend. I cried for Daniel's loss, for the woman he loved. But I also cried for the years stolen from us. Most of all, I cried for my son. If Yahweh wouldn't heal Zakiti, would He heal Allamu?

I don't know how long we wept in each other's arms, but I lifted my head when someone emerged from Daniel's chamber. Daniel, too, sat up and turned toward a dark-haired woman, her face tear streaked with grief.

Her eyes stole my breath. "Mert?" The name escaped on a whisper. "Is it you?"

The brave girl who had saved me from the assassin was now a woman with the same winter-gray eyes. Recognition softened the grief on her features. "Hello, Abigail." She arched a single brow. "Or should I greet Mistress Belili?"

"Both of you, please, call me Belili. My son, Allamu, doesn't know I'm Hebrew."

Daniel stiffened. "How will you explain our . . . friendship?"

I heard a sharpness in his tone, but when I looked into his face, there was only disappointment. How I wished for anger instead. "I'll tell him we met years ago because you and Gadi share the same craft. It's the truth."

"Gadi teaches incantations and magic, Belili. I interpret dreams through Yahweh's power alone, and we heal with herbs. I've never trained Chaldeans to use incantations or magic."

I turned away, ignoring the subject on which my husband and Daniel always disagreed. Noticing a washbasin and dirty rags in Mert's hands, I fairly leapt from the bench and reached for the basin. "Here, let me help—"

Mert jumped back like a skittish colt, the fear in her eyes palpable. I stood in the tension, wishing I knew what had changed my champion—yet thankful I didn't.

"I don't need help," she said. Looking at

238

Daniel, she added, "I've washed and wrapped Mistress Zakiti's body for burial. I'll be in my chamber if you need anything else." She hurried down the stairs and disappeared into a chamber immediately on the right.

"I found her in the slave market one day." Daniel's voice was barely above a whisper. "Zakiti was as pleased as I to give Mert a place in our home. We hoped to make her a member of the family, but she insisted on becoming Zakiti's personal maid. They've been together for nearly seven years now." He dropped his face into his hands and then scrubbed it, leaving his beard askew. He looked up, eyes red and swollen. "Why are you here, Belili?"

My heart leapt to my throat. The realization that he might refuse me had never been real until that moment. "My son is sick."

He looked at me, the sadness in his expression having grown deeper. "A son. Congratulations." He buried his face again. "Zakiti . . . Zakiti was barren."

I closed my eyes, wishing I could trust some god, any god. Gadi had begged me to visit the temple of Mithra, but I knew every priest's trick, every secret rite. None of it was real. I'd keep their secrets— as I'd sworn—but I'd never again worship a god who couldn't match the power I saw in that blazing furnace on the Dura Plain. And the only God worthy would never hear the prayers of a woman like me.

"Daniel, my son has the plague too."

Nothing. His face still buried, my friend didn't respond.

I knelt, pressing my forehead to his bare feet. "Please, my lord, I beg you. I would never ask for myself, but he's just a boy. Allamu is good. He's nothing like me. Please, Daniel. Please pray to Yahweh for my child—" Sobbing cut off my pleading, and I fell into a heap on the floor.

Strong hands gripped my arms, pulling me into a tight embrace. "Shhh, Belili. All right. We will pray. We will ask Yahweh together." His tears wet my forehead, sealing his promise, and then he held me at arm's length. "But you must understand. Yahweh will do what Yahweh will do, Belili. He takes one and leaves another. We will pray, but He will decide."

I shook my head, silently pleading that Daniel might tell me all would be well. He didn't. He held my gaze, unrelenting. My friend had never lied to me, and he was telling me the hard truth even now.

He led me to the chamber where his servant had taken my son and the eunuch. At least we had a roof over our heads—no thanks to the king and queen of Babylon. If I had been the one praying that evening, the plague would have struck Nebuchadnezzar and Amyitis dead. Instead, I sat beside my fevered son and watched Daniel pray.

He prayed. And prayed. And prayed. Until my eyes closed in a fitful sleep.

22

Let no one be found among you who sacrifices their son or daughter in the fire, who practices divination or sorcery, interprets omens, engages in witchcraft, or casts spells, or who is a medium or spiritist or who consults the dead.

—DEUTERONOMY 18:10–11

I had experienced the atrocities of war but never witnessed a battle like the one my son fought for his life during the week of his illness. Seizures, fever, seeping wounds, and hallucinations kept him in constant terror.

Finally, on the morning of the seventh day, he awoke from his first restful sleep with clear eyes. "Mother, I'm hungry."

Lying beside him, I hugged him close, laughing through my tears. "Mert will prepare any food you desire, my son."

Daniel bolted through the door, panic on his dear face. "I heard you crying. Is he—"

"He's hungry." I sat up and wiped my face, considering my unkempt appearance for the first time in a week.

Mert peeked around Daniel's arm in the

doorway. "What would the young master like to eat? Name it. I'll fix anything."

I chuckled and peered down at my son. "See? Didn't I tell you?"

Allamu's strength returned quickly under Mert's watchful care. A daily diet of bone broth, fruits, and vegetables—much like the food our four princes had eaten when we first arrived in Babylon—brought Allamu back to me. Within two weeks, he began eating the same rich foods Mert prepared for Daniel and me. She had become quite an accomplished cook, carefully following Daniel's Hebrew dietary laws so well that other guests would never have noticed.

Too soon, Allamu and I were standing beside a caravan headed back to Achmetha.

Daniel's hands were clasped behind him, mine clasped in front of me. The urge to cling to each other was stronger than ever. "Thank you seems such an insufficient offering for the gift you've given me." I stepped closer, but he moved back. Of course. Allamu was standing beside me. Gadi waited in Achmetha. Daniel was a righteous man. "My husband and I will forever be indebted to you, Lord Belteshazzar."

He bowed deeply and rose to meet my gaze. "The debt is mine, Mistress Belili. You offered someone other than myself to focus on during the darkest days of my grief. My villa will feel quite empty now." He cleared his throat and turned away, looking to the eastern hills. "I will pray the snow holds off in the mountains until after you're home. Safe journey." Again, he bowed, but this time he walked away without a backward glance.

"Come, Allamu." Tamping down frayed emotions, I busied myself with details for our return home. My son would ride with me in a luxurious sedan atop the second Bactrian camel, the safest place, behind the caravan master. On the ten-night journey, we slept in a two-room tent. Each afternoon, the master sent a servant ahead to prepare our temporary home at our overnight location. Lying awake each night, I listened to Allamu's deep and steady breathing and thought of Daniel.

Yahweh, I know You are real. I'm not worthy to ask, but Daniel is worthy of Your mercy. Comfort him as he mourns Zakiti. Give him a wife to love and care for him.

Praying for another woman to fill Daniel's empty arms felt like placing my own heart in an olive press. But he needed to be loved. He deserved a woman to love him. Mert appeared as a possibility, but I waved the thought of her away, refusing to believe she would betray me.

Betray you? my inner voice mocked. I had no claim on Babylon's governor of Chaldeans.

Our caravan approached Achmetha just before dusk on the ninth day of the eighth month. Built on the jagged Zagros Mountain peaks, Achmetha's multileveled stone buildings looked like mountains on top of mountains. The grazing meadows outside the city were empty of flocks, the villages strangely quiet, stirring a heavy foreboding I'd felt all day. Although the weather had turned chill, farmers should be sowing broad beans, and goats should be nibbling the last green shoots before winter.

As we climbed the cobblestoned road leading to Achmetha's gates, my fears went from blossom to bloom. The gates were closed, and the towers appeared empty. Our caravan master turned. "What do you suggest, Mistress Belili?"

"Did you send a messenger to alert my husband that we would arrive today?"

His single nod deepened my fears. I halted my camel and searched the parapets. There. A shadow of movement. But had I really seen it or only hoped someone was guarding the city?

"You there! In the tower! I demand you open the gates." No reply. "Do you hear me? I am Mistress Belili, wife of Lord Gadi, chief magus. You will open the gates immediately."

"Only you and the boy," a man's voice shouted, but still no one showed himself in the towers or on the wall. "The others must remain outside until someone inspects them."

The caravan master pulled back his cloak at his waist, revealing the *janbiya*—a curved dagger—he wore at his side. "They should not attempt to inspect me, Mistress. It will end badly."

"What would you have me do?"

Without answering, he shouted at the invisible voice, "Why the extra precaution?"

"Plague. The magi sent word from their school in Rhaga, commanding we refuse entry to anyone with symptoms. We must inspect you."

The answer landed like a rock in my belly and painted fear on my guide's face. "We escaped Babylon unharmed, Mistress. I have no wish to tempt foreign gods who are punishing this city with a similar plague. My men and I will go south and return to Babylon by way of Susa, since the mountain passes will soon close with snow." He clucked his tongue and reined his camel to retrace its steps toward the empty meadows we had passed earlier.

Everything inside me wanted to retreat with him. Allamu had survived the plague because Yahweh heard and answered Daniel's prayers. But neither Daniel nor his God lived in Achmetha. Who would protect us here?

The decision to stay was made for me when the gates opened and Gadi stood waiting for us. "It's Father!" Allamu squirmed as if he would leap from our sedan.

"Wait!" I tapped our camel's hindquarters

with the prod and cast a withering glance at the retreating caravan.

The caravan master shouted, "May the gods protect you and your boy, Mistress."

I righted myself on the camel, focused on my husband, and forced a happy countenance. We were home. Allamu was alive. Life would resume its normal rhythms. I stepped off the sedan and caught up with my son, who had already covered half the distance to Gadi.

As we drew nearer, I heard Allamu gasp. "Mother, look."

Gadi's neck was covered with sores, and he bent slightly as if standing straight might break him. "Welcome home, my dove." His smile was pained, but his joy was real. "Allamu, my son, you look well."

Allamu ran to his father but stopped short of embracing him. "Are your sores all over, Father? May I hug you?"

"You are nearly a man now, Allamu. Perhaps we should greet each other as men." Gadi reached for his son's wrist and winced only a little when Allamu locked onto his. My husband's eyes found mine. "Are you well, Belili?" The tremor in his voice exposed his fear.

I hurried to his side, pressing a kiss to his lips—the only place I was certain not to hurt him. "I am well, Husband. Let's get you back to the villa. You look like you need—"

"I have all I need right here." He gathered me under his right arm and Allamu under his left, steering us toward the palace complex. Like Daniel's villa in Babylon, the home of the chief magus in Achmetha was the most lavish villa on palace grounds. We climbed the cobblestoned streets, noting the beautiful colors of autumn's changing leaves. The streets were deserted and the market booths closed. Only a few servants busied themselves in their masters' courtyards, washing bandages and harvesting herbs.

"When did those in Achmetha first show signs of plague?"

Gadi ignored my question and lifted our son's pock-scarred arm. "When did our son show his first symptom?"

The guilt I'd felt returned. "A few days after the Judean captives arrived in Babylon."

My husband released Allamu's arm. "Nebuchadnezzar sent captives here as well— as a gift for King Astyages—before he realized they were so ill. The first palace servant died five days later."

"Is King Astyages well?"

"Yes. He's fine." His brows knit together. "Do you care nothing about the proof I've found that sickness spreads through proximity as well as the power of the gods?" He'd received much criticism from the whole Magoi tribe for his radical theory.

"Or perhaps," I countered, "Judah's God judges any nation who subjects His people to servitude."

He warned me with a glare. "You're being ridiculous. Their god has no power or he wouldn't have allowed them to be destroyed. Jews have been captives for years. Nebuchadnezzar favored them by rescuing them from that wilderness in Canaan."

Rescued? I needed to change the subject before I lost my temper and revealed too much. "I'll have the servants make bone broth for you when we get home. It helped Allamu recover."

"I think it was Lord Belteshazzar's Hebrew god who made me well," Allamu said. Our son looked up at his father. "He prayed a lot, and I got better. Perhaps we should pray for you, Father."

Gadi shot me an angry look, but I refused to be cowed. "Our son lived, when all others died."

I saw years of disregard turn to loathing in my husband's eyes, but his features softened when he looked down at Allamu. "I've made my oaths to Mithra, my boy, and one day, you'll hold the greatest power in the empire. Your mother is teaching you the rites of Mithra, and I'm teaching you the ways of the Magoi. Because you will have skills of both the sacred and wise, you will be the greatest chief magus the Medes have ever known."

When we arrived at our villa's fenced garden,

the untended plants and fetid water in jugs sparked more concern. Gadi hurried us to the front door and lifted the heavy cedar latch. We were met by only one servant, her skin pallid with a sheen of sweat on her brow. Gadi rushed past her. "My family is hungry, Tabni. Deliver our meal to my bedchamber."

She bowed and left without a word. Two other servants worked in the kitchen. Six were too sick to stand. Those six died the next day. Gadi and Tabni joined them three days later.

Allamu wept over his father until his strength left him. He stopped sleeping. Stopped eating. Not that I had much food in the house to feed him. With the city gates closed to traders, Achmetha's supplies dwindled quickly. Only a week later, our remaining two servants also fell ill. I sent them home to their families in a nearby village. Perhaps the gods were kinder in the countryside.

We survived for another week because I searched for and found Gadi's janbiya, used it to slaughter our only goat, and prepared bone broth the way Mert had taught me. The weather had turned, signaling winter's icy approach. A blessing and curse. I dug a hole in the frozen ground of our garden, then buried both the cooked meat and leftover broth. The cold kept it from spoiling but made us tremble day and night.

Gadi had stockpiled enough fuel and food to last only two weeks. Market stalls remained deserted. We burned wood furnishings for heat. We went to bed at night hungry, cold, and alone in an extravagant villa less than thirty camel lengths from a king's palace.

Two nights after our supplies ran out, we woke to the sound of horses' hooves and men's shouts.

I ran into the hall that connected the family's chambers, where Allamu stood wrapped in a woolen blanket. "Is it an attack?"

I pressed the hilt of his father's janbiya into his hand and herded him out like a mother hen. "Get back to your chamber. Lock the door. Use the blade if anyone comes in." I closed it and heard the lock fall into place.

The shouting outside stilled, and the pounding of horses' hooves stopped. The eerie silence proved we weren't under attack. But who would enter Achmetha in spite of a raging plague? Desperate to know who the gatekeepers allowed entrance, I hurried into my chamber and donned my finest robe. I would demand an audience with King Astyages. He knew me well. He'd even been to my villa to dine with his daughter.

I sat on my stool and released my hair from its long braid, wishing my handmaid was here to help brush and plait it with ribbons and pearls. I tried braiding, but my hands got twisted. I tried a knot, but my long tresses only tangled. Frustration set in, and I released a groan. I heard footsteps behind me and whirled on the intruder with my comb lifted, ready for battle.

Allamu chuckled. "Planning to comb someone to death?" Our tension drained as he reached for the comb. "Let me help." Tears pricked the back of my throat as he pulled the ivory teeth through my long hair. He'd never treated me so tenderly. Perhaps our journey to Babylon had been worthwhile.

He tied my hair at the nape of my neck with a string as leather soles scraped the tiled floor outside my door. Our eyes met in my hand mirror.

"I left the janbiya in my chamber." Fear filled his whisper.

"Stay here and lock the door behind me." I hurried across the room, slipped through the door and closed it, rushed into the hallway, and ran headlong into a man. I looked up. "Daniel?" I breathed the name. Was my mind playing tricks? The six soldiers behind him appeared shocked too, and I realized my mistake. "I mean, Lord Belteshazzar."

Before I could bow, my friend pulled me into a ferocious hug. "Astyages's guards assured me this was your villa, but when we found it deserted, I feared . . ." His voice broke, and he released me. Turning to the men, he cleared his throat. "Return to the palace. I will remain with Mistress Belili." They lingered only a moment before obeying Babylon's chieftain.

Daniel sniffed and wiped his nose before returning his attention to me. When he did, he seemed almost startled, his eyes traveling the full measure of my appearance. Seeming mesmerized by my waist-length, deep-brown curls, he lifted a lock between his fingers. "It's grown so long since we were young." His expression held a strange mixture of sorrow and trepidation. "Your king told me of your husband's death. I'm sorry."

I opened my mouth to speak, but there were no words, so I turned away. What should I say about a man I had tried to love but couldn't to the man I'd loved longer and deeper—to the man I loved still. "I suppose we both grieve now, don't we?"

"There is no time to grieve," he said, drawing my chin to face him. "Achmetha is nearing famine, and your son must have an abba. Marry me."

Startled, I choked on a laugh. "You can't be serious. Did you come all the way to Achmetha because you miss Zakiti?"

Indignation knit his brow and raised his voice. "King Nebuchadnezzar sent me—I mean, he sent me with Nabonidus, his son-in-law—

to provide wisdom and guidance on a treaty between the Medes and Lydians. We were told about the plague in Achmetha by some merchants after we crossed the mountains. Nabonidus wanted to turn back, but that night I dreamed of a ewe with her lamb, lost in a snowstorm in the mountains." His eyes softened and he stepped nearer, bolder now. "I knew Yahweh was telling me to find you."

His eyes lingered, searching me for something I'd lost long ago. "Daniel, I'm not—"

He laced his fingers through my hair. "I know you loved Gadi. I loved Zakiti too. But you can't stay in Achmetha. You have no food, and Allamu needs an abba. He'll soon be twelve, a man, and he must begin his training."

I closed my eyes, the musky scent of his nearness weakening my defenses. "Stay with us then. Give Allamu time to—"

"There's no time," he said. "King Astyages has refused the Lydian's terms and won't bend. We leave for Babylon at dawn. Nabonidus can resume negotiations with Astyages in spring after the Medes have had a cold, hungry winter to reconsider."

I opened my eyes and drowned in his. I longed to be held in his arms, to feel the security of a man who loved me and cared deeply for my welfare. I was tired of being strong, but I couldn't betray my son. He'd never forgive me if I took him away from the Magoi tribe and his dream for the future.

"Perhaps when you return in the spring, you'll visit Allamu and me." Even as I said it, I knew we wouldn't survive.

Daniel dropped his hands and stepped back, hurt etched on his features. "You and Allamu will die if you stay in Achmetha. Don't be foolish."

I stared at my trembling hands. Daniel wrapped his warm cloak around me and pulled it closed at my neck, drawing me near. My heart warred with my mind as I stared into his warm brown eyes. Daniel was my survival. But was I betraying my son? The promise of becoming chief magus coursed through his veins. Riding away with Daniel would answer my deepest longings—and shatter my son's life and dreams.

In the warmth and safety of Daniel's presence, I betrayed my own heart to search for a way to keep Allamu in Achmetha. "Will you allow me to speak with Astyages before I give you my answer?" With furrowed brow, he nodded and released me.

I knocked on my chamber door. "Allamu, it's safe. A contingent has come from Babylon on palace business, and Lord Belteshazzar has come to see if we're safe—"

The door flung open, and Allamu fairly leapt into Daniel's arms. "I knew Mithra would answer my prayers." He looked up at Daniel. "You must help me speak to my father. I have so many questions now that he's crossed over. And I miss him." His voice cracked, and he buried his head against my friend's chest.

Panic gripped me. I'd warned Allamu of Lord Belteshazzar's strict adherence to the Hebrew God, so he'd kept silent about his priestly training when we were in Babylon. But now? I pulled Allamu from Daniel's embrace. "Lord Belteshazzar must return to the palace, Son."

But Daniel reached for him again. "I have time, Belili. You go. I'll stay and talk with the boy."

They stood arm in arm, and I felt the familiar sting of exclusion. Could I trust an eleven-year-old boy to keep the one secret that could make Daniel rescind his offer?

"Very well, but Allamu . . ." I waited for my son to meet my gaze. "No more talk of Mithra. Do you hear me? You must show respect for Lord Belteshazzar and his God."

The spark in his eyes dimmed. "Yes, Mother."

23

You shall have no other gods before me.
—EXODUS 20:3

I rushed into the wintry day with only determination to keep me warm. The cold air cleared my head and gave me the words to speak. Astyages was a hard man but loved his daughter with a loyalty every bit as ferocious as mine for my son. Because Amyitis was my dearest friend, Astyages had grown fond of me, and I had no doubt he'd grant anything I asked—if it was within his power.

Approaching the palace entrance, I saw only one Median soldier joined by a Babylonian eunuch. The Mede nodded and stepped aside. The eunuch blocked my way. "No one enters the palace unless escorted by an official."

I let my eyes singe his face before I spoke a word. "Would you rather me tell King Astyages or Lord Belteshazzar you refused the chief magus's widow entry? Both will have you impaled by midday."

His bluster died with his bow. "Forgive me, my lady."

I charged past him and ran to the throne room, my emotions too raw to manage any more confrontations. Thankfully, the guards at those doors recognized me and flung open the doors at my approach. Only a dozen gathered around the throne where Astyages sat, head buried in his hands. He looked up, startled, when I rushed in.

"I apologize, my king." Dropping to my knees, I regretted my bold entrance. "May I approach your highness?"

"Lady Belili, this is a most unexpected visit." Silence stretched to awkwardness, but I would not reveal my purpose until I could look him in the eye. "Rise and approach, my dear."

Relief washed over me, nearly loosing the tears I'd contained for days. I must present my proposal with logic and tact. The king waved away the men gathered around him, but they hovered like vultures less than two camel lengths from the edge of the dais where I stood.

Astyages studied me, frowning. "You are shivering, woman. Where's your cloak?" His eyes lit with concern. "Is Allamu sick? Do you need the physician?"

"No, my king. Allamu is healthy and strong. Thank the gods." I choked back stubborn tears, losing the battle now. "Your kindness over-whelms me, and I can only hope it will extend to my next request."

He sat straighter, resting his back against the throne, suspicion now clouding his features. "What is it you want, Belili?"

His tone offended. Had I ever asked for anything from him or his daughter? "I need a husband, my king." I lifted my chin and held his gaze. "Lord Belteshazzar has offered to take Allamu and me back to Babylon and raise my son as his own, but I was certain you would wish to keep the son of Gadi—chief of the Magoi tribe—in Achmetha. I'm willing to marry whomever you choose in order for my son to take his rightful place as chief magus—when his training is complete, of course."

I saw a hint of amusement on Astyages's weathered face. He looked ten years older than he had when Amyitis and I left at the first sign of autumn. Perhaps a wedding celebration would help the city's morale. We wouldn't need a banquet.

"Go to Babylon, woman. Allamu is safer there." He leaned forward, eyes narrowed. "And you're a fool to think the Magoi would wait for your son to take his father's place. Already, two men have died in the power struggle to replace your husband. Nebuchadnezzar's governor will train the boy well."

Too shocked to speak, I bowed and turned to go.

"Belili." I turned again and found the king standing. "Tell Amyitis her father is well, and tell Nebuchadnezzar I won't be bullied to make peace with Lydia just because he's my son-in-law."

With an uneasy nod, I left the throne room and walked back to my villa. For nearly twenty years I'd dreamed of marrying Daniel ben Johanan—but not like this. Not while my son was in the throes of grief and loss. I lingered in my courtyard, dumping fetid water from jars and surveying the frosty dead plants. Allamu and I were leaving Achmetha. Perhaps we'd return to visit with Amyitis. A cold chill raced through me at the thought. I wanted nothing more to do with the woman who abandoned us during our deepest need.

Standing outside my chamber door, I heard Daniel's and Allamu's voices. No words, just low tones of peace and wisdom. I pushed open the door, and they looked up. My expression must have revealed my trepidation, because I now saw it reflected on Allamu's features.

"What did the king say?"

My son would become a man in less than a year. I must treat him like one. "King Astyages said two men have already died in the battle for succession to chief magus, Allamu. You will not inherit your father's position, and there is no man in Achmetha who would marry me to secure it for you."

Daniel's expression hardened. "You wish to marry another?"

"I was willing to sacrifice my happiness for my son's, but it appears . . ." I sniffed back the emotion that threatened to undo me and returned my attention to Allamu. "Lord Belteshazzar has offered to train you in the ways of the Chaldeans and can offer you a respected path in Babylon, and I am honored to become his wife—"

"No!" Allamu leapt off the couch where he sat with Daniel. "I'm not going to Babylon. I'll stay with the Magoi. They can teach me."

Daniel stood and started to address my son, but I interrupted. "Lord Belteshazzar, thank you for speaking with Allamu while I was tending to other matters. We'll be ready to leave at dawn." I inclined my head and extended my hand to the door.

"Belili, wait," Daniel said. "We have much to discuss and too little time. If you're to be my wife before we leave at dawn—"

I placed my hands on his chest and searched the depths of his soul, hoping for more grace. "Please, Lord Belteshazzar, would you allow my son and me to have the journey home to adjust to this decision?"

He glanced at Allamu and back at me. With a single nod, he slipped silently from my chamber.

"I'm not leaving." Allamu folded his arms across his chest. "You can't force me."

"We're both leaving, and I don't have to force you. King Astyages commands it—for your safety." It was almost true. "A Magoi never disobeys his king."

My son's swollen eyes filled with tears once more, and I pulled him into my arms. "I'm sorry, my love. My heart breaks with you, but we have no choice." That, too, was almost true. I was sorry that his dreams had died today and going back to Babylon with Daniel was our only choice for survival. But my heart had begun to mend in the promised light of Daniel's love. Only one thing could ruin it all.

I braced Allamu's shoulders and made him look at me. "In a few months' time, you'll begin learning the ways of governments and kings. I need you to maintain the secrets entrusted to you by your father—and me. Babylon's wise men never mix priestly arts with wisdom skills. Lord Belteshazzar knows your father had begun training you in wisdom, so you must never divulge that I was a priestess or that I began your qualification rites."

"But I heard Father tell Lord Belteshazzar often that combining the sacred and wisdom arts was a good idea and that—"

"Allamu, listen to me!" I didn't have time to argue. As my mind thrashed for ways to coax an eleven-year-old to give up all he'd dreamed of, my eyes wandered to a small pitcher and clay lamp on my dressing table. I hurriedly snatched up both and pressed them into his hands as if my ordinary pieces were the priestly items awarded to successful initiates. "Your father had hoped to get an authentic pitcher and lamp from the temple when you reached the age of manhood, but since you've already completed the first priestly rites, I'll give these to you now. These can be reminders of all he taught you in the land of the Medes, but allow Lord Belteshazzar to teach you the wisdom of Babylon."

His back straightened. "I'd rather stay at the temple of Mithra. I've seen children working at the temp—"

"No, Allamu!" He had no idea what they did to those children in the temple. "Lord Belteshazzar will teach you many of the things your father planned to show you: literature, politics, medicine, mathematics, astronomy, meteorology, alchemy. With knowledge, you can advise kings and guide nations." He opened his mouth to argue again, and I lifted my hand to silence him. "Enough. Go pack only what is necessary. You get one bag."

His lips pursed into a thin white line, and the look in his eyes chilled my blood. He stomped out of the room and slammed the door behind him.

Was Daniel's love worth my son's hate? No. But my son's life was worth everything.

Allamu hid in his chamber for the rest of the day and refused the meal Daniel sent over from the palace. I nibbled at the pistachios, almonds, and dried fruit while scanning my spacious chamber. Nothing felt like mine. The robes, of course, but Daniel had included a scroll with the food, telling me to pack only the clothing we needed for the journey. Everything else would be provided in Babylon. *Everything would be provided.* The words were like balm to my battered heart, and I sat in the middle of the floor and wept.

Clouds hung heavy with snow over the mountains that separated Achmetha from Babylon. The customary highway between the capital cities would be impassable this time of year. Nabonidus led us on the longer but safer southern trek, yet we still trudged three days through bitter cold, heavy snow, and howling wind before finally reaching a milder climate.

Allamu lay outside our tent, wrapped in woolen blankets, staring at an inky-black sky, counting his beloved stars. Only two more days and we'd transfer what little supplies were left to boats and sail upriver for five days to Susa. There we could enjoy fresh water, vegetables, and perhaps even a bath.

The escort with Daniel and Nabonidus was over four hundred strong, and the tent for Allamu and me was placed in the center of camp each night when we rested. I'd never felt safer— or more conflicted. Each day of the journey, I yearned more for Daniel's arms, yet I ached for my son's forgiveness. He'd barely spoken since leaving Achmetha, and I had no idea how to reach him.

Gadi had managed the discipline when needed, which had been very seldom, since Allamu worshipped his father. I sat at our tent opening watching my pensive boy. Gadi had sown in him a love of the stars and reaped Allamu's total devotion. Everyone should have at least one love no one could take away. They had each other, and I always had Daniel tucked away in my heart. Death had taken away Allamu's love. The thought gutted me.

"Are you waiting until we arrive in Susa to marry Lord Belteshazzar?" My son continued counting stars as if he'd asked about weather or the color of a flower. "297, 298, 299, 300."

"No, actually we'll marry in Babylon."

More counting. "301, 302, 303. Do you like Lord Belteshazzar?"

My cheeks warmed. "We've been friends a long time."

"Why are you waiting? 304, 305, 306."

"I'm wondering the same thing." Daniel's voice startled me and brought Allamu to his feet. "Good evening. I'm sorry to interrupt, but I wondered if I could speak with your mother alone."

He shrugged and laid back down on his mat.

"She's going to be your wife. Do as you please."

"Allamu!"

Daniel shook his head and offered his hand, ignoring the disrespectful child at my feet. I took his hand and walked with him a few steps before offering my apology. "He's still angry with me."

"Grief takes time." He looked up at the stars, and I knew he thought of Zakiti.

"Is your heart mending?"

A sad smile graced his handsome features. "Your presence helps." He glanced at me again. "You were partly right when you asked if I'd come to Achmetha because I was lonely. I needed to get out of Babylon, away from the memories."

He fell silent and led me to a clearing, where a blanket lay on the ground. Torches stationed at each corner stood sentry against wild beasts, and Babylon's soldiers were no more than a stone's throw away.

We stopped at the edge of the blanket, and he removed his sandals—and then mine. The tender act brought tears to my eyes. He wiped the moisture from my cheeks and invited me to sit with him on the blanket. He kissed my hand and then cradled it in his. "I had no idea Yahweh would return you to me. You are the single greatest gift of my life, Abigail, but I cannot marry you if you worship Mithra." His voice broke. "I wanted to ask you during Allamu's illness, but you were too fragile, and when he recovered, you left so quickly. I . . . I assumed the reason you wouldn't pray with me to Yahweh was because you worship Mithra."

His eyes pleaded with me to answer, but how much should I say? I wanted to tell him the truth—the whole truth. He could forgive me, couldn't he? But then he tucked a finger under my chin and lifted so that my eyes could meet his. I saw love there. Love. And it swept me into a world in which only we existed. I studied his heavy brows arched above eyes as warm as fresh-baked bread. The noble tilt of his head that framed an enigmatic half smile. And his bottom lip, fuller than the top, now begged me to kiss him. Focused on his mouth, I thought of nothing but him as I leaned slightly forward.

"Abigail." My name escaped on a moan, and his lips brushed across mine with aching tenderness. I circled his neck with my arms, needing him, wanting him more than my next breath. Our passion deepened, hearts beating as one—as they had been meant to pound since we were young and in love.

"Abigail, wait." He tugged at my arms. "Wait, my love." He pulled my arms from his neck and pushed me away. "We can't. Not here."

Humiliated, I stood to escape, but he grabbed my hand. "Wait. Please."

"Don't call me that." I kept my head down,

eyes averted. "I've told you. Allamu doesn't know I was Hebrew."

"You're still Hebrew. It's not something you can change." He waited in silence, but I couldn't look at him, even when he stood. "Forgive me. I won't lose control again."

Forgive *him?* I laughed, the sound cold and brittle. Finally, I looked into the warmth of his familiar brown eyes. I saw no judgment, no revulsion.

He brushed my lips with his thumb. "It's hard to resist a pleasure we enjoyed in our married lives. I'll walk you back to your tent."

I placed my hands against his chest and pressed a chaste kiss to his cheek.

"What was that for?" he asked, surprised but pleased.

"Because you are still my Daniel, and I have loved you most of my life." I turned and ran, unable to bear more unquenched passion. He had more than proven his love in his care for me and my difficult son, who would too soon become a man. How could I live a life of secrets with a man so good?

24

The heart is deceitful above all things
and beyond cure.
Who can understand it?
—JEREMIAH 17:9

Babylon

After a twenty-seven-day journey—on camels,
boats, and back on camels again—Nabonidus and
Daniel led our caravan into Babylon. No trumpets
announced our return this time, nor did crowds
sprinkle flowers under our camels' hooves on the
Processional Way. In fact, the plague-depleted city
felt like a hollow shell. Half the number of quffas
ferried people across Babylon's canals, and only a
third of the market booths were open for trade.

Allamu and I rode on a single camel in a
cushioned sedan, third in line after Nabonidus and
Daniel on their fine horses. The city gates opened
to receive us, but as the last of our four-hundred-
man escort entered, I heard the awful clang of
them shutting. When had they started closing
the city gates in the middle of the day? Niggling
dread ran through my veins, but I couldn't ask
Daniel. He'd become Lord Belteshazzar again,
riding beside the king's son-in-law.

Nabonidus lifted his fist, signaling the caravan to halt.

Allamu looked at me with wide eyes. "Why have we stopped?"

I didn't know, but dread turned to fear when I saw Ashpenaz approach with a contingent of the king's guard. "Greetings, lords." He bowed and turned his attention to the king's son-in-law. "Welcome home, Lord Nabonidus. King Nebuchadnezzar sends his gratitude for your service and commands you to govern Babylon in his stead while he brings the rebels at Tyre under submission."

Nabonidus's mouth gaped and then erupted with a string of curses I hadn't heard since I'd served coarse soldiers in the temple. Gathering control, he glanced over at me as if only then realizing a lady and child were present. "Forgive me, Mistress Belili." He leaned down and spoke to Ashpenaz in a tone his regiment couldn't hear. "My men and I must rebuild a plague-infested city while Nebuchadnezzar chases more glory for himself?" The eunuch didn't answer, so Nabonidus turned to Daniel. "Fine. Belteshazzar, you and I will take this city to new heights."

His stallion lurched forward through the palace gates, nearly knocking Ashpenaz to the tiled street. The chief eunuch scowled and moved aside, allowing Nabonidus past but halting Daniel as the rest of the soldiers rode their wearied animals to the royal stables. Daniel, Allamu, and I waited at the side of the street, watching them file past.

"I see you two are together again." Our eunuch friend looked at Daniel with a glint in his eye that could easily reveal my past to my son.

"Yes, Lord Belteshazzar arrived in Achmetha on the day our food ran out," I said, wrenching his attention to me. "My son and I are still grieving my husband's death, Ashpenaz, and Lord Belteshazzar has graciously agreed to care for us here in Babylon." *Please don't mention my Hebrew captivity.* I held my breath, hoping the formal address would signal caution.

Ashpenaz barely had time to look puzzled before Daniel pinned him with a stare. "Why would King Nebuchadnezzar suddenly decide to besiege Tyre, an island nation that will require more time and resources than he's ever been willing to expend?"

Ashpenaz scuffed his sandal on the blue tile, seemingly at a loss for words. Very unlike him. "You know my loyalty is always first and fore-most to my king." He looked up, meeting Daniel's gaze. "But because I believe you, too, are loyal to our master, I will tell you that Nebuchadnezzar left to avoid your return. He fears your god—and now fears you, Belteshazzar."

"I have no power, Ashpenaz. The king has nothing to fear from me." Daniel clucked his tongue at his horse to move, but the eunuch stepped in front of the palace gates.

Ashpenaz pointed to a street across the Processional Way—opposite palace grounds. "Your personal servants and belongings have been moved to the villa where you first lived when you arrived in Babylon. The king has deeded it to you as his gift. I've been instructed to ensure your comfort in Babylon for the rest of your days. In return, you must pray for your god's blessing on our great king and promise never again to enter his presence."

Daniel's face remained a blank parchment. Was he angry or relieved? "May I continue teaching the Chaldeans on palace grounds?"

"Yes." Ashpenaz answered with equal calm. "As long as you enter the school through the south gate and not through palace halls."

Daniel offered a respectful nod. "Please relay my agreement to King Nebuchadnezzar's terms." With a forced smile, he turned to Allamu and me. "Come, we'll get settled in our new home."

I prodded my camel to follow, issuing a glare at Ashpenaz, filled with the anger and betrayal Daniel's response lacked. After descending the animal ramp from the Processional Way, our camels lumbered along narrow streets that were once so familiar, churning up memories and emotions from a lifetime ago. When we neared the villa we had known as captives, Daniel let

271

out a sharp whistle. Two servant boys rushed to greet us. Perhaps eight and ten years old, the two boys were surely brothers and reminded me of Mishael and Azariah as young princes—with much dirtier faces.

They'd been playing inside a neighboring building that looked to be stables, built very recently. The villas on either side of our previous home had been demolished and our original building expanded to a more elaborate dwelling. Three stories now, iron gated, with gardens, waterfalls, a stable, and free-standing servants' quarters. When Nebuchadnezzar promised Daniel he would ensure his comfort, he meant it.

Daniel ruffled the boys' heads. "Where's your abba? We must tend the animals. They've had a long, hard journey."

The red-haired boy nodded. "I'll fetch him, Lord Belteshazzar. He's in the house." He ran inside. "Aahh-baah!"

Daniel started to correct him for shouting but shook his head, sharing a grin with me instead. The other boy—boasting a few more freckles—stood gawking and then pointed at Allamu and me. "Who are they?"

Daniel had dismounted his camel and gathered the little one's arm to his side. "It's not polite to point. This nice lady is Mistress Belili. She is to be my wife. And the boy is Allamu, her son and my friend."

I felt Allamu stiffen beside me. "I am the son of Gadi," he said, tapping our camel's right shoulder. The camel lowered itself, and Allamu hurried out of our sedan. My feet touched the ground for the first time since early morning, and I sighed with relief. Albeit, short lived.

Allamu nudged me aside and reached for his bag. "Which chamber is mine, Lord Belteshazzar?"

"You may choose whichever chamber is vacant."

My son stomped away, and I turned to Daniel apologetically. "He's tired. I'm sure he'll get used to—"

He pressed his finger against my lips and looked down at the boy. "You may go inside and tell Mert we'll have two extra mouths to feed."

"Are you going to kiss her?" The boy giggled.

"Go, Eli." Daniel made sure he was in the house before returning his attention to me. "Allamu is grieving. He loved and admired his abba, and he's committed to the Magoi people. We must come to terms with the fact that he may never accept being a part of our lives. If Allamu chooses to return to Media when he is of age, can you let him go?"

"He won't," I said, ignoring the wise man. "He'll come to love you as I d—" I stopped myself and looked down at my sandals. Why say it again? Daniel had never *said* he loved me.

He drew me close, and I pressed my head against his chest. His heart beat fast.

"I have loved you, Abigail bar Jonah, since the day we met as captives in Jerusalem."

"You are Hebrew?" Allamu's voice exploded behind me.

I pulled away from Daniel, feeling more exposed than if stripped naked before the king's court. Fire blazed in my son's eyes. "How could you lie to me, Mother? I thought you were Babylonian nobility."

"I didn't lie, Allamu. I just never corrected your assmptions. I let everyone believe as they wished." The words sounded hollow—even to me.

Revulsion marred my son's face. "You should have been Abba's slave." He spit on the ground and ran inside the villa.

"Allamu, wait!" I started after him, but Daniel caught me in his arms. Sobbing, I tried to pull away, but my strength was sapped by the long journey, the illness and death, the joy that had almost been mine—and now was ripped away. "I didn't mean to deceive them. I didn't. I feared losing too much with the truth." I pounded Daniel's chest. "I was his wife, Daniel, a Median noblewoman. I had to survive. I am Belili."

I fell against his chest, spent. Sheltering me under his arm, Daniel guided me into the villa, up the familiar stairs, and into the balcony chamber we once shared. I lay down on a soft mattress and turned my face to the wall. Whispers filled the room, but I didn't care who spoke, because none of the voices were my son's. The light through the window faded, and I drifted between sleep and wakefulness.

A knock on the door startled me. "Yes?" I sat up.

Daniel opened the door a crack and peered around the small opening. "You have a young visitor who would like to speak with you." He opened the door wider, and Allamu trudged in, eyes averted. Daniel followed him and shut the door. "We've been talking most of the day, and Allamu has chosen to stay here with us."

Rage warred with gratitude. Of course my son was staying! I drew a breath to say as much, but Daniel lifted a hand behind Allamu's head, warning me to be silent. "This very grown-up young man would like to say something to you, Belili."

Eyes still focused on his sandals, Allamu cleared his throat. "I'm sorry for the things I said to you, Mother. I was unkind. Will you forgive me?"

I wanted to leap off the bed and squeeze my boy till he popped, but when I scooted to the edge, Daniel shook his head and issued a forbidding look. Should I listen to my heart or to Babylon's chief wise man?

I stayed on the bed. "Of course I forgive you, Allamu. I know I should have told you and your father about my Hebrew heritage." I paused, knowing Gadi would have sent me to the slave market had he known a Hebrew slave deceived her way to the highest echelons of Mithra's service. "As chief magus, your father valued all people," I said instead. "He knew Lord Belteshazzar was Hebrew, yet he respected him more than any other Babylonian nobleman. Still, I should have told you both. Will you forgive me?"

He looked up then, his eyes intense and cold. "I forgive you, Mother, but I will never trust you. You are not Magoi. You aren't even Babylonian. How can you understand one born to be a seer?" Without waiting for my answer, he turned to Daniel and bowed. "I have been respectful to my mother—as is required of an honorable Magoi. May I return to my chamber to prepare for tomorrow's classes?" Daniel returned the bow, and my son left the chamber without a goodbye.

Cut to the heart, I sat on my bed, unable to form words. Daniel came and knelt before me. "I agreed to begin his training early."

"That's how you convinced him to apologize." The realization left me cold.

Taking my hands, he turned them over and kissed each palm. "These hands have scrubbed palace floors, emptied waste pots, and escaped the whims of corrupt priests at the Esagila." He traced the shape of my jaw, sending a shiver through me. "Your beauty captured my heart and won the love of the Medes' chief magus."

He stared into my eyes until I grew uncomfortable and turned away. He drew my chin back to face him. "Hard work and a pretty face can't define you. The love of another can't be your sole purpose." His fingers brushed gently from my chin to the hollow place between my breasts. "It's who you are here that gives you strength. Are you Abigail? Or are you Belili?"

I could barely breathe. I wanted to be Abigail, for I knew that's what he wanted of me. But my Hebrew self died somewhere in the streets of Achmetha, begging bread from strangers before the midwife took me in. Belili had survived and would continue to do so, never begging again.

"I am Belili." I pulled him into a kiss before he could ask more questions or speak more wisdom I didn't want to hear. This—loving Daniel—I knew how to do, and I would love Daniel ben Johanan until death took my last breath.

He returned my passion, laying me back on the soft mattress. But just as suddenly, he pulled away and stood by the bed, eyes wide as if waking from a dream. "No, Belili." He straightened his robe and averted his eyes. "I won't take you as my wife until we've drawn up the legal documents to secure Allamu's inheritance of Gadi's property in Achmetha."

"Achmetha? He'll be of age in less than a year. If you secure his inheritance now, he'll return to the Magoi the moment he's twelve." I choked on anger and humiliation. "My son is staying here in Babylon with us. He'll make his life here."

But Daniel was already shaking his head. "At the age of manhood, he must be allowed to choose, my love—"

Anger surpassed humiliation, hurling me off the bed to escape the chamber and go—I didn't know where. "He's a child. He can't choose. I'm his mother."

Daniel snagged my waist and pulled me close, burying his whisper in the bend of my neck. "You're terrified for him, I know, but I will love him like my own. I will teach him and train him, beloved, with the help of Yahweh. And when I take you to our wedding chamber, it will be with Allamu's approval and Yahweh's blessing. We will not hide in a guest chamber like impassioned teenagers—though that once described us." He placed a gentle kiss on my neck and bowed like the nobleman he was. "Good night, Mistress Belili. I will have our wedding documents prepared in the morning, and we'll secure Allamu's blessing by tomorrow's evening meal." He lifted an eyebrow. "Tomorrow night, you will lie in my bed, and our passion will find its true home."

25

I have come into my garden, my sister,
  my bride;
I have gathered my myrrh with my spice.
                    —SONG OF SOLOMON 5:1

The next morning, I hid in my chamber like a coward. Too wounded to face another of my son's rejections and too terrified something else would impede the second marriage proposal Daniel had offered in this chamber. When the low buzz of conversation in the courtyard below had died, I threw on my robe and opened the door a crack. Only the sound of clanking dishes and pouring water met my ears. Mert was washing the morning's dishes. Feeling safer, I padded barefoot onto the balcony and chanced a peek below.

"You can come down now," Mert said without looking up. "They're gone."

I'd forgotten she had knife-sharp intuition. Drawing my robe tighter and cinching the belt, I hurried downstairs and through the now-lavish courtyard to the back wall, where Mert still huddled in the cooking area. She'd saved me a bowl of barley gruel and a piece of bread slathered with date paste. I reached for the bowl and a spoon. "Thank you." The rich flavors of coriander and honey warmed my tongue and my heart. No one made gruel like Mert.

Before I had time to compliment her, she turned on me like a cross ima. "Why, in the name of Anubis, did you and Master Daniel sleep in separate chambers last night? Have you lost your mind?"

I might have been angered by her interference had she not sounded so ridiculous, calling on an Egyptian god in the house of Babylon's most pious Hebrew. A little chuckle preceded my answer. "Daniel wishes to secure Allamu's inheritance and approval before taking me as his wife."

She returned to washing the dishes, clucking her tongue and shaking her head. "Sometimes I think that man is too righteous for his own good. No one in Babylon would think any less of either one of you for marrying privately last night."

Mert was right. No one in Babylon would have judged us. But after Daniel left my chamber last night, I realized how wise he truly was. To marry without providing Allamu with a secure future would have driven the wedge between my son and me even deeper.

Mert had already begun replacing the dishes on the shelves, and I wasn't in the mood to chat. I took my bowl of gruel and wandered along the courtyard paths, noting the various plants and finding an ample herb garden in the northwest corner. After eating my fill, I set the bowl aside and began weeding, a mindless task that allowed my thoughts to peruse the possibilities of this day. Would tonight's meal be a celebration of my marriage to Daniel? Or would it be a tense gathering with a son who had disapproved of our marriage?

"We'll need some of that mint for tonight's lamb." I jumped at Mert's voice as if lit on fire. She knelt beside me, a coy grin on her face, and began weeding the herb bed. "Your hearing hasn't gotten any better."

I nudged her, enjoying the ease of our friendship. Silence built my courage to ask a question I knew my friend would answer honestly. "Should I return to Achmetha in the spring and marry a Magoi?"

Astonished, Mert looked at me as if I'd grown a camel's hump and then returned her hands to the dirt. "I heard Allamu and Daniel talking last night. You had no food in Achmetha. No one to provide for you. After this horrible plague there is no guarantee you would even find a husband. Why in the name of Osiris would you ever consider returning to Achmetha?" She leaned back on her knees and stared at me. "I'd say Daniel's God is watching out for all three of you."

I sat back for a moment too, wanting to believe her. Hoping Yahweh would someday include me in His watchful care. But I couldn't escape the feeling that I was somehow trading Allamu's happiness for my own. Everything my son had known or dreamed of had been connected to his father and the Magoi. The very fiber of his being, the beating of his heart, pounded to the rhythm of their secrets and traditions. Gadi had been the air Allamu breathed.

What was I to my son? I'd given him life, yes; provided protection for him as a babe. But the moment he could talk and reason and learn, he became his father's treasure. I was but a stream in the oasis of their fellowship, a source of provision and comfort while their kinship deepened. When Gadi died, Allamu lost a portion of himself, but could the Chaldean ways become a new identity? Hadn't Daniel and I adapted to new cultures, new food, new cities, new lives? Perhaps after a few months he would realize Babylon was our only survival.

I felt Mert's eyes on me and raised a hand to block the burning stare. "I don't want to fight." She couldn't understand a mother's difficult choices.

She pulled me close with her dirt-encrusted hand and laid her cheek atop my head. "Your son needs a man to help raise him. There's no man on earth better than Daniel."

Startled by her tenderness, I was unable to speak.

Mert patted my arm once and nudged me aside. "Good. Settled. Now, finish your weeding. You're slower than the stable boys."

I laughed at this friend parading as a servant, and my heart felt a measure of peace. The younger servant girl arrived in the afternoon to help Mert with laundry, beer making, and preparing for the evening meal. I joined them to keep my thoughts from turning dark. When the sun rested on the city gates, Mert said Daniel and Allamu would return from class. My stomach turned a nervous flip, and my hands trembled as I set out goblets, plates, bowls, and spoons on a low-lying table in the formal dining area east of the courtyard.

Mert had prepared a feast, so certain was she of Daniel's promise to me and Yahweh's good care. The roast lamb, simmered all day in broth and seasoned with onion, garlic, and cumin, would be served with mashed leeks and crocus bulbs on a bed of light-crusted bread. The bread, made from finely ground flour, was mixed with lamb's broth, a little fat, and coriander. The sauce for dipping both lamb and bread was altogether paradise, but she refused to give up that recipe. I was still attempting to coax it out of her when I heard the squeak of our iron gate by the street.

My first instinct was to race upstairs and hide

from another confrontation that could steal Daniel from me again. Had Allamu refused to give his approval? Had they somehow been unable to come to terms on his inheritance? Would hate linger in my son's eyes and disappointment shadow Daniel's features? I faced the courtyard's back wall, pretending to fuss over the food intended for my wedding feast.

"Belili?" Daniel's voice held both love and trepidation. I jumped like a virgin when he touched my shoulder. "Look at me, love."

"Tell me. Just tell me." I wrapped my arms around my middle and drew in more breath, too anxious to exhale.

He stepped closer, sliding his arms around mine and whispering in my ear, "Come, let's celebrate our wedding feast with Allamu."

I exhaled and turned in his arms, offering a kiss salted with happy tears. Wrapping my arms around his neck, I lost myself in a sweet intoxication and thought of nothing but my Daniel. He was finally mine—and I his. Years of longing met this night. Too soon someone tugged at my arms, and I realized it was him. Caught somewhere between embarrassment and disappointment, I released him, feeling heat rise in my cheeks.

"Oh. Oh yes." His breathing was labored, and he cleared his throat, seeming as affected as I. "We'll need to eat quickly."

I looked up then. Our eyes met. And we laughed at the passion neither could hide. "Mert has worked hard on the meal, my love. We can't disappoint her."

His eyes softened and he pulled me into a gentle embrace. "Of all the people in our world, Mert will understand."

I nodded, resting my head on his chest, listening to the heart that was finally and fully mine. *Yahweh—if You hear someone like me— thank You for giving me Daniel.*

I followed him into the dining hall, where Mert waited with Allamu. Both stood beside the ebony table. My son bowed stiffly. "I offer my sincerest congratulations, Mother."

His formality raked my heart, stealing some of the joy. I took my place at Daniel's right side and inclined my head in an equally polite reply. "Thank you, Allamu. I hope one day you'll understand we're doing what's best for you."

My son held up a rolled parchment. "Lord Belteshazzar has given his word to return with me to Achmetha when I complete the three-year training program." He looked at Daniel and then back at me. "Reclaiming my father's estate is what's best for me."

His rejection still stung, but I refused to let it dampen our celebration. My son would live under our roof for three more years, and I would be Daniel's wife. Surely Allamu's heart would soften and he would make new friends in Babylon.

Mert joined us at the table for our wedding feast, keeping the conversation lively with stories of Egypt and her childhood in Babylon's palace. Allamu was transfixed, which gave Daniel and me the joy of being alone while still in their presence.

He leaned over and pressed his lips against my ear. "I filed our marriage contract at midday after speaking with Allamu."

I'd been his wife all day long and didn't know it. The reality both thrilled and frustrated me. "You should have come home at midday. I would have been satisfied with bread and cheese—and the rest of the day in your chamber." I lifted my goblet and peered over the rim, hoping to tantalize him.

"I assure you, we'll have ample time to explore the reaches of our love." Before I could respond, he stood and addressed Mert and Allamu. "It's Hebrew custom that the bride and groom spend a week in their wedding chamber, uninterrupted by daily activities."

Allamu rolled his eyes. "I don't need to know anything about it."

Daniel bowed slightly. "Understandable. I'll see you next week in class." Allamu waved his hand, burying his face in his goblet of watered wine.

Mert began clearing the dishes. "Go, then. I'll bring a tray of food every morning and evening."

Suddenly feeling awkward, I noted the huge mess on the table. "Mert, I can help with—"

She huffed and pointed upstairs. "Get to his chamber, woman. You've waited long enough."

Laughing, Daniel swept me into his arms. "You heard her, woman."

Our eyes held each other as he climbed the stairs and carried me to his chamber at the end of the balcony. He stopped outside his door and set me on my feet.

I leaned back and stilled his hand on the latch. "Does Zakiti still linger in your heart?" His expression was pensive but not defensive, and I added quickly, "It's understandable."

Daniel placed his hands on either side of me, trapping me there in his love. "I have mourned Zakiti. She was dear to me, and I did love her. But Zakiti knew my heart always belonged to Abigail. Now it belongs to Belili."

I stared into his eyes, knowing this man spoke only truth. "You may call me Abigail if you wish."

He stroked my hair, the long flowing curls left free—as he'd requested. "I love you, and you are Belili now." He leaned down and brushed my lips. Teasing me with his gentleness. "And I will always be Daniel."

Our wedding week was the happiest time of

my life. Seven days with my best friend, my lover, my husband. A bliss beyond my wildest imagination. When we emerged from Daniel's chamber, the villa seemed brighter, my son darker. He seldom spoke to me, and when he did, it was in clipped formalities prompted by Daniel's instruction.

By mid-Šabatu, when farmers had planted onions and were sowing grain crops, another seed grew within me. I hovered over a bowl most of every day for a week, emptying my stomach and moaning.

At first, I thought I'd eaten bad figs or soured gruel, but Mert laughed at my suggestion. "Yes, and you'll get those bad figs out of your system in about seven months, squalling in a little bundle on birthing stones."

Startled at the realization, her joy was lost on me. At twenty-nine, I would undoubtedly lose this baby as I had the others. If I carried to full term, I'd be thirty, and many women died giving birth at such an advanced age. Perhaps this was Yahweh's plan all along—to give me Daniel, the one I loved most, and then kill me only months later. I deserved it, after all.

When Daniel and Allamu returned from class that evening, Mert could do nothing but smile. Allamu noticed it first and exchanged a wary glance with Daniel. "Why is Mert so happy? It makes me nervous."

I laughed, trying to smooth over her peculiarities. "Mert had too much wine this afternoon." My voice was unnaturally loud, and Daniel knew our friend drank only with her meals.

My husband looked at us both, suspicion knitting his brow. "All right, you two. What's going on?"

Just then, the smell of lamb stew wafted from the pot, producing in me a wave of nausea that sent me down a courtyard path to a tamarisk tree, where I emptied my stomach. I'd made it halfway back to our cooking area when both Daniel and Allamu met me, startled.

"What is it?" Daniel cupped my elbow and led me to a cushion. "Are you ill?" Allamu followed, close but silent.

Now I had to tell them. I sat down, Daniel beside me, Allamu and Mert across the table. "The midwife said I'd feel better in about a month—when the child inside gets a little older."

My husband's sweet face transformed from worry to absolute delight. "A baby?" He grabbed me, squeezing so tight I thought I might throw up on him. A little groan was enough to loosen his grip and send him into protector mode. "Oh, did I hurt you?" He held his hand in front of my stomach. What did he plan to do there?

I giggled and looked for Allamu's reaction

but saw only his back as he retreated upstairs to his chamber.

Covering my mouth to keep from crying out for him, I squeezed my eyes shut. Why couldn't he try to be happy? No. It was my fault. I lowered my hand and looked at my husband. "I should have told Allamu privately. I didn't realize how much this would upset him. I thought it might even give him something to look forward to."

He gathered me into his arms. "I'll talk with him. Change is hard for Allamu. He just needs time to adjust."

But Daniel didn't get a chance to talk with him, and I never saw my son again. When we woke the next morning, Allamu's chamber was empty. On top of his neatly made bed, we found the small pitcher and clay lamp I'd given him as symbols of Mithra's initiation lying on top of a note: "Don't need these. Will send word of safe arrival in Achmetha."

26

[Yahweh spoke to Moses and said,] "Put the altar in front of the curtain that shields the ark of the covenant law—before the atonement cover that is over the tablets of the covenant law—where I will meet with you."

—EXODUS 30:6

Babylon
October 539 BC

I led Allamu down the stairs to Mert's chamber, silent amid my roiling emotions, while the rest of our family continued to clean up after the Medes' invasion and the damage to our villa. Hesitating at Mert's door, I stared at the son who had broken my heart forty-six years ago. "You never sent word from Achmetha."

He knocked on her door, glaring at me with the same turbulent expression of the boy who had run away. "I never reached Achmetha."

"You never—"

The door swung open, and my son's countenance lit like the sun. "Mert!" He opened his arms tenderly. "I didn't believe it when I saw you were still serving Belteshazzar." She was consumed in his embrace, and I turned my back, unable to witness their easy relationship.

"You got old!" Mert chuckled.

"And you still have no manners." The delighted laughter that followed both warmed and condemned me. "Mother, come in with me. I have a few questions for you. I know Mert will tell me the truth even if you won't."

I took a deep breath, swiped away tears, and crossed the threshold like a soldier advancing in battle. I had a few questions for him too. "What do you mean you never made it to Achmetha? Your note said that's where you were going."

Mert sat on her favorite couch and patted the empty place beside her. Allamu started to sit down, but she shoved him away. "Don't be rude. This spot is for your mother, and it sounds like you owe us both an explanation."

Allamu grudgingly pulled up a cushion opposite the couch, while I took my place beside Mert. "We're going to listen to Allamu, Belili. No talking."

I started to protest, but her glare silenced me. The few times I hadn't listened to her counsel, I'd regretted it. She turned to my son. "Perhaps you should begin by telling us why you left without saying goodbye."

His features softened for her. "They took me from my home, Mert. I am nothing without the Magoi." His voice broke and he looked away, breathing deeply and exhaling through pursed lips. "You could never understand."

"I wouldn't understand?" She ran her hand across the couch we'd imported from Egypt for her, its cushions embroidered with colorful designs depicting the land of her birth. "For the Medes' chief wise man, you aren't very smart."

He stiffened. "It's different for me. My father raised me to inherit his position as chieftain of our tribe. When Mother took me from Achmetha, she took away my place as Gadi's heir."

"We were protecting you from the power struggle," I interrupted. "Magoi were dying to take Gadi's position, and they would have killed you if we stayed."

"You couldn't be sure." His eyes narrowed like a petulant child, and I knew then he would hear nothing from me.

"So what happened when you left here?" I asked. "You said you never arrived in Achmetha, but at some point you did, or you wouldn't be chief magus." My tone was as bitter as his, but did I give up the right to be angry because I was the mother?

My son's face lost all expression, but he started fidgeting with Gadi's janbiya, hanging from his belt. "I joined a caravan heading east but was appropriated by Persian soldiers when I reached Susa. They didn't care that I was a month away from manhood. They didn't believe my father had been chief magus in Achmetha. They only cared that their horses needed to be brushed and their camels watered." A mild snort escaped his cynical smile. "And my mother didn't care enough to search for her son."

"Did you wish me to find you?"

"No, but I wished for a mother."

His words pierced my heart—as was surely his intent. "Perhaps it doesn't matter to you, Allamu, but we did search for you. For years. Daniel sent messengers to every city in the land of the Medes." I looked away, shaking my head at the irony. "We never imagined you wouldn't make it to Achmetha. You were so determined."

"Perhaps I've learned both determination *and* deception from you, Mother." His condescending tone drew my attention, and I found a wry smile on his face. "I'm impressed that a priestess of Mithra has guarded her secrets so long. Lord Belteshazzar actually believes you worship his god."

"I do worship Yahweh, Allamu. Only Yahweh."

Shifting uncomfortably, his smirk changed to concern. "You swore a vow to Mithra, the god of oaths. You can't simply discard him like soiled linen, Mother."

In that moment, I knew my greatest failures as a mother hadn't been protecting my children too fiercely or even holding back secrets. My most dire mistake had been neglecting to trust Yahweh's power and sufficiency in both their lives and my own. "Mithra is a lie, Allamu. Only Yahweh has ever displayed the kind of power and love for His people that is worthy of worship and honor. He is the only true God. He is the only God I serve."

The Mede's chief magus straightened, seeming ready to pronounce judgment on me, but Mert leaned in to stop him. "Your ima has changed since you last saw her, boy, and you would do well to learn more before you speak more."

Red splotches crept up his neck, and his nostrils flared. I saw his thoughts whirling behind his eyes, building to a dangerous glint. Would he march upstairs and reveal my past to Daniel or announce it to everyone in the courtyard? I couldn't stop him, but neither could I bring myself to confess it to them myself. The possibility of losing them all was too terrifying, the consequences too over-whelming.

Finally, he stood, looking down on me as a mountain overshadows a valley. "I will send the guards to transfer yours and Daniel's personal belongings to the new villa. You and I have no need for further contact." He stalked out of the chamber, slamming the door behind him.

Mert squeezed my hand. "I think that went as well as could be expected."

"How can I fix things, Mert? My children hate me."

She crossed her arms over her chest. "What if telling them the truth—the whole truth—is the only way?"

"Well, I don't know . . . I . . . There has to be another—"

She rolled her eyes and shook her head. "Belili!"

"I can't tell them the whole truth."

"Because keeping secrets has worked so well all these years?"

"I don't need your sarcasm."

"Then why did you come to my chamber?"

I wanted to rail at her, but she was right. "I came because you're the only one who knows it all—you old crow."

Her mischievous grin told me she wasn't backing down. "Are you willing to risk losing your family to gain them fully?"

She wanted me to numbly say yes, but I couldn't. I wouldn't. I'd lived in the shadows so long that to emerge in light now could blind me. Mert was the only one I could trust with *all* my dark places because her shadows were darker still. She, too, had stayed alive by doing vile things that nearly killed her soul. She, too, held secrets that no one knew but me.

"I can't." I held her gaze, my voice barely a whisper. "I lost Allamu when he discovered I was Hebrew. I've known Daniel ben Johanan for nearly seventy years. I know what would happen if he discovered I met Gadi while serving as high priestess of Mithra."

"He would forgive you." Always so certain, but she couldn't know that.

I laid my head on her shoulder. "Daniel knows too much about a priestess's duties in Mithra's temple. He would realize how I won Gadi's heart. He'll know the countless men—" I covered my face, flaming with renewed shame. "I buried that part of my life years ago, Mert. I'm no longer that person."

She tugged my hands away. "Make your decision to tell them or not, but realize the consequences if Daniel and your family discover your history from anyone but you. Your betrayal will hurt worse than the truth."

Daniel had descended halfway down the stairs when he saw Allamu flee Mert's chamber. His stepson wore that expression only when he was angry with his ima. Perhaps this wasn't the best time to inform his family about the vision, but a sense of urgency compelled him.

He knocked on the door and heard slight shuffling inside. Mert opened only a crack. "What?"

She wouldn't win a prize for respect, but she was more like family than servant. "Tell Belili I've had another vision and need to share its message with everyone right away. I'll send one of the children to assemble the others in the courtyard."

"Now?" Her frustration confirmed his suspicions.

"I saw Allamu leave. Is Belili all right?"

"She will be." Mert closed the door.

Massaging the back of his neck, Daniel determined he and his wife would have a long talk about her son after the family meeting. He found one of his grandsons and sent him to fetch the adults from the second family villa. He then found Shesh, who was reattaching the rope to the bucket above their well.

"I need to speak with everyone around the table right away," he said without preamble.

Shesh set aside his mallet, beads of sweat running into the creases on his forehead. "Did something happen that you couldn't say in front of Allamu?"

"No. No. I've had a vision, and it affects us all." He squeezed Shesh's shoulder.

"What—"

"I'll tell you when everyone arrives. Please. Call everyone to the table."

Daniel ambled to the family's meeting place, using these few moments alone to search his heart before he burdened theirs. He'd known since he was a boy of twelve that he wanted to return to Judah. He'd worshipped in Solomon's magnificent Temple, eaten grapes from Jerusalem's palace vineyard, floated while sitting in the Salt Sea, and climbed Mount Hermon. His family had never stepped foot out of Babylon. When he and Abigail had vowed with Hananiah, Mishael, and Azariah to return to Jerusalem at the end of Jeremiah's prophesied seventy years, how could he have known that he'd be responsible for a family of sixty-one people?

Four daughters, their husbands, grandchildren, and great-grandchildren busied themselves with tasks all around him, trimming scarred trees, repairing damaged furniture, and restoring the many blessings Yahweh had rained down on them during Daniel's long life in a foreign land. Would the blessings become a millstone around their necks when it came time to return to the true gift of God's Promised Land?

He sat down heavily at the head of the first table as Belili emerged from Mert's chamber. "You've had another vision?"

"Yes, my love. The messenger Gabriel appeared again."

She turned a vacant stare to the family streaming into the courtyard, absently working her ruby pendant between two fingers. It was a nervous habit she'd picked up in Achmetha, where he assumed she received the necklace as a gift from Gadi. He never begrudged her the keepsake, but would mementos like these prove to be roots that grounded them in Babylon when Yahweh called them to Jerusalem?

Their children and grandchildren squeezed around the single table, leaving little ones at rest and play with servants to care for them. Even the question of servants tightened the knot in his gut. *Yahweh, will we return to Jerusalem the way the captives came to Babylon—with the clothes on our backs and a bag on our shoulders?* Bowing his head, Daniel silently recited the two things of which he'd been so certain after the vision. Yahweh would quickly bring the exile to an end, and the Temple would be rebuilt. *I trust You, Yahweh.*

When he lifted his head, everyone had stilled, their attention focused on him. "Thank you for coming so quickly. You know the story of Belili's and my captivity, how we were taken as children from Jerusalem." Affirming nods bid him continue. "Shortly before our capture, the prophet Jeremiah prophesied Babylon's attack and our exile. He also proclaimed the length of exile would be seventy years. When Belili, Shadrach, Meshach, Abednego, and I were faced with leaving God's holy city, we made a vow to return at the end of the seventy years."

Kezia shifted nervously beside Shesh. "I thought you were going to tell us about a vision you had, Abba."

"I believe the seventy years was part of this vision, Daughter." He turned his attention to Shesh. "I picked up one of Jeremiah's scrolls to show it to Allamu and opened it to the prophecy of seventy years. After he and Belili left our chamber, I was guilt stricken, realizing the ways I've failed to serve Yahweh faithfully in my sixty-six years in Babylon."

"Abba, no!" Shesh covered Daniel's hand. "Who in Babylon has been more faithful than you?"

"Our service to God isn't about comparing ourself to others, my son. It's about measuring obedience to our individual calling." Daniel studied the bewildered expressions on his family's faces. "I made a vow to return to Jerusalem, but was it based on Yahweh's will for me or confidence in my own strength and desires?"

Shesh laced his fingers together, his gaze intent. "Only you can know your own heart, Abba."

"And only Yahweh knows who will be among the remnant that returns to Jerusalem to rebuild His Temple in four years." Daniel returned Shesh's stare. "I want to lead the remnant, Sheshbezzar, but is it my will or Yahweh's?"

Like the calm before a summer storm, Kezia sat silent, her features churning like turbulent clouds. She shot to her feet. "You're being ridiculous, Abba. Our family is *not* leaving Babylon."

"Wait." Shesh tried to catch her arm before she rushed away, but couldn't. Sheepishly, he returned his gaze to Daniel. "What exactly was revealed in your vision, Abba? The seventy years? The rebuilding of the Temple? Did this Gabriel name the leader?"

"He spoke of seventy sevens," Daniel said to the group, "confirming Jeremiah's prophecy that I held in my hand when the vision began. Then he spoke of an Anointed One, the rebuilding of Jerusalem, and of sixty-two 'sevens' and seven 'sevens.' I believe the sixty-two sevens and seven sevens speak of the period in which we will rebuild the Temple, but I can't be certain." He directed his next words to Shesh. "I must confess, Gabriel didn't specifically name the man who would lead the remnant, but it must be someone with the unwavering respect of the elders."

Shesh leaned both elbows on the table, lips pursed tight in thought. The others sat in silence, showing varying levels of trepidation. Daniel felt it too, but he had nearly eighty years of Yahweh's faithfulness to lean on.

Belili's hand slipped into the bend of his elbow, and she asked in a soft whisper, "So you're sure, then?"

"Not sure, my love." He watched quiet

302

questions spread like wildfire over his clan. Fear bred dissension. They needed time to form good questions, and he needed time to ask for Yahweh's wisdom. "Jeremiah's scroll also confirmed that the Medes' invasion was Yahweh's judgment on Babylon. We don't yet know the details of the Medes' rule—how or if they're in league with Cyrus or fighting against him. Praise be to Yahweh that one of our own family members is among them. Return at dusk for a feast tonight. We'll discuss these matters with Allamu, and I'll try to answer your questions about the vision."

It seemed to Daniel as if the family released a collective sigh of relief as they pushed away from the table and began to disperse, but Belili's grip tightened on his arm. "When Allamu left Mert's chamber, he made it clear he wants no contact with me."

He pulled her close to kiss her forehead. "He's angry still, but I saw longing in him when he realized he had a family, beloved. He'll come."

27

"Lift up your eyes and look around;
all your children gather and come to you.
As surely as I live," declares the LORD,
"you will wear them all as ornaments;
you will put them on, like a bride."
                                    —ISAIAH 49:18

Belili left the family meeting to tell Mert about the impromptu feast, and Daniel climbed the stairs to continue packing. His wife returned to their chamber with reports of revolt among the servants—led by Mert, of course—at the short notice. They'd have difficulty gathering enough food after last night's invasion closed the market, but Mert would manage. She'd served more people with less.

Daniel started packing on his side of the chamber, but everything he placed in a basket, box, or chest, Belili removed. "We don't need that," she said. "Only take essential personal items to the new villa."

Finally, he sat on his favorite cushion in the corner, realizing he could be most helpful by watching his busy-bee wife buzz around. She was still the most beautiful woman he'd ever seen. At home she wore her hair, now a vibrant silver, in a long, thick braid over her left shoulder. Covering that tender heart she guarded so closely.

Seeing Allamu this morning had been hard on her, but couldn't she see Yahweh's hand in it? The Medes' invasion. Daniel's presence at Belshazzar's banquet. Allamu speaking on his behalf. Daniel's appointment to the royal council. Shesh finding Jeremiah's scrolls. The vision. Every moment had been skillfully shaped by the Master Potter. But how would they ever find enough gold, silver, and bronze to fashion the sacred items? *Help me trust that You can fulfill every prophecy and vision, Yahweh.*

Inhaling slowly, Daniel stood and approached his wife as if she were a wounded she-bear. "What did Allamu say that has upset you so?"

She steadied her hands on the sides of the basket. "Nothing he hasn't said before." Her quaking voice told him to tread lightly.

He stood behind her, where contents of the trunk lay strewn like fallen soldiers. Placing a hand on her back, he waited for her to stand and then drew her into a commanding hug. "Enough now. Tell me what's troubling you."

At first tense in his arms, he felt her body soften and then wilt like a flower in autumn's first frost. "I want my children to know Yahweh. Allamu still trusts Mithra, and our daughters were too angry when we returned from our Borsippa estate to see my new faith. I've failed

305

them. I've failed to convince the people I love most that Yahweh is real."

Daniel smoothed the gray strands out of her eyes and searched the deep lines of worry on her face. "You have not failed, and you can't convince them. Only Yahweh can work in a heart to help those we love to believe. We must simply love them with an honest and transparent heart."

"Honest and transparent?" She pushed Daniel away and started putting away the treasures she'd emptied from the wooden trunk. When she reached for the linen-wrapped bundle, she paused, holding it between them. "To be honest and transparent with our children, *you* must tell them about our seven years at the Borsippa estate. Are you willing to confess you chose to serve Babylon's king and queen instead of our own family? Can you share some of the blame our daughters assign to me for abandoning them?"

Daniel lowered his head, weighed down by the truth of her accusation. His wife shoved the bundle into his hands and began sorting a basket of robes. He unwrapped the linen, revealing Queen Amyitis's golden crown. She'd given it to them after they returned from seven years of caring for Nebuchadnezzar while Yahweh's judgment transformed him to a beast. They'd sworn silence, believing Yahweh's good work in Nebuchadnezzar would continue best if opposing political factions never knew. Daniel had kept that vow until Belshazzar's banquet—but it was time for secrets to end.

"Belili." No answer. "Belili, look at me."

She swiped at her eyes and turned with an expression of stone. "What?"

Yahweh, give me words to draw her close again. He held up the crown. "Tonight we'll tell our children of Nebuchadnezzar's transformation—and of yours—while we were in Borsippa. For the first time in our lives, we will share a meal with *all* our children. A meal without secrets."

Something he couldn't decipher passed over her expression, but she quickly crossed the void between them and threw her arms around his neck. "I love you so much my chest aches."

"It's probably sore muscles from packing all day."

She swatted him, and the air between them sweetened. Daniel felt his Abigail return to him. "It's time for afternoon prayers."

Holding his hand, she knelt first and then supported Daniel as he knelt beside her. They always faced Jerusalem, though it was a pile of rubble. In this, at least, Daniel and his wife had always been united.

28

[Nebuchadnezzar] said, "Belteshazzar, chief of the magicians, I know that the spirit of the holy gods is in you. . . . These are the visions I saw while lying in bed: I looked, and there before me stood a tree in the middle of the land. . . . The tree grew large and strong and its top touched the sky; it was visible to the ends of the earth. . . . Under it the wild animals found shelter, and the birds lived in its branches; from it every creature was fed."

—DANIEL 4:9–12

April 571 BC

My youngest three daughters sang David's psalms like crested larks this morning while the women in our household ground, roasted, and stored the freshly harvested barley Daniel purchased during Babylon's Akitu festival. But Kezia, our eldest, sulked in the corner alone. All four of the girls' nursemaids and three kitchen servants scurried about the courtyard, busy with tasks Mert had assigned.

My old friend elbowed me. "Go talk to Kezia.

She's a young girl in love and needs her ima's reassurance."

"I can't reassure her until Daniel reassures me." I hissed the reply and glanced around our little circle, praying my younger girls hadn't heard me.

Eva and Eden, our eleven-year-old twins, crooned the joyful litany of Yahweh's benefits from their favorite psalm, while Gia—age nine— pretended to strum a harp. Normally I would chide them for slacking—they were supposed to be grinding grain for today's bread—but I was too upset. Why hadn't Daniel returned from the palace yet?

Mert stilled my hands on the dough I was kneading. "He'll return, Belili." She glanced at the girls and then back at me, speaking so quietly I could barely hear her. "If Nebuchadnezzar wished to kill Daniel, he wouldn't summon him in the middle of the night to interpret another nightmare. He would simply order his execution."

"Is that supposed to make me feel better?"

I squeezed my eyes shut, remembering the terror on Arioch's face when Daniel opened our bedchamber door last night. "The king needs you to interpret a vexing nightmare—immediately."

Scoffing, Daniel's eyes narrowed. "King Nebuchadnezzar hasn't *needed me* for fifteen years, Arioch. He can wait until morning."

He tried to shut the door, but the king's bodyguard wedged his sandal over the threshold. "Please, Lord Belteshazzar. I've never seen him so frightened."

Need? Frightened? These weren't words I'd ever heard as descriptions for the King of the Earth. Daniel hesitated, as if considering the summons. My blood boiled.

I shoved him, forcing him to face me, and spoke in a strained whisper. "Nebuchadnezzar has avoided you like a leper since he destroyed Jerusalem. Tell him no, Daniel. We're discussing Kezia's betrothal and haven't come to a decision. We promised Sheshbazzar and his abba an answer by morning."

His silence and the set of his jaw told me his answer, but words confirmed it. "I should be home before dawn, Belili, and then we can finish our discussion." His hands slid down my arms, and he lifted my hands to kiss them. He grabbed a rough-spun robe off a peg and was out the door without a backward glance. I wanted to scream.

By the time dawn's pink tint softened the eastern sky, fear had mingled its dark possibilities with my seething. Now, at midmorning, I paused my kneading and looked up to see Kezia wiping her tears. I swallowed back my own, fearing for both our futures if Daniel didn't return.

Rubbing my throbbing temples with flour-dusted hands, I whispered to myself, "Why didn't he just drink the cup of blessing, accept the gold ring, and sign the betrothal last night?"

I knew the answer, but Mert looked at me as if I was cousin to a mule. "Daniel will never believe any man is good enough for his daughters." She stole the dough I'd been kneading and placed a new batch on the table in front of me. "But he must find husbands for them all someday."

"That's what I told him last night," I said, beginning to knead the fresh dough. "Shesh is a good man. He and Kezia love each other. What more could we hope for?"

She gave me a sideways glance. "What more *does* he want? He must have something in mind."

I shrugged and focused on my kneading, too embarrassed to admit that my husband was disappointed by the bride price Sheshbazzar offered. "My daughter is a treasure," he'd ranted.

"She's *your* treasure," I'd told him. "You coddle all the girls, making me the tyrant who must discipline." Our discussion spiraled into the same quarrel we'd rehearsed since the girls were old enough to disobey.

"You're too hard on them, Belili. They need an ima to love them, not an army general to berate them."

"And they need an abba who sees them more

than a few times a week, bringing gifts as peace offerings because he works too much."

My husband's face flushed crimson. "Perhaps we should stop before we say things we'll regret."

I raised my chin and leveled my gaze. "You mean before you accuse me of driving my own son away? Or before you admit you're afraid once our girls marry, they'll never come home because they hate me?"

His mouth gaped. "Belili, no! Allamu made his own choice, and our girls love you. They're just at a difficult age." He opened his arms and stepped toward me. "Come here."

"No!" I stepped back, and Arioch's urgent knocking suspended the conversation. *Yahweh, please bring my Daniel home so I can apologize for presuming my fears were his.*

"Abba!" Kezia's greeting drew my attention to the courtyard gate, where my husband entered, looking beyond weary. All four girls ran to greet him, surrounding him with hugs and bouncing curls.

He squeezed each one and placed kisses on their heads, then looked at me across the courtyard with a sadness that pierced me. "I must have a private word with your ima in our chamber about Kezia's betrothal."

"Please make Ima agree, Abba," Kezia whined. "You know how difficult she can be."

Daniel shot a surprised glance at me, but I kept my features placid. Was he surprised I hadn't revealed that her supposed champion was actually the one ready to crush her hopes? He tipped her chin. "Your ima and I will make the decision of your betrothal together. We both love you and want only what's best for you." Kezia cast a furtive sneer my direction as she and the other girls grudgingly released their abba to me.

He walked toward me, paused, and offered his hand. I noticed it shaking but grasped it without question. As we climbed the stairs, he spoke in barely a whisper. "We must betroth Kezia to Sheshbazzar right away. The king's dream will change all our lives."

When Daniel left his chamber with Arioch, he'd experienced a fleeting moment of terror that this time Yahweh might not give him the interpretation of Nebuchadnezzar's dream. The shock he felt now—after hearing the dream and receiving Yahweh's interpretation— filled him with more dread than he could have imagined.

He and Belili reached the doorway of their chamber, and she lifted his hand to her lips. "Should we invite Ater and Shesh for the mid- day meal? We could make a day of it. Celebrate the betrothal, begin plans for the wedding feast . . ." Her words disappeared as she searched his face. "What is it, Daniel?"

"We have more to plan than a wedding." Daniel opened their door and led her to the couch beside their bed. He kept his head bowed and began the difficult retelling. "When Arioch escorted me to the throne room last night, Nebuchadnezzar was waiting, pale and trembling. The first thing he said to me was, 'I'm going to tell you my dream, and you must be completely honest. Don't let its message frighten you, Belteshazzar. I vow, on the lives of Amyitis and our children, you will be punished only if you bend the truth to your will.' " Belili waited intently, but his mouth went dry. "I should have walked away then. Instead, I promised to tell only the truth, good news or bad."

Shaking his head at the memory, Daniel could barely believe it still. *Yahweh, the prophecy seems too fantastic, utterly ludicrous.*

"What was the dream?"

With a resolute sigh, he began the recounting as the king told it to him, and with each detail, his heart rose to a crescendo that silenced all doubt. "Nebuchadnezzar saw in his dream a tree that touched the sky and was visible to all the earth. Its leaves were beautiful, its fruit abundant. This tree provided shelter for wild animals, birds lived in its branches, and it produced food for all living creatures. But a messenger came down from heaven and cried, 'Cut down the tree, trim its branches, strip off its leaves, and scatter its fruit. The animals will flee from beneath it and the birds from its branches, but let the stump and its roots remain in the ground, bound with iron and bronze.'"

Belili's features hardened into a grim smile. "I can't say I'm saddened by the imagery of judgment in Yahweh's message, Husband. Are you? Nebuchadnezzar murdered your family, destroyed our homeland, and nearly ruined our lives. If anyone deserves to be cut down, trimmed, stripped, and scattered, it is Babylon's king."

"I agree, my love, but it was the second part of the dream that makes me tremble." He shook his head. "The interpretation shifted from speaking of a tree, saying '*its* branches, *its* leaves,' to a transformation of *him* that makes me shudder, Belili. I can't fathom it."

"How can you have pity on a barbarian? His cruelty has no limits. He's utterly inhuman in his cruelty—"

"And the Lord said, 'Let him be drenched with the dew of heaven, and let him live with the animals among the plants of the earth. Let his mind be changed from that of a man and let him be given the mind of an animal, till seven times pass by for him.'"

Belili's brows drew together, first seeming confused and then registering the misgivings Daniel himself had battled since the words left his mouth. "He'll become like an animal?" she asked, incredulous.

Slowly, tentatively, Daniel nodded. " 'Till seven times pass by,' which I think means he'll endure the judgment for seven years. However, Yahweh made it clear that if Nebuchadnezzar repented of his arrogance, He would forestall His righteous judgment. If not, and the king continues to boast that his own power and wisdom established his kingdom, Yahweh's judgment stands. Yet His mercy will be offered—as the iron and bronze stump of the tree implies—and Nebuchadnezzar will be given a chance at the end of seven years to humble himself and acknowledge that Yahweh gives kingdoms to whomever He pleases."

Belili choked out a sardonic laugh and turned away. "King Nebuchadnezzar will never admit any god *gave* him anything. He's seen glimpses of Yahweh's power but knows nothing of the divine passion that arouses it."

"Look at me," Daniel said, sharing every bit of her anger toward the destroyer of Yahweh's people. When their eyes met, he hoped the determination she saw there would convince her. "Seeing God's power at work in others isn't enough for some people. Those riddled with pride must experience God's personal discipline before they can feel the warmth of His love. We must be with Nebuchadnezzar—and Amyitis—for all seven years of his judgment so when his mind is finally capable of acknowledging Yahweh's supremacy, we can lead him to the One who deserves his praise."

Pulling away, Belili began shaking her head before he'd finished speaking. "Don't be ridiculous! I have no idea who is on the king's council anymore, but I'm sure any one of them will attempt to steal his throne the moment Nebuchadnezzar starts eating grass and begins to moo."

"No one must know, Belili. We must hide him."

He saw the wheels of thought spinning behind her lovely dark eyes. "You're mad. We have no room in our small stable for another—"

"We must take Queen Amyitis and the king away from Babylon. Arioch will go with us. No one else can know." He slid his fingers through her curly hair. Gazing intently, they exchanged all the impossibilities without words before Daniel spoke again. "The king is frightened and says he will humble himself. I hope he does, but experience tells me he won't. Arioch and I will begin forming a plan today. The king has reinstated me to serve at the palace, thinking having me near will somehow protect him from the coming judgment."

"No, Daniel! How can he expect—"

"He is the king, Belili. I have no choice." The truth silenced her, but how would she respond to Nebuchadnezzar's decision concerning her? "He's also given Queen Amyitis permission to resume her friendship with you. I was delayed this morning waiting for her to finish this correspondence to you." He retrieved the missive from the pocket of his robe and offered it to his wife. Belili simply stared at the small scroll.

When she looked up, her eyes were moist. "Do you know what it says?"

He couldn't lie. "Yes."

Her curiosity darkened to anger. "Why not just tell me, then?"

Daniel broke the seal, unrolled the parchment, and held up the short message for her to read. "It says the queen would like to help you and Kezia plan her wedding feast."

29

In the visions I [Nebuchadnezzar] saw while lying in bed, . . . a messenger, coming down from heaven. He called in a loud voice: . . . "Let him be drenched with the dew of heaven, and let him live with the animals among the plants of the earth. Let his mind be changed from that of a man and let him be given the mind of an animal, till seven times pass by for him."

—DANIEL 4:13–16

Twelve Months Later
April 570 BC

The sun had risen well above the horizon by the time Daniel ascended the grand palace stairway, taking two steps at a time. He'd stopped at the wine merchant's home to settle the bill for Kezia and Shesh's wedding feast. And what a feast it was. He'd never seen Kezia look lovelier or his family happier.

The week-long celebration had only been possible, however, when Belili relented and officially invited the king and queen. Since the vision of the tree and beast, Nebuchadnezzar hadn't allowed Daniel out of his sight for more than an afternoon. Short visits home, or when Belili and the girls visited Queen Amyitis at the palace, had been Daniel's only chance to see his family for the past year. So a full week in his home, enjoying the company of his wife in their chamber—well, it was almost like reliving their own wedding week.

Hurrying down the hallway to the throne room, Daniel prayed Arioch had kept Nebuchadnezzar distracted in his absence. The guards mumbled congratulations to the abba of the bride and opened the doors to the yawning, empty throne room. Odd. The king was usually preparing for his day of petitioners by now. Perhaps he was recovering from too much drink from last night's final evening of celebration. Daniel ascended the dais and exited the side door to the private hallway leading to the king's chamber. His royal eunuchs nodded their greeting but made no move to open the door.

"Is the king ill this morning?" Daniel asked.

"No, my lord. He and Arioch went to the roof early to break their fast and haven't returned." One of the eunuchs studied me. "Shall I go with you to check on them?"

"No, no." Daniel chided himself for letting his concern stir the guard's suspicion. He forced levity into his voice. "Perhaps the king and I will have our morning meeting on the rooftop." He hurried away before the eunuch could argue.

Daniel climbed the stairs leading to the palace roof, foreboding speeding his steps. Emerging atop Babylon's second-highest building, he found Arioch sitting on the low wall surrounding the perimeter of the rooftop, sobbing into his hands.

"Where is the king?" Daniel's coarse whisper startled the man.

He looked up, but before he could respond, Daniel's eyes were drawn to a sight his mind couldn't comprehend. A strange creature nibbled in the king's prized garden.

During the thirty-five years Daniel had known King Nebuchadnezzar, the man had been Daniel's ruler, Judah's destroyer, and Yahweh's instrument of wrath. He was a pagan. Prone to excess and extremes. As ruthless and blood-thirsty as any king in history. Daniel's hate for him had festered and grown into a writhing thing in his belly, and in Daniel's eyes, Nebuchadnezzar was no better than an animal.

But when God's judgment fell and he actually became one, even Daniel pitied him.

"I saw it happen." Arioch stood beside him. "A Voice, as clear as mine is now, called from the sky, repeating the exact words you spoke to the king on the night you interpreted his nightmare." He knelt and bowed to Daniel. "King Nebuchadnezzar was right. The spirit of the gods lives in you, Lord Belteshazzar. You have proven yourself faithful to my king, and

I am yours to command until he is restored to Babylon's throne."

Daniel placed a hand on Arioch's shoulder. "Stand up, my friend, I'm only a man. The only difference between you and me is the God we serve, and Nebuchadnezzar will be restored to his throne only when he admits my God gives kingdoms to whomever He pleases."

At Daniel's comment, the eunuch stood, nostrils flaring and jaw muscles flexing. Could he deny the proof that Yahweh was true to His word? God had mercifully given the king a year— to the day—to humble himself. Instead, Nebuchadnezzar had continued in his arrogance and kept Daniel at his side like a talisman, as though he could ward off Yahweh's discipline. No man, great or small, could preempt the fulfillment of God's relentless pursuit—or His perfect wisdom.

Daniel stared at the creature, repulsed but unable to look away. Coarse, thick hair was layered in the colors of an eagle's feathers all over his body and glistened with morning dew. His spine was curved, causing him to walk on both hands and feet. Long nails, pointed like talons, dug into the garden's rich soil and some of the king's prized vegetables.

Certain Nebuchadnezzar would never humble himself before Yahweh, Daniel and Belili had secretly made preparations necessary for this day. "We must amend my plan in order to get him safely and unnoticed out of the palace."

"You've planned for this?" Arioch's reaction seemed a mixture of shock and relief.

Daniel nodded, his emotions jumbled as he contemplated all that would change in this day. "We'll need to subdue him somehow in order to move him to the docks outside the Adad Gate."

"He cannot leave the palace."

As if the creature heard Arioch's protest, he lifted his tail and fertilized the royal garden. The king's bodyguard needed no further coaxing. "Where are we taking him?"

"I purchased an estate in Borsippa. It's completely private, and servants who have proven their discretion are prepared for our arrival at any time, day or night."

Thoughts raced behind the eunuch's keen eyes, and he gave a single nod. "How do we get him there?"

Daniel explained what they needed, and Arioch went to the royal chamber to retrieve a vial of imported lavender oil and several blankets. The lavender oil would calm the beast, and the blankets would hide his strange form while they secreted him out of the city. Arioch's high rank was enough to clear every guard from the king's private halls to the royal stables. There, they loaded the creature onto a cart—beside a heifer to stabilize the weight—

where a stable boy waited to accompany us to Borsippa.

He could barely believe they'd made it this far without being detected. "I must go home. Belili is the only one who can get the queen to the docks."

Arioch grabbed his arm. "No. The queen need not know."

"Of course she needs to know."

"He leaves her for military campaigns all the time. We can send word when the king is safe. Tell her he's on an extended siege and can't come home."

Daniel considered it. Nebuchadnezzar had been gone for a year, even two, but the king and queen had never been separated for seven years. "It's too long. He'll need his wife." He held Arioch's gaze. "You know how he loves her."

The eunuch pursed his lips, defeated. "Go, then."

"I'll send Belili to the queen and meet you at the Adad Gate."

Arioch left the stables, leading the cart through narrow streets.

Daniel hurried to the stables at his villa, where he instructed the servants to prepare two camels: one for his "journey to Canaan" with the king and the other for Lady Belili's "journey to Achmetha" with the queen. Once inside the villa, he found Mert playing the general, commanding her bevy of servants to restore their household to its prewedding calm.

When she spotted him, she laid aside the basket of soiled linen in her arms and met him at the base of the stairway. "What's wrong?"

"Where's Belili?" he asked.

"She's still dressing in your chamber."

Daniel kept his voice steady. "Perhaps you should follow me."

Her sharp gray eyes flashed. "Is this about the dream?"

Surprised for only a moment, Daniel realized his wife did nothing without confiding in Mert. "Yes. It's time."

She rushed up the stairs without further comment, and Daniel followed a step behind.

Mert entered the chamber without knocking, and Belili didn't even turn. Back to the door, she tried to fasten a gold-stitched belt around her waist. "Oh, Mert, I'm glad you came. I need help with—"

Daniel's hands slid around the belt, and she turned in his arms, startled. "What are you—" But the joy in her surprise faded with his silent sorrow. Realization dawned on her lovely features, replaced by pleading. "No, Daniel, no. Not today. We can't leave. Not when Shesh and Kezia have just entered their wedding chamber."

"We must, my love. We've talked about this."

"But we can't disturb them, and we can't leave without saying goodbye. And the other girls. I know we've talked about it, but the twins will need husbands in two years. Who will make that match? How can we just abandon . . ."

Her words disappeared into sobs, and Daniel pulled her into his arms.

Mert stood like a soldier prepared for a long siege. "You know I'll take good care of them." Disapproval laced her tone, but she patted Belili's back. "Shesh is a good man. He'll help me."

Daniel nodded his thanks and laid his head on his wife's. "Come, my love. We need to do this."

"Why?" She shoved him away, hugging her waist. "Why must I leave my children, my life, to help save a king I despise?"

"You know why." He let silence massage her heart, letting their year of preparation overcome this moment of doubt.

Yes, I knew why, but bitterness fed my defiance, and I matched my husband's determination. "I don't care if Nebuchadnezzar acknowledges Yahweh is sovereign. I don't care if he regains his throne in seven years. I don't even care to convince Amyitis to follow him into hiding."

Daniel looked as if I'd struck him. "Our lives in Babylon aren't for our own pleasure or purpose, Wife. We live for Yahweh, to fulfill His purpose for us on this earth."

"And what about your vow to Shadrach, Meshach, and Abednego, Daniel?" I shouted.

"What of preparing the remnant of Judah for the return to Jerusalem? How does protecting King Nebuchadnezzar fulfill Yahweh's purpose for our people?"

He whispered through gritted teeth, "Lower your voice, woman. Or perhaps you wish to tell the whole city of our plan—as you told Mert—and put all our lives at risk."

Quiet fury seethed. "Mert needed to know in order to care for our children, one of whom was married a week ago and will be devastated when she emerges from her wedding chamber to discover her ima has abandoned her for the most crucial year of her marriage. Three more daughters, who are coming into womanhood, will believe their abba abandoned them in the name of ambition and their ima chose a queen's friendship above their care."

My husband's anger drained like water from a cracked pitcher. He pulled me into a tight embrace. "Please, my love. I can't do this without you. You've raised our daughters to be strong. They're older than you were when you were taken into captivity, and they're surrounded by people who love them."

I fixed my eyes on Mert, who stood five paces behind us, tears streaming down her cheeks. She and I had spoken of that very parallel during the weeks of preparation—the scars of abandonment, the yearning for love and relationship, lifelong marks from early wounds. Mert held out my shoulder bag, her sign it was time for us to go. I'd made my choice when I began planning the escape. It had been easier to talk about leaving than to actually walk out, but she was right. The time for talking was over.

I wriggled from Daniel's arms and grabbed the bag from my friend. "Remind them every day how much I love them."

"You know I will." She wiped her face and fled from the chamber.

Daniel and I changed into servant's robes and double-checked the bag. Inside were two more servant's robes, a woman's head covering, pairs of sandals, and a plain robe, head covering, and sandals for the queen.

Daniel reached for my hand, lifted it to his lips, and kissed it. "Our daughters have Mert and each other. They'll be fine. We'll mend whatever's broken when we return." We left our chamber and escaped through the rear entrance like thieves—without a goodbye to anyone.

Our stable master's confused expression seemed to shout silent questions at our hurried departure but merely watched as Daniel rode toward the docks and I toward the palace. How would I convince Amyitis to leave Babylon in the same stealth when, by the king's command, she hadn't been told of his dream or the impending judgment it promised?

I hated Nebuchadnezzar. Not only for all the havoc he'd wreaked on my childhood but because of what he'd done to Amyitis and me. When Daniel and I returned with Nabonidus from Achmetha, Nebuchadnezzar refused to see us. And when I married Lord Belteshazzar, the king refused to let his wife associate with me. When my husband interpreted his dream last year, however, he not only reinstated Daniel to palace service but also reinstated me as friend of the queen—if I chose to be so. Though I was angry she abandoned me when Allamu was sick, I knew she'd been frightened of the plague and could never disobey Nebuchadnezzar. She was my dearest friend, whom I hadn't seen in nearly fifteen years.

Of course I forgave her and had been seeing her almost every day for the past year. She'd been a wonderful help while planning Kezia's wedding and even gave advice when my daughter turned into a turbulent bride.

Amyitis's husband, however, I could never forgive. Nebuchadnezzar was an arrogant bully who was finally getting a fraction of what he deserved. Let Yahweh pour out the burning sulfur of Sodom on his head.

Even as the thought lingered, concern for Amyitis tempered my anger. Like every woman who adored her husband, she saw beyond his public facade to the insecure boy inside—or the roguish gentleman, depending on the day. My friend would be devastated when I told her of his fate. Though their children were grown and had families of their own, she would leave them—as I had—and the lovely grandchildren she doted on.

Too quickly, I reached the palace stables. I carried my bag inside rather than leaving it with the stable boy. Hurrying past servants carrying pitchers and trays, I turned a corner and ran headlong into Ashpenaz.

"Oh! Forgive me, I . . ." Immediately, I stared at my sandals, searching for an excuse. "Amyitis and I are sneaking out to a vineyard for a midday meal."

His bald head wrinkled with his brow, making him look remarkably like a raisin. "Why sneak out?"

Before I could concoct another flimsy tale, the palace's chief official gripped my arm and pulled me into an empty chamber. He closed the door, and I jerked my arm from his grasp. "You will treat me with the respect I deserve or—"

"What happened on the roof this morning?" His hard-but-kind features were replaced with foreboding alone. "Where have Arioch and Daniel taken the king? If harm comes to King Nebuchadnezzar, you will suffer unimaginably."

I swallowed back my fear. Daniel said not to tell anyone. But surely Ashpenaz . . .

"I see that you know." His hand landed beside my head, rumbling the thick cedar door. "Tell me."

I stared at the half-crazed eunuch. Was anyone more loyal to the king? More trustworthy? "Yahweh has stricken the king. It was prophesied in a dream a year ago—to the day—and Arioch saw the awful transformation this morning on the rooftop. He will be returned to his throne in seven years—"

"Seven yea—"

"Yes, seven years. Arioch and Daniel have a plan to maintain his throne. Daniel has already sent messengers to key locations, telling them to expect the king's arrival any day. The confusion will take weeks to sort out, and by then he'll have another plan in place."

His mouth opened to speak, but words failed him. I patted his cheek and rose on tiptoe to kiss it. "If you escort me to Queen Amyitis's chamber, she'll feel better knowing we have an ally remaining in Babylon."

He stepped back and scrubbed his face, as if waking from a nightmare. He looked at me, his eyes glistening. "You said Arioch witnessed the king's 'transformation.' What did you mean? Transformed how?"

What could I say without adding to his torture? "In the king's dream, he saw a tree cut down, but the stump eventually flourished again. I promise

Arioch will return your king to the palace—in seven years."

His eyes raked me like blades scraping away anything false. Finally, he bowed and opened the door, leading me through the servants' dim-lit hallways to the harem stairs and finally to Amyitis's chamber.

Her guards knew me well but exchanged an uneasy glance when I approached with their chief eunuch. "Good morning," I said lightly, hoping to assuage their suspicions. "Ashpenaz and I were just—"

"You're dismissed," Ashpenaz said without gilding. "Your replacements are on the way."

"Yes, my lord." The guards marched down the stairs without a backward glance.

Ashpenaz stared down at me. "You're a terrible liar."

I grinned in spite of the circumstance. "I used to be quite good at it. I suppose I've lost the knack."

"You need to get better if you plan to keep a secret for seven years." He knocked on the door and announced our arrival, while my dread grew. Lying for seven years.

"Come in!" Amyitis's cheerful voice cut me to the core.

Ashpenaz opened the door and ushered me in first. Amyitis looked radiant as always, her hair coiffed and curled with beads and ribbons. We'd been friends for nearly thirty years, and

I'd never seen her in a plain or woolen robe. Always linen or silk for the queen of Babylon.

"Belili? Are you all right?"

"Yes, my friend."

She chattered on before I could explain. "What a lovely surprise! I thought you would hibernate for a month after that lovely wedding feast. Aren't you exhausted?" She stopped abruptly. "Ashpenaz, why are you lingering at the door?" Fear shadowed her lovely features, and her pleasantness fled. "Has something happened to Neb? Tell me, Belili!"

"I'll take you to him, but first—" I placed my hand at her waist, guiding her to the couch.

She shoved my hand away. "Tell me now!"

Heart aching, I met her fear with stubborn compassion. "I'll tell you everything, my friend, but first you must sit."

A thousand possibilities raced behind the windows of her soul. Finally, she relented, and I sat beside her. Words tumbled from my mouth. I don't even remember what I said, but I remember her reaction. First came disbelief. "A terrible joke," she called it. When I assured her it was the truth, anger settled in, and I endured her hatred while she changed into the plain robe I brought her and gathered a few essentials into her own shoulder bag. Her ivory comb. A polished bronze mirror. And, of course, her crown.

She reached for a jeweled pair of sandals,

but her hand stopped, poised over the satchel, trembling. She held them there, her anger morphing into despair. "Will he know me?"

She dropped the sandals and collapsed into my arms. I held her until Ashpenaz cleared his throat and offered the queen's bag, packed and ready. "You must hurry, my queen. You can trust me to support the king here in Babylon. I will work with Arioch and Lord Belteshazzar to keep his throne secure for as long as he must endure this."

Amyitis wiped her cheeks and patted his forearm. "Thank you, Ashpenaz. What would we do without you?"

I knew then that Yahweh had arranged my meeting with Ashpenaz for Amyitis's sake. It wasn't a mistake to tell him. A man I once counted my enemy had become my ally—and a display of God's mercy to Babylon's queen. He was dear to us both.

He led us toward the door. "You must leave the palace through the main entrance, Mistress Belili. If you take the queen through the servants' halls, as you came in, suspicions will rise."

The queen looked at me and back at her chief eunuch. "Won't we draw more attention by leaving from the main entrance?"

The right corner of his mouth twitched but stopped short of a grin. "A very skilled liar suggested you two might share today's midday meal at a vineyard. That's the story we'll tell."

30

You will eat grass like the ox and be drenched with the dew of heaven.

—DANIEL 4:25

We crossed the single bridge leading out of the city across the Euphrates and turned south, following the streets leading to the Adad Gate. We mingled with caravans of camels, donkeys, and ox-drawn carts, just two women dressed in servant's robes tromping through their daily lives. Finally, as the sun approached midday, Amyitis and I neared the gate.

"Where is he?" she shouted above the noisy sea of traders and merchants milling inside and outside the gates.

From atop my camel, I saw over the crowd to a copse of date palms in the distance. Arioch's stallion was tied to a tree, prancing nervously. Daniel stood beside a cart that carried two cows covered with blankets—wait. *Yahweh, help us!* One of those creatures was too small to be . . .

"Come, Amyi— Come, my friend." I nearly called her by name. I glanced back and saw Amyitis focused on the cart near the date palms. Daniel hurried out from beneath the shade, arms lifted to slow our camels' progress.

"I'm so glad you're here," he shouted in an unnaturally loud voice.

Amyitis removed her whip, ready to tap her camel to its knees for dismount. Daniel grabbed it. "No, stay in your sedan." His sharp tone startled her. Keeping his voice low, his features softened. "We can't cause a scene. We've placed him in the cart beside a heifer, both covered with blankets so people will assume we're moving two animals to Borsippa. It would be best if you could wait until journey's end to see him."

She looked at the cart again and covered a sob, bowing her head to hide her emotions. Daniel looked at me, silently pleading with me to say something. Anger at my husband still boiled beneath the surface. What comfort had I to give? My daughters were likely plying Mert with questions about my whereabouts, while my husband and I risked our lives to help save the man I hated most in the world. I returned my husband's silent plea with a defiant glare. The disappointment in his eyes pricked my heart but didn't soften it.

"Amyitis," he said gently, "we must continue the ruse as Arioch's servants moving livestock to Borsippa. We've fed both the king and the heifer poppy plants sprinkled with lavender oil to keep them calm for—"

"What?" Her head snapped to attention. "Do

you know how much to give . . ." Her words trailed off as she realized to whom she was speaking. Daniel was the foremost *asutu*—expert in medical wisdom—in the empire.

Daniel offered her a forebearing smile. "Perhaps you can see him after we've loaded the cart on a kelek and begin to sail—without a crowd to witness your reaction."

Amyitis dried her tears and lifted her chin. "I will never forgive your god for this, Lord Belteshazzar." Head held high, she fixed her eyes on Arioch, waiting for him to lead us.

I stared at my friend in awe. Even now, at the most desperate moment of her life, Amyitis was as elegant as an eagle in flight. Daniel and the commander of the king's guard resumed their mounts, and Arioch clucked his tongue to lead our little caravan. Daniel fell in behind the stable boy and cart. This time I followed the queen.

We arrived at the same canal that only a week ago had taken King Nebuchadnezzar downstream to celebrate the New Year's festival of Akitu. During the next six days, Nebuchadnezzar completed a series of rituals to ensure Marduk's favor on the empire, while all of Babylon enjoyed feasting and rest from their normal activities.

Sailors waited at the dock to assist merchants and travelers along the canal portion of their journeys. "Greetings, Lord Arioch," said a captain. "How far downstream are you traveling today?"

"To Borsippa, Eriba. My stallion, three camels, and an ox cart with two cows."

"Of course, my lord. All these passengers too?" He looked beyond the commander, surprised but pleased at the size of our party. "Two men, a boy, and two wom—" His eyes widened when he saw Amyitis, recognition dawning.

Arioch pulled him close with a fistful of the man's robe. "And no one learns their identities or destination."

"Yes. Yes, of course." The man bowed and backed away, struggling to take his eyes off his queen.

We dismounted our animals and led them one by one over the gangway and onto the barge. Once on board, Daniel reached in his bag to feed lavender-oiled grass to the heifer and more poppy flowers to the king, while Arioch paid the captain and his two oarsmen handsomely.

Arioch returned to Daniel's side. "I've confided in the captain that the king has made Nabu his new patron god for his military offensive in Canaan and has sent the queen with a secret offering to the priests in Borsippa. We're her guards." He pointed at Daniel, the stable boy, and me. "I've threatened his life if he tells anyone, but kelek captains gossip more than old women in the market."

Was this what our lives would be like for the next seven years? Constant lies and threats and fear? I reached for the basket Ashpenaz had given me back at the palace. "For your journey," he said with a wink. I looked inside and found enough bread, hard cheese, and dried fruit to feed all four of us and the stable boy during our sail to Borsippa. I closed my eyes and nearly wept with gratitude.

I offered Amyitis a small piece of bread and cheese. She barely took two bites while staring into the distance.

"What will Neb eat?" she asked Daniel, as if he were the expert on men turned to animals.

His Adam's apple bobbed twice before answering. "Yahweh said he would eat grass like an ox in the field."

No one spoke after that. What was there to say? In fact, I had nothing to say to my husband all day.

We arrived at Borsippa's docks at dusk. Most of the traders had gone, and only a few local sailors lingered near the canal. Arioch and Daniel spoke in low tones I couldn't hear. Amyitis stood alone, arms wrapped around herself as if she would fall to pieces if she let go.

I drew near and slipped my arm around her waist. "The estate can't be far."

She laid her head on my shoulder. "I want to close my eyes and never wake."

We watched in silence as the men unloaded the camels first and then the cart. A sound unlike anything I'd ever heard rent the air, and the creature bucked as the cart exited the kelek. The ox pulling the cart spooked, and the boy driver expertly gained control. But not before the creature-king released another unearthly wail and kicked open the cart's gate. Backing out, he stumbled and fell out of the cart. The blanket hung precariously over his back. If the blanket slipped away completely, how would they explain an otherworldly looking beast escorted by the king's wife and top two men?

Arioch approached the creature slowly, hands extended, speaking in gentle tones. It paced, agitated, tossing its head, skewing the blanket further.

"No!" Amyitis's coarse whisper was more like a plea. She looked at the growing crowd. "People are staring." Without warning, she raced toward the kelek and grabbed a woven papyrus rope dangling from a post.

I hurried over to Daniel, covering my mouth to keep from calling my friend back. "Is he dangerous? Will he recognize her?" My husband could only shrug, watching too intently to speak.

Arioch tried to block the queen's approach,

but she shoved past him. I couldn't hear what she said. I didn't need to. Arioch's bow made it clear she'd commanded him to stand down.

My friend began to sing as she approached with the dangling rope. She sang an old Sumerian lullaby—with a voice like a holy messenger. The creature calmed immediately. Approaching cautiously, Amyitis slipped the rope around his neck, adjusted the blanket to cover him, and led him calmly into the cart.

I watched in wonder. The Medes were a strong race, mustering fortitude I could never possess. Head held high, my friend placed the lead rope in Arioch's waiting hands. She then proceeded to the nearest date palm—and retched.

"Go," Daniel said, nudging me in her direction. He ran to prepare the camels, and I went to comfort Amyitis.

By sunset, we'd ridden the short distance from the city of Borsippa into an arid wasteland, where we stopped at the gates of a walled fortress.

Daniel turned in his sedan to the line of weary friends behind him, relief on his features. "Here we are."

"This? This is where we'll live for seven years? Fighting vipers and spitting dust?" If I'd been closer, I would have slapped him.

Amyitis ignored my comment and prodded her camel forward. "Open the gate, Lord Belteshazzar. I'm tired and need a bed."

Daniel lifted his fingers to his lips and whistled. The gates opened as if Yahweh Himself tugged on them. I heard Amyitis gasp—or was that my own astonishment when I saw the emerald kingdom inside the walls?

A corkscrew fountain, much like the ones Nebuchadnezzar had built in the queen's gardens, rotated bountiful water in the center of the estate's lavish courtyard. The sound of splashing water welcomed us as Daniel led us toward the barn. Arioch dismounted his stallion and led the creature off the cart first. Daniel, Amyitis, and I dismounted as well and followed Arioch into the barn, watching as he removed the rope and finally the blanket.

Repulsed, I tried not to turn away. The creature before us was massive. His spine hunched severely, requiring support from his hands to stand. Bones protruded from his back, covered only by a thin layer of skin. Thick feathery hair covered his whole body. Fingernails and toenails poked out long, curved, and pointed— like the claws of a bird. Cheekbones, elbows, and knees were sharp and bulging. The handsome king was only a vapor, blown away by the Creator's discipline. I realized I'd been staring and looked away, ashamed I'd so flippantly rejoiced in his discipline.

Arioch stayed busy, finding a pitchfork to toss in fresh hay for the king's evening meal.

Daniel ran his hand over the intricately carved doorframe of the stall. "The king's stall was built in the southeast corner so he would be greeted by sunrise each morning and shaded from afternoon heat. He is protected from the other animals but will never feel alone." Though I knew he was trying to allay the queen's fears, his tour created an incredibly peculiar moment.

Amyitis stood beside me, glaring. I reached for her hand, squeezing a little. "Daniel and Arioch are grieving too. This is not what any of us desire, but we're with you. We will get through this—together."

She pulled her hand away and wrapped her arms around herself again. "You have no idea what it means to grieve my husband, to see him reduced to—" She turned away, but I saw her whole body quaking in the torchlight. "Get me another blanket. I'll sleep in the stall with Neb."

"No!" My heart nearly leapt from my chest. "He could be dangerous. We don't know if he—"

She turned a blazing stare at me. "I'm not asking permission."

The anger had returned, and I couldn't blame her. I looked at Daniel and nodded toward the blanket that was taken from her husband's back. "Give her the blanket. I'll get another from my camel." Returning my attention to Amyitis, I asked, "Do you want anything to eat?"

"No."

Nodding, I left the barn to do as she'd asked. And nothing more than she'd asked. I knew my friend and understood the Medes. They didn't like to be pampered. They were a proud people, and seeing her husband in this state was almost more than she could bear. To the daughter of King Astyages, helplessness was worse than death.

The stable boy was still watering the camels, but he'd unpacked our sedans before beginning the long and taxing chore. I reached for my blanket at the same time I heard my friend's air-splitting scream. Arioch and Daniel began shouting, and I ran to the barn in sheer panic.

Blood. Everywhere. The creature raged and roared inside the stall, smashing against the reinforced walls. Daniel held Amyitis across his lap, pressing a cloth against her left calf, while several other wounds bled through her robe.

"Tend to Arioch!" he shouted, pointing at the commander, who lay with his back against the stall door. A long, deep gash on the inner part of his left bicep gushed blood.

His eyelids fluttered, but I patted his cheek. "Stay with me, Arioch. You can't die. The king would never forgive me if I lost his best friend." I removed my belt and tied it between the wound and his heart, as Gadi had shown me when one of our servants was injured in a riding accident. "And I will never forgive you if we see only the barn of this beautiful estate. Come, now. We must get you inside the villa." I tried to help him to his feet, but he'd lost consciousness.

I glanced Daniel's direction, and he was patting Amyitis's cheek with the same fervency. "My queen? My queen!"

Afraid to ask, I stared at him in silence, waiting for his pronouncement.

"She's fainted, Belili. That's all."

"That's all?" In that moment, I would have given all I owned for a little Median fortitude.

The creature continued roaring, and every shred of courage left me. I fell against Arioch, sobbing. It didn't matter that he couldn't comfort me. It didn't matter that my husband held another woman less than two camel lengths away. All that mattered were my tears, and they would not be stopped.

Everyone slept in the barn on our first night in Borsippa, too exhausted to move. It was a foreshadowing of my life in what was now my third exile.

31

Cut down the tree [Nebuchadnezzar]. . . .
But let the stump and its roots, bound with
iron and bronze, remain in the ground. . . .
Let his mind be changed from that of a
man and let him be given the mind of an
animal, till seven times pass by for him.

—DANIEL 4:14–16

Borsippa

As the first rays of dawn shone into the open
barn doors, I woke to joints and muscles that
ached from yesterday's long journey and my
restless sleep on the dirt floor. The first sound
I heard was the creature's inglorious snoring
inside his stall.

According to Daniel, when Amyitis entered
the stall with her blanket last night, the beast
had become agitated, and the queen feared it
might harm itself. She'd charged inside despite
Arioch's warnings, and the commander threw
himself in the path of the creature's attack to
protect her.

The creature. It. I could almost forgive the
beast, but never Nebuchadnezzar.

Sprawled across my lap, Arioch moaned,

waking Daniel and Amyitis. Our faithful stable boy, who had accompanied us from Babylon, was curled up and still, sleeping soundly on a nearby pile of straw. My attention returned to Daniel, who mouthed "I love you," bringing tears to my eyes.

Before I could respond or even speculate on our dire state, two men appeared at the barn door. Daniel's expression brightened with recognition. "Ezra, Samson. Praise be to Yahweh."

Faces painted with shock and concern, the two men stepped inside. One of them looked at the large eunuch lying across me, then back to Daniel, and then at the queen. "Where is the king?"

These men knew?

"In the stall." Daniel pointed in the direction of the creature's stirring. Their voices must have wakened him. "The king's guard and the queen had some trouble with him last night. We'll need your help moving them to the villa."

"Of course." Both men spoke in unison as if they'd practiced the reply and immediately helped Daniel with Amyitis. Moments later, they returned with Daniel to carry Arioch into our new home. Bearing a strong resemblance to each other, the young men were most certainly brothers. They were likely in their early second decade, too young to have accumulated a bride price through a skilled trade. Had they left their family behind, as we had ours?

Following them out the door, I paused to scan the estate in daylight. The fountain splashed, revealing a spring at its source, and lush green grounds spread in every direction inside a high bricked wall. Poplars grew around a modest villa positioned about twenty camel lengths north of the barn. Between the two structures was a vast orchard, extending farther than my eyes could see, full of fruit trees: apple, pear, pomegranate, and fig. Northeast of the villa lay sprawling fields that looked as if they had recently been harvested—broad beans and barley, no doubt. Would we be planting and harvesting next year's crops?

Daniel and the two young men disappeared into the house with our injured eunuch, and I hurried to catch up. Once inside, I stood in a common room, where we would all likely gather to eat, cook, visit, and generally live as a family. A single hallway extended to the back of the villa, and I caught a glimpse of a deep red robe vanishing inside a door on the right. "Put him in here," said an unfamiliar female voice.

I hurried across the packed dirt floor and down the hall, stopping at the second doorway, and watched as Daniel and the brothers lowered the hulking eunuch to a straw-stuffed mattress on the floor. Arioch moaned pitifully. A dark-haired young woman knelt beside him, wringing out a cloth over a clay bowl of water. She dabbed his forehead, speaking soothing Egyptian words. I recognized them from Mert's ministrations.

Daniel looked up and saw me. "Belili, my love, this is Hasina. She'll help you and Amyitis in the house and fields." He pointed to the broad-shouldered young men while my mind absorbed the word *fields*. "I'm sorry I didn't officially introduce you to Ezra and Samson. These are Solomon's brothers."

"Solomon?" I said, trying to fit all the pieces together.

"Yes, Mistress?" Our stable boy stood behind me, rubbing sleep from his eyes.

My heart softened toward the little man who'd shown great courage during yesterday's journey. "I've just met your brothers."

He ran into the arms of the taller brother. I watched my husband tease and banter with the three boys and ached that I'd given him only daughters. Every man wished for a son. Memories of Allamu came to haunt me on this turbulent morning. My family, now cast upon the four corners of the wind, would grow and change without my direction, without my care. *Yahweh, why have I been forced to give up my children? Am I such a terrible ima?*

Hasina's hand rested on my arm. "Your tears mean you are as good as Master Daniel."

I laughed and shook my head. "No one is as good as Master Daniel."

Her black eyes sparkled, and I liked her immediately. She wasn't Mert, but she was sharp, and I suspected she would feel like family soon in this cramped villa. "In which chamber did you put the queen?"

Hasina pointed. "Down the hall. Last room on the left."

Thinking I should check on my friend, I turned and ran into Amyitis. "What are you doing out of bed?" My tone was sharper than intended.

"Get out of my way. I'm going to see Neb."

I almost snapped back but remembered everyone's nerves were frayed. Pausing to poke my head into Arioch's room, I caught Daniel's attention. "I'm going to accompany Amyitis to the barn."

He gave me a wary frown at the same time Amyitis voiced her objection. "I'm perfectly capable—"

"We've come here to hide Nebuchadnezzar from the world," I said to her, "but we've also come to care for you." I reached for her hands, drawing them both to my lips. "Let me care for you, Amyitis. Let us care for you."

The queen swallowed audibly and nodded. "Thank you." Without another word, she stepped around me, off to see her husband. I followed, casting a triumphant glance at Daniel.

We walked in silence out the door, down the flat-stoned path, and across the courtyard toward the barn. Amyitis limped a little. The wound on her left calf was likely sore this morning. I slowed my steps to match hers and noticed Borsippa's heat rising in waves from the ground. "I'll miss your palace servants with their ostrich-plume fans to keep us cool."

Amyitis choked out a laugh. "I'll miss more than the fans."

There would be no more small talk. The queen hesitated when we reached the barn, bracing herself against the doorframe.

I laid my hand against her back. "Perhaps you should wait before you see him again. Rest a little first."

She shook her head. "Neb gets no rest from this awful curse."

I could have argued, offered facts or logic. But why? When a heart hurts, only another heart can heal it. "I'm with you, whatever you decide."

With a deliberate sigh, she marched into the barn, and I followed. Our eyes adjusted from bright morning sun to the dusty haze of an alley of stalls, where we'd spent our first nightmarish night. Solomon had somehow slipped in before us and was forking soiled straw into a dung pile. When he saw us, he leaned on his pitchfork and bowed to Amyitis.

She stopped beside him, examined the dirty smudges on his cheeks, and lifted his chin, turning it left and then right. "Thank you for helping us yesterday. Shouldn't you get home to your ima?"

"My brothers and me work for Lord Belteshazzar now because my abba owed lots of debt when he died. I lived in Babylon with Ima last year, while she cooked for the Chaldean students. I just found out yesterday I would drive the cart for the king and live here with my brothers." His expression fell. "I'm sorry about the king, and I'm sorry he hurt you. I don't think he meant to."

Amyitis bent and kissed the top of his head. "You're right. He would never harm me intentionally, Solomon." I watched her strength return at the reminder of the truth. She lifted her chin and strode toward Nebuchadnezzar's stall with renewed purpose.

I followed with less enthusiasm and reached for her arm. "Please don't go in there again."

She stopped, staring at the locked wooden door that separated her from the husband she no longer knew. "You saw him on the barge yesterday. He knew me. Last night in the stall was different. He was frightened out of his mind." She turned to face me. "He's still my Neb, Belili. If it was Belteshazzar in there, you would go into the stall."

I released her arm. Would I? My anger and bitterness toward my husband had built steadily during the past year. I'd agreed that Amyitis would need my presence to encourage her through the seven years of hiding and that the king would need his wife's coaxing to admit Yahweh's sovereignty at the end of his judgment. But I was still angry. At Daniel and . . . I couldn't bring myself to admit any negative feelings toward the God who had forgiven my past, wed me to Daniel, and given us four beautiful daughters. How dare I grumble against Him? So my anger smothered Daniel and dimmed the flame of our once-passionate love.

As Amyitis and I neared the stall, we heard a strange grinding, crunching—the creature's chewing. Rising on our toes, we peeked through the iron-barred window and saw him eating a pile of fresh hay. He seemed utterly calm and content. He even glanced at us, pausing before resuming his morning meal.

Amyitis and I exchanged a surprised look. She squeezed my hand, took a deep breath, and unbolted the door. Slowly she crept inside while I stood in the doorway, holding my breath. The creature looked up momentarily but, again, resumed his meal. She eased closer, hand extended, until her fingers barely swept over his coarse black hair. His hide twitched at her touch, but he didn't stop eating. She laid her hand on his side and began stroking. Speaking in soothing tones. Assuring him of her love. Promising him a future.

If it was Belteshazzar . . . I couldn't imagine how I would react if Yahweh had chosen such a judgment to mete out on my husband. Would I see Daniel beyond God's judgment, as Amyitis saw Neb? In our current circumstance, could I love him unconditionally, trusting his proven relationship with Yahweh to be trustworthy and to lead us back to a healthy family? As I stood outside the stall, feeling utterly useless, I considered my husband's purpose for me on this journey. What did my friend need from me at such a dark hour? I heard no Voice from heaven, but I knew what I must do.

Hand shaking on the door, I stepped into the stall with Amyitis and approached the creature she loved. Both looked at me with surprise, and I nearly turned and ran.

My friend held out her hand. "He won't hurt you, Belili."

I took her hand, my heart beating like a thousand chariot horses in my ears.

She drew me close and placed my hand on his side. "Feel that?" I nodded, and she said with a smile, "It's the same heartbeat I heard each night when I laid my head on Neb's chest to fall asleep." She leaned over to press her ear against his side. "He's in there, Belili. My Neb is still there."

32

[The messenger in Nebuchadnezzar's vision said:] "The holy ones declare the verdict, so that the living may know that the Most High is sovereign over all kingdoms on earth and gives them to anyone he wishes and sets over them the lowliest of people.

—DANIEL 4:17

Eleven Months Later

Daniel sat beneath a tamarisk tree, feeling a little guilty about enjoying the cool spring morning with their flock of sheep and goats while Solomon, Ezra, and Samson harvested the broad beans. Adjustment to life on the estate had been more difficult than he'd expected. The first night's disaster had kept Arioch abed for a month, and Amyitis spent most of her first week in the barn with Nebuchadnezzar. Daniel feared Belili might demand to return home, but she stayed, her anger somewhat abated, though he couldn't imagine why. Blisters and open sores plagued Amyitis, Belili, and Daniel for weeks until their hands developed calluses from the long hours of work in the fields, barn, and kitchen.

Even more painful, however, were the frantic letters from their families, at first asking and then demanding they come home. Winter lessened the demands, both families realizing that the snow in the Zagros range would blockade their mothers in Achmetha at least until spring. No doubt, the letters would begin again soon.

Yahweh had provided for all their needs during the first winter in Borsippa, and Ezra and Samson had established key friendships with local merchants to trade for goods in the city market. Their estate's goats provided wool, milk, and cheese for trade, and the sheep provided wool and meat. They'd added ducks to their estate shortly after they arrived that now produced eggs and meat for an occasional celebratory meal. The orchard, fields, and gardens would provide the rest of their fruits, vegetables, and herbs. *Jehovah-jireh, our great Provider.*

Three figures approached in the distance, and Daniel shaded his eyes to see that Arioch accompanied Belili and Amyitis. All three wore simple rough-spun robes with rope belts. Daniel chuckled at the sight of the giant eunuch in a woolen robe and the memory of his first meal in the presence of his queen.

Hasina had insisted they move the round leather mat used for their meals into Arioch's chamber so he could at least join them for their first evening meal together. He lay in his bed, conscious but blurry eyed from the poppy tea Daniel had given him.

"We'll live as a family," Daniel had begun, trying to explain gently that they must all serve one another. "Everyone will be called by first names, not titles." Pointing to each one, he recited the unfamiliar names in case anyone had forgotten since early morning. "Hasina, Solomon, Ezra, Samson, Arioch. I'm Daniel, of course. My wife is Belili, and this is Amyitis."

The queen looked as uncomfortable as her new acquaintances. "I am still Astyages's daughter and queen of Babylon, Lord Belteshazzar."

Daniel's patience with her Median pride had worn thin. "Indeed. But you are also one of seven adults and a stable boy who will tend fields, cook meals, and protect a king's throne. We will all do things we've never done before, *Amyitis*."

Babylon's queen hesitated only a moment before nodding. "It will be as you say, Daniel."

The woman walked toward him now with the same Median resolve, but she could now pluck a duck faster than Hasina. The Egyptian girl had taught them all new talents in house and field, her spunk adding life and joy to the toil and sorrow of this place. Daniel noticed Belili's sober countenance as she drew nearer and saw the same on Arioch and Amyitis. Perhaps everyone would need a generous dose of Hasina's joy today. Daniel raised his hand in silent welcome.

Arioch raised a scroll in return. Belili carried one too. Dread churned in his gut, and he wondered which bad news he should ask for first.

His wife's tears won without hesitation. "Come, my love. What's happened?" Belili faced most of the Borsippa hardships with her jaw set and eyes narrowed for the challenge. Tears meant a new rip in her heart.

"You must do something." She shoved the open scroll into his hand, and he recognized Shesh's familiar scrawl. The first section reiterated the familiar summary of their household with little variation from his last five letters: Mert continued to lie about their true whereabouts; Kezia remained angry at us and the world; Eva and Eden were fine because they had each other; little Gia was despondent and had withdrawn into a world of her own. With the heavy weight of responsibility on his shoulders, Daniel read the last section more carefully:

Nabonidus told the high priest of Marduk that King Nebuchadnezzar had sent him to Borsippa with a large offering to Nabu and his priests in Borsippa. The priests of the Esagila were outraged. Nabonidus has now begun meeting regularly with the high priest to stoke his anger, and I've heard other priests vow their support should the king's son-in-law make a play for the throne. Everyone knows General Nebuzaradan will oppose Nabonidus. But the king's son-in-law has raised support from some in the army. Babylon's streets will run with blood if the king doesn't return soon, Daniel. I beg you. For the safety of your daughters if for no other reason, convince King Nebuchadnezzar to return to Babylon—soon.

Daniel gathered his wife in his arms and nodded at the scroll in Arioch's hand. "Is it from Ashpenaz?" The eunuch nodded once, his silence foreboding. "What does it say?"

"It's as you predicted, Belteshazzar. Nabonidus will make a play for the throne at next month's Akitu festival with the support of Marduk's priests." He paused only a moment. "Since you predicted so accurately, let's hope your plan to stop it proves equally accurate."

Amyitis looked at Arioch, her face a mask of calm. "Tell Ashpenaz he has my permission to kill Nabonidus."

"Amyitis!" Belili lurched from Daniel's arms. "Any instability at the palace will cause bloodshed in the streets and put everyone's family at risk."

Arioch ducked his head to hide a grin. "Though I like your plan, my queen, I must agree with Mistress Belili." He'd never abided by the first-name rule. "We've already coordinated a false military campaign in Canaan with Ashpenaz, who has been communicating the king's locations to key Babylonian officials each month. The ruse has worked for nearly a year, but the Akitu festival draws near, and the whole city grows anxious to celebrate with their king. Ashpenaz has managed to distract the council members by instigating riots in Babylon's outer city and stirring rebellion in the heart of Lydia's king."

"Ashpenaz is starting riots?" Belili's shrill voice frightened sparrows from a nearby tree.

Arioch lifted his brows, challenging her tone. "Yes, and a rebellion in Lydia."

Belili turned to Daniel with an accusing glare. What did she think he'd been doing with the king's seal around his neck? He tugged at the leather string, pulling the engraved stone cylinder from under his robe. "The best way to keep our families safe is to create distractions in other places. It's the essence of war, Belili. You send troops to distant lands so your own family never witnesses the atrocities."

Arioch tapped the leather-bound scroll in his hand. "Ashpenaz says only Nabonidus challenges the king's throne, but if General Nebuzaradan senses the slightest crack in the foundation of Nebuchadnezzar's empire, he'll swoop in like a falcon on a mouse. We need a distraction that can keep all that ambition occupied elsewhere."

"Neb only misses Akitu," Amyitis said, "when he's detained by war. You must start a war, gentlemen." She was as calm as if she'd commented on the weather, but Belili looked like she'd swallowed an egg sideways.

Impressed with the queen's political prowess, Daniel turned his attention to Arioch. "We'll invade Egypt. Ashpenaz reported rumblings of Pharaoh's rebellion to the council in Babylon months ago. It makes sense."

Arioch's slow, deliberate smile showed a war plan already developing. "General Nebuzaradan will lead the campaign, and we can place Nabonidus over his own regiment."

"Nabonidus is a statesman," Daniel scoffed. "Placing him over a regiment is like putting me in command."

"With any luck the Egyptians will kill him for us." Amyitis waved her hand as if dismissing him easily.

Daniel exchanged a hesitant glance with Arioch. Now was the time to tell her who they'd chosen as interim king. "Amyitis, in order to keep the throne secure, we've chosen a man we believe will serve Babylon rather than himself. Someone who can willingly give up the power and glory when Nebuchadnezzar returns to Babylon in six years."

Wary, her eyes shifted from one adviser to the other. "Tell me."

Arioch knelt before her and pressed her hand against his forehead. "We plan to place your daughter's husband, Neriglissar, on the throne." He looked up then, releasing her hand but remaining on his knees. "Your seven sons are fine men, but placing one of them on the throne could cause dissension. Neriglissar is . . ."

"He's a lamb." Amyitis studied Arioch and then Daniel. Surely if she trusted them with her life, she could trust them with her husband's kingdom. She lowered her head and breathed out a sigh. "My son-in-law is as fragile as a flower, but my daughter Kassaya is strong. She rules him, so he can rule Babylon without my sons feeling threatened."

She straightened her robe as if doing so could arrange the scattered kingdom. "I'll tell Neb about your plan. He'll be pleased to know our Kassaya is in charge." She was gone before the two men could respond.

Concerned, Daniel noted his wife's silence during the war deliberations. Was she angry with him again? He'd seemed the object of her wrath quite often recently. He cautiously reached for a single finger, not her whole hand.

She didn't pull away, so he drew her near, and she melted against him. "It feels wrong somehow to thank you for instigating a war in Egypt to protect our family—but thank you." Her voice was strong, not the broken words of weeping.

"War wasn't my first choice, Belili. It was our only choice." He pulled her arms from his neck so he could see her face. "You claim I never say no to our daughters, which requires you to do all the discipline. You're right."

Her look of surprise was almost worth the confession and spurred him on to lay his heart bare. "Part of the reason is as you suspect—because I enjoy being the fun parent since I see them less often—but the greater reason is I fear my judgment could be too harsh. For many years, I spent my days teaching students facts, black and white, right and wrong. After the king's dream, I lived in the world you just witnessed—riots, wars, and trading men's lives for political efficiency. I feared bringing that calculated, unfeeling person into our children's lives. Even worse, applying it to the moment of discipline, a point at which they should see Yahweh's love and mercy reflected in their abba." He brushed away a tear from her cheek with his thumb. "Will you forgive me?"

She nodded emphatically and laid her head on his chest. "Yes, I forgive you, and I must ask for your forgiveness and patience as I continue to sort out my own fears and failures. Only now am I realizing how different are the worlds in which you and I live. While on this estate, you create havoc all over the empire, but my thoughts are consumed with our children almost every moment of every day." As he formed his defense, she placed a finger over his lips, and a sweet smile graced her lovely face. "And I'm sure you have no idea that there's a miracle transpiring in the barn."

"Arioch and I just checked the king this morning. If something is happening . . ." Alarmed, he exchanged a glance with Arioch, who sat beneath a tamarisk tree ten paces away. The guard raced over. "What is it?"

Belili stepped back, her smile gone. "See? Neither of you has witnessed Neb and Amyitis together recently, or you'd know there's nothing to fear." She turned toward the villa and barn, waving over her head. "I'll see you at mealtime."

"Should I go with her?" Arioch asked, watching Belili go. Indecision reared its ugly head, and Daniel hesitated. How many times had Belili assured him, "I don't think he'll ever harm her again." But Nebuchadnezzar was a beast with the mind of one. If he sensed tension or felt fear, he could turn on any perceived threat—including Amyitis.

"No, let her go. I think the king feels safe with Amyitis." Wasn't that the reason they brought the queen to Borsippa? To bolster the king's spirits? During this most terrifying transformation, perhaps he could find strength in the refuge she gave him and confess God's sovereignty at the end of his chaos.

• • •

I left Arioch and my husband to discuss their invasion of Egypt, feeling both relief for their efforts and guilt that my relief would cause others pain. When I'd tearfully read my scroll aloud to Amyitis, her reply had been calm. "Don't worry, Belili. Your husband and Arioch will take care of your family, even as the troops of Babylon have taken care of mine all these years."

It seemed ludicrous to begin a war in Egypt to avoid bloodshed in the street outside my family's villa in Babylon. But to Amyitis, the decision was no more than was expected from a king's wise counselors to protect a throne and empire rightfully his. Would my children ever know the sacrifices made for them? Of course not. Had I ever known the dozens of decisions that kept war from our front door in Babylon? Was it sympathy I felt for kings who made such decisions? Revulsion? Both? And for their wives who must love them, live with them, support them—or at least submit to them—how did they cope with the weight of knowing their children would be first to die in an invasion but were also the cause of so much suffering in their own kingdom and around the world?

Suddenly, Amyitis's love for Nebuchadnezzar seemed almost a sacred thing, and the work Yahweh was doing in their relationship during this incomprehensible testing was nothing short of miraculous. On some level, the creature-king seemed to understand he belonged to her, and he grew agitated if Amyitis was away from the barn too long. It was beautiful and heartrending, glorious and tragic.

I took the path toward the house, planning to fill my pocket with grain to feed the ducks on my way to join Amyitis in the barn.

Hasina met me at the door. "The messenger returned with another scroll. He said it had gotten lost in the bottom of his bag."

Kezia's writing. My heart pattered an irregular beat, and I tucked the scroll into my left pocket. I filled the right pocket with grain as planned and started for the barn. The ducks gathered around me, delighted with a midday snack. When I neared the barn, I heard Amyitis's low murmur. Peering inside, I let my eyes adjust to the dim light and saw she'd led the creature outside its stall to comb its long hair with her favorite ivory comb. He was standing still, mesmerized by her voice.

She stroked first with the comb and followed with her hand to smooth his thick coat. Young Solomon sat in the corner less than two camel lengths from the queen, but he was watching me. As Amyitis's self-appointed guardian, not much escaped him. I smiled and pressed a finger to my lips, sharing my intention to leave my friend and her husband in peace.

I turned toward the house, left to ponder the scroll in my pocket and the strange circumstances in which Yahweh had placed me. Why was I here? Arioch and Daniel pretended to be king. Amyitis calmed the beast. But what about me? Was I merely here as a hired hand, or had we all come to share in Nebuchadnezzar's punishment because we'd somehow participated in his sin? No, I had plenty of my own sins for which to atone.

Rather than return to the house, I took the footpath toward the fields and found a shady spot to read the first scroll addressed only to me from my eldest daughter. Pulling it from my pocket, I broke the seal and braced myself for the venom.

Ima,

My son was born today. His name is Samuel. Mert was there to catch him between my knees since you thought it more important to be with your friend in Achmetha than with me. When you return—if you return—you need not pretend to care about your grandson.

In your last correspondence, you encouraged us to be adults and take care of ourselves. We will heed your advice. Shesh has taken it upon himself to find matches for my sisters. We will inform you of their betrothal dates and weddings.

    You need not write so frequently.
          Kezia

I pressed the missive against my chest, weeping, rocking, grieving the death of my relationships with my daughters. Why couldn't I go home—for even a few days? I knew the answer. Amyitis would never leave Nebuchadnezzar, and I could never leave Amyitis. Our Borsippa refuge was hidden behind a teetering wall of lies built on the assumption that Amyitis and I were together as were Daniel and Nebuchadnezzar. For either Daniel or I to appear at home without the king or queen could raise suspicions and bring Babylon crashing down.

My daughters' faces flashed across my mind's eye and then Ima's face tormented the edges of memory. Though blurred by years of separation, I remembered the most important things about her. At least she locked me out of that chamber in Jerusalem's palace to *save* me. At least she'd said goodbye. But I'd abandoned my girls. No goodbye. No explanation. Every letter was a lie, sent from an estate less than a day's sail from home. How could our absence ever be made right?

Yahweh, what is my purpose in Borsippa?

Surely if You are good, as Daniel insists, we must see something better than riots and war from these months of lying and hiding. What is my part to play in the years to come?

I heard no Voice from the sky. The Man from the fiery furnace didn't appear. I was alone and heard only birdsong in my despair. Tears were my midday meal, and I fell asleep to the sound of my own weeping.

When I woke, my world hadn't changed. The scroll lay pressed between my hand and face like a jagged pillow, leaving marks on my cheek as it had on my heart. I tucked it in my pocket, stood under the tamarisk, and saw Ezra and Samson in the distance, still bent over rows of broad beans. They were good workers. Their parents had raised them well. I pressed my hand against the scroll in my pocket, heart aching afresh. I needed to tell Daniel about our new grandson.

But I felt suddenly drawn to the field. Walking twenty paces north, I inspected the first ground I'd ever tilled and the first seeds I'd sowed. I knelt beside a plant with young beans forming and felt an unexpected awe at the realization that these plants were food for our unlikely family. "Miraculous," I whispered in reverent wonder.

Ezra had explained the multiphased harvest of this particular crop, and it hadn't interested me until this moment. I pulled a single bean off the plant, inspected it, bit off a piece. Tender and sweet. This was the first harvest. We'd harvest as many as we could eat and cook the whole pod before the beans grew large and fibrous. In a few weeks, we'd harvest more, shucking the beans from toughened pods and eat the beans alone or dry them for later use in stews. The tough pods we would trade for silver with a nearby pig farmer to feed his animals through the hot summer when grass was scarce.

I scanned the field, imagining baskets and baskets of beans, our harvest complete. Some we would sell. Most would provide our sustenance through the summer, fall, and winter. In the last step we would chop the stripped plants and turn over the soil. The plants and dirt would become one as time prepared the land for next season's tilling.

I bit off another small piece of tender pod, tasting the first fruits of our labor—my labor. Perhaps this was part of my purpose, to experience the process. In Babylon, I lived what felt like a rather fruitless routine, oblivious to plan and process. I plodded from one day to the next. I woke every morning to dress and primp. My daughters did the same. Servants tended us, and we helped with some household tasks. But where was the greater purpose—seeing a seedling from start to finish?

Yahweh's plan for His people had seasons—

sowing, growing, harvest, and rest. Had I ever pondered my relationships in the context of their seasons? I thought of our new grandson, Samuel. I had missed his birth, but Daniel and I would water and tend that little seedling from the moment we returned home to the day we left this earth. Had I ever tilled up the rotten fruit of my past to prepare for a life of healthy new growth? Could the anticipation of future seasons lift the heaviness I felt about more years in Borsippa?

I fell to my knees and dug my fingers into the rich dark soil. *Yahweh, Master Gardener and Creator of all things, I plant, but You water. I hoe, but You stretch the plants tall with the warmth of the sun. I wait for harvest until You kiss each crop with perfect ripeness. Forgive me for trying to plant my life on the rotten remains of unconfessed sin. Give me a new planting, Yahweh, a new sowing, growing, reaping, and resting with my family when we return.*

I lifted my face to the sun and bit off more of the tender pod. The sweet, earthy taste satisfied me completely. Standing, I inhaled a cleansing breath and set out toward the villa with new determination. I would become a student of process on this estate. I would sow seeds in the lives of my new Borsippa family and become more aware of what seeds Yahweh was sowing in me. The Master Gardener had much to teach me. *Speak, Lord, Your servant is listening.*

33

I, Nebuchadnezzar, raised my eyes toward heaven, and my sanity was restored. Then I praised the Most High; I honored and glorified him who lives forever.

—DANIEL 4:34

Six Years Later
563 BC

Amyitis and I needed the warm spring sun to lift our spirits this morning. I woke, desperately missing my girls, and remembered the letter we received last fall about our youngest daughter's wedding and pregnancy. "Gia has almost certainly given birth by now," I said, my voice nasal and pathetic.

"Do you know what day this is?"

Surprised by Amyitis's distraction, I found her staring at Neb. Had we planned a walk with him and I'd forgotten? Since our lives were dictated by weather and crops, I looked to the sky. Clear. We would undoubtedly work the fields this morning, harvesting a few early broad beans and whatever onions were ready, but we could walk this aft—

Reality struck like a bolt of lightning. "Today! Today marks the seventh year."

"He didn't come back to me, Belili." She turned her head slowly, showing me the enormity of her accusation. "Yahweh changed Neb at dawn seven years ago but didn't restore him as He promised."

I opened my mouth to speak, but all words drowned in the depths of her despair. Wrapping my arms around her, I held her. Both of us dry eyed. Wondering in silence.

As if sensing the unease, Neb lumbered over to our shady spot and nudged Amyitis's shoulder. He'd become as meek as a lamb under her years of love and care. Still a terrifying sight, he was now loved by us all, and my heart ached at the thought that he could remain like this forever.

Yahweh, please. Restore him—as You've promised.

Even as the prayer winged heavenward, peace settled in my spirit. Didn't the prophet Isaiah say Yahweh's thoughts and ways are higher than ours? Feeling an inner nudge to recount some of the promises Amyitis and I had discussed over the years, I pulled from her embrace. "Who can know Yahweh's plan, Amyitis? Were God's promises to Abraham, Isaac, and Jacob fulfilled in ways they expected?"

Hesitating at first, she laid her hand on her husband's elongated face and caressed his jaw.

"No, I suppose Yahweh can fulfill His promise in unforeseen ways." Pressing her forehead against Neb's neck, she let tears fall. "Belili, do you think . . . I mean, when I said . . ."

"What?"

"When we left Babylon, I told Daniel I would never forgive Yahweh for what He'd done." She raised her head, tears streaking the dust on her cheeks. "I didn't know the stories of Yahweh's love in the midst of discipline, His faithfulness to complete all He begins. I didn't know Him then." She covered her face. "Will He punish Neb for my—"

"No, Amyitis." I gathered her in my arms. "Yahweh is not capricious. He knows our hearts better than we know ourselves."

A huffing sound drew my attention, and I peered at the creature who had once been King of the Earth. Neb was growing agitated, tossing his head, no doubt sensing his beloved's angst. Though he'd become calm and gentle under her care, he was still capable of unspeakable violence.

"Amyitis, I think Neb needs calming."

She wiped her eyes with a sleeve, gathering her emotions like a tattered robe. "I must be patient. The seven years could mean anytime. Yahweh doesn't use some cosmic water clock." We both smiled at her attempted humor until a thunderous thud launched us to our feet.

"Neb!" Amyitis shouted. Her husband had collapsed on his side, panting and shaking.

"Daniel! Arioch!" I screamed, running. They came from the barn with Ezra, Samson, and Solomon. Hasina emerged from the house, and I shouted, "Bring the herb basket and honey, Hasina. Something's wrong with Neb." I hurried back, asking Yahweh what could have caused Neb's collapse. A poisonous plant could have induced trembling and weakness. Had we been remiss in pruning and left a dogbane bush in his path?

The others reached me, and we must have all caught a glimpse of Amyitis at the same moment. Everyone stopped short. Rooted to the ground. The queen sat on the ground, gently stroking a man's face.

"Nebuchadnezzar." Daniel uttered the name on a breath. The rest of us stood in silent horror.

The misshapen face of a man we once knew protruded from the body of a creature we'd known for seven years. He lay still while his wife spoke quietly—too quietly for us to hear. When he tried to speak, we heard only a roar. His eyes grew wide with terror, but Amyitis continued stroking his overgrown beard and tangled curly hair. Calming. Soothing.

Arioch took a step toward them. "I must help him."

"No." Daniel stepped in front of him, meeting

his stare with a gentle hand against the big man's chest. "Remember what Yahweh said. The king will be restored only when he acknowledges that the Most High is sovereign over all kingdoms of the earth and gives them to whomever He wills."

The eunuch glanced at his king, part beast, part man. "Nebuchadnezzar will never. He knows it is the power of Marduk and men that delivers kingdoms into our hands."

"I believe you're wrong, Arioch." Daniel stepped aside, watching. "Amyitis believes Yahweh is who He says He is. If the king hears the truth from her lips, he might just believe it."

Seven of us stood thirty paces away, gawking at the strangest sight on earth, holding our collective breath. Eavesdropping on soft whispers was excruciating, thinking I heard the grass growing or a bird's flapping but not a word of the conversation that would determine our future. Every time the king roared, my heart fell, sensing his determination to refuse the truth.

Daniel's arm slipped around my shoulder, and he pulled me close. "It's because of your obedience that King Nebuchadnezzar is hearing the truth right now, my love. Because you spoke of Yahweh to your friend."

The memory of my day in the broad-bean field came rushing back, and emotions instantly prickled my cheeks. *Yahweh, how far we've come, You and me.* Though I would never wish to relive the seven years and was anxious to leave Borsippa forever, my relationship with Yahweh—and with these people—had grown in ways I could never have imagined.

The king's guttural roar startled me, a mournful cry building to an exultant "Ahhh . . . I . . . aaaacknowledge You, God Most High! Sovereign God over all the earth. Your dominion is eternal. Your kingdom endures for all generations, and I will not say to You, 'Why have You done this thing?'" Curling into a ball like a newborn, the creature groaned and shrieked. He rolled to his hands and knees—yes, hands and knees.

Hasina and I turned away from his nakedness while the men covered him with one of their cloaks. Amyitis cried and rocked and sang praises to Yahweh. I hugged Hasina, joining Amyitis in the songs of David I'd taught her. Even Hasina joined us, surprising me at how much she'd picked up by quietly listening.

"My king, can you hear me?" Arioch was first to test his master.

All fell silent.

Hasina and I found the king covered and clear eyed, staring at his wife. "I hear you, Arioch, but it was Amyitis's voice that offered the only light in my living death." He pulled her into a fierce embrace, their weeping like a melody sung in harmony.

I knew then I was witnessing pure and

unconditional love. A life lived for another without demands or regrets. Yahweh made only one Amyitis.

"Come," I said to the six other gawkers. "Leave them to refresh their love. They deserve all this day can give them."

Arioch returned to the barn with all three brothers to gather the things we needed for our return home. Daniel and I changed into new robes, preparing for our first visit to Babylon in seven years. We would need new clothes for the royal couple and ourselves before sailing the half day's journey to resume our lives.

Hasina would remain at the villa for as long as she wished. Daniel had erased the three brothers' family debt last year, but Solomon refused to leave Amyitis. I suspected Ezra had his eye on Hasina for a wife, but I couldn't guess when he'd gather the courage to ask her.

The king and queen returned to the villa late that afternoon looking like newlyweds emerging from their wedding chamber, their countenances glowing with joy—and a little shyness at our teasing. Although the king's raven-black hair was now streaked with gray, he was still as handsome and as imposing as ever. He kissed his wife's forehead, and her cheeks bloomed like roses. He stood in the doorway, watching as she sat on a low stool beside Hasina and lifted a hand mill into her lap. She reached into the sack of last year's barley and filled the small trough to begin grinding for this evening's bread.

"What are you doing?" His loving glow turned to a glower.

"I'm grinding grain for this evening's bread." She met his disdain with her typical mettle. "Would you rather do it?"

His answer was a short huff before stomping through the kitchen toward the dining table, where Daniel and Arioch prepared for the imminent storm.

The king jabbed both fists at his waist and aimed his ire at my husband. "While your God made His point, you made my wife a slave?"

"While the one God revealed Himself to you, we've taken care of you—and each other."

Nebuchadnezzar's fury drained like the silent tears of a child. He noticed the trading silver and financial scrolls spread out on the dining table. "What's this?" His fingers skimmed the columns of numbers, realization darkening his features. "This is all we have to buy our supplies to return to Babylon?"

Arioch started to answer, but Daniel lifted his hand, silencing him. "It is enough for tomorrow's purchases in Borsippa and the following day's journey to Babylon." He reached up to place a hand on the man's shoulder. "Yahweh said He would restore you to your kingdom. Trust Him."

PART 3

Daniel prospered during the reign of Darius and the reign of Cyrus the Persian.
—DANIEL 6:28

34

Hear, O Israel: The LORD our God, the
LORD is one. Love the LORD your God
with all your heart and with all your
soul and with all your strength. These
commandments that I give you today are
to be on your hearts. Impress them on
your children. Talk about them when you
sit at home and when you walk along the
road, when you lie down and when you
get up.

—DEUTERONOMY 6:4–7

October 539 BC

My son arrived for the evening meal at dusk,
escorted by twenty of General Gubaru's men,
ready to move our few personal items to the new
villa on palace grounds.

I bowed and addressed the soldiers in their
native tongue. "We're honored you've come with
Lord Allamu. Please join us for a simple meal
we've prepared in his honor."

Allamu marched past me through the iron
gate. "My men will wait in the street until we've
finished eating." His personal guard followed
him, and I started to apologize to the others,

but they'd already formed two straight lines, a human pathway leading to two lavish palanquins. Allamu obviously hoped to avoid a leisurely evening. I was shamefully relieved.

Scooting around his guard, I caught up to him and kept my voice low. "Please don't cause trouble tonight."

He halted abruptly when we reached the tables where the rest of the family waited. "Why is Mert still serving after all these years?" His tone was more command than question. "She should be treated as family." In less than five strides, he crossed the room and reached for the tray of fruit and cheese my friend was holding.

"Go sit down." Mert slapped his hands away and nudged him toward the empty cushion between mine and Shesh's. "Who do you think you are, walking into this house shouting orders? I'd rather slit my own throat than sit in this stuffy courtyard with the lot of you!" Mert slammed down the tray and marched back to the cooking fire.

I ducked my head and glanced at our guest. Allamu grinned at Daniel, cheeks flushed. "I suppose I deserved that."

"Yes, you did." Daniel looked around at the family before him. "Could we all lay aside our ragged emotions and simply get to know each other this evening?" Wary nods soothed a few harsh expressions, and Allamu settled on the cushion we'd reserved for him. His bodyguard stood like a pillar behind him. "Good. Good," Daniel said. "Belili, my love, would you begin our meal by giving Yahweh thanks for His provision?"

With a timid smile, I turned on my pillow toward Jerusalem, closed my eyes, and began the familiar refrain. "Hear, O Israel: The LORD our God, the LORD is one. Love the LORD your God with all your heart." The words felt sweet on my tongue until "serve Him only and take your oaths in His name—" My breath caught, robbing my mouth of moisture. Allamu's stare felt like a flame on my cheek.

Daniel's hand covered mine. "What is it, love?"

"Nothing. I'm sorry. I—"

"Perhaps she's forgotten the words." Allamu's tone was cynical. "Am I to assume it had something to do with keeping oaths?"

"I didn't forget. I will take oaths *only* in Yahweh's name." I met his mocking smile and saw the angry boy who crept out of our villa without a goodbye. My heart constricted. I couldn't blot out the damage I'd done in Allamu's early years, but I could begin to change our relationship tonight—as well as the relationship I'd lost with my girls.

I offered a meaningful glance to each of my daughters before sharing a piece of my heart they'd never heard before. "When I lived with the Medes, I learned about their god Mithra. Worshippers presented *oaths* with their sacrifices that made the oaths binding. I stuttered over my prayer tonight because Allamu's presence reminded me of those days in Media and how thankful I am to worship Yahweh, who is completely sufficient in all things—even oaths."

Allamu lifted a single brow, and I waited, certain he'd reveal my darkest secret. At that moment, it barely mattered, so light was my heart at the joy I saw on Daniel's face. My husband was proud of me, and I, too, felt as if the wind of God's pleasure had breathed on me during my strong witness to our family. Those opportunities had been few since our return from Borsippa twenty-four years ago.

Shesh broke the uncomfortable silence. "Shall we begin our meal now?" He picked up the tray Mert had deposited on the table. "Would your guard like to join us?" He turned to address him. "I'm sorry. What was your name?"

The man bowed and offered a pleasant smile. "I am Zerubbabel ben Shealtiel, grandson of Jehoiachin."

"King Jehoiachin—my cousin?" Daniel choked on his first bite of lentil stew.

"Indeed." Zerubbabel bowed again, a faint grin cracking his granite countenance.

"Please, join us!" Daniel wiped the stew from

his beard. "I must hear how you became Allamu's friend."

"Forgive me, Lord Belteshazzar," he said, "but it's not a story worth telling. Please continue with your meal as if I'm one of the lovely trees in your courtyard." He averted his gaze and stared straight ahead at a distant nothing, affirming his decision to end the conversation.

Shesh exchanged an intrigued smirk with Daniel and returned his attention to Allamu. "Perhaps we could speak more with your guard at a later time. Tonight, we're anxious to know you better, Allamu, and help you know us. My wife, Kezia, is Daniel and Belili's firstborn, and I work as a scribe at the Esagila. Please let me know if I might be of service to the new administration. I believe you'll find most of the citizens in Babylon are relieved to see the end of Belshazzar's reign. We're all anxious to know more about our new ruler."

My son-in-law had honed his gift of peacemaking to a fine tip by mediating between Kezia and me. Remarkably, the conversation turned safer when it veered into politics.

"King Cyrus has a good plan for Babylon," my son said without hesitation. "He and the general trust each other implicitly, and you'll find Gubaru far more reasonable than the rumors we heard of your King Belshazzar."

Daniel leaned forward. "So Cyrus and General

Gubaru will reign in Babylon as co-regents without the arrogance of either man causing a power play?"

"They will not be co-regents," Allamu said. "Let there be no mistake, Lord Belteshazzar. We will all serve Cyrus the Great, sole ruler of the Persian empire, but he will give Gubaru, the Mede, oversight of the Babylonian province."

I saw the concern wrinkle Daniel's brow, but I had my own concerns. "What will Daniel's role be, Allamu? He's not as strong as he once was. He gets tired if—"

"I don't know Gubaru's plan," Allamu interrupted. "Are you capable of serving on the high council, Lord Belteshazzar?"

Without hesitation, Daniel inclined his head. "I would not dishonor you by offering less than my best after you graciously spoke on my behalf."

Seeming unnerved by my husband's respect, he stood in a sudden rant. "Was I invited tonight simply to gain information about your new rulers?" Even his stone-faced guard raised a brow. What had we said to make him so angry?

"Please, Allamu, don't go." I was afraid he'd leave, angry and disappointed again.

Mert and three other maids carried in the meal. My friend shoved a tray into my son's hands with a mischievous grin. "Thank you, Allamu. We don't usually allow the guest of honor to help serve, but since you've offered . . ." She scurried away before he could protest, her brashness once again snapping the tension. Zerubbabel bowed his head to hide a laugh.

Kezia rose from her place and took the tray from him. "Has she always been this rude," she asked, "or is it getting worse as she gets older?" They shared a brief grin, and my heart sang.

"Please, Allamu." Daniel extended his hand to his empty cushion. "We invited you because you're a part of our family."

My son glanced at his guard, and the man raised both brows as if challenging him. Some understanding passed between them, and when Allamu turned back to Daniel, I saw resolve had replaced his anger. Why would my son consider the opinion of a servant before making a decision? He obviously respected Zerubbabel, a Hebrew. I determined then to find out more about the man who guarded my son.

Allamu resumed his seat. "I have no need of a family, Lord Belteshazzar. For years, I served King Astyages until his grandson, Cyrus, marched against Achmetha and made the Medes errand boys of the Persians. Family betrays." He laughed, seeming to have surprised even himself with the transparency. Lifting his goblet as if toasting, he added, "My life is dedicated to King Cyrus and ensuring the traditions of the Magoi tribe live forever." He took a few long, slow gulps of our strongest wine.

Kezia reached for her wine and prompted her sisters. "Perhaps we should all drink to Allamu's sentiment. I think we can all agree." She lifted her goblet. "Family betrays."

Allamu pointed at Kezia with his goblet, sloshing a little wine on the table, and I exchanged a glance with my husband. There could be no better introduction for our confession.

He lifted his goblet and nodded at me to do the same. "Let's drink to the poor parenting choices that have left all our lives in shambles." Daniel took a gulp and I a quick sip, but our offspring were too surprised to join us.

Allamu looked like a cat that had just spied a mouse. "Surely you haven't made parenting mistakes, Lord Belteshazzar."

"Every parent makes mistakes, Allamu. The difference between healthy adults and broken ones is the willingness of parents to apologize." He turned his attention to our four daughters and their husbands. "Shortly after Shesh and Kezia were married, your ima and I abandoned our family for seven years. We apologized when we returned yet said nothing more. Because we were bound by honor to King Nebuchadnezzar, we couldn't reveal the truth, so our apologies were empty. After Nebuchadnezzar died, the upheaval in the royal family and our need to hide Amyitis from the warring factions made it necessary to continue the ruse."

Shesh shrugged. "You were on a military campaign with King Nebuchadnezzar. It's understandable that you couldn't share more detail."

Kezia cast a searing gaze at me. "It was Ima who chose to be with Queen Amyitis in Achmetha instead of—"

"Your ima and I were together," Daniel said, "hiding the king and queen at an estate we own in Borsippa." Our children couldn't have appeared more shocked if I'd stripped naked. Daniel lifted his goblet again. "Until I revealed the secret at Belshazzar's banquet, we'd never told a living soul, but it's finally safe to tell you the truth."

Shesh was first to recover. "Why would you hide Nebuchadnezzar and Amyitis? And why so secretive about an estate in Borsippa?"

Daniel cleared his throat before beginning the explanation. Starting with the king's dream and its meaning, he began to describe Nebuchadnezzar's transformation.

Our children's mouths gaped as the details unfolded. "He had talons and attacked the queen?" Kezia grimaced. "It sounds like his appearance became as hideous as his essence."

Daniel looked at our daughter with the shock

I felt. "I think that describes his condition profoundly, Kezia. He was in every way the most piteous creature I'd ever seen."

"Why would you help him, Abba?" she asked. "He destroyed Jerusalem, killed its royal family—your family. He treated you horribly."

I happened a glance at Allamu's guard, whose stare nearly burned a hole through my husband. It seemed he, too, waited to hear. Even after all these years, I still didn't understand why Daniel had insisted we must care for them. I knew what it was like for a girl to grow up without an ima. They would celebrate every first with a stab of longing. I'd experienced it my whole life. For our girls, every first reminded them of an ima who'd chosen her best friend over them.

Daniel lifted his head, tears on his cheeks. "At the time, I thought by helping Nebuchadnezzar, I was serving Yahweh. But now?" He gave a self-deprecating grin. "Now I realize I did it to see Nebuchadnezzar suffer and prove myself right."

"Prove yourself right?" Kezia stared at her abba as if seeing a stranger. "Right about what?"

"Right for hating him." Even I was stunned by my husband's rawness. "I wanted to be the first face he saw when—if—Yahweh restored his mind, so he would be humiliated before me and never mistreat me again."

"Did he?" Even Allamu seemed drawn in by my husband's confession. "Mistreat you, I mean, after he was restored?"

Regaining some of his tenderness, Daniel nodded. "He did, but somehow it mattered less."

"You let the man who ruined your childhood ruin ours as well?" Kezia's voice trembled with rage, her eyes lit with indignation. "I could believe Ima's heart so cold, but yours?"

He braced both elbows on the table and leaned toward our eldest daughter. "Your ima begged me to stay in Babylon and let others care for the king and queen, but I refused to listen." He slowly met each of our daughters' eyes as he spoke. "Since my vision this morning, I've pondered the time I wasted during my life in exile. Why so many long nights away from my family? Why such striving for things of no eternal value? Why didn't I focus more on the census records, teaching the Law, and making more written copies of our sacred texts?" Clenching his fists, he let out a growl. "If only I'd been more faithful, we could be better prepared when the remnant returns to Jerusalem."

Allamu's brows shot up. "Why would anyone go back to Jerusalem?" I heard warning in my son's voice and prayed Daniel would use wisdom.

He paused before answering, which was a good sign. "After you and Belili left the chamber this morning, a heavenly being appeared to me." Allamu grinned and rolled his eyes. Daniel continued, undaunted by his skepticism. "His name was Gabriel, and he confirmed that a remnant of our people will soon return to Jerusalem, where they'll rebuild both the city and Yahweh's Temple."

My son laughed now, looking to his siblings for support. "He must be joking." Then back at Daniel. "Tell me you're joking."

"I'm quite serious."

"Jerusalem is a jackals' haunt. It will never be inhabited again."

Daniel smiled patiently. "Gabriel disagrees."

Allamu sobered. "Do you have any idea how much planning and wealth would need to be—"

"Actually," Daniel interrupted, "I was hoping, since you've spent time in the highest echelons of Median and Persian royalty, you could tell us if you've seen a golden box that was taken from Yahweh's Temple during one of the attacks on Jerusalem. We Hebrews call it the Ark of the Covenant and believe God's presence rests on its lid between two replicas of cherubim."

Allamu's eyes narrowed. "How small is your god if he rested on a box and allowed himself to be stolen?"

No one was laughing now, but Daniel still offered a gracious smile. "Grant me a few moments to compare our gods, will you?"

Allamu nodded and spread both hands, as if giving Daniel permission to make his futile attempt.

"As chief magus, you rely on the stars to guide you in decisions, and though I've heard only whispers of Mithraic rituals, I suspect their priests—like many others—rely on omens, animal entrails, and casting lots to make predictions."

"Yes, I rely on the stars," Allamu conceded, "and I'm not at liberty to discuss the rituals of Mithra shared with me by a high priestess when I was a boy." He shifted his attention to me. "You remember that woman, don't you, Mother?" Without giving me time to answer, he spoke again to Daniel. "What does any of this have to do with Hebrews returning to Jerusalem?"

"As followers of Yahweh," Daniel said without distraction, "we don't rely on stars or sheep guts to reveal God's will. We rely on Yahweh to reveal Himself, to speak, to draw nearer as we walk with Him in the process. For centuries, our people have kept meticulous records of their experiences with El Shaddai, and centuries-old prophecies predicted both our exile from Jerusalem to Babylon and our return. I showed you one of those ancient scrolls this morning while you were with me in our chamber. Do you remember?"

Allamu sighed, making no effort to hide his

disinterest. "Yes, I remember. From a prophet Joseph or something."

"The prophet Jeremiah. I picked up a scroll at random—or so I thought—and turned to the exact passage referring to the exiles' return from Babylon. Moments after you left with your mother, I was caught up in a vision, Allamu." He leaned closer. "I know the Magoi give special credence to dreams and visions, so this should give the validation you need to believe me when I say I am certain a remnant will return to rebuild both Jerusalem and Yahweh's Temple. I'm asking you, Allamu, will you help us locate the Ark?"

Every eye was focused on him, and I held my breath, watching Daniel's words etch hard lines into my son's face.

Allamu stood, bumping the table and nearly knocking over everyone's wine. "It's getting late. Have you packed all the items you wish to move to the palace villa?" Without waiting for an answer, he bowed to those still seated. "Thank you for allowing me to invade your family gathering." Zerubbabel's gaze remained on the distant nothing.

I stood slowly with a heavy heart. "I hope you'll join us again someti—"

"We should settle you in the new villa quickly if you hope to get a decent night's rest. General Gubaru will expect Lord Belteshazzar in the throne room by dawn. I'll fetch the guards and send them upstairs." He bowed curtly, suspending all but official conversation, then hustled out of the courtyard. Zerubbabel followed without a backward glance.

Daniel and I excused ourselves from the meal and started toward the stairs. Mert waited for us at the rail. "I suspect the evening didn't go as you'd hoped," she said. "I also suspect you're leaving me to care for your tribe again." She shook her head and started up the stairs ahead of us.

Stricken, I pressed my palm against my forehead. I hadn't even talked with her about staying here when Daniel and I moved to palace grounds. Allamu said servants would be provided for Daniel and me. With the distractions, I'd neglected to consult her, assuming she'd want to stay with Kezia and Shesh.

Hurrying to catch up, I tried to explain. "I'm sorry, Mert. I should have at least—"

"I'm not angry, Belili. I love the children, and I wanted to stay." Quirking one side of her mouth, she added, "Not that anyone asked." She placed a kiss on her palm, transferred it to my cheek, and continued up the stairs ahead of me.

I watched her go, feeling both relief and sorrow that she would stay behind with Kezia again. She was the glue that held our family together.

Daniel met me on the stairs. "That woman may be Yahweh's greatest blessing and His most persistent test."

He took my hand, and we continued to our chamber with lighter hearts, finding it as we'd left it. Stark and impersonal with a pile of baskets, bags, and wooden boxes piled near the doorway. Allamu came charging in shortly after us, leading twenty strangers into the most intimate room of our home.

"Is this all?" He pointed to the small pile we'd prepared. "I won't send another contingent of guards to move things you've forgotten."

"Yes, Allamu. We've packed all we need." I breathed slowly to control my annoyance, while he followed his men downstairs to lead them to our new villa.

I stopped a guard before he grabbed the last basket, and I opened the lid. Mert peered inside with me. "What are you looking for?"

I withdrew Allamu's baby shoes, placing them in the large pocket of my robe. "Right now, I need a reminder of the boy I loved to soften the edges of a man I don't like."

35

Now, our God, hear the prayers and petitions of your servant. For your sake, Lord, look with favor on your desolate sanctuary. . . . Open your eyes and see the desolation of the city that bears your Name. We do not make requests of you because we are righteous, but because of your great mercy. Lord, listen! Lord, forgive! Lord, hear and act! For your sake, my God, do not delay, because your city and your people bear your Name.

—DANIEL 9:17–19

A week on General Gubaru's royal council—up before dawn and home after dark—and Daniel could barely drag his weary bones home from the palace each night. Tonight, Allamu sent the king's guard, Zerubbabel, as his escort, but Daniel suspected he was sent as a human walking stick. Daniel was grateful. The man carried a lamp to light their way in one hand, and Daniel leaned on his other arm.

"I've never felt so old in my life." His voice echoed in the narrow street leading to their palace villa, lined on both sides with multistoried buildings. His journey home was dark and discouraging after a day of noblemen's grousing. "Do you suppose every royal council is the same, Zerubbabel? Does every empire complain of too little wealth, too many beggars, and unreasonable enemies?"

The man chuckled, a rough, rolling noise like a child's ball on a cobblestoned street. "I've witnessed three royal councils: Astyages's, Cyrus's, and now Gubaru's. So far, yes. They all worry about the exact same things." His teeth shone bright white amid a bushy dark-brown beard, and a dimple made him look quite boyish, though he was as wide as a mule was tall.

"You hardly look old enough to have served three masters."

He gave Daniel a sidelong glance. "Are you trying to flatter me so you can offer me an ugly daughter you've hidden somewhere?"

"No, no! Four daughters are enough, and they're all happily married." They walked a little farther, and Zerubbabel remained silent. Daniel wasn't so easily put off. "So, how have you managed to serve three masters at such a young age?"

His smile dimmed, but a slight indentation of that dimple remained. "I don't often tell my story. Why should I tell you, Lord Belteshazzar?"

"Because I'm a nosy old man, and perhaps I'll forget by tomorrow."

He considered his reply carefully before he spoke. "I grew up in Erech. My abba and your friend Abednego were like brothers. They spoke of you often, almost as often as they spoke of Yahweh." He glanced down at Daniel and seemed pleased at the shock on his face. "I was fourteen when I rebelled against their teaching and went to Susa to follow my dream of joining the great armies of the East. I rose quickly through the ranks and found my way into palace service in Achmetha during the last days of King Astyages."

"When Cyrus betrayed him."

Zerubbabel stopped abruptly, halting Daniel with him. "That's what you've been told, but I assure you, it was Astyages who betrayed his grandson. Cyrus simply made him regret it."

"I see." Indeed, Daniel saw many things in this soldier's past. A passion for justice. Deep loyalty. And an intentional rejection of Yahweh's truth. "May I ask what made you rebel against the teachings of Yahweh?"

He secured Daniel's arm around his and continued their journey. "I was a foolish boy with wanderlust in my blood. Isn't that enough?"

"Have you ever returned to Yahweh?"

"What is there to return to, Lord Belteshazzar?" They reached the garden gate of Daniel's villa, and the burly soldier met him eye to eye. "I've seen Jerusalem in my military travels. Allamu was right. It's a jackals' haunt. Where would I worship the true God when there is no Temple?"

Zerubbabel opened the iron gate. "You should go inside, my lord. It appears you have guests." He was finished talking of Yahweh.

Lights from the courtyard braziers streamed into the dark street, and the sounds of laughter reached them. Daniel wanted to talk more with his new friend, excited to find a true believer among General Gubaru's men, but curiosity drew him. The courtyard was usually dark, with Belili waiting in their bedchamber by now. "Please come in and join us, Zerubbabel. Whoever it is, I'm sure we'll have enough for one more."

Zerubbabel bowed. "Thank you for your kindness, but I must return. I've promised to beat Allamu at another drinking game."

Still contemplating the intriguing character, Daniel entered the gate and passed the sprouting plants in their garden to the heart-stirring sound of his children. He stood in the shadow of a tamarisk tree and watched all four daughters and their husbands teasing one another and telling stories, while Belili watched with a contented smile. Shesh sat beside Belili, and Kezia beside him. Their eldest daughter always placed herself so she needn't meet her ima's gaze.

Their youngest, Gia, seemed most comfortable with her ima and began relating a childhood memory of harp lessons. "For everyone's health, I practiced my harp while Mert taught the other girls to cook. I still can't boil water."

"That's not true." Belili patted her knee. "You've become a very good cook—but still a better harp player." Everyone exploded with laughter.

Daniel stepped from behind the tree and opened his arms wide. "What a wonderful surprise!" His children hurried from their cushions to greet him, while Belili remained seated.

She tilted her head up when he approached, eyes sparkling. "Our children brought the evening meal to share with me." Her eyes grew moist. "Wasn't that thoughtful?"

Daniel kissed the top of her head and sat beside her. All the splendid chatter fell to silence. "Please don't let me stop your storytelling. You were having such a pleasant visit."

"Actually, Abba," Shesh, the family spokesman, began, "we brought the meal for Ima because she'd been eating alone all week, but we also wanted to learn more about your vision."

Daniel felt the renewed guilt of a scattered focus. Once again he'd let his position as a councilman steal his thoughts every waking moment. He couldn't define his schedule, but he did have reign over his thoughts—and he'd failed to focus on family and eternal matters as often as he ought. "Of course, yes. Let's make a plan. What do you have in mind, Shesh?"

Shesh exchanged uneasy glances with his brothers-in-law. "We'd like to discuss your idea of exiles rebuilding Jerusalem and the Temple. We don't see how that's feasible. We've been thinking. You've been here sixty-six years, which means by Jeremiah's prophecy, the Temple will be rebuilt within four years. Who would make such a decision—Cyrus or Gubaru? How would such a project be financed, especially the vast resources needed to rebuild the Temple?" He left his couch and knelt before Daniel. "Do you see how far-fetched a return to Jerusalem seems, Abba?"

The weariness of his day returned, and Daniel longed for his bed and a cup of hot spiced wine. He sensed Belili's tension and didn't dare look at her. If she lost her temper and defended him, she could forfeit the healing they'd gained through tonight's laughter. He remembered Zerubbabel's comment, that he'd seen Jerusalem, the wilderness it had become. Was it harder for Daniel himself to believe the vision or his children who had *never* seen God's chosen city?

Affixing his most patient expression, he met Shesh's concerns with the truth. "You're absolutely right. The vision is entirely far-fetched. It's unreasonable to imagine that an empire on seemingly wobbly legs can stand, let alone gather resources and allocate them to a small band of foreigners to rebuild an extravagant Temple to their invisible God." Daniel let his family rest in their satisfaction just long enough to unseat them with his next words. "And that's exactly the circumstance in which Yahweh works best. Don't you understand? If *we* could organize the path to take, we wouldn't need a miracle-working God to create it."

He placed his arm around Belili's shoulders and drew her near. "We've seen Yahweh do impossible things, which has strengthened our faith to endure more impossible things. We've grown spoiled and lazy in our freedoms, making us afraid to trust Yahweh for the uncomfortable." Daniel felt energized after his speech, but when he searched his children's faces for signs of faith or resolve, he found none.

Shesh had donned his mask of patience for Daniel. "Abba, we know Yahweh can do miracles. We just don't want you to hold on to a childhood dream and be disappointed at this stage of your life."

Daniel wanted to laugh—and cry. "Disappointment is the bridge to awe, my son. I've witnessed too much of Yahweh's power in my life to ever be disappointed again," he said. "I've felt His presence when He reveals a dream or vision. I saw Him standing in a brick furnace with my three best friends. And I watched Yahweh transform an arrogant king into a beast and then turn him into a ruler who acknowledged his limitations. It has never been Yahweh who disappointed me, Sheshbazzar."

With those words, he stood and offered his hand to Belili. He looked at their children once more. "Your ima and I are old and tired. We're so thankful you came for a visit. Please, let's do it again—and we'll talk more about returnin to Jerusalem." He led his wife up the stairs to their bedchamber, ignoring the whispered protests in their courtyard below.

36

Restore us to yourself, LORD, that we
    may return;
renew our days as of old.
                —LAMENTATIONS 5:21

Two Weeks Later

The smell of singed hair interrupted my
brooding. "Oh no!" I released the bronze curling
tongs from Daniel's beard.

"That one's a little crispy," he said with a wry
grin.

I swatted him. "Shall I start under your arms
next?"

"No!" Arms tight against his sides, he chuckled.
"I need *some* hair left to meet King Cyrus."

King Cyrus's arrival had stolen my attention.
I applied scented oil to Daniel's singed beard,
hoping to mask the smell. "Is the council still
divided on how to approach Cyrus with their
demands?"

"From what I've discerned from the various
members, no one *demands* anything from
Cyrus." He checked his beard in the mirror. "You
missed a spot."

I rolled my eyes and reapplied the bronze

tongs. He was fussier about his beard than our girls about their braids and curls. It was that meticulous nature that made him indispensable to the Medes' General Gubaru. When his soldiers began grousing that today's Persian arrival would steal their victory over Babylon, Daniel suggested pairing a Median soldier with a Persian guard to engender trust between the troops and build a "Medo-Persian" force.

"I want our family to stand close to the south gate when Cyrus enters the palace courtyard." His reflection in the handheld mirror was grim, his levity fallen away like the last leaves of autumn. "Keep everyone together and stand in the back row if you must to ensure a quick and clear exit if needed."

Setting aside the bronze tongs, I tried to steady my breathing. "Do you expect violence?"

A small V formed between his brows. "I don't expect it, but I want to be prepared should the Medes' resentment toward Cyrus turn bloody. They believe this city belongs to them, to General Gubaru. When they successfully invaded Babylon three weeks ago, Cyrus promised to set Gubaru on the throne and give him a new title." Daniel shrugged. "I've never met Cyrus, but I've known dozens of kings. They all disappoint. If he reneges on a single promise . . . well, you know that loyalty is what makes a Mede—a Mede. And betrayal is dealt with swiftly."

The trembling I'd felt all morning worked into my chest. "Should we leave the babies at home with servants? The smaller children too?"

Daniel set aside his hand mirror and pressed a gentle kiss on my lips. "Keep them all with you, my love. You'll know what to do. You've survived worse." Was that supposed to make me feel better?

He rose from his stool, looking every bit as regal as a king. His linen robe was exquisitely patterned, his dark outer robe of finest wool. Reaching for his short white overcoat, he shrugged it on and then absently straightened the two layers of sleeves underneath while he spoke. "Cyrus plans to honor General Gubaru by giving him the throne name Darius. He is to reign over Babylon, Syria, Phoenicia, and Palestine. If he follows through, I suspect it will be enough to assuage the Medes' grousing, but I've never seen a successful shared government."

I offered no reply, letting my husband process his thoughts aloud, while I feared my own demise in silence. Other than Allamu and Mert, Cyrus the Persian was the only one who could identify me as Mithra's high priestess. The Cyrus I remembered was a spoiled prince. His mother was Amyitis's sister, a woman much too gentle to be a Mede. Cyrus and his mother were forced into exile when old king Astyages dreamed Cyrus, his grandson, would plot to kill him someday. One autumn, when Allamu was seven, Amyitis detoured our return to Babylon by way of Susa, insisting Allamu and Cyrus meet. The boys were instant friends, though Cyrus was three years older. In an effort to impress the young prince, Allamu told him I'd once been high priestess of Mithra. Now the little boy who knew my secret ruled the empire.

Flustered at my thoughts and Daniel's musings, I reached for a simple gold-braided belt to tie around Daniel's waist and then searched the jewelry box for accessories. He pointed to a gold pendant and sat on his stool again so I could fasten it around his neck while he talked. "We must remember that Yahweh has already determined which king will send a remnant back to Jerusalem and is currently in the process of placing that man—or men—on the proper throne. Or thrones."

He picked up the hand mirror again and peered at me in the reflection, but I avoided his gaze, choosing instead to pillage the jewelry box again. I'd successfully avoided offering my opinion on his vision. Our children had tried that, and their doubts had been abruptly dismissed. They hadn't returned to the villa for a meal or visit since.

Our chamber was suddenly quiet. I looked up from the jewelry and found that Daniel was staring at me. "Will you help me convince

Allamu to search for the Ark?" he asked. "His connections to Mithra's temples could be the link we need if it's in Media."

"Absolutely not!"

He pulled me into his arms. "If Allamu won't help us, I think the Hebrew bodyguard—Zerubbabel—might be willing. I've coaxed a bit of his story from him. Evidently, he's served Astyages, Cyrus, and Gubaru."

My heart skipped. "He hardly seems old enough to have served Astyages."

"I said the same thing, but he changed the subject."

Before I could concoct an excuse to abandon the search, he released me and began rummaging through the jewelry box himself. "Let me choose something for you, my love. If Cyrus sees you today, he might remember you as his aunt Amyitis's best friend. You should be well dressed."

"Thankfully, Amyitis didn't live to see Cyrus assassinate her father," I mumbled as he chattered about the jewelry.

"This one!" He lifted out a string of carnelian beads with a lapis-inlaid pendant. "The red beads and blue inlay will bring out the roses in your cheeks when I tell Cyrus that I've loved you all my life."

I turned my back to him so he could fasten the necklace and I could hide my fear. Lost in what-ifs, I let my fingers glide over the necklace. Daniel's arms enfolded me, and he leaned over to still my hands. I hadn't realized they were shaking. "Tell me what you're thinking."

"Please don't be upset." I should have asked him first. "I sent a messenger to Mert this morning to send me our wooden trunk of keepsakes when the family comes today."

I faced him, and his expression softened. "Belili . . . why?"

"Why?" *Because if Cyrus recognizes me, and you divorce me, I'll need Amyitis's crown to survive.* I found myself telling my husband half truths again. "Because you've told me there may be war between the Medes and Persians, and you've cautioned me to gather our family by the south gate for a quick escape. How can you ask why I want our wealth transferred here for easy trading?"

He sifted the jewelry from our box through his fingers. "We have enough here to get our family to safety if things go badly with Cyrus."

I squeezed my eyes shut. "You said I know how to survive. It's true, but surviving pushed me into places I never wanted to go." I opened my eyes and voiced my decision. "I can't return to Jerusalem, Daniel. I won't. Our lives are here in Babylon."

He couldn't have looked more wounded if I'd stabbed him with his short sword. His hand went to his middle as if removing the blade. "But why? Jerusalem was our home. It's Yahweh's jewel. It's—"

Mert appeared at our doorway. "Kezia and Shesh have arrived with the trunk. The rest of the family is following close behind. Where should the messenger put it?"

"Have him put it in the library," Daniel said before I could speak.

I turned a burning glare on my husband. "I don't want to go into your library today, because I don't wish to discuss scrolls or visions. There's enough tension with Cyrus's arrival."

He drew breath to speak, but I joined Mert at the door, escaping my husband and the renewed guilt clawing at me.

"What's wrong?" my friend asked, giving me a sideways glance on the stairs.

"I can't talk about it now." Daniel had fallen into step behind us. Our children were coming in steadily from their side of the Processional Way. "Good morning," I said brightly. They called back greetings with smiles to both Daniel *and* me, and I felt warmth from those dearest to my heart. They'd been strangers too long. Yahweh was working to restore our kinship. How could I even think of parting from them again—vision or not?

As Mert and I reached the bottom step, Eva rushed ahead of her sisters with a bundle wrapped in cloth. "Ima, we've been so busy with sesame harvest and making oil that we haven't been back to share a meal." She offered me the wrapped bundle. "But we wanted you to try the bread recipe Kezia wheedled from the new breadmaker in the market. We baked it earlier this morning. I'm sorry it's cold."

"No apologies," I said. "I'm sure it's wonderful." I received the aromatic bundle from our older twin and unwrapped it.

Daniel came to my side, placing his arm tenderly around my waist. The tiny gesture assured me we could work out my fears with his faith. He leaned over and broke off a small bite. I did the same. At first the flavor was dull. Flour and sesame oil, a little water and perhaps some salt. I dared not pronounce the recipe mediocre when our girls seemed so enamored. In the next moment, the loaf in my hands warmed as if fresh from the oven and sweetness filled my mouth. The flavor was unmistakable. I stared down at the small round loaf in my hand. *It couldn't be.*

Then at Daniel, who seemed utterly unaffected. "I taste a hint of cumin," he said.

Cumin? I tore off another bite from the now-blazing loaf. The flavor of the Temple's sacred bread burst in my mouth, the aroma from my childhood undeniable. There was no cumin in Temple loaves.

"Yes, a little cumin and some fennel-flower sprinkled on top before baking," Eden added.

I shook my head, tears stinging my eyes, and offered the loaf to my husband again. "Touch it, Husband."

Noticing my reaction, concern wrinkled his brow, but he did as I asked. The moment his fingers met the bread, his eyes widened—and a slow grin revealed both his joy and strong faith. "Yahweh is at work, my love. Tell us what's happening."

My tears had overflowed their banks, and I covered an awe-filled laugh. In *my hand* was proof. Yahweh was at work, indeed. It was time to tell my children that I'd experienced His presence in Jerusalem's Temple. "My bite of bread was rather bland at first, but when the loaf began to warm in my hand, the faint taste of olive oil and honey burst in my mouth." I held out the small loaf for my daughters and their husbands to touch. While their eyes grew round with wonder, I relayed my story of my sacred loaf in the Holy of Holies.

"And this bread tasted like that to you?" Kezia's question was sincere wonder, not suspicion.

"Yes, Daughter. I might have doubted it myself had Yahweh not warmed the bread for everyone to experience with me."

Daniel turned to me as silence settled over

our family. "Are you with me, my love?" He offered his hand to me, and I knew he wasn't just asking me to follow him to meet Cyrus the Great. He was asking me to follow him to Jerusalem. My mind raced back to Jerusalem's captive camp when he and his three friends made their promise, wrists linked, hands piled together.

With the warmth of Yahweh's presence in one hand and Daniel holding the other, I nodded. "Yes. I'll be with you, Daniel ben Johanan, whether we go or stay."

Before Daniel could respond, Shesh stepped around our daughters. "I've done more research into the old records at the Esagila but found no mention of the Ark."

I felt both relief and sadness. Perhaps if the Ark was never found, we could stay in Babylon, but I didn't wish the Ark to be lost forever. Kezia—as usual—reacted with anger first. "Why would you look for it?"

Daniel lifted his hands to silence them both and spoke to the whole family. "I'm encouraged that Sheshbazzar began the search before today's display of power. It tells me he felt the touch of Yahweh's feather before the Lord used His holy mallet." Even Kezia grinned at her abba's word picture. "The remnant *will* return to Jerusalem, my children. Begin searching your hearts now to decide if you'll be among them.

Can you give up your comfortable routine to live in the tension of God's uncharted plan?"

Daniel returned his attention to Shesh and put a hand on his shoulder. "Perhaps you'd be willing to speak with some of Marduk's retired priests who served during Nebuchadnezzar's reign. Ask them if they recall hiding the Ark without recording it for some reason." My husband wiggled his eyebrows. "Retired priests might enjoy sharing their secrets."

37

This is what the LORD says to his anointed,
to Cyrus, whose right hand I take hold of
to subdue nations before him.

—ISAIAH 45:1

Daniel left the villa before everyone else to join Cyrus's processional with the other council members. Sheshbazzar led our family from my palace villa and began the short journey to the south gate of the palace courtyard. I walked amid my growing tribe, determined to remain hidden among them. Shesh and Kezia seemed equally determined to find a place closest to the grand stairway.

"Wait!" I shouted, frightening the infant in my arms to tears. "Didn't Daniel tell you he wanted us to stay near the south gate?"

"No, he didn't mention it," Shesh called back to me. "Don't you want to get close enough to see Abba and Allamu's faces? I'm sure Gubaru's council will stand close to the stairway." The thought of seeing Allamu again nudged me against better judgment. He'd made no attempt to see me after moving us to our new villa. I wasn't surprised, but my heart still ached.

A distant roar announced the processional's

beginning. "Hurry, Ima. The courtyard is filling up fast." Choosing to surrender, I squeezed through the burgeoning crowd behind my determined son-in-law.

The roar in the distance came in waves as King Cyrus drew nearer through the poorer sections of Babylon. How much praise was for Cyrus, and how much would have been offered to anyone providing relief from King Belshazzar? Belshazzar's reign had stifled trade and drained the city's resources. For the peasants in Babylon's streets, Cyrus was the great savior, come to restore their city to life and health.

Neighborhoods nearer the Processional Way grew wealthier, and as the parade drew closer to the Ishtar Gate, the roar dulled to polite applause. To the nobility, Cyrus and his Medes were vipers in the weeds. Men killed at Belshazzar's feast left countless widows and orphans, the homes and women claimed by Median soldiers only days after the attack. Those claimed stood silent around us, bruised and humiliated. Those unwanted were sold to temples or sent to slave markets.

Four carts clattered into the palace courtyard, drawing my attention with the sound of growls emanating from them. The sight of lions in iron cages stirred mixed reactions among the onlookers. Some pulled their children closer. Some cried out in fear, others in excitement.

We'd heard rumors of Cyrus's fascination with the beasts, not only of him hunting them but also of how *they* hunted—and devoured—humans.

A battalion of Mithraic priests followed the growling beasts—at a safe distance, of course. The priests swung giant censers in rhythm with the low thrumming of their chants, filling the air and my mind with unwelcome memories. Two Persian guards led a pure white bull before the bevy of priestesses.

One of our great-granddaughters leaned close and spoke in a loud whisper, "What will they do with the bull, Savta?"

Images played in my mind, and I could see the exact details of the ceremony. Every word of incantation. Every rite at each of seven levels. The price the high priestess charged for an oath by nobleman or king. All came flooding back in a nauseating rush of pain and regret. "Perhaps they sacrifice the bull." It was a safe answer, but empty. I should teach her the timeless truths of Yahweh, but I could barely keep this morning's meal in my belly.

Behind another contingent of Persian soldiers came King Cyrus himself, riding a dazzling black steed. General Gubaru rode beside him on a brilliant white stallion.

Cyrus had gotten old. The thought helped ease my angst. Would I have known him in a crowd? In a different city? A different life?

I stood a little straighter, fear of recognition dimming with each imperfection I saw in the boy I'd met only once years ago. He and Allamu had shared barely a week together when they were boys. How could he remember me all these years later?

"There's Allamu." Shesh pointed. "And Abba." Of the three men marching behind King Cyrus, two belonged to me. What once would have yielded a sense of security now filled me with dread.

My eyes rested on Daniel, the only stoop-shouldered, gray-headed man among hundreds of black-haired, curly-bearded warriors and priests marching into our city. *Yahweh, what are You thinking? Why throw him into the fray at his age?*

I heard no rumble of thunder or heavenly messenger. Not even a stolen glance from my husband. But my spirit enjoyed complete settledness. There would be no blood in the streets today. No battle between our conquerors. Not even an uprising of rebellious Babylonians. A cool breeze swept across my cheeks like a divine kiss, and I knew in that moment that Daniel and I would never leave Babylon—even if some in our family joined the prophesied remnant that returned to Jerusalem. We were rooted here, like Nebuchadnezzar's hanging gardens, to the foundations of this city.

Shesh leaned close. "Ima, why are you crying?"

I swiped at the tears I hadn't realized were falling. "They're grateful tears. So grateful. Thank you for leading our family well during the years we were in Borsippa and in the years of nearby separation."

"Nearby separation." He rested his head on mine. "That's a good description of some very hard years. Years that are behind us now, Ima." He kissed the top of my head covering.

Kezia stood on the other side of her husband, as usual, but this time instead of avoiding me, she peeked around him and smiled. The simple gesture gave me hope.

I bowed my head, overwhelmed at God's goodness and grace. *Yahweh, oh my God and gracious Redeemer, thank You for turning darkness into light and death into life.*

The clanging of palace gates wrenched my attention back to the courtyard as the last of the processional stepped onto palace grounds. King Cyrus rode his steed up the palace steps, and I feared he might continue right through the doors. Amyitis would swat him were she alive to see it. Stopping short of the entrance, he dismounted and stood as tall as Nebuchadnezzar had been. An imposing figure. A giant among men.

Must all kings be tall?

"I have closed the gates to speak with the

noblemen and women of Babylon." His voice was low and smooth, rolling over us like mulled wine on a cold mountain evening. "Those of you who lived in peace under Belshazzar's reign, I bid you continue." He drew his sword, the sing of it a threat. "Those of you intending rebellion, I bid you fight and die."

King Cyrus descended the palace stairs and halted in front of a nobleman to my left. He lifted his sword and rested the point at the base of the man's throat. "Do you choose peace?" he asked with a smile.

The man tried to nod, but the sharp tip broke the skin. He stilled. "Yes, my king. I choose peace."

"Good. Good!" Lifting his sword, Cyrus commanded one of his men, "Get this man a cloth to wipe his neck," and then found another nobleman with whom he repeated the game. Countless times he tested both men and women, and everyone, of course, answered peaceably.

Seeming satisfied with the results, Cyrus returned to General Gubaru and motioned for him to dismount. That's when I discovered all kings were not tall. Gubaru was built much like the guard Zerubbabel, but Gubaru's girth—unlike the Hebrew guard's—seemed derived from too many banquets.

Cyrus waved him toward the Ishtar Gate's watchtower. The general's attendant scampered behind them, carrying a basket the shape and size of a roast duck. The nobility stood spellbound, waiting for the two leaders to emerge at the top of the parapet. One a Mede. The other the grandson of a Mede—now a Persian.

Gubaru and Cyrus appeared at the top of the Ishtar Tower, now visible again to the peasantry outside the gate as well as we who stood inside the courtyard. Cyrus grabbed Gubaru's hand, raising his arm high, and the commoners roared their praise, shaming those inside the gates to join the celebration.

"Cyrus knows how to manipulate," I said to Shesh, shouting over the noise. My son-in-law quirked his mouth, unimpressed.

Our new king lowered his arms, motioning for silence. "I am Cyrus, king of Persia," he said when the crowd stilled. "I will create an empire greater and more prosperous than any the world has seen—but our kingdoms must work together." He let silence build tension and then, with a booming pronouncement, reeled them in with what rumors had baited. "Today I appoint King Darius, the Mede, as ruler of Babylon and the Lands Beyond the River!"

The announcement roused cheering from the Median soldiers, men loyal to their general unto death. They clanged their spears against shields when Cyrus called the attendant from the watchtower's shadows and placed a gold crown on Darius's head.

"I crown you, my brother, King Darius," Cyrus said. Then he did something that shocked even me. He bowed, stirring jubilant praise from even the most skeptical among the nobility around me.

The new King Darius returned the bow and then drew Cyrus into a respectful embrace. Was this a show, or did these two men truly believe they could rule together the largest empire the world had ever known?

King Cyrus stepped to the edge of the watchtower, facing his soldiers within the confines of the palace courtyard. "My comrades and friends, please turn your attention to the grand stairway, where King Darius's chosen leaders have gathered." Three men stood on the top step while all eyes had focused on the watchtower.

Shesh had to steady me. "It's Saba!" My great-granddaughter's delighted cheer drew the ire of several around us. She bounced and clapped, oblivious of the stares.

"Yes, I see." My Daniel stood on that top step, elevated above the satraps, the nobles, and the soldiers. His gray hair glowed like the moon in a night sky of oiled black beards.

King Darius's voice rose above the murmurs. "The one hundred twenty satraps will govern cities, collect taxes, and enforce the laws throughout Babylon and the three provinces in the Lands Beyond the River—Syria, Phoenicia, and Palestine. I've chosen three overseers—a Mede, a Persian, and a Jew—who will supervise the satraps and ensure their efficiency and productivity. King Cyrus's empire is a *world* empire in which all nations will live at peace." He bowed to Cyrus, who then lifted his sword over the courtyard, and once again, the crowds outside the gates roared their approval, though they couldn't see for whom they cheered.

Those inside the courtyard offered compulsory applause, knowing too well who would pay the empire's heaviest taxes and suffer its strictest laws. Whispered grousing surrounded me, and I worried for Shesh, his standing among the elders, and our other sons-in-law in their positions at the temples. Kezia's hens at the market dared not cluck about the new kings. Medes and Persians had little tolerance for nonsense. As for my children and grandchildren, what abuse would they endure? What hurtful words and hidden attacks?

As the emperor and king descended the tower, I looked again to my son. Tall and regal, he drank in the applause and recognition like a man born for royalty. He was stunning. More handsome than his father. With silver hair at his temples and perfectly arrayed in Median finery, he exuded confidence and diplomacy. His political cunning was as sharp as Cyrus's sword. He would do well in the multicultured political climate, but what of his heart? I looked at the man and saw my little boy, lost and alone in a sea of wealth and success. *Oh Yahweh, show me how to reach him.*

Darius and Cyrus continued their endless flow of words, now fawning and flaunting directly in front of the Babylonians and Medes gathered in the courtyard. "We have fought together and lived together, and we will now rule together," Darius shouted, raising his fist in the air like a victor. The satraps joined him, hands held high. When two of the three overseers also beat their fists in the air, I looked at my Daniel and found his head bowed, praying.

Oh Yahweh, protect him, for even now he stands alone.

38

It pleased Darius to appoint 120 satraps to rule throughout the kingdom, with three [overseers] over them, one of whom was Daniel. The satraps were made accountable to them so that the king might not suffer loss.

—DANIEL 6:1–2

Next Day

Daniel heard a trumpet blast as if in a dream. Maybe it was a dream. His body felt like iron weighted to the bed. His eyelids, equally heavy, refused to open. The trumpet again, this time louder. Someone shook his shoulder.

"Daniel. Daniel!"

"What?" He bolted upright in bed. The chamber glowed in predawn gray.

Belili placed a calming hand on his chest. "The king's trumpet. Why would they call a meeting so early? Let me send a message that you're ill. You're too tired to go."

He took her hand from his chest and kissed her palm. "I'm fine. Stop fussing." Actually, he was exhausted, but he couldn't let her know. She'd march into King Darius's courtroom and demand he be allowed afternoon naps. "I'll be home as soon as I can." Dressing quickly, he grabbed a piece of stale bread as he walked past the cook fire and food baskets.

The morning air cleared his head, a hint of night's chill lingering before the sun chased it away. Cyrus and Darius had kept the satraps and overseers until after the moon's zenith on their first day of organizing territories and dividing responsibilities. It was exhilarating. While serving as Nebuchadnezzar's governor of Chaldeans, Daniel had held sway over immediate decisions, sometimes determining life or death, war or peace, a nation's rise or fall. But to be involved in the foundational planning of an empire . . . he couldn't stop smiling.

Barely thirty paces from the palace entrance, he skirted a large, deep pit apparently still in process. Torches burned inside it as men filled baskets with dirt and hoisted them up to be carried away. The size and depth of the hole was impressive, but he was too practical not to shudder at the destruction of Nebuchadnezzar's beautiful blue-glazed tile street.

Eight lions paced in iron cages around the pit's perimeter. Daniel suspected the deep hole would be their new home since he'd heard the beasts' sharp claws and teeth were Cyrus's preferred method of execution. Why did kings make executions as unique as their seals? As a warrior, Nebuchadnezzar favored torturous deaths.

Nabonidus and his son Belshazzar enjoyed the entertainment of public executions. A lion's roar hurried Daniel's flight up the stairs. He hoped the lions would be allowed to do their work privately.

Reaching the palace entrance, he greeted the first guard with Darius's newly prescribed greeting, "Prosperity and honor to the empire." He was a bit too cheery, judging from the scowl he received. Perhaps a more refined demeanor was befitting a king's overseer.

Hurrying toward the throne room, he planned to lower his voice and erase the smile but recognized Zerubbabel as one of the guards. "Prosperity and honor to the empire."

Zerubbabel's wide smile greeted Daniel with equal zeal. "Prosperity and honor to the empire, Lord Belteshazzar." He offered his hand, and Daniel gladly embraced his wrist in friendship. "I've been promoted to one of three top men myself," he said, pride beaming. "King Darius chose three personal guards: a Scythian, a Hebrew, and a Medjay. Guess which one I am?" His laughter echoed, earning scowls from the weary satraps forming a line behind Daniel.

He liked this man more each time they spoke. "I'm proud to find a fellow Hebrew protecting our new king."

Zerubbabel welcomed the overseer and the line of satraps into the courtroom, where surprising changes had been made since last night. The kings' thrones sat in the middle of the elevated dais, which was the same, but three exquisite couches, gilded and covered with plush pillows, fanned out beside them. One was placed at the right side of Cyrus's throne, and the other two sat at the left of Darius's throne.

Only five other officials had outpaced Daniel this morning. Allamu was one, and he approached with an outstretched hand. "Prosperity and honor to the empire." Finally, someone who matched his enthusiasm.

Gripping the younger man's wrist, Daniel sensed a newfound camaraderie after yesterday's long hours of unified vision. "Did you sleep well?"

Allamu shook his head. "Didn't sleep at all. I saw only maps and lists of satraps when I closed my eyes. What about you?"

He laughed. "When you're my age, you can sleep anywhere, anytime—even when you don't intend to."

"Good morning." The sound of King Cyrus's voice wrenched everyone's attention to the dais, where both impeccably dressed kings approached their thrones. Darius and Cyrus looked well rested and expertly polished for their first full day in Babylon's court.

"Please be seated," Darius said. "Satraps, on the cushioned benches. Our three overseers, on the couches beside us on the dais."

Allamu headed for the couch closest to King Cyrus, but Daniel hesitated.

Noting the delay, Darius leaned forward on his throne. "Is there a problem, Lord Belteshazzar?"

He glanced at the double doors, where another twenty or more satraps were just now entering. "I wondered if I might ask your permission to sit among the satraps rather than on the couch, my king." Those entering the room froze in place, and all talking ceased.

"Why?" Darius seemed impatient.

"I'd like to speak freely with the men I'll rule over. I want to know who they are. Find out about their families. Discern their character through a simple conversation." He pointed to the two empty couches on the dais. "I can't do that if I'm sitting up there."

A few chuckles started behind him, and some whispered wagers on the form of his execution.

Darius exchanged a smile with Cyrus. "I like your idea, Lord Belteshazzar," Darius said, "but you will sit on the couch prepared for you."

"Of course, my king." He hurried up the aisle and climbed the six steps of the dais, choosing the second couch beside Darius. He'd purposely left the one closest to the king empty.

"Afraid I'll bite?" Babylon's king asked with a wry smile, eliciting nervous laughter from the satraps filing into the room.

"Not at all, my king. I simply left the place of honor for your third overseer." Lowering his voice, he spoke only for Darius to hear. "You'll likely wish to speak with him about being more prompt."

The Mede's laughter boomed in the courtroom, garnering a curious grin from Allamu and dubious glances from the rest of the satraps. The third overseer sprinted up the aisle. "Forgive me, lords and kings. My wife was in labor all night—" His foot reached the first step of the dais, and Darius sprang from his chair to meet him.

Daniel recognized the gleam in the king's eyes and saw the glint of sunlight on his dagger. In what seemed to the audience of satraps to be a left-armed embrace, Darius sank his dagger into the young overseer's belly with his right hand. When the young father crumpled on the steps, many quieted. When they noted the bloody dagger, the courtroom fell silent as a stone.

But Darius's smile never dimmed. "I hope I've made it clear that promptness is of utmost importance when you hear the king's trumpet. No excuses. No delays." When the room remained silent, his good nature turned sour. "I should hear, 'Yes, my king.'"

"Yes, my king!" A unified shout rattled the cedar rafters.

A contingent of soldiers proceeded up the aisle.

"What are you doing? Did I ask you to remove the body?"

One of the eunuchs bowed. "No, my king. We'll return to our posts and wait for your command." He turned promptly, as did the others.

"Better. Much better. Now bar the doors. Any satrap who hasn't arrived by now will be executed, and another leader will be appointed to take his place." Darius returned to his throne, shaking his finger at Daniel. "I liked your suggestion, Lord Belteshazzar."

"My suggestion, King Darius?" Daniel hoped he hadn't thought speaking to the overseer about promptness meant killing the poor man.

"Yes. I will speak with each satrap and overseer about their families. Get to know them. Discern their character through a simple conversation." He pointed to the dead man. "Perhaps we can avoid more mishaps with young fathers who assume I'll be lenient because of a woman's labor pains."

"Avoiding further mishaps would be commendable, my king. Any kingdom has only so many fine overseers."

Again, the king grinned. "I like you, Belteshazzar. I suspect you've earned your gray hair with wit and cunning. King Cyrus and I will interview you first."

"As you wish, my king." Daniel pointed at the dead man lying on the steps. "Shall I remain seated since the location for supplicants is occupied?"

Darius laughed aloud. "Yes, Belteshazzar. Remain where you are and tell me about your family."

"I'm married and have four daughters," Daniel began.

"Is Mistress Belili still living?" Cyrus interrupted. Though the emperor had final authority in all matters, Cyrus had remained silent during most of yesterday's proceedings. Why the sudden intrusion?

Daniel trained his features into a calm facade. "Yes, King Cyrus, my wife is alive and quite well. Thank you. Would you like me to communicate your well wishes?"

Cyrus's eyes narrowed. After an excruciating pause, a slow smile sent a chill through Daniel's veins. "No thank you, Lord Belteshazzar. I'd like to offer my regards to Mistress Belili in person." He motioned the guards toward the dead overseer. "Take him away and escort Lord Belteshazzar's wife to the throne room—immediately."

He elbowed Darius. "She was my aunt Amyitis's dearest friend, you know. I remember Mistress Belili as having the same spit and fire as I've seen in Lord Belteshazzar." He then turned to Allamu. "I'd forgotten your mother lived here. Have you seen her since you've been in Babylon, or has Gub—has King Darius kept you too busy?"

Daniel cleared his throat, interrupting the impromptu reunion and hoping to keep Belili out of Darius's court. "Of course the emperor may speak with my wife when he pleases, but she could visit anytime. You wish to interview one hundred twenty satraps—whose wives are far more likely than mine to cause tardiness with birthing pains." He tried to chuckle, but it sounded more like a nervous groan.

Cyrus leaned toward Allamu. "Is there a reason Lord Belteshazzar doesn't want me to see your mother?"

Allamu shifted uneasily on his couch. "I can't imagine. She would be delighted to see you."

"It's settled, then." He waved his hand at Darius. "Proceed with other interviews while we wait."

The guards cleared the overseer's body, and Darius began his interviews. Daniel tried to remain attentive, studying the mannerisms and cues of Babylon's new king in order to learn his moods and responses. Would he wield his dagger again? Or had it been a shock tactic to gain their attention? If so, it had certainly worked. Daniel hadn't looked away. At the thought, he stole a quick glance at King Cyrus and found him intently watching the large entry doors. Perhaps his motives were pure in wanting to see Belili, a woman he seemed to include in fond childhood memories. Daniel tried to relax his shoulders, hoping Darius would keep his dagger in its sheath when Belili arrived.

After the third satrap's interview, Darius turned to Daniel. "I believe I'll begin your interview now, Belteshazzar. Get it out of the way before your wife arrives."

"As you wish, my king." Daniel descended the dais and offered a bow. Darius began with questions of his childhood captivity, training as a Chaldean, and Nebuchadnezzar's appointment as governor over them.

Seemingly frustrated that too many answers led back to Daniel's singular and focused faith in Yahweh, Cyrus scooted to the edge of his throne and leaned forward. "You talk in circles, wise man."

"Yes, my king. I've been accused of that many times." He bowed again, awaiting the next question.

Darius spoke again. "How is it that you've remained calm when others half your age complain of changes to a city they've lived in half as long?"

"My peace comes from two sources, King Darius. First, I realize when I leave this earth, I'll go to paradise, where I'll be surrounded by the faithful and will fellowship with Father Abraham. Second, Yahweh showed me two visions during the reign of Belshazzar. Both confirmed in vivid images that a divided kingdom would conquer Babylon. We stand here today amid Yahweh's fulfillment through your combined kingdoms. Why would I grow anxious now?"

The courtroom door banged open. "Take your hands off me!" Belili's voice echoed in the near-empty hall.

Daniel whirled to see if she'd been hurt and was relieved to find her angry instead. Rushing toward his flustered wife, he realized she was more frightened than angry.

She fell into his arms and looked beyond him to the dais. "I thought they'd hurt you or Allamu."

"Shhh, beloved. We need not fear. Cyrus simply wanted to see his friend's mother again after so many years." He dried her tears with her head covering and offered his arm to escort her. He placed his right hand over hers to steady her shaking but realized he was trembling as well. Cyrus seemed a reasonable man, but he couldn't say the same for Darius. The words he'd said moments ago echoed in his mind. *Why grow anxious now? Why grow anxious now?*

Daniel stopped at the edge of the crimson carpet, less than a camel length from the dais, and we both bowed. My heart slammed against my chest, and I gripped his arm tighter.

King Darius spoke first. "It is impolite in Persian court for a woman's head to be covered, Mistress. Please remove—"

Looking up, I avoided Cyrus completely, fixing my gaze on Darius, the Mede. "Forgive me." I pushed my red scarf off and bowed deeply once

438

again. When I rose, King Darius seemed transfixed by my gray curls. I hadn't had time to plait them or even tie them back with a leather string.

A mischievous chuckle broke the silence, a familiar sound. Cyrus batted the Mede's shoulder. "Stop staring, King Darius. Lord Allamu's mother will take a strap to you." I turned to the emperor, terrified his familiarity would draw my secret from his lips and saw kindness in his eyes. "Mistress Belili, you are lovely. As lovely as the day Auntie brought you to Susa when I was but a child. I've heard whispers of conspiracy regarding Nebuchadnezzar's death, but no word reached me about Aunt Amy's end. Do you have information to share?" Brows turned down slightly, he conveyed a gentle warning to speak only truth.

Daniel reached for my hand between the folds of our robes. "King Cyrus, though we have no proof of Nebuchadnezzar's assasination, we believe the rumors of conspiracy. His young heir was on the throne only two years when Neriglissar, the man who had co-reigned peaceably during Nebuchadnezzar's absence, usurped the throne in a violent coup. It was then that the faithful chief eunuch, Ashpenaz, secretly conveyed Queen Amyitis from the palace to our home in a meat cart—"

"A meat cart?" Cyrus's eyes went wide. "I can't imagine Auntie riding in a meat cart."

I grinned at his interest. "Your aunt was the toughest Mede that ever lived, Cyru—my king." Realizing I'd nearly called an emperor by his first name, I relinquished the telling to my husband.

"We hid Amyitis in our family's villa through the turbulent years of change in the palace," Daniel said. "She enjoyed our grandchildren and lived well until lung sickness cut short her sixty-third year."

Cyrus rested his elbow on the armrest. "I owe you two much. She was dear to me. I must ask. Was she alive when I—" He cleared his throat and shifted nervously on his throne. "Did she know I conquered Achmetha?"

"Amyitis died before you killed her father," I said. Daniel squeezed my hand hard, but what was I to do? The words were said.

Cyrus glared at me. "I didn't kill my grandfather. I conquered King Astyages, the man who exiled my mother and me only days after my birth because of a silly dream."

"Might I ask about that, King Cyrus?" Daniel drew his attention from me, and I was both relieved and terrified. "Was it not the Magoi who interpreted your grandfather Astyages's dream that resulted in your exile? Yet Allamu is chief magus and now sits at your right hand. How is it that you've remained friends all these years?"

Cyrus leaned back on his throne, eyes narrowed

at my husband. "You are as tactful and wise as Allamu boasted, Lord Belteshazzar, to divert my annoyance from your wife. Long before I met Allamu, his father, Gadi, was the faithful friend who revealed my grandfather's ill intentions to my mother and sent us fleeing to safety. It's why Auntie wanted Allamu and me to meet. It's why I will always trust Lord Allamu."

Daniel bowed deeply, and when he rose, there was a glint of mischief in his eyes. "It would appear the Most High God was at work in your life as well, my king. When Gadi alerted your mother, he also sent a messenger to me with a scroll detailing the Magoi's conspiracy with King Astyages and his part in helping your mother and you escape. In the message, he also asked me to care for his wife and son if anything ever happened to him." Daniel wrapped his arm around my shoulder. "As you see, my king, Yahweh has given me the privilege of fulfilling Gadi's wishes."

Cyrus laughed and clapped his hands. "You have found a way to bring the matter back to your god again, you old dog." My husband beamed at the emperor's congratulations. I bathed in the peace I saw on Daniel's face, feeling as if we'd walked through a field of vipers without being bitten.

39

Now Daniel so distinguished himself among the [overseers] and the satraps by his exceptional qualities that the king planned to set him over the whole kingdom.

—DANIEL 6:3

Six Months Later

The fifth day in a row, Lord? Daniel heard no clear answer but knew from his medical training that his red, swollen, and painful feet were likely related to the rich food he'd been eating since his appointment to the royal council.

He stared at the ceiling, watching dawn's glow brighten their bedchamber as the aroma of myrrh stung his eyes. Or was it frustration that caused him to swipe at tears before they rolled into his ears? He'd tried to get out of bed at the rooster's first crow but fell back to the mattress in pain when his feet bore the slightest weight. Belili had awakened when he landed hard on the mattress.

"I'll get my herb basket." She kept clean bandages and a small pot of myrrh-and-coriander unguent in the table at her bedside. Grabbing the basket, she hurried to his side and knelt. "Do you know the cause?"

His legs hung over the side while she applied ointment to bandages. "We only see the condition among nobility who eat meat more than three times a week." He chuckled, trying to lighten his dreary mood. "Perhaps I should return to the diet Shadrach, Meshach, Abednego, and I ate when we first came to Babylon."

She paused her ministrations and looked up without a shred of amusement. "A change in diet would be good, but a man your age can't work from dawn till the moon's zenith every day. Must I go to court myself and tell King Darius you need rest?" She applied the bandage gently to his left foot, and he sucked in a breath. Even the slightest touch felt like the stabs of a thousand daggers. He counted heartbeats until the tingle of myrrh provided some pain relief. "Yahweh ordained a Sabbath for our benefit," she added, "not His."

Her words treated the true illness. Daniel had been so meticulous in teaching and obeying other commands in this foreign land, yet he'd completely ignored the fourth of God's ten commandments. "You're beautiful when you speak for Yahweh." Daniel brushed the feathery-soft wrinkles on her cheek.

"Phssst." She waved away his compliment, busy wrapping his feet with her blue-veined hands. Her fragile, translucent skin bruised easily when she bumped a table corner or stumbled into a doorway.

"How did we get so old?" he mused.

She looked up, a spark of mischief dancing in her eyes. "We didn't die."

Laughter draining his strength, he helped her off her knees and guided her back into bed. She lay in the bend of his arm, their bodies molded into the same shape, and suddenly Daniel didn't feel so old anymore. This felt right, the way they were meant to be. Her nearness, her love had never gotten old or tired.

"I want you to tell Darius you need more rest."

"I know you do, love." But how could he demand a Sabbath from a king who executed satraps for tardiness? Surely Yahweh understood his added responsibilities. "Darius has divided supervisory responsibilities of the one hundred twenty satraps among himself, Allamu, Orchamus, and me. Darius oversees the satraps of Babylon, Allamu the ones assigned to Syria, Orchamus those bound for Phoenicia, and I'm training those going to—"

"Palestine?" Belili raised up on one elbow. "Oh, Daniel, it must be part of Yahweh's plan to restore the remnant to Jerusalem." The spark in her eyes dimmed as understanding dawned. "That's why you can't rest. You feel responsible. To King Darius but also to train the satraps who will rule our people in Palestine."

"I know Yahweh will care for His people, but I must also serve faithfully. Shesh continues his search for the Ark, so I must train satraps who understand its significance in our culture."

She raised one corner of a lopsided grin. "Have your satraps realized that you're teaching them about Yahweh, not just culture?"

"Hebrew culture sounds less offensive to Medes and Persians. No one has complained yet." They laughed together, and he pulled her into a tender kiss, enjoying their first leisurely morning in months. The trumpet's call interrupted his warming passion, and he offered his wife an apologetic shrug. "I'll wake you when I get home."

"You'd better," she said as he scooted off the bed. "And make sure Orchamus does his share of the work—the little whelp."

"I'll likely leave off that last comment. You've been spending too much time with Mert." Daniel reached for his robe, chuckling. Oh, how he loved his wife. One more kiss, and he was dressed and on his way to the palace before the second trumpet warned of the king's impatience.

Allamu met him at the palace entrance, their relationship becoming easier each day they spent together. How Daniel wished it could be so between Allamu and his mother.

"You look like walking death." Allamu laid his arm around Daniel's shoulder. "Perhaps you should ask King Darius for a day to rest."

"Did your mother pay you to say that?"

Orchamus, the overseer appointed after Darius stabbed the tardy young father, waited for them at the entrance. Having heard their banter, he fell in step beside Allamu. "Maybe King Darius should declare a day of rest since he canceled the Akita festival. The whole city is ill tempered. Already this morning, I've dealt with two merchants, a physician, and an oarsman for my quffa who would have benefited from a New Year's festival to regain their good humor."

"I'm sure King Darius will make the right decision." Allamu cast a warning glance in Daniel's direction, but he'd already determined to keep silent. Orchamus was ten years younger than Allamu, and only his ambition surpassed his energy. Allamu and Daniel knew better than to offer a word that could later be twisted by their counterpart into betrayal or treason.

They approached the large double doors of the throne room, and Daniel looked for Zerubbabel. The Scythian guard was on duty instead. Tattooed and always wearing his ornate bow and quiver strapped across his back, the stone-faced warrior was so imposing no one dared mock him. He opened the door without command, and Daniel patted his shoulder as he passed.

The overseers had arrived before most of the satraps. Those already present gathered in small huddles, faces weary and grim. Allamu, who walked between Orchamus and Daniel, lowered his voice. "I think we three can agree that the whole city needs a break, but it makes no sense to hold a festival that worships Marduk and Nabu, patron gods of Babylon and Borsippa, when our king and emperor worship Mithra."

King Darius entered the room from a side door, gaining everyone's attention. "Be seated," he said without preamble. "We begin."

More satraps hurried in and took their seats. Only one place on the benches remained empty, and Daniel prayed the man would arrive before the third and final trumpet sounded. Darius's no-excuse policy, established on his first day, hadn't relaxed but had been refined. The first trumpet called the officials, the second warned time was short, and the third signaled the doors closing. Three more satraps had died in six months. Darius was not to be tested.

The last satrap ran through the doors as the final trumpet blared. Barefoot, disheveled, and carrying his jewelry and sandals, he hurried to his empty place and sat down, trying to appear attentive.

Darius's eyes narrowed, but he left his dagger sheathed. "It has come to my attention that canceling last week's Akitu festival left Babylon and Borsippa in mourning."

Daniel hadn't heard it phrased that way, but it was an apt description and offered more than a little relief that he wasn't the only one finding it difficult to keep pace with their new king.

"It's our job," Darius continued, "in the first year of my reign, to establish traditions and systems that will propagate peace and health throughout Babylon and the Lands Beyond the River. King Cyrus will not hear of a grieving Babylon." He let silence grab their attention. "I said . . . King Cyrus will not hear of a grieving Babylon."

His lifted brows invited the practiced reply. "Yes, my king!" the men responded.

With a single nod, he continued. "Before you eat your midday meal, you will suggest a celebration to replace Akitu. Something equal in splendor and significance. Something to capture people's hearts, pique their interest, and tantalize their senses. Begin!" He sat down on his throne, and the satraps scooted together in groups, conversations growing lively immediately.

With a wave, Darius called Allamu, Orchamus, and Daniel nearer. Servants appeared from the shadows with their customary three stools, placing them in a tight arc in front of the throne. Like baby birds waiting to be fed by their mother, the overseers waited for Darius to speak. Only twice had he gathered them like this. Once, when he assigned their territories, and five months ago to announce Cyrus's departure.

"Our current structure is ineffective. King Cyrus and I have corresponded and agree that I will rule the whole of my kingdom, rather than administrating details in Babylon alone. To administrate those details, I've chosen Lord Belteshazzar. He will also rule over the overseers and our one hundred twenty satraps." He met Daniel's gaze. "You have distinguished yourself in the past six months, my friend, above all others. Will you serve me in this way?"

Daniel wished he could say, "With all my heart, no!" But wisdom won over desire. "Of course, my king. I am honored." He ventured a surreptitious glance at Allamu and Orchamus, finding their reactions varied.

Allamu extended his hand with a warm smile. "Prosperity and honor to the empire." Gripping his wrist, Daniel felt the warmth and affirmation of a son's pride.

Orchamus offered his hand as well, but his expression was trained in political rightness. "Yes, prosperity and honor to the empire." The words were correct but forced, and his grip lasted barely the length of a heartbeat.

The king was last to offer his hand and held Daniel's wrist as he spoke. "You will accompany me to my chamber, Lord Belteshazzar. We will speak of your duties while the others continue to form a plan for our replacement festival." He pulled on Daniel's arm, hoisting him to his feet.

"Of course, my king." Giving the fire in his feet time to cool, Daniel bowed a quick good-bye to Allamu and Orchamus and then followed Darius out the side door.

Daniel felt the stares of his comrades like daggers in his back. Looking back, he found Orchamus scowling. Envy was an insidious master, and it appeared to have bound Orchamus with heavy chains.

Daniel followed Darius down a narrow hall-way toward the private suite that had once been Nebuchadnezzar's. Now eight guards stood watch at the door, one of whom was Zerubbabel. The Hebrew guard opened the door as they approached and nodded as Daniel followed the king inside. Daniel nudged him in jest without drawing attention.

Still looking over his shoulder at Zerubbabel, Daniel heard a low growl. "Yahweh help us!" he yelped when he saw a lioness lounging on a goatskin rug barely a camel length from the king. "Quick, my king!" Daniel grabbed his arm and pulled him toward the door the way an ant might tug at a boulder.

Darius laughed and patted the hand that assaulted him. "Nergala is my toy, Lord Belteshazzar."

The beast stood, and Daniel nearly left a wet spot on the king's tiled floor. Darius lowered himself to one knee, and the giant animal lumbered closer, rubbing her rich golden coat against his chest like an Egyptian cat. He stroked her, hand over hand, and she melted to the floor, submitting to his petting.

"Come, Lord Belteshazzar," he coaxed. "Pet her yourself. She is friendly to those I deem a friend."

Daniel took a step toward the lion, hand outstretched, but Nergala's ears flicked. She turned her head and roared, the sound of it vibrating his chest. Stopping where he stood, his knees nearly buckled. "I think not, my king. Should I return after Nergala has eaten her midday meal?"

Darius gave her a vigorous two-handed scratch behind her ears and instructed his chamber steward to remove her. The well-muscled man attached a heavy chain to Nergala's jeweled collar and led her out an alternate door.

The king's impish grin said he'd relished the interchange. "Should I have Nergala's sister delivered to your villa?"

Finally breathing again, Daniel could chuckle. "Only if you wish to face the wrath of Mistress Belili."

His eyes widened. "I'd rather face Nergala's sister!"

Their familiarity felt right, nothing forced. Daniel had grown cautiously fond of this young man. Though he bore the unyielding harshness of a Mede, he'd shown some teachability and could become a fine leader.

"Sit down, Belteshazzar." Darius pointed to a stool opposite the couch where he now rested. Daniel obeyed and waited while the king studied him.

A long silence ensued, both men skilled in waiting. "I've heard rumors," Darius said finally. "Rumors that trouble me."

Daniel thought they'd entered the private chamber to discuss his new duties. "Rumors are often lies begun with a seed of truth."

Darius nodded and scratched his chin. "The rumors I've heard are that you worked evil magic on King Nebuchadnezzar and King Nabonidus—that you changed them into oxen."

Daniel had to stifle a laugh at the absurdity, but the fear on the man's features sobered him. "I am Hebrew, King Darius. I led Babylon's Chaldeans as an asutu—a physician—and an astrologer. I interpreted dreams *only* through the power of the Most High God. It would be an abomination to Yahweh were I to use magic, as the *asiputus* do in their incantations."

The relief on his face was likely the same as Daniel's when Nergala left the room. Daniel leaned forward, resting his arms on his knees. "My God did, indeed, transform Nebuchadnezzar into the form of an ox for seven years. I witnessed the day Nebuchadnezzar acknowledged Yahweh's sovereignty over all kingdoms on earth and regained his throne. However, I've only heard the rumors about Nabonidus. If it was judgment, however, I've heard nothing of it ending."

A shadow of fear returned to the king's features. "So you admit to using your God's power to manipulate Nebuchadnezzar?"

"No, my king."

"You are wily, Chaldean." Darius sat back, eyes narrowing. "Will you threaten your God's vengeance if I don't do as you say? Will I become an exiled king like Nabonidus?"

"I don't even know if the rumors of Nabonidus are true, and I did not threaten any vengeance. I'm only a mouthpiece."

Darius appeared unconvinced, his features darkening. "What am I to do with you, Belteshazzar? If I kill you, your god will turn me into an ox. If I promote you to chief administrator—as I planned—you will rule my kingdom."

Daniel turned his wrinkled hands palms up in surrender. "I assure you, King Darius, I have no interest in ruling your kingdom, and I have no more power than any man in your court." He straightened and offered his most penitent smile. "Only the God Most High holds all kingdoms in His hands. Occasionally He announces His plan through my lips. If you kill me, He'll simply raise up another to be His voice."

"He already did."

"Raise up another prophet?"

"Another Yahweh magician." Darius waved his hand in a circle as if conjuring someone. "My soldiers told me about another Hebrew who claimed he spoke messages from your god. He lived in a southern province by the Kebar Canal."

"Ezekiel, yes." Daniel's chest constricted. "He died several years ago."

"You knew him?"

"I knew of him, but we never met. Ezekiel was taken from Jerusalem in Nebuchadnezzar's second attack. His message from Yahweh was always the same: Jerusalem will be completely destroyed, but Yahweh is with those who remain faithful in Babylon, and He will lead us back to restore Jerusalem at the proper time."

"It sounds as if Ezekiel was inciting rebellion, hoping to overthrow his captors and lead an army back to Jerusalem."

"No, no, my king. Just the opposite," Daniel said. "He worked with the Hebrew governors, Abednego and Shadrach, to help our people put down roots in Babylon. They built homes, married, and started lucrative businesses, which in part will provide for a remnant of Yahweh's people to return to Jerusalem."

Darius leaned back on his couch, his features frozen in a scowl.

Daniel watched closely, waiting for him to reach for his dagger, and considered how he might soften the lines across the king's forehead. "Perhaps you know more details. Did Ezekiel somehow unite an army before he died? Is that why you thought him a magician?"

The king shook his head, his tension easing. "I thought him a magician because he did exactly as you said. He instilled peace in his province—and the provinces around him. Why would he do that in the land of his enemies?"

Yahweh, is this the open door to ask for our remnant's return?

Trying to tamp down his excitement and keep his voice level, he began. "Ezekiel believed, as do I, that our exile was discipline from our God that would last only seventy years. At the end of that time, Yahweh, in His mercy, will place a ruler over this empire who will allow a remnant of Hebrews to return to Jerusalem and rebuild His Temple—the place where His presence dwells on earth. The prophet Jeremiah spoke this message to our people when I was a boy, and the same vision was given to me." Daniel's stomach fluttered as though a dove had taken wing inside it. "It's been nearly sixty-seven years, King Darius. Have you considered sending a remnant of Hebrews to our homeland with the satraps you've chosen?"

Daniel wanted to say more but let the weight of his question settle into Darius's heart.

The king held his gaze, his expression never changing. "I've spent my whole life learning to read men, Lord Belteshazzar, and I don't see any deceit in you. No guile or hatred toward me or the ambitious men in my courtroom who would rather cut your throat than eat at your table." He shifted on his couch, cradling his chin in his hand as if deep in thought. "You're either the most ignorant man in the empire or the most favored by his god—and a man who's lived this long in Babylon's court can't be ignorant. I will consider what we've discussed before officially installing you as my administrator."

Daniel nodded respectfully. "I believe that's a wise decision, my king."

Darius reached across the small space separating them and lifted the hem of Daniel's robe. "I noticed your limp," he said, pointing to both heavily bandaged feet. "Perhaps after we plan the new festival, you should let your pretty wife take care of those feet, Lord Belteshazzar."

"I believe you would win much favor with Mistress Belili if you forced me to do so, my king."

Darius stood and offered his hand to help Daniel to his feet. "Perhaps it is your wife I should fear more than you, Chaldean." He chuckled and led Daniel out of his chamber.

40

The royal [overseers], prefects, satraps, advisers and governors have all agreed that the king should issue an edict and enforce the decree that anyone who prays to any god or human being during the next thirty days, except to you, Your Majesty, shall be thrown into the lions' den.

—DANIEL 6:7

They exited King Darius's chamber, and Zerubbabel led them down the hallway and through the door leading to the dais's side entrance. The council's lively chatter instantly ceased. Zerubbabel marched onto the dais with a hand on his sword, muscles taut, while Darius and Daniel followed. The king's heavy footsteps were the only sound in the uncomfortable silence.

When they reached the throne and overseers' couches, the king looked over his audience of averted eyes. "Your conversation appears to be something you'd rather Lord Belteshazzar and I didn't hear."

"On the contrary, my king." Orchamus left the huddle of Phoenicia-bound satraps he'd been consulting and cleared the dais steps in two large strides. "I believe we've settled on a replacement festival that will erase the Akitu celebration from your new kingdom's collective memory." He kept glancing at Allamu, who sat sullenly among his Syrian group of satraps.

"I'm anxious to hear." Darius's impatient tone barely dimmed Orchamus's enthusiasm.

"We haven't yet named the festival, but we'll construct an image much like the one of Nebuchadnezzar's day on the Dura Plain. Except this image will be your likeness, my king. Then for thirty days hence, anyone who prays to any god except you, King Darius, will be immediately thrown into the pit of lions."

He stole a glance at Daniel before motioning for the king's scribe to approach the throne. Daniel felt the sharp blade of fear slice through his middle. Every one of his Palestine-bound satraps knew he prayed only to one God. They'd undoubtedly informed the Syrian and Phoenician groups of the fact, and Orchamus used the information to trap Daniel.

"The decision was unanimous," Orchamus was saying. "Praying to you alone will unite the kingdom, and feeding the lions will provide some sport for those in the city who've never witnessed the sight."

The decision was unanimous. Allamu's eyes were downcast. His stepson's betrayal cut him to the bone.

Darius joined in Orchamus's excitement. "We

could set several days during the festival for executions. I'm sure it would draw large crowds."

Orchamus bowed deeply and slammed his fist to his heart. "This festival will teach our children—and men and women of all ages—the importance of magnifying our king, no matter what gods or goddesses they worship. No matter what cultures separate us, we can be united in our worship of Darius." Orchamus turned his attention toward Daniel, and the eyes of everyone else followed suit. "Don't you agree, Lord Belteshazzar? We knew you would laud the idea since it elevates the king who has so graciously elevated you."

Daniel's thoughts raced at the pace of his heart. "Our king is indeed most gracious, Lord Orchamus, and we would do him a great disservice if we neglected a single detail in planning this festival. Perhaps—"

"Yes, and for that reason"—Orchamus motioned the king's scribe—"we must have the royal scribe enter this historic moment into the records of the Medes and Persians."

Working to keep panic from his voice, Daniel turned and bowed to Darius. "Might I ask a few questions to clarify before the king speaks into law a decision that cannot be repealed?"

Annoyance shadowed the king's eagerness. "Go ahead. Ask your questions."

Daniel directed his questions to Orchamus.

"Since King Belshazzar's reign left Babylon's coffers empty, has the cost of the statue been considered?" When Orchamus stumbled over an uninformed guess, Daniel pressed him with another question. "Perhaps you intend to request the silver, gold, and bronze from King Cyrus. Since the statue will honor only King Darius, how much metal should we request from the emperor for a statue that honors the king of Babylon and Lands Beyond the River alone?"

Orchamus glared at him with open disdain, while the king ignored them both. "Daniel is right, of course. Building an image is foolish. Too expensive and takes too long. A festival replacing the old tradition of Akitu should celebrate the new unity of my kingdom. Using the lions as part of the festival is brilliant. The people have been intrigued by them since they arrived."

Daniel's mind grasped for more objections, but he'd served enough kings to know Darius's mind was made up. He watched the scene unfold as if it was another vision—except this one was more horrific than Yahweh's glorious truths. This was the nightmare of vain men seeking fleeting glory from divided hearts.

Darius offered his hand to Orchamus. "Cyrus will approve of a festival in which our people pray in unity to the new king of my unified lands. You've done well, my friend."

The ambitious overseer gripped the king's wrist and then bowed to one knee, placing his forehead on their locked hands. "I seek only to serve you, my king."

Barely noticing his groveling, Darius pulled from his grip and turned to the scribe. "My council has three days to coordinate the details of this new festival, but you will record its future dates for celebration as identical to Akitu—beginning on fourth Nisannu. All of Babylon's temples will accept offerings made only to me for thirty days. Anyone caught praying to, presenting offerings to, or in any way worshipping another god will be arrested and held for execution on a date and time of my choosing."

The scribe's reed scratched the parchment, keeping time with the king's dictation. When he looked up, nodding the completion of his task, Darius turned to his court of eager satraps. "You've done well, men. Send messengers to traders. I want plenty of food and supplies brought into the city for feasting. I'll provide a loaf of bread to every family in Babylon, and we'll starve the lions between now and then to make sure their first meal is especially entertaining."

The raucous room of nobles clapped and shouted, openly celebrating their king's approval with unbridled relief as the king descended the dais to congratulate his satraps.

Zerubbabel followed Darius into the fray. A quick and concerned glance over his shoulder told Daniel he understood his predicament. Many in the city strolled past Daniel's open west window at midday and had seen his regular practice. Allamu also knew he prayed toward Jerusalem three times a day. *"The decision was unanimous."* The words pierced Daniel afresh, and he searched the jubilant crowd for his stepson's face.

Allamu sat alone, head in his hands, and Daniel's hope rose. Perhaps "unanimous" had been overstated.

Weary to the bone and with feet on fire, Daniel felt an unbearable pull toward home. For the first time since accepting a place on Darius's council, he must admit his weakness. "Forgive the interruption, my king." Daniel lifted his voice, and the celebration quieted. Darius turned, and Daniel swallowed the bitterness of age as if he were drinking a cup of vinegar. "I am unwell. Might I be excused from this afternoon's session?"

Concern propelled the king up the dais steps two at a time. "Of course, but we'll likely name the festival and settle on details. Are you sure . . ." He looked down at Daniel's feet. "I'll call for my palanquin, my friend."

Daniel nodded in defeat. "I would be most appreciative, my king."

"I'll secure the palanquin and escort him home." Allamu's voice startled him.

"That's a good idea." Darius's brows drew together. "Shall I send my physician?"

"Thank you, but that's not necessary," Daniel said, offering a wan smile. "Mistress Belili has become quite proficient with herbs."

Allamu supported his elbow and helped him stand. Daniel clenched his teeth to keep from crying out. "Wait, please," he said, the pain stealing his breath. When it subsided enough to take a step, Allamu helped him down the stairs. Humiliated, Daniel walked down the aisle of Darius's throne room, while every satrap averted his eyes. An overwhelming sense of finality swept over him that today would be his last day to serve in Darius's court.

Daniel leaned heavily on Allamu's arm. Neither spoke until they descended the grand stairway and stood, awaiting the promised palanquin.

"What's happened?" Allamu asked. "Why are you limping like this?"

Daniel lifted the hem of his robe, revealing his bandages.

Allamu released a frustrated sigh. "What is it? Did you burn them?"

"No. I believe it's what we call Rich Man's Disease."

Allamu nodded. "Have you stopped eating meat?" He ducked his chin and gave him a "you should know better" look from hooded brows.

Consternation locked Daniel's lips into silence.

"How long have you been like this? You shouldn't have come to the session this morning." Then he mumbled, "Perhaps none of this would have happened."

"Are you referring to my swollen feet or the law commanding me to pray to Darius?"

Allamu kept his eyes focused on the approaching palanquin. "You know exactly what I'm referring to, and we'll speak of it when we get to the villa."

Allamu had dismissed him as if he were a ten-year-old child, but his feet hurt too much to protest. The soldiers lowered the conveyance on its knee-high stilts, and Daniel fell onto the cushioned elegance with a relieved sigh.

Allamu walked beside the lead soldier, stoic and brooding, but his concern had sparked a glimmer of hope that perhaps he'd maintained some loyalty to his mother and Daniel. Perhaps a greater proof that he hadn't joined Orchamus's conspiracy was his willingness to face Belili. Surely he wasn't foolish enough to vote to kill Daniel and then confess it to his mother.

They arrived at the villa before Daniel had time to consider how to tell Belili about the new law. Allamu appeared at the curtain as the soldiers lowered the palanquin. "Let me tell Mother."

Daniel eased himself from the seat and cried out when his feet touched the ground. "Wait. Please." Breathless, he stood still, adjusting to the pain. Bowing his head, he prayed silently— for himself, yes, but also for Belili. *Yahweh, give her courage to support my decision.*

"All right," he said, leaning on Allamu. "Let's go tell your mother."

Allamu matched Daniel's slow pace and called out to the soldiers, "Return to the palace. I'll walk back later."

"Thank you, Allamu."

"It's the least I could do."

"You mean since you agreed to let them kill me?"

"I didn't agree—"

"What's this?" Belili swung open the court-yard gate. "Allamu, what happened to him?"

"He didn't tell me his feet were swollen, Mother."

"Daniel, my Daniel . . ." She cupped his cheeks and then pointed toward the courtyard. "Help him in. Help him. Thank you for bringing him home, Allamu. You're a good boy."

Her son obeyed without a word and eased Daniel onto a cushion in the shade of two date palms. He stood and clasped his hands behind his back in uncomfortable silence.

Belili alternated glances between them. "What is it? Which of you has bad news?"

Daniel patted the cushion beside him. "Sit down, my love. Allamu and I had a very difficult morning. I think he should tell you about it."

"Wine," Belili said. "Do we need wine?"

"Sit down, Mother." Allamu grabbed another cushion and placed it opposite them. "King Darius made Belteshazzar the single administrator over his entire kingdom, placing the overseer positions and one hundred twenty satraps under his authority."

"No, no!" Belili covered a gasp.

"That's not the bad news." Allamu looked at Daniel, completely bewildered. "Any other wife would be proud—overjoyed."

"Haven't you seen the way the other noblemen look at Daniel?" she asked. Allamu closed his eyes and nodded.

Daniel actually felt sorry for him. He had no idea how perceptive she was. When Allamu opened his eyes, his expression softened. "You're right, Mother. Orchamus and the other officials hate Daniel, and now they've found a way to kill him if he continues to flaunt his faith in Yahweh."

"What do you mean, flaunt?" Belili sat a little straighter. "How does anyone *flaunt* the one true God?"

Faint splotches appeared on Allamu's neck. "Aren't you more worried about how they plan to kill your husband?"

"Of course, but first I must know why you

used the word *flaunt,* because you said he was flaunting—"

"Enough!" Daniel covered his ears, unable to endure their verbal sparring today. "Orchamus instigated a new law in which everyone must pray to Darius for thirty days. Anyone who prays to any god or human except our new king will be thrown into the lions' pit."

Belili's mouth flew open, but no sound escaped. Allamu's head fell forward. Perhaps their bickering would have been better. Daniel reached for his wife's hand. "You know I must continue to speak with Yahweh three times a day, kneeling toward Jerusalem. It is who I am, not just what I do, beloved."

Tears gathered on her lashes as she pulled his hand to her lips. "I know, my love, but couldn't you pray with the shutters closed? Just for thirty days?"

Close the shutters. Such a simple solution. Pray in secret. Nothing in the Law prescribed shutters being open or closed.

Allamu's eyes sparked. "Yes, thirty days with your shutters closed, Belteshazzar. Secret prayer inside your chamber."

The relief on their faces twisted his gut. What would happen to Belili if he was arrested? To Shesh and Kezia—to the whole family living in the villa deeded to him by Nebuchadnezzar?

But secret prayer?

The creation story flickered through his consciousness, and he remembered Adam and Eve's reaction after they sinned. They *hid* from Yahweh. Deception allows sin to lurk in the shadows. To hide his daily practice would be to deny his God and deceive his king. For him, it would be sin.

His decision made, he brushed his wife's soft cheek. "I'm sorry, my love, but I cannot live a lie. How could I boldly testify to King Darius of Yahweh's faithfulness if he thinks I was unfaithful to my God when it served my purpose?"

Something in her expression changed. Daniel couldn't define it or even describe it, but she sat up straighter and turned to her son. "I cannot ask my husband to live a lie and die inside."

Allamu's neck mottled crimson. "Mother! Did you hear the penalty? The lions. He'll be thrown—"

"No, Son." Belili studied her hands. "The penalty if Daniel betrayed Yahweh would be far worse than a pit of lions. My husband would cease to be himself." She lifted her eyes to meet her son's. "Our God can protect my husband if He chooses. The way He protected all the Chaldeans by giving Daniel the interpretation of Nebuchadnezzar's dream. As He saved our three friends from the fiery furnace. Our God saves His faithful ones, Allamu. Daniel has always been faithful."

Allamu's anger smoldered into seething. "Look at his feet, Mother. Yahweh can't even dull Daniel's pain—"

"You must go." Belili stood, towering over him. "I love you, but in this matter, you must either be silent or leave."

Daniel wanted to counsel moderation, but years of failed mediation between mother and son told him to hold his tongue. *Yahweh, You must be their mediator.*

"I cannot be silent, Mother, when a man I respect is being foolish."

At this, Daniel looked at Lord Allamu, his peer and friend. "When my ancestor King David was mocked for dancing before Yahweh in worship, he said to the mocker, 'I will become even more undignified than this in His name.' Allamu, my son, if Yahweh grants me more years to proclaim His faithfulness, you can call me a fool every day of my life."

Daniel tried to stand but couldn't. "Help me up before you go. I'm going to our bedchamber to pray—as I do every day."

Allamu set his jaw and offered his hand in silence. Daniel pulled against it, stood, and hobbled toward the stairway. The steps felt like a mountain today, but he would climb them, praising Yahweh with all his strength.

41

[Daniel] went home to his upstairs room where the windows opened toward Jerusalem. Three times a day he got down on his knees and prayed, giving thanks to his God, just as he had done before.

—DANIEL 6:10

My husband's feet had worsened over the past two days until he could barely walk with two sticks to help balance him. Even with myrrh bandages, changed four times a day, he found the pain hard to bear and sleep nearly impossible. He'd sent word to the king of his illness and was pardoned for three days from his duties. I sent word to the family villa that I needed Mert's help but didn't inform them of his condition. I didn't want to alarm the children by telling them about Daniel's feet until they could see him in person, see his resilience and determination. A report on the physical condition without witnessing his joyful countenance could lead them to wrong conclusions. Today was different. There was no joy, and the conclusion was grim.

Kezia accompanied Mert, which didn't surprise me. I met them in the courtyard. "It's his feet,"

I said while we climbed the stairs. "Worse than I've ever seen them."

Without waiting to hear more, Kezia bolted up the remaining steps and through our chamber door. I heard her knees hit the floor and then . . . "Abba, your toes are so swollen the skin looks as if it might split." When Mert and I arrived at the doorway, Kezia was kneeling by our bed, unwrapping her abba's bandaged left foot.

My daughter looked up, pouring out her worry in anger. "These bandages are obviously old rags. Didn't you call for the king's physician?"

I knelt beside her, trying to hold my temper. "Kezia. Daughter. Your abba has been governor of the Chaldeans for nearly seventy years. He knows more than any physician in the land and has shown me how to—"

"Surely the second-highest official in the land can afford to have a trained physician tend his feet." She began unwrapping his other foot, more concerned about telling us what to do than with the pain on her abba's face. "Look at his joints!"

"Mert?" But my friend was gone. I hoped she had gone to gather two bowls of water to soak my husband's feet.

"Ima, did you hear me?"

"What, Kezia?" I shouted. Daniel patted my shoulder, his encouragement to be calm. He didn't speak much, since the pain drained his energy. I would try to keep the peace. "I'm sorry, Daughter. What did you ask me?"

She knelt, head bowed, hands in her lap. "I'm sorry I was impatient." She swiped at her cheeks and looked up at her abba. "We never get to see you since you've been appointed to the king's council. Your family misses you terribly." Turning to me, her pleading changed to accusation. "Why did we have to hear about Abba's promotion from my friends in the market?"

Daniel's hand tightened on my shoulder, and I grinned at his silent warning. Normally, I would make a harsh comment about Kezia's gossiping, but not today. None of us could stand the usual grousing. "Your abba's new position hasn't been made official yet, and it shouldn't have been shared outside the king's council."

Mert arrived with two bowls of cool water, the scent of mint oil filling the air. She set them on the floor in front of Kezia and me. Kezia and I each cradled one of Daniel's feet and lowered it into a bowl. He released a shuddering breath. The pain was chipping away at him. I was losing him a little more each day.

Our daughter didn't seem to perceive it. "I heard in the market that the king has ordered the new festival to begin tomorrow. He's named it the Hidati, the Unity Festival. The stalls are packed with goods from everywhere. I saw a new stall filled with pottery from Egypt. The bowls, the amphorae and vases—beautiful."

I nodded. She needed no reply. She'd begun the inane chatter that won the hearts of her gossiping friends in the market.

"And did you hear, Abba? King Darius has commanded everyone in his kingdom to unite in prayer to him alone for thirty days. It's why he named it Hidati, so all peoples and tribes under his authority can celebrate unity as a single nation." She shrugged. "I suppose we don't actually have to pray to him. Maybe it's not such a bad idea—"

"Don't you dare!" Daniel pushed himself to his feet, towering over Kezia and me with one foot in each bowl. "We are to have no other gods besides Yahweh. Do you hear me, Kezia bat Daniel?"

Mert chuckled. "Well, don't you look silly, Lord Belteshazzar, standing in two bowls of water?" I had desperately missed my friend's candor, but now wasn't the time to reintroduce it.

Kezia looked up, her expression a mix of surprise and offense. "I wouldn't actually pray to the king, Abba." She bowed her head only a moment and then stood. "I should return to the villa. Shesh will arrive for his midday meal . . ."

It was barely midmorning. I rose to my feet. "Kezia, don't go. We need to talk."

She turned to her abba, waiting. He sat back on the bed and rolled over on his side, dragging his wet feet onto our clean blankets. I would have killed him if he hadn't been hurting so badly.

"Please, Kezia, my love. We must talk." She looked longingly at her abba and walked toward the door. Mert followed us down the stairs.

"Let's go to the open courtyard," I said when we reached the bottom step. "It's a lovely morning." Mert stopped by the kitchen and asked one of our maids to bring something cool to drink. When Mert arrived in the courtyard, I'd already directed Kezia to the plush cushions beneath the date palms where Allamu and Daniel had told me about Darius's terrifying law.

Had it really only been two days? I'd nearly drowned in a sea of guilt. Me, the one who'd been hiding my whole life, must tell our daughter that her abba would willingly die rather than hide behind shutters to worship the God who could heal but chose not to. He'd never been stronger in his faith, nor weaker in his body.

"Ima?" Kezia's soft tone shattered my brooding.

How long had the maid been standing over us with the tray of watered wine? "Yes, thank you. You may set the tray here." I waited until the Egyptian girl left before reaching for a goblet, unable to lift my eyes and meet the inevitable questions.

Kezia's hand stayed mine on the goblet. "Ima." She waited in silence, holding me there.

I felt tears sting my throat. The secret pounded at my heart's door, begging to be freed. *I can't tell her. Not Kezia.* She'd hated me longer and stronger than any of my daughters. I inhaled a deep breath to relieve the urge to confess, but still my secret screamed inside me. I pulled my hand from Kezia's grasp. "I should explain your abba's mood."

Both she and Mert looked at me in surprise. "What is there to explain?" Kezia asked. "He's in pain."

"It's more than that." I took a slow sip of my wine and set the goblet down. "You both know his routine. At dawn, midday, and dusk, he goes to our window facing Jerusalem, opens the shutters, and prays."

Kezia's expression grew wistful. "He's always done it."

I let my silence inform them both what his faithfulness would cost us all.

Realization hardened Mert's features first. Kezia, though slower to understand, was quicker to react. "But he can't! Not during Hidati, Ima."

I found myself fidgeting again. Daniel usually settled me. I laced my fingers together and curled my hands into a white-knuckled ball. "Your abba continues his daily routine, and since he's missed the last two days of council meetings, his prayers at our open window have drawn quite a crowd."

My throat tightened. *And every moment of his faithfulness condemns my choices in Achmetha. How did I think I could save my life by denying Yahweh?*

"He must stop, Ima, if only for a few days!" Panic launched Kezia from her pillow. "You must convince him. He could do so much good for our people as the king's chief administrator. And what about the vision and Jeremiah's prophecy? He can't return to Jerusalem or help others do so if he's executed for praying to Yahweh! Why not mumble a few meaningless prayers to Darius if it can save his life?"

Shaking, I stood to meet her fury. "Because uttering meaningless words to a false god shriveled my soul."

My daughter looked as if I'd slapped her. "When did you pray to a false god, Ima?"

The secret became a living thing within me, now clawing, shrieking, ranting to come into the light. I shot a panicked glance at Mert.

"Tell her, Belili. She needs to know."

"Someone, tell me." Kezia looked from Mert to me.

Feeling light-headed, I returned to my cushion.

The decision I faced now was different than in Achmetha. Then I'd feared for my life. Now I feared my family's rejection and Daniel's hatred. In Achmetha, I'd chosen to survive by my own wits and will but lost the living breath of my soul. Wouldn't Yahweh provide if my family rejected me? Hadn't He proven His power and mercy again and again?

I looked up at my daughter still towering over me. "When I was exiled to Achmetha, I became high priestess of Mithra."

Her face lost all color, and she collapsed onto her cushion.

"Your abba doesn't know."

"No. No, you couldn't. You . . . How . . ." She looked away. Shook her head. Then looked at Mert. "You knew." My friend nodded. Kezia's face clouded with unspoken sorrow, and then she broke into sobs.

"Kezia, let me explain." I knelt beside her.

She continued shaking her head, silent no after no. Mert rubbed her back and fought her own emotions. Though I felt lighter, cleaner, free of the beast that had stained me for most of my life, I was tortured by the pain I'd inflicted on my daughter.

My own tears began to flow, a stream at first that gushed into waves of confession and repentance to the only One who could save me from myself. *Yahweh, forgive me for bending*

477

a knee or offering worship to an idol that can't see or know me. Forgive my anger and doubt when You showed me mercy. Give me courage now to love You above all others and be forthright and true—even if it costs me Daniel and my family.

A tender touch on my hand startled me, and I lifted my head. Mert and I were alone. I scanned the empty courtyard. "Where is she?" And the consquences of my confession began to churn in my gut. "Why did I tell Kezia first? What if she tells Daniel? Or the other children? She'll tell her friends at the market. The whole city will know before the evening meal, Mert." Wild with regret and fear, I couldn't breathe.

"Look at me, Belili. Look at me!" She grabbed my arms and shook me. "Kezia won't tell anyone." My friend's eyes were red rimmed, but her tone was even. "Kezia needs time to process what you've told her. She loves you. She'll be all right—as will you. I'm proud of you." A tender smile graced her lips. "Do you want me to go with you to tell Daniel?"

With the single question, the beast returned to wrap its chains around my heart again. "I . . . I can't . . ."

Mert dropped her hands. "You have to tell him."

"I will, but not right now. How could I add to his pain? And he could be arrested any day."

"All the more reason to leave nothing unspoken between you."

I turned away. How could Mert know what was at stake? She'd never known a love like mine and Daniel's. *Yahweh, forgive me. I can't risk losing the one who led me back to You.*

A dense fog floated into my bedchamber window on the Borsippa estate, and the lavender glow signaled time to help Hasina and Amyitis start our morning meal. I hurried through the kitchen and outside to rob the ducks' nests of eggs. While running across the barnyard, I tripped over something.

"Daniel!" He was kneeling, praying. I tugged at his arm, trying to interrupt. "Daniel, get up!" But when I looked behind me, a lion lunged at us both. "Noooo!" I flailed in the grip of the giant beast, but its claws pinned me to the ground.

Lifting its head to the sky, it let out a roar that sounded like Daniel.

"Belili! Belili, my love, wake up!"

I bolted upright in bed, clutching the husband I'd loved since my youth. "I can't lose you, Daniel." I couldn't stop trembling. "Please, please don't leave me."

"If I must leave you, it will be for only a blink of eternity."

I squeezed him tighter and realized the room in my dream was the same lavender in which we now sat. Dawn had come on the day of Darius's ridiculous feast, and my husband was already dressed. He was ready to kneel at our window. "No!" Panic clutched at my throat, and I clutched at Daniel.

"Shhh. Shhh." He held me, smoothing my hair. "Yahweh rules over kings and kingdoms, Belili. He sets rulers in place and knew the number of my days before I was born." He kissed my forehead and winked. "I don't think this is my last day."

"Well, that would have been good to hear three days ago." I pulled him into a ferocious hug. "Did you receive a vision? A dream? Are you sure?"

"No, I'm not sure."

All my relief was shattered by another wave of fear, but I couldn't let him see it when I released him. "Well, we can be sure of this. Yahweh is good."

The sweetest smile brightened his features. I kissed him, hoping to be steadied by our love and cleansed by his purity.

"I'm going to pray now," he said when we parted. I simply nodded, my throat too tight to speak.

Daniel stood on painful feet and walked with the regal air of a king to kneel humbly before our God. He opened the shutters and invited in the cool morning air.

Voices below our window sounded low and rumbling.

"Who—" I started to ask.

Daniel turned to me with lifted hand and a stern gaze. I was to remain in our bed. He'd told me last night, "Even though you pray near me each day, there's no need for you to be seen through the window now."

Protecting me. It's what he'd done since the day we met. And I'd told him half truths for just as long. How could I ever tell him the whole truth now, on a day that could be his last?

My Daniel braced himself against the windowsill as he knelt. With eyes closed, he lifted his hands and then his voice:

Hear, O Israel: The LORD our God, the LORD is one. Love the LORD your God with all your heart and with all your soul and with all your strength. These commandments that I give you today are to be on your hearts. Impress them on your children. Talk about them when you sit at home and when you walk along the road, when you lie down and when you get up.

He continued the Shema and sang two psalms before ending his worship with supplication for King Darius and the prosperity of the empire that would return a remnant of Israel's faithful to their home in Jerusalem.

I did as he'd asked of me, sat on our bed and prayed with him. Silently but fervently.

I prayed for his safety, for Darius's leniency, for Allamu's realization of Yahweh's truth. I prayed for Kezia's mercy on an ima who had failed her again. And last of all, I prayed Yahweh could somehow forgive me for surrendering my whole heart and then snatching it up again.

When Daniel rose from his knees and closed the shutters, I patted the mattress beside me. He sat down and laid his head back, sighing as if he'd done a full day's work.

"Do you know how it pained me to stay in this bed?" I asked.

"I know. You wouldn't have wanted to see."

"How many were outside our window?"

He paused two heartbeats. "Many."

I thought about the lion in my dream and closed my eyes, trying to unsee the image. "Are you hungry?" I was hoping he'd say yes so I could go downstairs and busy myself with something.

"No. Would you stay with me awhile?"

I turned on my side and curled my body around his. "I'll stay until you tell me to go."

He snuggled his head against mine, and in a short time I heard the slow, steady breathing of sleep.

When I opened my eyes next, the air was warm and sticky. The shutters on the window were open, and my husband was on his knees once more.

"Hear, O Israel: The LORD our God, the LORD is one. Love the LORD your God with all your heart and with all your soul and with all your strength . . ."

Again after his prayer, he refused to tell me how many people stood outside our window, but at least this time he ate a meal. Mert coaxed him downstairs to enjoy the shade of the courtyard before his evening prayer. But when the sun touched the western horizon, my husband made his trek upstairs to kneel before our open window once more. This time I didn't go with him. I spoke from our courtyard to Yahweh, the great God who sees all, knows all, and is sovereign over all. This time I prayed only for my husband's deliverance.

Daniel emerged from our chamber after his evening prayer. "I'm not hungry, and I'd like to spend some time alone in prayer." He grinned. "With the shutters closed."

I tried not to be concerned, but I could tell he was troubled.

Mert was good company. She asked if I'd spoken with Kezia. I changed the subject. We finished our meal sharing stories about my grandchildren and what a joy they'd become in our lives.

Our words were light, but my thoughts were heavy. If Kezia revealed my secret, would I be cut off from my family? Would the children and grandchildren who had finally accepted me now send me into an exile of the heart? I winced inwardly. Where was the courage that prodded me to tell Kezia in the first place? Where was my faith?

"Where is Lord Belteshazzar?" Allamu stormed through the courtyard gate.

I'd endured enough heartache for one day. "You will call him Daniel in this house. He is resting upstairs, and you will not disturb him."

"The whole council saw him, Mother. All of them. I've come from a meeting in which they unanimously agreed to accuse Lord—Daniel—before the king's court."

I had expected to feel the same panic I'd experienced after confessing to Kezia, but a surprising peace settled over me. I looked up at my tall and handsome son. "I'm sad to hear it was unanimous. I'd hoped you would have spoken in his defense." Patting his arm, I left him standing sullenly in Mert's care.

Our bedchamber was lit by a single lamp, flickering on a small table near Daniel's side of the bed. The shutters were closed, the bed empty, yet I heard a faint whisper. I took three steps closer to the bed and saw Daniel lying facedown on the floor, his arms outstretched. I'd entered holy ground without realizing it and bent to remove my sandals.

Kneeling beside my husband's prone body,

I began my own silent vigil. Sometime during the night, I woke with a start, lying in a ball on the floor. My bones creaked as I unfolded, stretching sore and weary muscles.

"Nebuchadnezzar's story in his own writing." Daniel's voice startled me. Sitting on the couch beside the bed, he lifted a scroll he was reading. "Quite valuable, but don't ever sell it, Belili. Amyitis's crown, yes, but even if they take the villa after I'm arrested, don't sell this. Yahweh will provide for you and the family. This scroll must be kept for future genera—"

"Allamu said the council will present their charges as the first order of business in the morning."

He nodded once. "They'll come by midday." Sighing, he turned toward the shuttered windows. "Perhaps I can pray twice more by then." He looked at me and winked. There was still fight left in him.

Pushing to my feet, I groaned a little and started toward the door. "I'm hungry. Do you want something?"

He snagged my hand as I walked past him, opened it, and kissed my palm. "You are braver than any warrior."

I bent to kiss the top of his gray head and fled before my tears proved him a liar.

42

Then they said to the king, "Daniel, who is one of the exiles from Judah, pays no attention to you, Your Majesty, or to the decree you put in writing. He still prays three times a day."

—DANIEL 6:13

Daniel opened his eyes after morning prayers and glanced down at the council members. The group was small, and Orchamus wasn't among them. A few satraps from the Palestine group came and two or three from each of Syria's and Phoenicia's groups. He closed the shutters, wondering why any of them came. They already had plenty of eyewitnesses to testify. *Yahweh, let their interest be spiritual curiosity rather than political malice.*

Making his way to the couch, he nudged Nebuchadnezzar's scroll aside and began unwrapping the bandage from his left foot. Yahweh had answered his prayers, easing his pain enough to walk with help. He removed the right foot's bandage as well, hoping he'd be able to stand before his accusers instead of being carried on a couch.

Kezia's and Shesh's voices filtered up the

stairs, and he closed his eyes, speaking aloud to the Giver of joy and peace. "Thank You, Lord, for surrounding me with family today."

Footsteps on the stairs tightened his shoulders, but he remembered Allamu's report. No arrest until later. Belili appeared at the door with a smile. "Shesh is here with news you'll want to hear." She looked at the uncoiled bandages on the floor. "Your feet look better."

"They feel a little better."

Nodding, she came near to offer her arm as support. "This is becoming a surprisingly good day." He accepted her help, then walked arm in arm with her down the stairs and to the open courtyard, where all four of their girls waited with their husbands. Mert poured something from a pitcher into silver goblets.

"Wine at this hour?" Daniel knew he sounded like a prude.

Mert kept pouring. "It's watered, and you should hear Shesh's news before you judge."

Their son-in-law's smile nearly swallowed his face. "We've found more sacred items from Yahweh's Temple in other temples in Babylon."

Daniel hugged him. "Praise be to Yahweh! What did you find?"

Shesh helped Daniel to a cushion, where he sat down beside him. "We discovered more lampstands, wick trimmers, and gold and silver bowls." His enthusiasm dimmed. "The lampstand was the only thing of significant size. We found most of the treasure in the two main temples, the Esagila and Nabu's temple."

Daniel scratched his chin, contemplating both the thrill of discovery and the dread of finding only small items. Would Nebuchadnezzar dared to have destroyed the Ark of the Covenant? Shaking the thought from his head, he reached for a goblet of wine and lifted it toward heaven. "We praise You, Yahweh, for Your faithfulness. We asked for Your help, and You answered. Now we ask for continued guidance to prepare the remnant of Your people to rebuild and restore Your holy city." He took a sip of sweet nectar, allowing the taste to satisfy both body and soul.

His family drank a quick sip, but their jabbing elbows and pointing turned Daniel's attention toward Shesh. "What are you up to?"

Without a word, his son-in-law stepped aside, revealing a small pile of dusty leather scrolls hidden behind him. He pulled one out, blew off some dust, and sneezed as he delivered it into Daniel's hands. "Pardon me, Abba."

"Of course, but what are they?"

"Nabu's priests found all of them beside the lampstand," Shesh explained while Daniel unwound the leather tie. "I don't know why they were there, but I'm grateful they were."

Daniel read the first lines aloud. "The words of Jeremiah son of Hilkiah, one of the priests at Anathoth . . . in the thirteenth year of the reign of Josiah . . ." The dawning understanding of the significance began in his belly. "Are these the remainder of Jeremiah's writings?"

Shesh nodded. "As well as sacred words of other prophets."

Daniel dropped the scroll to his lap and wept with joy. Belili cradled his head against her chest and began singing the song of Miriam. "I will sing to the LORD, for He is highly exalted . . ." Her voice carried him into a private place of worship. "The LORD is my strength and my defense; He has become my salvation—"

"How can you celebrate?" Allamu's voice raked against the melody and wrenched Daniel from God's presence. The man stood at the courtyard gate with Zerubbabel, and joy vanished like grass in summer's heat.

Daniel stood, wincing at his still-tender feet. "If you were here to arrest me, you would have brought more than our Hebrew friend. What news from court?"

But he knew by Allamu's and Zerubbabel's faces the news wasn't good. Zerubbabel lagged behind, and Allamu braced Daniel's shoulders. "Orchamus and the satraps presented their accusations this morning, reminding the king that you are a captive from Judah, that your slave name is Daniel, and that your first loyalty is to your native god. But your open rebellion—

praying to your god beside an open window during the Hidati festival—is the only charge that matters. The council demanded your immediate arrest and execution."

Daniel's relieved sigh turned into a grin and changed Allamu's concern to anger. "How can you smile? Over a hundred witnesses stand against you."

Daniel looked beyond Allamu to Zerubbabel at the gate. "And yet I'm not under arrest."

Zerubbabel stepped up beside Allamu. "Darius doesn't want to lose his best administrator. He's distressed, Daniel. He commanded his scribes to find a way to reverse the law."

Belili jumped from her pillow and hugged Daniel with a stranglehold. "It's wonderful news."

"It's not a reprieve," Allamu cautioned. "Don't celebrate yet. Court reconvenes at sunset."

Mert appeared with a tray full of bowls. "Aren't you a fly in the wine." She shoved the tray into Allamu's hands with a mischievous grin. "I'm glad you brought your guard. He can help you set the tables. I've made your favorite—gruel with date paste." She patted his cheek and whispered, "Your ima needs you."

Allamu glanced at his mother, and her expression brightened to a welcoming smile. "Please stay, Son."

"Come, Zerubbabel." He nodded in the

direction of three long rectangular tables. "It appears we have work to do."

"I'll help too." Kezia exchanged a meaningful glance with him and followed the two men to the dining area.

Daniel pulled his wife close, watching Mert marshal the family into action and then set to work at her cook fire. The sweet aromas of feasting wafted through the courtyard all day long. Though Daniel's mouth watered to sample the roast duck and lamb mounded on his family's plates, he was obedient to his conscience, knowing the diet he'd eaten as a captive prince was the answer to his aching feet. Mert had gone to great lengths preparing tasty chickpea stew with onions, garlic, and leeks, seasoned to perfection. Fresh fruits would soon ripen as the Akitu festival—now Hidati—signaled the beginning of spring in Babylon.

He laid his head in Belili's lap and patted his rounded belly, laughing at the antics of their great-grandchildren and enjoying easy conversation with the whole family around them. His wife, however, appeared deep in thought, her smile distant. "Yahweh can deliver me," he said quietly. "Lions are no more challenging than a fiery furnace."

She lowered her eyes to meet his, blinking away tears. "What if He doesn't?"

Daniel sat up and drew her chin toward him,

forcing her to meet his gaze. "Yahweh delivered Shadrach, Meshach, and Abednego from Nebuchadnezzar's lunacy on the Dura Plain but allowed them to die at the hands of Nabonidus years later. Who can know the mind of God or the reasons behind His salvation? But we *can* know two things for certain." He held up one finger. "We know God is good no matter what tonight holds, and"—his second finger went up— "nothing can make me deny the one true God."

Belili's countenance crumbled. Covering her cries, she scooted from the bench, fled from the courtyard, and disappeared upstairs. Several of their children saw her hurried departure and exchanged puzzled glances. Kezia's eyes met Daniel's with something more than concern. Something that tied a knot in his belly.

He called her over with a wave. She obeyed but stood silent before him, head bowed.

"Your ima is upset about more than my arrest, isn't she?"

After a slight pause, she looked up, her eyes filled with tears. "Talk to her, Abba. Don't let this day pass without talking to your wife."

I lay across our bed, weeping, Daniel's words gouging my soul. *"Nothing can make me deny the one true God."* His faith was unshakable. Even on the eve of his arrest, even while remembering the unjust deaths of his best friends, he could say without pause that he would *never* deny Yahweh.

How could he ever forgive a wife who had?

I'd planned to tell him today. After we broke our fast, I almost took him aside, but Shesh wanted to show him one of Isaiah's scrolls. After our midday meal, I was going to walk with him in the garden and tell him of my idolatry then, but he played Hounds and Jackals with one of the grandsons. Moments ago, the words were on my tongue to confess my life of bondage to Mithra. He was peaceful, and Yahweh had restored my faith and peace. I was ready to trust in Jehovah-jireh—God, my provider— when Daniel's declar-ation snatched away all hope that he could ever understand or forgive.

"Belili?" My husband's voice sent a shock of terror through my veins.

"What is it, my love?" I wiped my eyes and tried to gain control as he lumbered across the room on swollen, painful feet. How could I explain my departure without telling the whole truth now? *Yahweh, he is Your most precious gift to me. How could You ask me to give him up?*

A clear but silent voice resonated like a drum in my mind. *Is he more precious to you than I AM?* The thought stripped away all pretense, exposing the filth of my excuses and half truths. No fear of physical or emotional pain could compare to an everlasting separation from the One who always showed me mercy. My choice was finally made, my surrender complete.

He hobbled across the room, sat on the bed beside me, and pulled me into his arms. I felt his heartbeat against my chest as if it were my own. "I must confess my sin to you, Husband, because your courage has been a light shining on my darkness." I pulled away and held his gaze. The same fear twisted my tongue. "I . . . When I . . ." I bowed my head and inhaled a sustaining breath. "When I was abandoned by Ashpenaz's eunuchs in Achmetha . . ." I faced him and continued, "I begged on the streets until I was taken into the temple of Mithra and nursed back to health. I was expected to serve in order to pay my debt. Within a few years I became the high priestess of Mithra."

I let the weight of the revelation register on his expression before I went on. "I rejected Yahweh in Achmetha, certain He had rejected me—or I thought perhaps that He was simply limited to His presence atop the Ark or with good people like you. By the time Gadi paid the exorbitant price for my dowry, I was hardened toward any god and never worshipped at Mithra's temple again. After several miscarriages, Allamu became my sun and moon, and then even he was taken from me."

"Stop!" Daniel's face grew crimson. "You're

494

telling me you didn't believe in Yahweh even after we were married?"

Fear rose up again at the anger smeared across his features. "I . . . Yes, I believed . . . that He answered *your* prayers. But not mine. I believed I was too broken, too stained. I thought Yahweh could never hear the prayers of a woman like me, but then I saw Him humble Nebuchadnezzar. And I witnessed Amyitis's love. I knew then that if a woman—flawed as my friend was—could love her husband while he was a brute beast, harming her and those she cared for, somehow Yahweh could love me too."

Daniel's lips were pressed into a thin white line, but I had to finish. I needed to assure him that my heart was secure with Yahweh now. "He has become to me like water and air. I am changed because of the love He has shown me. Because of the love *you* have shown me."

I reached for his hand to lift it to my lips, but he pulled away as if I were leprous. "How could you deny Him, Belili? You witnessed His power in the Holy of Holies. You saw Him rescue our friends from the fire on the Dura Plain. It's not as if Yahweh was a story you heard from traveling merchants. How could you ignore His power, His presence?" His voice rose with every accusation. "You *knew* Him, Abigail!"

The disdain I'd feared blazed from his eyes

and sent my heart reeling. "But I didn't know Him. Not really. Not until—" The sound of rhythmic footsteps outside our bedroom window stole my breath, and I saw the same recognition on his features.

Daniel pushed himself off the bed and cried out when his feet touched the floor. I supported his arm, but he pulled away. "Leave me, woman."

I backed away, covering a sob as the shout came from the courtyard.

"By the order of King Darius, Lord Belteshazzar is to be taken immediately and without mercy into the custody of the royal guard."

We stared at each other while listening to the words. Without comment, he turned to go.

I rushed after him. "I'm going with you."

"No!" He whirled on me, his hand raised in warning. "You will remain with Shesh and Kezia."

In a flash of memory no longer than a blink, I thought of Amyitis combing that creature's hair with her ivory comb, and I knew where I belonged. "I'm going with you to witness Yahweh's deliverance and bring you home."

43

So the king gave the order, and they brought Daniel and threw him into the lions' den. The king said to Daniel, "May your God, whom you serve continually, rescue you!"

—DANIEL 6:16

Four hulking soldiers barged into our bed-chamber and unceremoniously carried Daniel downstairs. Allamu followed them, shouting, "Take care with his feet."

I was two steps behind them. Kezia intercepted me with a hug, pressing her lips against my ear. "Did you tell him?"

Holding her tight, I whispered, "It didn't go well. Please pray. I've upset him at a time when he needs peace."

She held me at arm's length, infusing me with her approval. "He needed the truth, Ima. You've both shown great courage today. Yahweh will deliver."

Allamu returned after settling Daniel in the palanquin and looked at our family, his expression grim. "No exception was found. Pray to your god, and I'll send word when we receive the final verdict." He nudged me toward the gate. "Come, Mother."

"We will send word of Daniel's deliverance," I corrected, refusing to consider another outcome.

He didn't contradict but rather hurried me to the street, where we caught up with the guards who carried my husband toward the palace. We walked alongside for the short distance, but rather than entering the palace courtyard through the south gate, the guards continued down the street.

I pointed in the proper direction and shouted, "Wait, where are—"

Allamu wrapped a strong arm around me, prodding me to follow the straying palanquin. "It's all right, Mother. They're taking a different route." He looked behind him as if being chased.

I looked back too but saw nothing unusual. The guards turned into a narrow alleyway and set the palanquin on the tiled street at the top of the stairway I recognized from years ago. "Why are they taking him through the servants' entrance?"

Allamu pulled me close, kissed the top of my head, and whispered against my hair, "I'm sure they're following orders, Mother. Please keep silent."

The guards helped Daniel out of the palanquin and, though he tried to refuse their help, they fairly carried him down the stairs and through the narrow passageways to the wide public hall leading to the courtroom.

Daniel greeted each soldier by name along the way, receiving surprised and respectful nods in return. I offered my hand to support him, but he pushed it away. "I will lean on Yahweh alone."

His words, intended to harm, hit their mark; but I refused to be dissuaded. "He will be your shield, your sword, and your strong tower."

As we approached the throne room doors, Zerubbabel was one of the two guards stationed there. He spoke in a whisper as we passed, "May Yahweh save you, Daniel ben Johanan."

"Thank you, Zerubbabel." Daniel's voice quaked as he passed, but the man's presence was encouraging. Yahweh's people, scattered all over Babylon, would hear of Daniel's faithfulness and recount the stories of his deliverance. *Please, Yahweh, let there be deliverance.*

Allamu offered me his forearm, and I placed my hand there, afraid my knees would buckle as I followed my husband into King Darius's courtroom. The crowded room smelled of stale sweat and rancid wine. Men sat shoulder to shoulder on councilmen's benches, and others stood tightly packed to the walls, leaving only a narrow aisle. Daniel limped down the crimson carpet amid the whispers of jealous men. When he reached the foot of the dais, Allamu stood on his right, I on his left. We bowed as one and waited to be addressed, while the audience stilled.

"Lord Belteshazzar,"—King Darius's voice sounded like cymbals in the silence—"you have been accused of wantonly disregarding the law of Hidati, praying to your god rather than to your king. What say you in defense?"

"I respectfully vow, before you and these witnesses, King Darius, that I serve you to the best of my ability, but I serve Yahweh with every beat of my heart. He commands that I pray to none but Him, and His law is higher than the law of any man."

"Treason!" one man shouted.

"To the lions!" yelled another, jabbing his finger at the air.

King Darius stood, his very presence quieting the onlookers. "I will see you in my private chamber, Lord Belteshazzar. Now!"

"My king!" Orchamus stood. "Why not sentence him? Has he not confessed his crime? Your law is irrevocable. What further discussion is necessary?"

King Darius's eyes narrowed. "Perhaps I wish to discuss who else will join him in the pit."

Orchamus resumed his seat, and Darius stalked toward a side exit. Daniel followed the king, and I followed Daniel. Allamu reached for my arm, but I pulled away. "I'm going!"

When I took another step, the king's hard stare met me. "You weren't invited, Mistress Belili."

I returned his gaze but kept my voice low. "You should invite me, King Darius. Young

Cyrus discovered I was quite stubborn, and so will you."

The king's lifted brow questioned Daniel, and I held my breath, waiting to see if my husband would shut me out. His apathetic shrug gave permission.

As the guard was about to open the king's chamber door, Daniel pulled me into his arms. "Wait!" His hands trembled, his face pale as milk. "I beg you, contain Nergala before we enter."

Darius's features softened. "It's done, Lord Belteshazzar. I can't save you, but I won't make you face Nergala or parade you past the lions' pit on your way to your trial."

Daniel held me between himself and the king as if frozen, unable to respond. Filling the silence, I said, "Thank you, my king. You are most kind." It was then that I realized we'd been taken through the servants' entrance to avoid seeing the lions' pit. Though I appreciated his thoughtfulness, my heart nearly failed when he said, "I can't save you." Was that what had changed Daniel's demeanor so drastically?

I looked back at my husband and spoke gently while prying his fingers from my arms. "We must follow the king, my love."

Like waking from a dream, he blinked several times before following Darius into what had been Nebuchadnezzar's chamber. The old hunting trophies were gone, replaced with tasteful tapestries and Persian pottery.

"Mistress Belili, please sit down." Darius pointed to the couch where Daniel sat, and I realized I was the only one still standing. The king heaved a sigh and fixed his gaze on my husband. "I had no idea you prayed to your god three times a day until Allamu told me on the day of my decree that you would never stop. So I sent messages through carrier pigeons to Achmetha on that very day, asking Cyrus to overrule my premature edict."

"Thank you, my king," Daniel said. "But as I'm sure you're aware, the laws of the Medes and Persians are ir—"

"Irrevocable. Yes, I know. Orchamus has reminded me of it at least a thousand times. He wants to make your execution public. Light torches around the pit. Invite the whole city. He even suggested jugglers and dancers."

I covered an involuntary whimper, my heart melting in my chest.

"Truly, Mistress Belili, I've done all I could to save Lord Belteshazzar." King Darius's tone bordered on frustration. "First, because he is the best administrator in my kingdom, but also because he is your husband, and King Cyrus holds a special fondness for you. I'm not anxious to kill a man who's wife nursed the emperor's beloved aunt during her last days."

Shocked, I didn't know if I should be flattered or offended, but at this point I was grateful King Darius had tried to save my husband.

Darius pulled his fingers through his hair, sweat glistening on his forehead. "I hope, Mistress Belili, when the emperor next visits Babylon, you will speak to Cyrus about me with the same mercy I've shown your husband in his last hours."

Could I somehow use King Darius's fear of Cyrus to change my husband's fate? I glanced to my right to see if Daniel had noticed the same opportunity, but my husband had suddenly grown old. He was round shouldered and frail, and his head and hands bobbed with the tremors of the aged. I laid my hand on his arm, and he jumped as if he'd forgotten I was there.

His eyes darted from me to Darius and back to me. "I don't want to die, Belili. I don't want to die."

Any advantage I thought we might have had fled when I saw the terror on Daniel's face. There would be no negotiation from him. My husband was going to the lions.

The edges of his vision darkened, and Daniel saw only his wife's face. Mouth dry, he couldn't speak. He accepted King Darius's help to stand and shuffled his feet as if in a dream—no, a nightmare—allowing the king to lead him back to the throne room. Panic had seized his body like a vise the moment he'd approached the king's door and remembered Nergala. Every detail of the lioness's powerful frame rushed into his mind's eye. Claws. Teeth. Even the sinewy muscles that flexed each time she moved.

"Courage, Lord Belteshazzar." Zerubbabel was now at his side. Where had he come from? They passed three guards on their way to the throne room's side door, each one staring as if Daniel were a leper escaped from the colony.

He glanced behind him. Darius followed, Belili on his arm. Betrayers, both of them. Darius wished to save him only to save face with Cyrus. And his wife—had everything been a lie? No. She loved him, but could love be true when all else was a lie?

Zerubbabel opened the side door, and the roar of conversation stilled. Daniel's footsteps grew shorter and slower. Darius and Belili crowded him from behind, and Zerubbabel coaxed him to a quicker pace. "Don't rush me!" Daniel snapped.

"Shhh, my love." Belili left Darius's side to accompany Daniel down the six steps of the dais while Zerubbabel remained on the platform with the king.

Darius sat on his throne, waiting for Daniel, Belili, and Allamu to settle into place. Daniel felt as if the floor were shifting beneath him, but when he looked down, he realized his legs were shaking violently, causing him to sway. What was happening to him? He'd never been afraid to die.

Well, not exactly true. Death itself seemed a welcome friend. He looked forward to entering paradise, to spending eternity with Father Abraham and the other faithful who were waiting. It was the *dying* that terrified him. The pain. The suffering. The lingering fear of being torn apart by lions.

"According to the law of the Medes and Persians to which I am bound," King Darius bellowed over the silent crowd, "Lord Belteshazzar is guilty of breaking the law of Hidati and is hereby stripped of all official titles. He is henceforth known as Daniel, the Hebrew, and will be lowered into the lions' pit this night and sealed up until morning."

His eyes narrowed, searching the men on the audience benches. "Orchamus, stand."

Daniel considered asking the king to make Orchamus the new chief administrator. Perhaps, then, the covetous overseer would end this vendetta and Daniel could be set free. He dared glance over his shoulder and noted his terror mirrored on the overseer's face.

"Yes, my king?" Orchamus stepped toward the dais.

Darius held up his right hand, displaying the

cylinder ring he wore. "When the guards roll the stone over the pit to secure it with wax, I'll impress my seal to ensure the rock isn't disturbed overnight. Every council member who signed the written accusation against Daniel will also press his seal into the wax. Is that clear?"

Orchamus turned to scan the men nodding their approval behind him and stood taller. "We will be honored to do so, my king."

Darius directed his next command at the prisoner. "Daniel, the Hebrew, you will now turn and face your accusers. Scribe, read the names."

Daniel's feet felt rooted to the floor, and his knees were too weak to support him. Allamu helped him turn, and Belili laced her arm through his while the man seated on a cushion beside the throne began shouting names. Each man stood as his name was called—one hundred twenty-one in all—and Daniel felt each one like a blow.

The scribe announced the conclusion of his list, and Belili released a cry that came out on a sob. "Allamu's name was *not* among them." A small victory, but still a gift, on the darkest day of Daniel's life.

"Guards!" Darius's shout made him jump. "Seize the prisoner, lower him into the pit, seal the stone, and lock the gates. Court is adjourned."

An excited buzz swept over the crowd as six guards approached Daniel from every direction.

One separated him from Belili as if with an ax. Another bound his wrists. Two more removed Daniel's outer cloak and jewelry. The last two started to take his sandals but saw the condition of his feet and decided not to touch them.

Allamu stood five paces away with Belili, while Daniel was stripped of his title, his dignity, and his courage. This wasn't supposed to happen. He felt the first shove toward the lions' pit, and panic gripped him. His knees gave way, and he began to whimper like a child.

"Pray, beloved," Belili called out over the ruckus.

"Get out of the way." Zerubbabel shoved two guards aside and gently lifted Daniel into his arms. "We are sons of David, men of honor. You will meet Yahweh in this pit, Daniel ben Johanan—one way or another." He began marching to the rhythm of King David's shepherd song. "The Lord is our shepherd. We shall never want. He makes us lie down in green pastures . . ."

Daniel closed his eyes to hide himself in the words. Too soon, his human conveyance stopped, and he opened his eyes to King Darius standing beside them. Zerubbabel lowered Daniel's feet to the glazed tiles in the courtyard, where he'd been delivered as a captive sixty-seven years ago. Flaming torches lined a rectangular pit the length of four horses, the width of two. A huge slab of limestone rested on two long timbers, ready to roll over the opening. Lions roared, and Daniel's skin crawled. A guttural moan escaped him.

"Be strong, Daniel," Zerubbabel whispered. "You must be strong for our brother Hebrews in the crowd watching. Perhaps next time we will be as courageous as you when our faith is tested."

His words, like a splash of cold water, silenced Daniel. Still paralyzed by fear, the thought that his Hebrew brethren were near somehow gave him a measure of peace. He searched for Allamu and Belili and found them close by. Despite his harsh judgment, his wife remained. Who stood with her when she faced death in Achmetha?

"Hear, O Israel: The LORD our God, the LORD is one." His wife's voice rent the night air. "Love the LORD your God with all your heart and with all your soul and with all your strength." Daniel sent her a warning look. *No! Stop! You'll be arrested too.* But she kept praying. "These commandments that I give you today are to be on your hearts. Impress them on your children. Talk about them when you—"

Allamu gripped her arm. Angry words passed between them, and then . . . "Hear, O Israel: The LORD our God . . ." Her prayer continued while Zerubbabel and another soldier took hold of Daniel's arms, fairly carrying him to a large basket connected to a rope and pulley system.

The roars increased as they drew nearer, and Daniel caught his first glimpse of one of the large males when it leapt halfway up the wall and fell back into the pit. Fear had weakened him completely. Unable to stand and shaking violently, he could barely comprehend his surroundings. But he heard his wife's voice and the prayer that had been engraved on their hearts.

"Love the LORD your God with all your heart," he whispered, "and with all your soul and with all your strength."

Zerubbabel alone lifted Daniel into the basket, eyes moist and his voice low. "Now would be a good time to remind Yahweh of His promise to return you to Jerusalem, my friend." Daniel crouched into a ball inside the basket, unable to clarify that Yahweh hadn't promised it would be *him* who returned.

More lions jumped, perhaps sensing the increased activity above them. Zerubbabel lingered at Daniel's side, his presence like a shield.

King Darius called him away, but Zerubbabel gripped Daniel's shoulder before leaving. "May the Lord bless you and keep you."

He was gone in a moment, and three other guards began lowering Daniel into the pit as two lions lunged for the basket. The king's voice echoed in the darkness. "Daniel, may your god, whom you serve continually, rescue you!"

44

At the first light of dawn, the king got up
and hurried to the lions' den.
—DANIEL 6:19

I was grateful Darius ordered a wide perimeter,
so only soldiers were near enough to see what
happened when they lowered my husband into
the pit. The lions' roars were deafening. Daniel
was silent.

I buried my face in Allamu's chest, overcome
by fear and unable to continue my prayers.
Soldiers moved the stone over the opening and
immediately poured hot wax around all but a
few places, allowing air for the lions to breathe.

I tried to resume my prayer, but bile rose in
my throat, and I nearly lost the day's feast on
Darius's jeweled sandals. He quickly fled to
impress his seal on the wax, as did one hundred
twenty-one other men.

Allamu remained at my side, his hand resting
gently on my back. "Come, Mother. I'll escort
you home."

"No, I'm staying." I hadn't planned to say it;
in fact, the declaration seemed to startle us both.

"Mother, you can't stay."

I stood silently, refusing to argue, watching the

crowd disperse. King Darius trudged away like a child who had lost his last friend.

My son stood there gawking like a toad, mouth open waiting for flies. "I can't convince you to leave, can I?"

I shook my head but couldn't speak. Tears were too close to the surface.

He brushed my arm, his voice soft. "You realize, don't you, what lions do to a—"

"Stop!" I waved away his words. "You don't realize what Yahweh can do with lions." I folded my arms over my chest and sat with my back toward the pit while the moon shone overhead.

Though the city outside the courtyard walls was still bustling—grinding more grain in the gossip mills—the lions in the pit below had grown disturbingly quiet. I wanted to shout Daniel's name but was terrified I'd hear no reply.

Allamu's touch startled me, and he lifted his hands in surrender. "I'm sorry. I . . . You're trembling. Are you cold?"

"No, no. It's fine. I'm just . . ."

He removed his cloak and wrapped it around me.

My son sat with legs folded, forearms resting on his knees, his eyes looking everywhere but at me. He looked toward the palace. Then up at the stars. Over my shoulder. Still my little boy, all nerves and awkwardness when faced with emotion.

I rescued him from the silence. "When you walked into the Esagila on the morning after the invasion, I thought you were Gadi, raised from the dead." Finally, he looked at me. "You're so much like him, you know."

"So I've been told." He picked up a pebble and focused on scraping it against the blue-glazed tile. "But I didn't inherit his talent for interpreting dreams, Mother. I'm not as gifted as other Magoi."

"Is that why you hate me so? Because my Hebrew blood robbed you of a pure Magoi gift?"

He slapped the pebble against the tile. "I don't hate you. Why must you twist—" He stopped himself and drew in a breath. "Can we simply look at the stars?" Leaning back on one arm, he tilted his head to the sky, perusing the miracles of a God he refused to acknowledge.

"I'm sorry, Allamu."

His head snapped toward me. "What do you mean?"

"I'm sorry I taught you to deceive and be angry."

His expression softened. "Mother, I didn't mean—"

"I didn't actually sit you down and tell you to do those things, I know, but you've always been a smart boy. I've been angry since I lost my ima in Jerusalem and then was forced to leave Daniel in Babylon." Now I wanted to look away, hide myself in a distant glance, but

I studied the son who had been cheated out of a mother. "My life has been a lie since the eunuchs took me from Babylon. I became Belili and never looked back."

The gravity of my wasted life weighted me, and the image of Daniel praying on the floor of our chamber played in my memory. On his belly. Facedown. Arms outstretched. I bowed my head. *Yahweh, my heart and soul are prostrate before You now. How can I fix a life so broken?* I would surely have to confess to all my children about my past.

"Mother?"

Allamu's touch lifted my head, and I knew Abigail must be reborn. "I must ask for your forgiveness, Son. Hiding the truth of my heritage hurt you deeply, and I'm sorry. I've wronged Daniel in the same way. Perhaps if I'd told him from the beginning that my faith in Yahweh was an interrupted journey, not a continual climb like his own, he might have been able to forgive me."

"He wouldn't forgive you?" Kezia stood in the shadows, not ten paces behind us, clutching a blanket to her chest.

"It doesn't matter. Now there are no more secrets between us." I patted the tiles beside me. "Bring your blanket and let's get some rest."

Allamu leaned on one hand, ready to stand. "I'll leave you two alone."

I deferred to Kezia since she was the one who had been slower to warm to her brother. "No," she said, placing a hand gently on his arm. "Please stay. We should all be here at dawn to see Yahweh's great deliverance."

My awareness grew, though sleep still lingered. Something dragged over a cobblestoned street. My body ached. The noise grew louder as wakefulness heightened my senses. My eyes shot open, and I sat upright—beside a lions' pit. The cobblestone noise was actually snoring, but not Allamu, as I'd first thought. Kezia lay sprawled on her back, making the same awful racket as her abba with his winter cough and drainage.

Allamu sat two paces from me. "She's been doing it all night." His smirk said she'd likely hear his teasing when we all got past this morning's fears.

I looked at the pit. Wax seal unbroken. Nothing had changed, and my heart ached. What had I expected? Maybe a bolt of lightning to strike the rock? Perhaps Daniel to be miraculously sucked through the small air holes while I slept? Yahweh chose to do neither, and I struggled this morning to forgive Him for it. What would I do if they removed the rock and my Daniel was—gone?

"I checked your palace villa this morning."

Allamu kept his voice low. "Darius hasn't sent anyone to seize it yet, but we must face reality. I'll order your things moved to my villa by midday."

"To your villa?" Surprised at his generosity, I saw his tentative gaze return to the tiles.

"I'm sorry," he said. "I'll have them moved to Kezia's—"

"No, no." How could I convey my shock without sounding ungrateful? "I, uh . . . Daniel and I wouldn't want to be a bother, but we'd be happy to live at your villa, Allamu."

His dark eyes held me, the waning moonlight glistening off gathering moisture. "Mother, you've got to face the possibility that—"

"I'll face it if it becomes true, but not before. You didn't see Shadrach, Meshach, and Abednego in that blazing furnace, Allamu. Yahweh is a miracle-working God."

He cupped my cheek, and I leaned into his rare affection. "But I saw Daniel's feet. Yahweh chose not to intervene."

Men's bawdy laughter sent a chill up my spine. The king's soldiers changing guard. Kezia startled awake. "Is he . . . Did they . . ."

"It's almost dawn, love." I patted her leg and stood, returning Allamu's cloak and folding the blanket. "The king should join us anytime now."

As if summoned by my words, King Darius appeared at the palace entrance and fairly sprinted down the long staircase. "Have you heard anything?" At least twenty guards trailed behind him.

I wasn't sure what he thought we might hear. "No, it's been quiet."

He looked at me as if I'd lost my mind. Perhaps I had. Complete peace had overtaken me. Not a single skip of my heart, even when the soldiers began breaking away the wax seal. It was as if Yahweh Himself had cradled me in His arms and held me.

I still chose to stand twenty paces from the pit while the soldiers used ropes and pulleys to hoist the slab of rock, swing it onto the two timbers, and roll the stone away. Kezia and Allamu stood behind me, and Darius knelt at the edge of the open pit. "Daniel, servant of the living God, has your god, whom you serve continually, been able to rescue you from the lions?"

First I heard a groan, the sound Daniel made when standing after he'd sat too long. Then, "May the king live forever!" His strong voice rose from the pit. "My God sent His angel and shut the mouths of the lions. They haven't hurt me, because I was found innocent in His sight. Nor have I ever done any wrong before you, my king."

Allamu staggered back. Kezia jumped and squealed, then pulled him toward me, jostling us both until we all laughed like children.

"Get him out! Get him out!" Darius shouted at the men with ropes and then peeked over the side. "Is the angel still down there?"

Curious myself, I extricated myself from my children and rushed to the pit, looking over the side. Lying calm as Egyptian cats, seven lions watched my Daniel rise with the rope looped around him and under his arms. I rushed to where the men untangled him, and nearly tackled him. The moment his feet touched the ground, the beasts began wildly pacing and roaring. One even leapt upward, swatting at the rope that dangled over the side.

Daniel skittered away from the edge, drawing me with him. Eyes wide, he looked at me and then King Darius. "Well, there was certainly none of that last night. They were calm as kittens."

Darius grabbed Daniel and pulled him into a fierce hug but released him quickly. "Are you injured? Let me see you." He lifted his arms. Turned him around to inspect his robes. When he knelt to look at Daniel's feet, his jaw dropped. "Daniel, your feet are no longer—"

"Swollen, my king?" Daniel lifted his robe.

I bent to inspect the feet I'd pampered and bandaged, now perfectly normal. "Yahweh healed your feet too?" All redness and swelling around his joints was gone.

"I think they were healed sometime in the night." He offered his hand and helped me stand.

"I woke to someone's snoring." He looked at Allamu. "Was that you?"

"I wouldn't know." My son turned to Kezia, whose cheeks instantly pinked. "Perhaps it was Yahweh's way of notifying you of His healing."

Kezia offered a grateful nod, but the small deceit reminded me of the larger one I'd confessed to Daniel last night. "Daniel, I . . ." My words died as I searched his eyes for the disgust I'd seen last night. "We need some time alone—to finish our talk."

He turned to King Darius, head bowed in submission. "I must return home for my morning prayers, my king. Please know that when I pray toward Jerusalem at an open window, it is not out of defiance. I remain your faithful servant, Daniel ben Johanan." He looked up then. "But perhaps Belili and I should move our personal belongings out of the palace villa."

"You have served me well, but I agree it is time for you to move out of the palace villa and return to your family's home." Darius stared at him hard. "The Hidati festival will continue, and the law still stands; however, I will issue the following decree in every part of my kingdom to ensure your freedom to worship:

People of all nations, tribes, and tongues must fear and reverence the God of Daniel, for He is the living God and He

518

endures forever. His kingdom will not be destroyed; His dominion will never end. He rescues and He saves; He performs signs and wonders in the heavens and on the earth. He has rescued Daniel from the power of the lions.

Darius grasped my husband's wrist firmly. "You're a good man, Daniel ben Johanan. Live at peace."

As we walked away, I heard the king order his guards, "I want every man who signed Lord Belteshazzar's arrest warrant in my courtroom immediately—with his entire family."

"Yes, my king."

I didn't dare look back. I didn't dare let my mind wander to what Darius would do to those men and their families. I was focused on the man walking beside me, the miraculous deliverance of our God, and how the confession I'd made would affect the rest of our days.

Allamu and Kezia strolled several paces ahead, chatting as if they were old friends. Daniel raised his brows in silent question, and Belili answered with a tentative smile. Yahweh had given him ample time to hear their stories in the days to come. It seemed the whole world had changed while he was in that dark hole, but the biggest change was his own heart.

He reached for his wife's hand, hiding the affection between the folds of their robes. The sparkle in her eyes both thrilled and pained him. "I understand now, Belili." He kept his eyes forward, afraid he wouldn't be able to get through his confession if he looked at her. "When my fear overwhelmed me, I had a moment of regret. A moment when I realized if I'd been faced with your choices in Achmetha, I could have made the same mistakes. If I'd been alone as you were. If I'd been betrayed and abused and abandoned as you'd been. At my lowest moment, Zerubbabel reminded me I wasn't alone. There were other faithful Hebrews around me, and then your prayer, beloved . . . Your prayer . . ." Daniel's emotions choked his words.

"Nothing can excuse the choices I made, Daniel." Her voice was flat, drawing his attention. Though her cheeks were damp with tears, her features held a peaceful glow. "At least I know what I'd choose now." She stopped atop the Processional Way and faced him. "Life with idols or death for Yahweh? Belili chooses Yahweh. *Abigail* chooses Yahweh. I've become the sum of all my choices, and now I choose Yahweh over you, over our children, over life itself."

He held her gaze, the clear-eyed beauty of the girl he once knew. "As do I, *Abigail*. As do I." He looked left and right, considered his status as a simple citizen of Babylon, and kissed his wife's cheek in public. Scandalous. He removed his sandals and turned his face to the rising sun, feeling the cool tiles beneath pain-free bare feet. "I'm alive, and you are forgiven. Let's go home and inform Shesh and Kezia that they must share the villa with us again."

They turned left, and soon the tiles beneath their feet changed to bricks in the city of nobility on the other side of the Way. Servants shook rugs and emptied waste pots, while nobles tried not to stare at Yahweh's undeniable miracle. The story of Daniel's deliverance would surely spread like wildfire through the provinces—praise be to Yahweh—making the gathering of Hebrews for the return to Jerusalem much more likely.

As they neared the villa, Daniel glanced at the woman he adored and found her brows downturned. He pulled her to a stop. "What is it? Are you anxious about living with Kezia and the children again?"

She shook her head and choked on a laugh. "I haven't thought that far ahead. Actually, Allamu invited us to live with him, but I think he was carried away in the moment."

"Allamu?" Yahweh had been busier than he'd realized. Watching Allamu and Kezia walking ahead, he considered their children's newfound camaraderie. How might their parents' choice of lodging affect it? "Do you want to live with Allamu?"

"Ima! Abba!" Kezia shouted from the villa courtyard. "Hurry! Shesh and the children will be anxious to see you."

"We should go." His wife offered a wan smile. "But I'd like to talk with you alone about it before we announce a decision."

Daniel chuckled inwardly. What a wonderful conundrum to be so desired by one's children that they must choose.

As they approached the villa, he was overwhelmed to see every member of their family—including Mert—standing at the court-yard gate to welcome him. The grandchildren and great-grands celebrated with cheering and dancing, while Mert greeted Allamu with a hug and Shesh swept Kezia into his arms.

With every embrace, every kiss, every encouraging word, Daniel wondered, *Who among them will be left when the remnant leaves for Jerusalem?* He staggered back at the thought, feeling his own mind had betrayed him. Wouldn't Belili and he also be among the remnant?

Belili steadied him. "Are you all right, love?"

"Yes, yes. Just a little dizzy."

Daniel's family snapped into action as if he'd fallen down dead. Mert, of course, took charge. "A little gruel will fix you. Kezia, you and your sisters set bowls on the table. Grandchildren, follow me. Today we feast again!"

Allamu watched them and chuckled. "At least Mert didn't make me set the bowls this time."

"Allamu," Mert called out. "You're going to the market for feasting supplies."

Daniel and Belili laughed with him, but before he obeyed Mert, he clamped Daniel's shoulder. "I've offered that you and Mother can stay at my villa, but I see the laughter and love you have here. Please don't feel obligated. This is your home, and I'll visit as often as I can." He was gone before they could answer.

Belili squeezed Daniel's waist and looked up with joy sparkling in her eyes. "Our cup overflows with blessing, Daniel ben Johanan, and Yahweh has given you back to me *again*."

He kissed her forehead and hugged her to his side. "We have so many gifts, my love, but I believe God is teaching us both to hold them loosely."

45

I am the LORD, the Maker of all things, . . . who says of Cyrus, "He is my shepherd and will accomplish all that I please; he will say of Jerusalem, 'Let it be rebuilt,' and of the temple, 'Let its foundations be laid.'"

—ISAIAH 44:24, 28

One Week Later

Since Daniel was no longer chief of Babylon's Chaldeans or King Darius's chosen administrator, he'd spent the past seven days teaching their grandchildren lessons of immense national import.

"Saba, where did the elephants poop while they were on the ark?" Little Daniel, his four-year-old namesake, studied him with intense dark eyes.

"Anywhere they wanted." The reply tickled his fifteen giggling students, soothing the ache in his soul that grew stronger each day. Shesh and the elders had begun the necessary processes of coordinating an empire-wide search for willing Hebrews to return to Jerusalem.

Was it the palace activity he missed, or was it a

gnawing unrest to return to Jerusalem? Since the day of Yahweh's deliverance, Daniel had prayed fervently for Yahweh's clear direction. Were he and Abigail to return to the land of their birth? Or had he been called to teach future generations the foundational knowledge on which Jerusalem and its Temple must be built?

"Who wants bread and date paste?" Abigail stole his class's roving attention with her tray of morning snacks. She lit up when the children crowded around her at the table, clamoring to see what treasures she bore on the silver tray. She had become Abigail again, free to love in a way Belili never dared. Yet she was still his Belili, with the strength and courage that Abigail never possessed. He loved her regardless of the name, but because her heart had changed, she now wished to be called Abigail—the name of the girl who had won his heart.

"We must all say thank you to Savta." Daniel delighted in the chorus of fifteen grateful voices.

Abigail bowed, then tickled, hugged, and snuggled children as she walked over to Daniel. She pulled a small rolled parchment from her pocket, laid it in his hand, and held it there. "It bears Cyrus's seal."

Her words both excited and concerned him. He had no desire to be drawn back into the web of an empire led by two such strong men.

"Open it." Abigail removed her hand.

Daniel's stomach clenched as he slid his finger beneath the wax seal and unfurled the short missive:

> *From King Cyrus the Great. Emperor of the World and King of All.*
> *To Daniel ben Johanan.*
> *It pleases me to speak with you and Mistress Belili immediately at Allamu's villa.*

He handed the small scroll to his wife, giving her a moment to read it. "Why meet at Allamu's? And why no processional when he entered the city?"

Brows furrowed, she rolled it and returned it to him. "Why summon both of us?"

"I have no answers," he said with a sigh. No one could know the mind of Cyrus the Great.

Abigail found Kezia, who agreed to finish the children's lessons, giving Daniel and his wife time to change into formal robes. His feet had remained healthy through Mert's diligent dietary care, so they would walk to Allamu's villa on the other side of the Way. Springtime in Babylon was spectacular, but Abigail nearly ruined their peaceful stroll by speculating on the gravity of Cyrus's clandestine arrival.

"Allamu didn't mention Cyrus's visit at last night's meal. Do you think he knew, or did the emperor surprise even the new chief administrator? Does King Darius even know Cyrus is here?" She gasped and pulled Daniel to a stop. "Don't let Cyrus snare you back into palace politics."

He framed her cheeks. "I'll do what Yahweh asks of me, my love. Remember David. He tended sheep. He slew a giant. He played a harp for King Saul. He was faithful in all this before he became king."

"And he lived in constant fear for his life during the last years of Saul's reign."

Daniel kissed her nose and sighed. "Do you suppose what awaits us at Allamu's villa is worse than lions?" His wife's wrinkled brow changed to a rueful grin, and they resumed their walk.

The guards at the palace gate greeted them both by name as they walked past. As they continued down the street toward Allamu's villa, a slight breeze stirred the palm fronds and sent gentle ripples across the river next to his courtyard. Daniel pushed open the gate, but Abigail's grip tightened when only Allamu's guards greeted them. If the king were in residence, where were his bodyguards?

"Prosperity and honor to the empire," Daniel said, suspicion rising.

Allamu's men bowed. "Prosperity and honor to the empire, Daniel ben Johanan. Lord Allamu is expecting you."

Daniel nodded, clutching Abigail's entwined

arm tightly. Why was there no servant to escort them to the audience chamber? Cautiously, they walked through Allamu's outer courtyard, following the sound of voices.

When they arrived at the doorway of the audience chamber, the mystery was solved. All of Allamu's servants were serving their master and his guest. King Cyrus and Allamu were so deep in conversation, they hadn't noticed their guests' arrival. Daniel cleared his throat.

"Lord Belt—" Cyrus stumbled over the title but waved it away, embracing the new name. "Daniel ben Johanan. We've been expecting you and Mistress Belili. Welcome to you both."

A measure of relief relaxed Abigail's grip on Daniel's arm and sent them both to cushions around a low-lying table, where the king and Allamu were already seated. Daniel sat on the king's right side and Abigail on his left.

"Wine for my ima and Daniel." Allamu cast them a meaningful glance after using their Hebrew titles. Daniel nodded calm approval, though his heart did a flip.

King Cyrus, oblivious to the tender moment, eagerly began his agenda. "I called you both here—"

"My king," Daniel interrupted, "might I ask how you entered the city without being noticed and why we're meeting here—rather than the palace—without your royal escort?"

"I see you're still Belteshazzar, protector of the king." He chuckled. "I sent word to Darius alone. My fifty-man escort entered the city last night, and my royal guards are here, I assure you." At his words, fifteen men stepped out of the shadows like specters from Sheol.

Abigail gasped, but Daniel grinned. "Very effective, my king, but why the secrecy, and why meet here at our son's villa?"

"What I have to say is . . . delicate. Even at the palace, the walls have ears."

Daniel didn't appreciate the position in which he'd placed Allamu. A man could get crushed between two powerful kings. "Am I to understand, then, that what you're about to say is something you wish to keep from Darius?"

"Oh no. Darius will know exactly what we decide. I simply don't wish to offend him in the way I decide it."

"I see." Indeed, Daniel understood the under-currents too well. The divided Medo-Persian kingdom was beginning to show its cracks. *Yahweh, keep Allamu safe when it crumbles.*

The king turned to Abigail. "Mistress Belili, I brought you here to apologize in person for the mistakes of King Darius during the Hidati festival. Though noble in his effort to unite, Darius was too inexperienced in ruling to recognize the manipulation of his council members. Darius will restore the Akitu festival next year for Babylon and Borsippa, as tradition demands, rendering the law of Hidati obsolete. He learned a hard lesson, unfortunately, at Daniel's expense. The responsible council members and their families have been disposed of." The emperor bowed his head to Belili, proving his sincerity.

Daniel held his breath, wondering if his outspoken wife would chastise the emperor for Darius's rash execution of the noblemen and their families, but she didn't. Instead, she rested her hand on Cyrus's forearm and squeezed it gently. "You need not apologize, my king. I daresay we all experienced things that night we'll never forget."

He returned her gracious smile. "Indeed, I learned of your god's power, though I wasn't even here. I received Darius's messages and was so intrigued by Daniel's miraculous deliverance that I desired to know more of your Hebrew god." He turned his attention to Daniel. "That's why I brought you and Belili here today, my friend. I believe your god has chosen me to send a delegation of your people back to Jerusalem."

Daniel choked on his wine, thinking surely he'd misheard. Still sputtering, he set down the goblet. "Could you repeat that, my king?"

A servant dabbed the spilled wine from Daniel's robe, while Cyrus's grin stretched ear to ear. "I thought you might react that way. You heard me correctly, Daniel. Your god chose me to send this delegation back to Jerusalem."

The amusement in his voice coaxed the obvious question from Daniel. "How did you come to such a conclusion, my king?"

He took an excruciatingly slow draw of wine before explaining. "After hearing Darius's wild claims about your deliverance from the lions, I remembered the old Hebrew scrolls Nebuchadnezzar had given to my grandfather Astyages. Grandfather sometimes read them when he couldn't sleep."

Daniel grinned. "I can see how some might find the scrolls boring if the subject matter is unfamiliar."

"I began reading the scrolls written by your prophet Moses and soon found a scroll written by your prophet Isaiah," Cyrus said, his voice softening with wonder. "Daniel, have you read his scroll?"

"My sons-in-law recently discovered a few of his writings in one of the temples here in Babylon, but I was a boy in Jerusalem when I last had access to the full writings of Isaiah." He hoped the hint would move Cyrus to donate his scrolls to the burgeoning collection in Daniel's library. "Isaiah was a distant relative of mine. We are both descended from the tribe of Judah."

Cyrus looked at Daniel with unfiltered awe. "Now I know why you hear the voice of your god. You are like the Magoi, a chosen tribe among your people."

Daniel wanted to clarify the differences between Judah and the Magoi, but Cyrus's intensity overwhelmed him.

Cyrus rested his elbows on the table and held his head with both hands. "I myself can barely believe what I'm about to say." He shook his head. "Isaiah spoke of *me* in his prophecies, Daniel. He called me by name. He said I would return people to Jerusalem so that it would again be inhabited. He said I would allow it to be rebuilt and the foundations of a new temple laid."

With shock equaling the king's, Daniel looked to Allamu for clarification and found Abigail's son's face alight with anticipation. Allamu removed a scroll from beneath the table, unrolled it, and pointed to a section already marked. Abigail rose to her knees and leaned over the table while Daniel read it aloud: ". . . who says of Cyrus, 'He is my shepherd and will accomplish all that I please; he will say of Jerusalem, "Let it be rebuilt," and of the temple, "Let its foundations be laid." ' "

"See?" Cyrus said with a satisfied grin. "Even your god knows Cyrus the Great."

Daniel sat back. Breathless. Speechless. Awed at the sovereignty of his God. Letting the significance of this moment settle into his spirit. "Consider, King Cyrus, every detail Yahweh orchestrated to bring you to this moment in history. The generations past and present. Every detail of your life and others around you to give you the world's thrones so you can do this marvelous thing." He watched the king's smug expression fade as the Creator's sovereignty took root.

It was time to ask the question Isaiah didn't predict the answer to. "Will you choose the delegation yourself, my king? Or will you allow any Hebrew who longs for Jerusalem to go back?" The hairs on the back of Daniel's neck stood on end. Perhaps this was the way Yahweh would reveal His will for him and Abigail. If Cyrus commanded them to go, their decision was made.

The king held Daniel's gaze for the span of a breath before answering. "What about you, Daniel ben Johanan? Will you return to a land of rubble and weeds after living in Babylon's luxury all your life?"

Daniel noted his evasive response. Abigail squeezed Daniel's hand and nodded toward Allamu. Frustration and fear etched deep lines between her son's brows. They'd spoken of the journey at length during last night's meal, but none of their family could agree on a verdict about their parents' participation. No matter whether they went to Jerusalem or stayed in Babylon, the family would be divided, and Daniel and Abigail would never see some of their children again.

"I'd like to hear the wisdom of Cyrus the Great on the matter," Daniel said. "I've longed to see Jerusalem for nearly seventy years, but my wife and I are old and haven't made a long journey since we were children." He turned to Abigail while speaking to the king but made his vow to her. "If Cyrus allows me to choose, my wife and I will make the choice together."

The king laughed. "You are undoubtedly the wisest of my empire's married men." Sobering, he clapped Daniel's shoulder. "I must choose someone to lead the Hebrews back to Jerusalem. Someone wise, a man they know and trust. Though you are most capable, your age disqualifies you. Is there another among your people who is capable and trustworthy?"

"You want me to name someone now?" Daniel could think of no one more qualified than Sheshbazzar, no one who better understood preserving Yahweh's pure truth among foreign neighbors. But to appoint him now, without preparing him or Kezia for the decision?

Cyrus nodded. "I intend to go immediately from our meeting to speak with Darius about the decision. Whomever you choose will need to come to court this afternoon to request permission for the exiles' return." Cyrus leaned forward. "So, yes, Daniel ben Johanan. Appoint someone now so my name will be remembered among your people forever."

"Our son-in-law Sheshbazzar would serve you well, King Cyrus." Abigail surprised them all with her input.

Cyrus's eyes widened with amusement. "Is this son-in-law someone you wish to be rid of, Mistress Belili?" His features softened. "You realize it's unlikely you will ever reunite with those who make this journey."

"I don't wish to be rid of any of my children, my king, and Shesh has been like my right arm since he married our daughter." She turned to Daniel, peace tempering the sadness in her eyes. "But Shesh is the prince of our tribe in Babylon, well respected, and his passion for Yahweh and the restoration of His Temple is unequalled among our people. He is the right choice to lead the remnant home."

"It's settled, then." The king received her comment as if it were Persian law. "Sheshbazzar of Judah will lead the *remnant,* as you call it, as soon as we locate and gather Judah's treasure from Babylon's temples."

"The locating has already begun," Daniel said. "Yahweh spoke to me about this day in a vision the day after Darius invaded Babylon."

Renewed wonder lit the king's face. "We'll make every effort to send an initial group within a year."

"So soon?" Panic laced Abigail's tone, but she turned to Daniel and seemed to draw strength

535

from him. "Yes, I mean . . . a year. So soon . . . that's wonderful."

Daniel heard the tremor in her voice and knew he must get her home. "Was there anything else you needed from us, my king?"

"No, Daniel. Inform Sheshbazzar to make his plea before Darius today. I'll allow Babylon's king to approve the decision, whereby he'll save face in his city after his poor decision on the Hidati festival. A proclamation in my name will be read throughout the empire, inviting all Judeans from any province to return to Jerusalem."

"Thank you, my king." Daniel stood on shaky legs and helped Abigail to her feet so they could bow to a foreign king who listened to Isaiah's words better than God's own people.

Cyrus nodded his acknowledgment, and Allamu rose to escort them. As they reached the courtyard gate, Allamu stopped them, but he wouldn't look at them. Daniel had seldom seen him so unnerved. "What is it? Has Cyrus planned something he didn't tell us? Are we in danger?"

"No, no!" Allamu's denials brought his gaze to Daniel's, and he saw the same frightened expression of the eleven-year-old boy he'd once known. "You can't go. You simply can't g—"

Abigail pressed two fingers to his lips. "Daniel and I will discuss our decision on the way home, but it must be our decision, Son. No one else's."

She removed her fingers, and Allamu bent to kiss his mother's cheek. "I don't want to lose you again. I can care for you both here in Babylon. Cyrus assured me I'll remain Darius's chief administrator."

Abigail brushed his cheek, tears shining in her eyes. "Thank you, my sweet boy. Your care means more than you can know, but we must make the decision based on God's promises alone, not on anyone else's."

Allamu turned to Daniel, pleading. "What about the others? I just . . . surely *all* of them aren't going to Jerusalem, are they? Not the little ones too." He clasped both hands behind his back as if not sure what to do with the emotions they held.

Daniel wished he could embrace the awkward man before him, knowing he dare not show such affection—yet. "Not everyone has decided who will go and who will stay, but why don't you join us for as many meals as you're able. You will want to spend as much time as possible with your sisters and their families."

The muscles in his jaw worked as he considered Daniel's invitation. Then, without warning, Allamu pulled Daniel into a fierce embrace. "Thank you." Before Daniel could reply, Allamu released him and strode away, waving a hand over his head. "I'll see everyone tonight for our meal."

46

In that day the remnant of Israel,
the survivors of Jacob,
will no longer rely on him
who struck them down
but will truly rely on the LORD,
the Holy One of Israel.

—ISAIAH 10:20

When Daniel and I returned home, Kezia was marching around the courtyard in front of the children, reenacting the story of Joshua and the walls of Jericho. Oh, how I wished I could paint the picture and tuck it away with our keepsakes. I tried to etch every sweet face in my mind, knowing our lives would too soon become quieter in Babylon.

Daniel waved our daughter toward the library. "Kezia," he said, "let the older children teach the younger ones for a while. Your ima and I must speak with you." Fear shadowed her features immediately.

Mert came from the kitchen at the sound of Daniel's voice. "Well, you're alive. Was it good news or bad?"

"Good news," Daniel said, looking to me for affirmation.

"Yes, good."

Mert sensed my hesitation. "Huh. I'll fix a nice meal tonight in case someone goes to the lions."

"Mert!" I meant to chastise her, but she'd already retreated to the kitchen. Daniel winked at me. Kezia stood beside me, pale as parchment. "Is someone going to the lions?"

"No one is going to the lions," he said, leading us both to the small room off the courtyard, where we sat on cushions in a circle. "Kezia," Daniel began without preamble, "King Cyrus summoned us to meet him secretly at Allamu's house."

"But why? Is Allamu all right?" The fear for his safety both warmed and crushed my heart. They'd just found each other, discovered they *liked* the other, and worked out a way to live at peace. *Yahweh, prepare my family's hearts for the difficult days ahead.*

"Allamu is well, my girl. King Cyrus called for your ima and me because he discovered his name in Isaiah's prophecy. A king named Cyrus would return our people from captivity to rebuild Jerusalem and Yahweh's Temple."

Her mouth flew open, joy and awe drawing out a laugh. "How can it be? Abba, hadn't you read this in Isaiah's scrolls?"

"Not all his writings have been available to me. King Cyrus, however, has many of our ancient writings that I believe he'll donate with other sacred texts and Temple items for the remnant's departure as early as next spring."

"The remnant?" Shock tempered her excitement. "Next spring? He'll allow the Jews to return to Jerusalem? Hasn't it only been sixty-eight years?"

Daniel nodded slowly. "I suspect it will take two more to rebuild the Temple. Jeremiah's prophesied seventy years will be fulfilled."

Kezia covered an excited gasp. "Wait until Shesh hears! I can begin harvesting and drying vegetables, fruit, and fish right away." She turned to me. "We have much to prepare, Ima!"

"Your ima and I will not return with the remnant, Kezia." Her abba's blunt declaration stilled her. "Cyrus said I would not lead the returning exiles. I agreed, so he asked who I would recommend. I suggested someone honorable. Trustworthy. Respected. A leader who could balance his passion for Yahweh with the peacemaking skills necessary for that area of Palestine—"

"No, Abba. You didn't."

Daniel nodded once. "Shesh is the best man to do it, Daughter."

"No!" She looked at me. "Ima, how could you allow it? You know what happens when men are called to lead."

"Kezia," Daniel said, "we believe Shesh is Yahweh's choice—"

I placed my hand on his leg, quieting him before emotions escalated further. "Will you let me speak with Kezia alone?"

Both husband and daughter looked surprised. Usually her abba handled our emotionally charged girl, but Daniel agreed, kissing Kezia's hand before he left. Her jaw was set like flint.

When her abba closed the door, I kept my eyes focused on my hands. "I thought I'd lost you the day I confessed my past, and I was afraid I'd lost your abba when he was lowered into that lions' pit. But those two experiences have taught us one thing, Kezia bat Daniel. We must hold loosely to the things on this earth—both possessions and the people most precious to us."

I looked at her to see if my words had any effect. Slowly, almost imperceptibly, the sharp lines of her brow turned upward, softening. I continued. "Our family has been planning to return together for months, but your abba has ached to return for years. He made a promise with Shadrach, Meshach, and Abednego that they would return together. It's been difficult for him to let go of his dream." I laid my hand on her cheek, remembering the baby girl I'd held in my arms and drinking in the amazing woman I'd come to know. "I suspect your dream is to surround yourself with family and remain in a comfortable villa until your great-grandchildren close your eyes in death."

"That *was* my dream," she said, pouting.

"Which is more important? Your comfortable dream or leaving a legacy for the nation of Yahweh's people? You and Shesh will lead our people home, representing high and low, rich and poor. I am the daughter of servants. Your abba is the son of kings. It is an honor beyond reckoning."

"But Jerusalem isn't the city you left, Ima. It's a pile of rubble. There's nothing left after Nebuchadnezzar destroyed it." Her eyes filled with tears, as did mine.

"You're right. It will be the most difficult thing you've ever done. But remember this: Jerusalem isn't merely a city; it's Yahweh's Promised Land. Of all the patches of dirt on this earth, Yahweh gave it to His chosen people, who have been called to reveal Him to other nations."

Tears finally spilled down her cheeks, and she reached for my hand. "I don't want to leave you. I finally like you."

We both chuckled at the truth of it. "And I, you. But you must go, and I fear you must take at least some of my grandchildren and great-grandchildren with you. Teach them the truth of Yahweh's laws and stories—as you've been taught."

She pulled away, swiping at tears. "I don't like it." Searching my face, she hesitated for a while, and I let the silence do its work. "But we'll do it."

I couldn't rejoice. I could only drop my eyes to my fidgeting hands and nod. Pain tore at my heart. Devastating, thoroughly wrecking pain. The kind that comes only to those wholly devoted, those who've held nothing back. I looked up and saw my daughter's heart breaking too. We fell into each other's arms, sharing the exquisite brokenness of loving well.

Shesh arrived home from the Esagila for his midday meal, and Daniel shared the news. His reaction? Astonished. Overwhelmed. And thoroughly committed. He and Daniel went together to present the prescribed plea before Cyrus in Darius's courtroom. They returned with a signed decree and plans to search every temple in Babylon for Jerusalem's lost treasures. Everything, that is, except the Ark.

"Why not search for the Ark?" I was more than a little perturbed. "How can our people return to Jerusalem without Yahweh's presence?"

"Come! Follow me." Daniel grabbed my hand and pulled me toward the library again. He called to Shesh and Kezia. "Both of you, come!"

We marched like a captive train into the room he'd filled with scrolls and parchments. Still lying on the table was Jeremiah's scroll, to which Daniel now pointed and read, " 'In those days, when your numbers have increased greatly in the land,' declares the LORD, 'people will no longer say, "The ark of the covenant of the LORD." It will never enter their minds or be remembered; it will not be missed, nor will another one be made.' "

He looked at me with fiery eyes. "You and I remember it because we're old, but most of the remnant knows the God who saved Shadrach, Meshach, and Abednego from a fiery furnace and me from the den of lions. Yahweh's disobedient children were exiled from Judah and came to Babylon a broken nation. With no Temple in which to worship, no sacrifices to cleanse our sins, and no priests to present our offerings, we learned that the true power of Yahweh's presence dwells among His people. The remnant will return without the Ark but not without Yahweh's presence."

I felt both loss and freedom in his words, grief and hope. "It seems wrong to rebuild the Temple without the Ark in the Most Holy Place."

Shesh's brows knit together. "Jeremiah's words and our experience of Yahweh in Babylon make it clear we don't need to find the Ark to return His presence to Jerusalem. Perhaps it's we ourselves who carry His presence within us." Daniel's single nod bore witness to aged wisdom and silent assurance. He would give the younger leader space to wrestle with Yahweh and with the people he would lead.

While our men spoke of great plans, my mind wandered to how our lives were about to change. I glimpsed the weathered trunk in the corner and hurried across the room to dig in my favorite treasures. When I drew out Amyitis's crown, Kezia, Shesh, and Daniel stood beside me, curiosity written on their faces. "I think Amyitis would be honored to give her crown to Yahweh." I presented it to Shesh. "Use the gold and gemstones to help replace any Temple items that aren't found. Since Yahweh worked boldly for His people in Babylon, let Babylon's gold glimmer brightly for His Temple."

Daniel was reinstated as Lord Belteshazzar. His chief role, according to Cyrus, was to advise King Darius. His actual duties consisted of teaching the returning exiles—including our grandchildren and great-grandchildren—the laws of Moses and the words of Yahweh's prophets.

Allamu continued as chief administrator and remained true to his word, caring for us in ways that continued to endear and amaze.

During the eleven months after Cyrus's decree to return the exiles, many more Temple items were found, recorded, and placed in Babylon's palace treasury for safekeeping. To celebrate, King Darius planned a banquet, inviting all the nobles from Media, Persia, and all outlying provinces.

"Must we go, Ima?" Kezia fussed with the pearls Mert braided into her hair. "I always say the wrong thing when speaking with noblemen's wives."

It was true, but I had learned to deal more gently with my eldest daughter. "Perhaps you and I should both listen more than we speak tonight. It's the first, and likely the only, royal banquet you'll attend in Babylon. Let your husband receive the honor he deserves, and allow the other women to compliment you." I continued working the juniper-scented lotion into her feet.

"That's good counsel, Ima."

I exchanged a surprised glance with Mert, thankful my daughter had received my comments without offense. Yahweh was doing a good work in us both.

The banquet was like every other royal feast I'd attended. Drunken men. Half-naked dancers. And too much rich food. Kezia held her tongue and represented her husband well. I, on the other hand, forbid my husband the rich foods and sent not-so-subtle pleas to leave shortly after they lit the torches at dusk. Allamu played his political games, but at least now I knew there was a tender heart beneath the painted smile.

"Mistress Belili." A deep voice called from behind me.

The king's Hebrew bodyguard, Zerubbabel, bowed low. "I haven't seen you since Lord Belteshazzar's trial, Mistress, and I wanted to say how much I admired your courage that night." When he rose, he offered me a small scroll, wrapped in a finely designed leather case. It looked very expensive.

"Zerubbabel, I can't accept—"

"Please, Mistress." His smile drew me in. "I've written the Shema on the scroll inside and had the case fashioned especially for you. Your faithfulness that night and the faithfulness of your husband inspired many of our people to return to prayer. You and your husband have done a great work in preparing the exiles for their return." He bowed again and was gone before I could argue with such a compliment.

I stared at the small treasure, no larger than the length of my hand, and felt Daniel's arm wrap my shoulder. "Open it, my love."

Noise and chaos assaulted my senses, creating a wider chasm between the world around me and the holy thing in my hand. "I can't, Daniel. Not here. Please take me home."

Making some excuse about the rich food and his feet, my husband excused us from our table and escorted me from the palace into the cool night air. The freedom of it was palpable.

Daniel wrapped me in his woolen cloak for the walk home. I let my head fall back to look at the stars as Allamu had taught me. "Tell me what you know about Zerubbabel, Husband. He seems like a lost soul. So kind but alone."

"I believe Allamu mentioned on the first night we met him that Zerubbabel is the grandson of Jehoiachin, so we are cousins. I know little else."

"Is he returning with the exiles?"

"Oh no, love. He's a eunuch. His loyalty is to the king until death."

The thought saddened me. Zerubbabel's greater loyalty was obviously to Yahweh. He'd obeyed Darius unswervingly on the night of Daniel's arrest yet showed me compassion through it all. Jerusalem needed men like him. Shesh needed leaders like him.

The thought nagged me in my sleep and while I helped Mert make bread the next day. I slammed my fist into the bread dough.

She grunted at me. "What happened at that banquet? You're as sad as a two-legged dog."

I'd never heard that one. "Well, I don't believe I'm quite that sad, but I'm thinking about—"

"Does the king require my presence?" My husband's voice distracted me.

Mert and I exchanged a wary glance and rushed

to the courtyard gate, finding there the Hebrew guard who had consumed my thoughts. "No, Daniel ben Johanan. I no longer guard the king."

I might have been frightened were it not for the joy on his face. "Come in, Zerubbabel." Daniel caught sight of me following our guest. "Abigail will get us something to drink."

Zerubbabel shook his head. "Thank you, but no. I'd like to see Lord Sheshbazzar. King Darius gave me permission to join the exiles."

I covered a gasp, but Daniel clapped his shoulder. "Congratulations! How did you manage it?"

"I'm sure it was Yahweh's hand. I suggested a contest of wisdom with the king's other two bodyguards last night after King Darius had gone to sleep. We each wrote on a piece of parchment the one thing we thought most powerful in this world. The king and his council judged my answer of greatest wisdom and offered me rich gifts and great honor, but I chose the thing I hold in greatest honor. I asked to return to Jerusalem with my people."

I stared at the man in wonder, so many questions racing through my mind. I wasn't sure which to ask first. "What were the most powerful things you and your friends listed?"

His eyes sparked at the chance to retell it. "Utultar, my red-haired Scythian friend, wrote 'wine' because it forces people to both folly and violence. The Medjay, Ikeno, believed the king to be strongest. Most likely he chose this because he's been enslaved his whole life, never knowing the freedom to do as he pleases."

"And your winning answer?" Daniel's amused tone baited the man.

Zerubbabel let out a jolly laugh. "Women, of course. They give birth to the king and baker alike. Men fight for gold and glory but then see a beautiful woman and relinquish all to gain a wife."

Daniel and I laughed with him, this man who led my husband to the lions and offered me high praise. How strange is this life on earth? How odd the random patterns that somehow curve into a portrait of ourselves.

Zerubbabel's laughter faded, and he raised a finger. "But I added a note to my answer that overruled even women." He paused, whetting our appetites for more. "Truth. It is the only purely righteous thing on earth, giving it power over the excesses of wine, unrighteous kings, and disagreeable women. Truth alone prevails forever without partiality or preference." He bowed, finishing his recitation. "Truth conquers all."

I pressed my hands together as if in prayer to the God of truth. "Indeed, my friend. Truth has set us both free."

EPILOGUE

In all, there were 5,400 articles of gold and of silver. Sheshbazzar brought all these along with the exiles when they came up from Babylon to Jerusalem.

—EZRA 1:11

AUTHOR'S NOTE

Thank you for taking this journey through sixth-century BC Babylon with me. I hope you discovered things about the Bible, Daniel, and ancient Israel and Babylon that spur your curiosity to search the Scriptures. Some readers may have hoped to discover more about Daniel's prophecies in these pages, but my purpose in writing was to explore the deeper truths of the prophet's *life* and let other Bible teachers take on the meaty challenge of interpreting those complex visions in God's Word. For a well-researched, thoughtful study on Daniel's biblical text, please consider Dr. David Jeremiah's *Agents of Babylon: What the Prophecies of Daniel Tell Us About the End of Days.*

As with all my books, writing takes on a three-layered approach. First I read the biblical accounts of the time period to build the foundation (Daniel; 2 Kings 24–25; 2 Chronicles 36; Jeremiah; Isaiah; Ezekiel; and Ezra). Second come the historical facts that support the truth of God's Word, taken from archaeological records, maps, scholarly articles, commentaries, and so forth. Creative fiction is the third element, the mortar that holds historical fact and biblical truth together.

Because expert opinions vary, I try to find a golden thread of agreement that runs through my research in order to create a believable *fictional* account of Scripture's truth. In Daniel's case, I had believed for years that when Daniel and his friends were taken to Babylon, they became eunuchs because of Isaiah's dire prophecy to Hezekiah: "Some of your descendants, your own flesh and blood who will be born to you, will be taken away, and they will become eunuchs in the palace of the king of Babylon" (2 Kings 20:18).

After researching the original Hebrew further, I found *eunuch* also described Potiphar, interpreted as "chief official" in Genesis 39, the man whose wife made overtures to handsome Joseph. Potiphar may not have been a great husband, but he wouldn't have been married had he been a eunuch—in the way I'd understood the word all those years. This singular finding allowed me to imagine Daniel as a husband and father, opening my heart to the story you've just read.

Three mysterious characters made *Of Fire and Lions* an especially difficult book to decipher.

Nebuchadnezzar/Nabonidus—Daniel 4 gives an incredibly detailed account of King Nebuchadnezzar's miraculous transformation from a prideful king to an animalistic beast and then his re-formation to a ruler who acknowledges the sovereignty of the Most High. This is biblical truth. Indisputable. As I researched the historical context of his change—looking for a period of seven years when Babylon might have been without Nebuchadnezzar's leadership—I dis-covered historians' conflicting accounts. Some Babylonian legends say that Nabonidus, the father of King Belshazzar (see Daniel 5), was stricken with the same malady as Nebuchadnezzar. Other records say it was Nabonidus—and *not Nebuchadnezzar*—who suffered the physical condition called boanthropy. Rather than focus on a bunny trail, I made a small mention of the rumor and moved on. Again, in my heart and mind, biblical truth is foundational.

Cyrus/King Darius/General Gubaru—Perhaps the most difficult characters to sort out were the Medo-Persian kings Darius and Cyrus. Scripture is clear that King Darius *the Mede* cast Daniel into the lions' den (see Daniel 5:31). The Bible is also clear that in King Cyrus *of Persia's* first year he made a proclamation that any Jew who wished to do so could return to Jerusalem to help rebuild the Temple (see Ezra 1:1–4). Scripture and time lines put both kings in power during the days of Daniel. "Daniel prospered during the reign of Darius and the reign of Cyrus the Persian" (Daniel 6:28). When I began researching their roles and histories,

General Gubaru—a Median general—popped up as the identity of Darius before he assumed the throne name of Darius. Though that's not the only explanation for the three names, it felt most plausible with what we know to be true from biblical text.

Sheshbazzar/Zerubbabel—Some commentaries proposed Sheshbazzar and Zerubbabel to be the same person because of the formation of their names in the original Aramaic text. I found them treated very differently, however, in both Scripture and history. Sheshbazzar is a prince of Judah in Ezra 1:8, and Zerubbabel's winning competition among his fellow bodyguards is recorded in the apocryphal book of 1 Esdras 3–4.

I purposely did *not* include what might have happened to the Ark of the Covenant. If you'd like to hear more about that, you can read my novella, *By the Waters of Babylon*, which focuses on the destruction of Jerusalem and gives a glimpse into Jeremiah's flight to Egypt (where some suspect he hid the Ark in a cave—see 2 Maccabees 2:4–8).

I hope you've enjoyed Daniel's epic journey. If I strayed from Scripture, please forgive my unintentional oversight. I pray truth will shine brightly and the Most High God will give us all courage to stand strong in the presence *Of Fire and Lions.*

READERS GUIDE

1. How does the metaphor of the sesame seed in the opening paragraph forecast the differences in Belili and Daniel throughout the story? their personalities? their relationships? their faith?

2. In chapter 2 we don't yet know why Belili's family shuns her or why she can't forgive herself, but Mert seems confident the relationships could be mended if Belili would simply explain the past to her adult children. After reading the whole story, in what ways was Mert right? In what ways was she wrong? What traits can we learn from Mert that would strengthen our relationships with friends and family members?

3. Toward the end of chapter 3, Abigail experiences Yahweh in a personal way while hiding in the Holy of Holies in Jerusalem's Temple. She could have tried to explain the shimmer and missing bread with natural causes—like Ashpenaz eating the bread—but she quickly acknowledges the miraculous. Why do you think this little girl believed in Yahweh though most of Judah worshipped pagan gods? When others try to dismiss God's intervention in our world

today, how do you choose faith over doubt?

4. At the end of chapter 7, Abigail wonders if Yahweh will be able to find her in Babylon. Her doubts mirrored the overall fears of all the exiles. Why then was it so significant that Yahweh appeared with the three brothers in the fiery furnace (see Daniel 3)? Have you ever felt abandoned by God or perhaps felt like an exile in a place where God seemed absent? In what ways did Yahweh prove His presence in various locations and/or seasons of need?

5. In chapter 5 when young Daniel realized he was headed for exile in Babylon, he remembered Jeremiah's prophecies and said, "The royal court ignored Jeremiah's warnings, but we won't ignore his promise." Today, the Bible is to us what the prophets were to Daniel—God's living Word (see Hebrews 4:12). In what ways might we ignore its warnings? Do we ever ignore its promises? What are some practical steps we can take to heed the warnings and embrace the promises of Scripture?

6. Chapter 19 reveals Daniel's faith at a low point. What events chipped away at his confidence in Yahweh? Have you struggled similarly? Are you encouraged or discouraged that a "hero of the faith" might have experienced moments of doubt, despair, or even rage? Please explain.

7. (See chapters 31–33.) Do you think Belili needed to leave her children when Nebuchadnezzar became a beast? What did Belili discover was Yahweh's purpose for her at Borsippa? How did she change and grow during that time? What hard decision have you made that important people in your life might have disagreed with? In what ways did God redeem your decision by giving it purpose and/or strengthening you?

8. (See chapters 40–41.) How did Belili's view of family and friendship change throughout the story? In what way did those changes affect her decision to support Daniel's choice to ignore Darius's edict and continue praying to Yahweh? If you were Belili, could you have supported Daniel's decision? Why or why not?

9. (See chapters 39 and 43.) How did Daniel win King Darius's favor? What stands out the most to you about Daniel's witness of Yahweh to others? What stands out most to you about Daniel's personal relationship with Yahweh? What steps can you take to be more like Daniel in your witness to others and strengthen your personal relationship with Yahweh?

10. (See chapter 41 and others.) What did Belili fear her confession would cost? What did she gain from it? When have you hesitated

to confess for fear of the cost? When have you gained from a hard confession? Is there something the Lord is nudging you to talk to someone about right now?

11. (See chapters 43–44.) How did Daniel's night in the lions' pit change him? How did it change Belili and her children? Think of a difficult relationship in your life right now. How might it change if lives were at stake? What would become most important, and what issues would become insignificant and petty? Share if appropriate.

12. Some commentators believe that Isaiah 44:28, which mentions King Cyrus's involvement in rebuilding Jerusalem, was penned over a hundred years after Isaiah's death (during the exile by a faithful student). However, I chose to write the scene in chapter 45 as if our miracle-working God told Isaiah the name Cyrus decades before the Persian king seized the throne. Why? Because I couldn't imagine any other reason that a foreign king—in the first year of his reign—would allow nearly fifty thousand Jews (Ezra 2:64–65) to return with such vast wealth to rebuild a city and a temple to an unknown God. Can you think of other plausible reasons Cyrus might have sent the Jews back to Jerusalem?

13. What do you notice about Belili's personal

growth as she tells her story? In what ways did the events of her life change her actions, attitudes, and faith? How have events and circumstances in your life changed your actions, attitudes, and faith?

Thanks for pondering what Daniel's life might have been like in *Of Fire and Lions.*

Center Point Large Print
600 Brooks Road / PO Box 1
Thorndike, ME 04986-0001 USA

(207) 568-3717

US & Canada:
1 800 929-9108
www.centerpointlargeprint.com